# SHADOWS LOST

By B.K. Cavaleri

The West Isles
Finlandia
Inquus Isles
Red Cap Mountains
N
W E
S
Andromeda Island
The I

Nocturnes Mountains
City of Night
City of Light
Wildwoods
Balsam Plains
HEN'S WALL
Faerie
Under
Southern Mountains

# INTRODUCTION

A curse that drove a queen mad.
A heroine that failed to stop her.
A shifter that refuses to give up.
A world that needs them both again.

***

One hundred years after the Queen of Faerie sacrificed her own people in the name of salvation, the fae are on the verge of extinction and a suspicious power is on the rise. Remnant Ezra Solaire Dark, the once legendary war general, is the last of the shadow fae. Living in exile, only she holds the power to save the kingdom of Faerie. Enter Emon, a tempting shifter fae they call "The Golden One" who has been hunting Remnant for the past century. When an unnatural power comes for them both, they must join together to reset the wrongs of the past in order to heal the future, not only for the world of Faerie but also for themselves.
Be warned. Remnant and Emon will journey through desolate lands long abandoned, to the shadowy underworld of the ocean, and into the dangerous kingdom of the shifters. This is no innocent adventure story. This is the dark world of the fae—power, vengeance, and half truths are the laws of the land. And the worst monsters are the ones hidden within.

# Content Warning & Trigger Warning

This is a dark fantasy romance with themes of language, violence, assault, sex, rape, and infertility complications. Content may be sensitive to some readers.

# Dedication

*For Me.*
*Only I know how powerful this is to say.*


*For My Husband.*
*For supporting my power.*

# JOURNAL
# EXCERPT

*Gerald S. Gio*

*Head Researcher of The National Fertility Institute.*

*Tuesday, May 5th, 2055*

At first we were all awed by her silver beauty. Eyes of aqua, skin that sparkled, silver hair that cascaded like a waterfall with every graceful movement. Her body left you wanting, her voice the sweetest of symphonies, and her touch made you shudder with unyielding pleasure.

We thought...perhaps she was where the stories of angels came from...

She brought her own people here. Some to assist with the work she tasked us, others she brought for *experimentation*. Her goal...if one could call it that, was to cure their barren wombs and bring life back to her world. They once were a great people, she said, flourishing, prosperous, and fruitful. Until the goddess abandoned them and left them impotent. She wants our science to change this. To prevent the extinction of her people. All of us are so enraptured by our need to please her, we never really called her *experiments* for what they really were.

Torture, rape, murder. She wants results and we all are too eager to deliver them.

Two new specimens were brought in. One light and one dark. Words cannot describe how imposing their presence is...and it angers the silver haired angel with each passing day.

The golden one's roars shake the very walls of this facility. His strength is insurmountable and his golden eyes, so unique in their color, are always watching, burning, hunting. I feel that he has marked me as his next prey. If he survives this, I know I will be a dead man.

Then there is the one who resembles the moon in the blackest of nights. Darkness surrounds her, calls to her, defines her. Her quiet strength and graceful beauty is something of which I have never seen before and it has broken the fog I have been living in these past few months. But my colleagues are still bewitched—and God help them, they found *something*.

Unlike all the others, these new prisoners might be the saviors the silver haired angel has been searching for. Except this displeases her...it enrages her. She is determined to make them suffer while taking from them both the very essence that will create a new race. She is fanatical about destroying them, the very quintessence of light and dark, and I find I can not allow that to happen.

I try to help her...the dark one. Her torture has escalated, specifically, it seems, to invoke the fury of the golden one. The more she screams, the more his raging roars shake the very lands. He begs for them to stop and she begs for her life to end. But I cannot give her what she desires...I want to save her. Her screams haunt me...if she were my daughter, I'd pray that someone would fight for her in this God forsaken place.

This silver haired being is not an angel.

She's a monster.

No, she's worse.

Fae.

She calls herself the Queen of all Fae.

# PROLOGUE

*Remnant*

100 years ago

Dust.

Dust was everywhere and it continued to sprinkle down from the sunlit sky, so thick in the air that I could scarcely breathe without inhaling the grit fully in my lungs. Yet here I stood, on a half crumbled balcony.

Waiting. I was waiting.

Sunlight broke through the thick air, highlighting the utter destruction of my home. The capital, the City of Light—it was gone.

A harsh rattling breath escaped me as I took in the desolation. Gone were the elegant shops, luscious gardens, sparkling fountains. Just crumbled marble, tints of gold, and lush splintered wood covered our once sacred city.

Worse, there was no sound. No cries of pain, no harsh sobs of loss, no chickadees trilling wildly looking for the comfort of their perches. Even the corrupted inner city, where the most wicked fae resided was silent, buried beneath the rubble.

Waiting. I was still waiting.

Desperate for just one cry...to know that one pitiful soul still lived—still *existed*.

It just couldn't be.

I was part of an already dying race. Abandoned by our goddess and cursed with infertility after a long bloody war over a thousand years ago. Our extinction was inevitable but it could have been slow. I could have made sure that what was left of the fae lived a long, prosperous, and happy existence.

Except...I failed.

I was their hope, their salvation, their dark hero...and I failed. And yet, I felt nothing. Nothing but hollow emptiness. I wasn't even able to feel the warmth of the sun's mocking rays.

Waiting. I was still waiting.

Not for hope. It was clear that time had passed.

A dark, inky blackness oozed from the ruined city and gathered like a plume of smoke from a campfire.

Finally, they were here.

Infinite.

Ominous.

Dark.

Shadows.

So life-like, they moved through the air with a sentient purpose—a deadly power unlike anything this world had ever seen.

And they were *mine*.

Instinctively, I reached outward to their darkness allowing them to swarm my hand before wrapping themselves around my body as if to thaw the now frozen heart inside of me.

"She is gone." I whispered to them and closed my eyes that burned with unshed tears. She was just dust now, forever gone just like the rest of the fae that lived here.

Opening my eyes, I took one last look at the city I had dutifully served and destroyed. I was not the general they had hoped for and I sure as goddess was not the heroine they had loved.

I never deserved such love anyway.

After all, monsters never did.

And I was the worst monster around.

Alive—but dead inside.

***

I stared at the utter desolation with nausea threatening to rise from my churning gut. The sun set low on the destroyed City of Light, casting a peaceful glow that was mocking in the chaotic turmoil roiling inside of me.

A long low whistle speared the silence from my best friend, his violet eyes glinting with admiration. "Fucking Faerie," he cursed. "She did this?"

I shook my head as an all too familiar feeling of desperation flooded my tired eyes. I stumbled forward on the verge of collapsing when a strong hand from my other side gripped my shoulder. I could not hide the flinch his touch created.

"You are not healed enough for this Emon, let us return you home. You cannot keep going on, my cub."

I shrugged off the support from the healer who had joined me here. "I'll be fine Jar and there is no time, if I am going to find her I must leave tonight."

Out of my periphery, I could see the healer give my friend a look, jerking his head towards me and hissing under his breath, "Tyr, talk some sense into him."

Tyr scoffed. "He practically dragged himself here and we couldn't stop him then, healer. What makes you think we can stop him now?"

My tears spilled down my face, only half listening to their continued squabbling about my current state and I growled out, "I have to find her. Where is Penina?"

"I'm here," a gentle voice called and the deadly silhouette of Faerie's most infamous assassin stepped forward into the remaining sunlight. "I brought you something," she smiled brightly and shoved two bound fae onto their knees before me. "I found these two searching through the rubble."

I peered down at the grief stricken fae. Their heads hung low and their shoulders slumped in defeat. Their hands clenched in front of them bound by a leather cord that was clearly not needed.

They were broken...like me.

Clad in heavy black leather, caked with grime and dust, the one with bright wavy green hair looked up at me through his low hanging locks. Stormy hazel eyes glared, recognizing me for what I was.

A shifter.

His partner didn't bother. Hair white as snow covered half her face and it slung sharply towards the ground where her tears stained the crumbled earth.

"Who are you?" I growled low.

Green hair narrowed his hazel eyes on me. "We don't answer to shifters," he spat.

I smiled, my fangs glinting in the low light, "So there is still some fight in you. That's good," I nodded. "Penina?"

Jerking him back by his hair, the assassin flipped down the collar of his uniform, where a delicate silver pin, crafted to look like a swirl of smoke, was clasped on the inside.

I inhaled. "Shadow forces," I nodded to Penina, who dropped the fae's head and quickly moved to flip the collar of his partner, revealing the same pin beneath. "Captains, by the looks of it," I growled and crouched low, catching both their gazes this time. I stared into a singular stormy gray eye of the fae with white hair. "Where is your master?"

"Dead," she hissed back.

I shook my head, they didn't know. "Your queen is likely dead, yes. But that is not the master I speak of. Yours is very much alive and I will find her."

Neither could hide their shock nor the new hope glimmering in their eyes.

Green hair laughed dryly, "If what you say is true, shifter. Then may the goddess help you. If the general doesn't want to be found, you won't be finding her, she will be finding *you*."

Distracted, I barely recognized the threat before his meek partner lunged for me with a snarl. Penina was faster. A blade stopping the shadow force captain mid attack.

"Easy little elemental," Penina purred down at her.

I frowned, assessing them both again, recognizing them from the stories I had gathered. "Elementals? As in the elemental twins. The captains of *her* inner circle. Riley Dragoon and Xi Chin."

They glanced at one another then. A thousand words spoken in one look. I should know it, it was the same for me and my friends here today.

"What is your plan if you do find her, shifter?" The fae with white hair didn't bother to flinch away from the blade caressing her exposed throat.

Xi. Her name was Xi Chin. The earth elemental. I recognized her now. It was said that only the dead knew what the other half of her face looked like.

I rose and took in the destruction again, sadness seeping into every pore of my body. I could feel everyone's eyes on me now...waiting.

I was so tired. Jar's firm grip caught me again and my body shuddered. I blinked to stop the world from tilting and shook my head hard, fighting to stay upright.

Growling, I stared out beyond the horizon, gripping hard to the leather strap of my satchel slung across my shoulders. "I'm going to bring her back home..."

# Chapter 1

S HE FOUND *ME*.

Riley Dragoon would be laughing his ass off right now. Goddess damn that fucking elemental for being right.

Through the pain of the imbecile sawing out my insides and the haze of my life being drained out of me, I felt her again—my soulmate.

I couldn't keep the grin from spreading across my face even as the sickening squelch of a knife punctured my body. All this fucking time and *she* was the one who found me—chained to a tree with irons, in the middle of the Wildwoods, bleeding out, and dying. How embarrassing.

I glared at my torturer with renewed strength. "What's wrong Jurin, have you tired already?"

Spitting out my own blood, I watched as it splattered on his already disgusting boots—it improved them.

"You know there are herbs that help you with stamina," I snickered despite the black dots dancing across my vision, "I'm sure your bed partners would appreciate it, although with that face, I doubt you have any."

The shifter named Jurin sneered. "Shall I make it the same for you? I believe you don't need this to talk..." His knife followed the trail of blood seeping down my torso and pressed threateningly against my dick.

I wrenched on the iron chains draining my shifter power and snarled as it seared my flesh. The pain was worth seeing the flicker of fear flash in my torturers muddy brown eyes.

Iron. A stupid weakness. Why our Goddess Faerie even gave us any weakness at all was beyond my understanding...perhaps it was some sort of kink she had.

"If you're so worried about my dick, Jurin, then take these irons off and let me show you how a real male performs." I bared my teeth at him, feeling my own blood drip from my mouth, too bad it wasn't his.

Jurin laughed up into the dark night. "You hear that boys?" he called over his shoulder. "Our poor, dear, *golden one* would like me to take off his irons."

The other three shifters in the camp laughed along with him.. The fae were otherworldly creatures. Dark, vicious, deadly...but still enthrallingly beautiful, powerful, enchanting. Unfortunately, for these four, their grotesqueness on the inside had festered to the outside.

Repulsed, I spat again on the forest floor.

Jurin dogged it, his face contorting into a sneer. "How fucking stupid do you think we are? We knew who you were the moment you stepped into our camp."

I attempted to shrug, the smell of my flesh burning sending me flashbacks of a time passed. Those memories did not control me...that's what the healer had said.

I swallowed down the nausea. "Stupid enough to fool you four into actually thinking you could capture me unwillingly."

Although, bleeding out, on the cusp of death, hadn't been part of the goddess damn plan.

Our heads snapped up at the long howl that pierced the cold night air. The sound sent Jurin stumbling from me with alarm and the other shifter scrambling to their feet, looking wearily around them. They were too stupid to notice the way the silver branches of the Wildwoods leaned hungrily inward and the shadows around the firelight darkened with anticipation.

I chuckled. A cù-sìth call. Faerie could not have provided a better opportunity.

"What in the Sheol was that?" One of Jurin's cronies, Tomac, whispered fearfully.

I snorted. How were these bastards even shifters if they couldn't distinguish a cù-sìth howl? A call from these massive black hounds of Faerie meant your death was forthcoming. A true shifter would know that which was why it was a mistake for them to come here. Shifters resided in The West Isles for a reason and we were at the top of our food chain there.

But not here in Faerie.

From the gentle time warping wisps, to the smallest needle biting gnomes, and the great fierce weretrees of old, everything here was a beast that wanted to kill you first and ask questions later.

I smirked when three more howls joined the first.

Four howls.

Four deaths.

There was no guarantee that one of those howls wasn't for me, but at least three of these assholes were going down with me. Plus I had the weretree, keeping my mission safe in its silvery gnarled branches. If I didn't survive, he would make sure it was delivered to her safely.

I spat out the bitter taste in my mouth, regret splintering my chest like another knife wound. I had wanted to see the blazing emerald green of her eyes—eyes that everyone whispered about but I never had the pleasure of seeing. I had wanted to touch her soft pale skin—to feel it reverently against my lips and purge it of the invisible scars I knew were there.

My vision blurred, darkness creeping in my periphery. I felt the hot sting of a single tear slide down my face and I closed my eyes. I was not ready for Sheol but it was here for me anyway.

Darkness swirled around me. Then I gasped—a punch in my gut full of golden light spilled into my veins, it thrummed in my body, it blasted my senses.

Was this Sheol?

My eyes snapped open and I inhaled sharply. I was still in Faerie, still in this goddess forsaken camp, still chained to the damn tree but instead of dying...I was healing.

I groaned at the pleasurable tingling of my injured body knitting itself back together, my fractured bones snapping back into place, and the pulsating energy that sent my heart racing.

This power was...reverent, it was euphoric, it was life. It tasted of our long lost goddess—a goddess who had abandoned us to our cursed sterile fate thousands of years ago.

A fate that had driven the Faerie queen mad, destroyed the life of the one destined to save us, and sent me on a one hundred year search to find her again.

And yet...here the goddess power was. Present and alive—and saving me.

"What the Faerie fuck? Who healed him?" Jurin snarled, whirling around and pointing at his comrades. "I told you idiots to not fucking heal him."

"It wasn't us," one of them cried out.

I chuckled, the power of the goddess making me higher than the Red Cap Mountains—I fucking missed those looming peaks of my homeland.

"She'sssss cominggggggg," I slurred, seeing the shadows darken unnaturally. "Whatsss do you do when the darknessssss comes," I started singing boisterously at the top of my lungs, "Dooooo you hide or dooooooo you runnnn." A long slurring laugh escaped me before I shouted, "Nay. Neither...what you neeeddd is the rising ssuuuunnnn."

"Shut him up. Something is out there," one of Jurin's goons whispered, a bear shifter with curly brown hair and dark brown eyes that were almost black. I wanted to rip his traitorous face off.

Almost one hundred years ago, they had joined the queen of Faerie, betrayed our people, and attempted a coup against the shifter throne. Until the queen abandoned them here...a lunatic if I ever saw one, the Faerie queen's obsession to cure the fae courts of their infertility ultimately led to her own death.

At least that's what most believed. I believed otherwise.

All four of the shifter traitors startled when the furious flapping of a chickadee swooped into the camp.

I could not control the blast of laughter booming deep from my belly at their skittish reaction.

"Doooo youuuu hide or do youuu ruuun," I whispered, my eyes latching on to the appearance of the sexy silhouette stepping out from the rolling darkness.

Shadows fell away from her fine figure like a silk dress falling off her bare shoulders.

My mouth went dry, my lips parted with awe.

Bright emerald green eyes, piercing and fierce, striking and gorgeous, connected with my own for the very first time, and I never saw anything more beautiful.

I never would again.

Finally.

On my death's door, the one I had been searching for, the one I was dying for.

Remnant Ezra Solaire Dark

The last shadow fae.

My lost soulmate...found at last.

# CHAPTER 2

I T HAD BEEN ALMOST one hundred years since I'd last seen her. The moment had brought me to my knees—and it would have this time too if not for the chains that bound me.

One hundred years of dreaming, wondering, imagining, and now my power-induced high made me ravenous for her.

I hadn't forgotten a single detail of those curves, they were the only thing that got me through my many dark nights, except my memories had not been accurate enough.

Not even fucking close.

My soulmate wore fitted black leather that wrapped her body much like the shadows who were poised at her back, hovering like cobras of darkness ready to strike.

Her leather top was cut off at the shoulders, baring the pale skin of her tattooed arms to the fire's light. I licked my lips hungrily, imagining my lips trailing over those black swirls of ink from her fingertips up. I wanted to worship every spiral, contour, and etching along their path.

Tracing the long line of her neck up to her heart shaped face, I memorized her petite nose, the lush fullness of her lips that parted ever so slightly—my gaze snapped up and the world melted away when I met her stare. I inhaled at the faint hitch in her breath, the soft flutter in her long dark lashes then I growled hungrily, watching those emerald depths dilate, glowing with a need only I could give her.

Another slow blink in a moment of chaos. She would not understand it, our connection. Nor should she. The bond was undetectable, to her at least. Masking the soulmate bond was the only way to ensure her safety.

I smiled at the small furrow that formed when she frowned, her head tilting to the side, the tips of her black-blue tresses kissing her leather clad ass sinfully. An endearing curiosity clashing with her hardened warrior exterior.

"Who the fuck are you?" Jurin sneered. "We don't need no bitches intervening unless it's to suck our dicks."

I barked out a snarl at the fae that would dare come between me and my soulmate.

Slowly, she turned her dangerous gaze away from me and on Jurin while the shifters in the camp laughed at her expense.

"Is that so?" she walked towards him, her hips swaying seductively. "I have been watching all of you quite intimately you know."

Their eyes dilated with arousal and Jurin snickered with self satisfaction.

"Unfortunately, not even a hag would want to suck your worthless cocks. Dirty shifters do not belong in Faerie lands and I find that I am more than obliged to rid her of your filth." Her pearly white teeth flashed in the firelight with disgust. "You. I'm going to savor killing you first," she waved her hand lazily, "Go."

A blur of darkness struck the camp, followed quickly by sudden snarls and cries. A wide grin crept across my face, relishing the sight of my four captors as they struggled violently against shadows that anchored them to the forest floor. Each one of them clawed and pulled against the unyielding darkness that chained them, but nothing could break that power—nothing they had in their arsenal anyway.

Twirling her hand at her side, the shadows snaked their way up her body, forming a long lethal black sword in her hand. Slowly, with dark amusement twinkling in her eyes, she stalked them all with perfect ease, admiring her work and tapping her black shadow sword against her thigh with pursed lips.

I leaned in with starved anticipation.

"You fucking bitch. You're a shadow fae aren't you?" Jurin pulled at his bonds and drew his sword strapped to his side defensively. "Your kind should be fertilizer for Faerie right now. I personally made sure of that. Who the fuck are you?"

She stopped in front of him, tilting her head to the side. "Who am I?" A sad smile spread across her face. "A betrayer. A monster perhaps. A ghost of a time past. But you'll likely know me as Dark. Remnant Dark."

Lunging against my bonds, a garbled warning ripped from my chest when I saw the subtle shift in Jurin's body and his arm raising quickly, his shifter speed sending his sword blurring through the night.

She was faster. A thud hit the ground. The five of us all stared at the severed arm laying there, Jurin's hand still clasped tightly around the hilt.

The shifter blinked slowly down at the bloody stump of his shoulder before his anguished howl pierced the night.

She grinned, "Shut him up."

The shadows around his legs blasted upwards in a fire of darkness, flickering with the last sounds of his tormented screams only to be replaced by the soft cackling of the fire.

Remnant broke the shocked silence, kicking at his severed limb, "You missed something, my loves."

I hummed my approval watching the shadows devour the severed limb like a juicy fae steak and then gazed at her vengeful face unable to hide my love for her. This was a side of her I had only heard tales of but never saw for myself, and I adored every bit of it.

"The shadow fae were supposed to be honorable," Diego, the bear shifter snarled. He pointed at the shadows anchoring his feet and then at the blood stained ground where Jurin once stood. "I'd say using your pathetic minions to kill us is spitting on your family's grave. Traitorous bitch."

The shadow fae threw her head back laughing and goddess, the way her body arched—I groaned.

"This..." she smirked, waving at his person, "coming from a fae that has one of his own chained so prettily to that tree over there. If I didn't know better, I'd say you are afraid of him. Why else would irons be needed?"

I full out grinned when they all turned to look at me, my fangs bared before I shot them a lazy wink. Something splattered to the forest floor and her nose wrinkled ever so slightly.

Was that drool?

Diego sneered, "General Dark or not. You have no idea who you are messing with, shadow bitch."

She smiled back lethally, "Then who exactly am I *messing* with, shifter? I'd love to meet them. I'm in need of a real challenge." She spun slowly with her arms outward in a mock search. Stopping, she raised her brows. "Or is it that you are referring to yourself, do you think you'd be able to meet my *needs*?"

"Nuh uh, sweetheart. The real question would be can you meet all of mine?" The bear shifter growled, his claws lengthening and fur rolling across his body.

Remnant snorted and rolled her eyes, the pretend amusement gone from her striking features. "Shifters are so disgusting. Why the goddess even created you is beyond my comprehension. But have it your way." She waved her hand and the shadows released Diego without any hesitation for their mistress's safety.

I sputtered out another warning when the fae shifted and a fucking demented teddy bear now stood over her, twenty five feet tall with over 600 pounds of bear muscle clawing outward with a savage swipe. Growling, I fought against the iron chains, feeling my flesh burn, desperate to help her.

Undeterred, emerald eyes shot towards me with glittering amusement before dancing gracefully away from his attack.

"Too slow baby bear." She blew a kiss at him.

"Get her Diego!"

Cheers rose from the remaining two shifters while they continued to struggle against their bonds. Frowning, I tilted my head when the shadows stretched out from their anchored darkness towards me and then proceeded to rub against my chained legs in what seemed like a silent greeting.

I chuckled down at them, "Niccee meet you tooooo, little fiendsssss. Do me favorsss, don't tellsss her 'et."

They swirled excitedly up my body, around my head in a cool caress before fluttering back down to the ground. A content black puddle of darkness at my feet, not at all worried for their mistress.

Fond of her shadows already, I smiled. "Thanksss."

A roar from Diego, that shook the very trees, drew my attention back to her. The bear had reared up on his back legs and his tawny head disappeared into the silver foliage of the woods. Drool dangled from his mouth and splattered straight into the shadow fae's upturned face.

"Gross." She wiped the drool off with the back of her hand and sneered.

He roared again and lunged, his giant paw lashing out in several directions while she twirled and danced out of the way with perfectly coordinated movement.

"Your attacks are predictable, baby bear," she shook her head disappointedly, "How you lived this long is beyond me." Finally, flicking her sword up, her eyes glowed villainously. "Allow me to remedy that. Give my best regards to the god of Sheol."

The bear shifter roar's shook the woods. Silver leaves fell down around us like confetti before he charged her. Without hesitation she met him head on, sliding under his swiping paws with her shadow sword raised.

Hot steaming entrails tumbled out from beneath him like a waterfall, her slice fatally long and deep. The shadow fae cleared his large frame, sliding to her feet, without sparing a glance at the bear shifter tumbling to the ground behind her.

Satisfaction rose within me as the goddess's light extinguished from his deep brown eyes.

"Uhg," she said, wiping Diego's blood off her shadow sword onto her black leathers. "That was messier than I wanted it to be. Who's next?"

The other two shifters were silent, transfixed on the bloody pile of guts that was the fiercest of their little company.

Laughter bubbled up deep from my chest. Goddess she was a sight to behold. My slurring rumbles earned a small smile from her that had me practically glowing with happiness.

"Please miss," a small shifter, named Tomac stammered, "Please, General, have mercy. Let us go. We won't tell no one what happened. We won't mention we even saw a shadow fae here in the woods. Jurin and Diego just got eaten by some animal."

"Shut the fuck up Tomac," hissed his friend. I never did get his name. I didn't care. She was going to kill him anyway.

Four howls, four deaths, since the goddess so graciously decided to save my dying ass today, there were only two obvious candidates left.

I was going to enjoy this.

Remnant pursed her lips in contemplation, ignoring the other protesting shifter, "What's your name again?"

"Tttommac, General."

"Just Remnant if you please. Well Tomac. You've been out here for Goddess knows how long, destroying and pissing in my woods, and torturing one of your own kind with those two sadistic bastards," she tossed her thumb towards the dead bear shifter, "which tells me exactly what kind of mercy you deserve." She leaned in and whispered, "None."

Tomac dropped to his knees awkwardly in his shadow restraints. "Plllease miss. I'll do anything you ask of me. Please don't kill me," he sobbed.

"Goddess, just fucking kill him bitch—he's an embarrassment to his own kind," his companion spat at Tomac's prone form. "Let me go to fight. I'd rather fight for my life then beg to the likes of ya like that little cunt there."

"You're going to regret those words, shifter." Her hair swayed when she sidestepped away from him, shadows pulling inwardly toward her, a small smile dancing on her plush lips.

It wasn't until Tomac lunged for his companion with bloodlust in his eyes and a dagger in his hand did I understand her game. The mad shifter, convulsing with rage, plunged his dagger deep into the chest of his unsuspecting friend over and over again. Lost in his animal, having been pushed to the point of breaking, the bloodlust consumed him, and Remnant Dark wielded it like she wielded the shadows swirling behind her—with cold calculated precision.

The Wildwoods shuddered with delight, relishing in the blood feeding its deep roots, its silvery canopy glowing brighter around us.

Disturbed by the sudden glow like an alert predator, Tomac stood with a snarl. His eyes, just as red as the blood trailing down his face turned on the shadow fae.

"Watch snout," I slurred with fear just as Tomac charged. "Bloodwust."

Throwing her hand out the shadows contracted inward, opening a pit of darkness. The force of their draw thrusted me against my chains, burning my flesh anew while the canopy bowed to her great power.

Mindlessly, Tomac charged head first into the swirling black-hole with savage intensity, the shadows closing with a loud snap behind him.

Released from the drawing force, I sagged back against my tree, away from the sharp sting of the irons while the forest lurched back to its natural resting state.

A rumble rolled up from deep in my chest and bursted out of me in loud booming laughter.

Goddess, she was phenomenal and she was mine.

Bright emerald green eyes turned on me—cutting through the dark night like the stars in the sky. Amusement and a tinge of worry dancing in their reflection. I soaked up every ounce of her undivided attention.

My only life purpose for the past century was to find her, forsaking all my duties and obligations—and now here she was. An avenging remnant of the past with her terrifying shadows and deadly blade.

# CHAPTER 3

## Remnant

"THAT WAS—" I WRINKLED my nose at the bloodied camp. "Disturbing."

I flicked my sword back into the void my shadows held for me and turned towards the last remaining shifter. Surprisingly, still alive.

I didn't envy him that—being alive. I had imagined and hoped for my own death more than once in my self exile. Except the fae were immortal...unable to die of natural causes, including taking our own lives, I was forced to live my many years with the knowledge of what I had done and what I had become.

A monster.

I glared at the slumped form of the shifter hanging in irons that seared his skin, recognizing the power that had flared around him just moments before I stepped into this camp.

27

The goddess had come, after thousands of years and abandoning us with a curse that was a slow torturous extinction, she had come.

*For him.*

Compelled, I took a step forward. The blood on him was more than a few days old but it did nothing to mar his beauty. My stomach flipped with anticipation with every step I took, the draw to be near him heady in its pull.

Even in his fae form, I could tell he was a powerful beast of a shifter and it was no secret of my undeniable draw towards powerful beasts. From the deadly creatures of the northern night, to the sunbathing dragons of the south, I had always been drawn by their ferocity, their deadliness, and their loyal instincts to protect. A weakness that had always led me into trouble and this time would be no different.

When his gold eyes had met mine, it took every bit of my focus to ignore the compulsion he stirred within me. Let alone the hot desire that rushed into me.

At that moment, I was more alive than I had been for almost a hundred years.

It made me want to kill him.

I did not want to *feel*. I deserved the lonely, lifeless exile I now lived. And this unknown shifter, with his gorgeous body and alluring gold eyes, was threatening my very non-existent life with his intoxicating power.

Power, unlike anything I had come across from any other court of fae. From the stubborn fae elementals with their ability to wield earth, fire, wind, and spirit, to the siren singing water fae that controlled the riverways, the tides, and all ocean life, I thought I had seen it all in my two thousand and twelve years.

Even the shifters, with their vast strength, quick speed, and lethal predator instincts never manifested power quite like him...as far as I knew.

Consuming in its hot need, it called to me.

I shook my head to clear my senses. I was a shadow fae. My power was cold, glacial, and infinite. I had no need for this burning hot power. The last of my kind, the shadow fae once controlled all the dormant shadows of this world and manipulated them as we saw fit. We controlled the night.

I frowned. This shifter was pure limitless light.

"Perhaps he has evolved?" I waved my hand, talking to the shadows that appeared beside me. Floating with satisfaction from their fae meal.

Immortal life had a way of preventing stagnant eternity, although we still were classified by our courts, some of our powers had morphed to become uniquely individual. Our previous queen could control all four elements, my mother had the power of foresight, it was said even the shifter king of old had the power to see truth, making him an admired leader. My own had evolved as well, with the ability to see auras of fae around me. I read their souls just as easily as I took them.

"I wonder what his aura is like," I glanced at them, watching them swirl happily. "You agree then? One little peek shouldn't hurt?"

Their smokey tendrils bobbed excitedly.

"Except that's what you said about those shifters and their auras just about made me throw up in my mouth."

The shadows shimmered in a laughing manner that almost seemed mocking.

"You're insinuating I'm a coward. You didn't see what I did." Shaking my head at them, I turned to the shifter, "This better be worth it."

Peering deeply at the last shifter alive in this camp I engaged my sight only to find myself gasping and stumbling backwards by the blinding light emanating from his very soul. Swirls of shining, glittering, golden light surrounded him in a perfect halo so bright that it was almost white in nature.

Sharply, I turned away, clutching at my chest to steady my racing heart and switching off my aura sight. His soul...goddess his soul was beautiful. The color was divine in nature with the mark of the ascended and in mere seconds, it cracked the monstrous darkness surrounding my own in its fiery blaze.

The shadows draped around me and I clutched at their darkness, spinning in confusion to face his unconscious form again, seeing him now in a whole new way.

My gaze raked over his bronze sculpted body, caked in dried layers of blood. Strong wide shoulders outlined a tall frame, and the nakedness of his chest revealed every delicious cut of newly healed muscle. His pants hung deliciously low off his hips, baring the provocative chiseled v of his abdominals down to his strong dark brown leather encased legs.

He was irrevocably the very definition of fae and I found myself enraptured by the very presence of him. For the first time, I understood what it was to be ensnared by our kind... much like all the humans of Earth who came in contact with us.

Humans were a plaything for the fae in their immortal boredom and we had manipulated their culture for centuries. From Atlantis and mermaids stemming from the water fae, legends of werewolves originating from the shifters, the fear of vampires from the long extinguished blood fae, even the stories of dragons, enchanted swords, gigantic sea creatures...it was all fae. Of course there were also a select fae who craved human worship and thus legends of the Tuatha Dé Danann were created.

I drew the shadows closer to me. Those times were over now. The gateways to other worlds and even realms within our own world had been sealed shut one hundred years ago.

Morta.

The day I destroyed our queen, murdered our people, and leveled the capital city of Faerie.

All that was left of the fae now were a scattered few elementals within the continent, the water fae hiding in their mysterious watery depths of The Under, and the shifters across the vast ocean in The West Isles.

Isolated, we lived out the rest of our lives within a massive world without the hope of ever having a legacy of our own. The curse prevented us from procreating and brought out the savages that laid within.

Without purpose to cull our violent nature we were nothing more than sophisticated animals, miserable in our own existence, killing in boredom, waiting for the day when there was only one of our species left.

A soft touch of shadow brought me back to the forest and I blinked slowly at the unconscious shifter, my lip curling in a silent snarl.

"What is he doing here anyway?" I hissed to the shadows. "They have their own damned continent, with their own murderous king to rule them."

They were savages. The whole lot of them.

Except this one didn't feel like a savage. He felt like something...*more*. More beautiful, more powerful, more commanding, more dominant. I just wanted to bathe in the glory of his shadow like a besotted fool.

Reaching out, I held my breath and cupped his face where the soft stubble of his beard prickled my palm. Only shifters grew body hair. The other courts of fae had no need for it. We were not animals outright.

His mouth parted in a sigh when my touch trailed over his smooth lips and his warm breath washed over my face leaving behind the scent of chocolate and spice. I licked my lips at the hunger that pooled deep in my belly at his delicious scent and forced my hand to trace the crooked contour of his nose with my fingertips. Enjoying that one *perfect* imperfection of him and wondering why this specific injury hadn't ever healed.

His long dark lashes fluttered on his chiseled cheekbones and I reached up to sweep back the light brown hair that had fallen over his brow. Long only down the center of his head, the sides of his head were shaved short, the texture of it much softer than the coarse bristle of his beard.

His tormentors had called him *the golden one* mockingly. If they only knew how true his aura was to this name they wouldn't have dared slander it. They would have trembled in fear before him. An ascended fae, goddess touched, a leader of all, the light within the darkness.

Snapping my hand back I finally exhaled and stared at the iron chains binding him. Memories of that cold metal burning my wrists and the emptiness I felt at being disconnected from my shadows made my stomach churn with revulsion.

Shaking my head, I rubbed at my wrists. "I am free…somehow I got free." The mystery of that day, the broken iron shackle, was something I had never solved. Clenching my teeth, I glared at the chains. "*Separ.*"

Black tendril shadows immediately obeyed, severing the iron chains that held the powerful shifter. A singular breeze rustled my unbound hair and blew through the Wildwoods, the silver foliage whispering excitedly at my newly sealed fate.

Irritated, I kicked the iron chains that had thudded to the ground away from him and then looked up to see over two hundred pounds of pure limp muscle falling directly towards me.

"Shit!" I cursed, unable to sidestep the bronzed glory falling on top of me, I braced for impact.

# Chapter 4

Remnant

I FLUNG OUT MY arms in panic and shrieked when the unconscious shifter laid me flat, effectively crushing me beneath him. Only a growling snore indicated he had been disturbed by the event at all.

Hissing my agitation, I spat out the hair his chocolate scented snores had blown across my face and peeked around his massive body to glare at my shadows. "I do believe you did that on purpose!"

My shadows, sentient in nature, danced excitedly around us with silent laughter. I did not need words to understand that they were highly amused. I could read them as well as they could read me...after all, they had been with me since my birth.

Unlike my other shadow fae family, who controlled dormant shadows casted by light, my powers were alive, sentient...infinite. The elemental fae seers called it a dark omen, the shadow fae called it a blessing. Neither really knew where or how they came into being or why they chose me in particular. Even my own mother, who was a powerful ancient with the gift of foresight didn't quite understand why I gained such a power although she considered them a loving blessing all the same.

*"A mothers greatest wish,"* she would say, *"is to make sure their children would always be safe even when they were no longer able to protect them."*

Then she would laugh and joke that perhaps the shadows were really a blessing for her rather than one for me.

Closing my eyes, I shut down the well of grief that threatened to overflow and focused on my current problem.

Pushing at the shifter's heavy form, I attempted to disentangle myself from his massive body but my movement only caused him to nuzzle closer, straight into my cleavage. The prickling stubble of his beard on my vulnerable skin sent my heart racing.

"Help," I gasped, frantically shoving at the shifter and wriggling my body away from his touch.

My shadows, sensing my panic, threw the shifter across the forest floor.

Gasping, I rolled to my hands and knees. Gulping air through my panic.

"Sorry. Sorry," I choked, controlling the trembling within me.

In what seemed like hours but was mere minutes, I was finally able to breathe and sat back on my heels to gaze up at the night sky. The coolness of the shadows embracing me calmed the tension in my shoulders.

Looking at them, I gave them a wry sad smile. "Not your fault, my loves."

A few moments passed before I chanced looking over my shoulder at the large fae male snoring contentedly in the dirt. I groaned, rubbing a hand down my face. How was it that his back was just as sexy as his front and that even in my panic, I still felt desire for him?

With a shaky sigh, I rose and waved dismissively at my shadows. "Just for that you are carrying him." Kicking over one of the shifters bags, I sniffed with disgust at the contents. Black lace underwear—disgustingly stiff from the goddess only knew what, molted dried provisions, and an odd string of...goddess were those teeth?

My eyes traveled over to the last dead shifter, shredded to bits by his own companion, still bleeding all over the forest floor. "For

Goddess sake clean that up! Damn bloodlust ruined a perfectly good kill."

Bloodlust. A shifter's curse as well as his greatest strength. When pushed past their emotional breaking point, a shifter's power was amplified. It was said to be the sole reason why the old shifter king had fallen—so driven by it from the loss of his soulmate, his own son had to put him down to take over the throne. A shame. He was a worthy foe during those times and I regretted never meeting him in battle.

My lips pulled back over my teeth when my gaze fell on the blazing fire. Fire in these woods drew unwanted attention—attention I could already feel was moving towards us. I had managed to live in these woods for over one hundred years without detection...many of the beasts here were my friends but that didn't mean I trusted anything in the Wildwoods. They were called wild for a reason.

Summoning nearby dormant shadows, I doused the fire in a blanket of black, and allowed the moonlight to fill the small clearing. Inhaling deeply, I tilted my face up to the glow of the three moons of Faerie and basked in the peace their presence brought me. I would need it for whatever was to come next.

Cool wind blew playfully at my loose hair, whispering its secrets—a friend not foe was nearby. Then the subtle creak and groan of a werewood tree echoed in the clearing and I smiled.

"Hello old friend."

Opening my eyes, I gazed at the rare monstrous tree towering over me with its silver leaves and graying gnarled branches. Its sharp, thorny teeth grinned widely at me, slick amber sap oozing from each pointed tip, and dripping down his gigantic trunk of a body.

One drop of that sap in my system would render me cursed forever. Bound to the weretree for all eternity as a starving, restless, wolf, guarding its master.

Except, I did not fear this one, we had met once before. Back when I was a young fae of ten summers with a fanciful goal to spend the rest of my life as a wolf with a powerful werewood tree. Together we would rule these very woods. Free and vicious. All would fear us.

I spent three weeks in the Wildwoods, dodging my mothers guards at every turn, in search of werewood tree that would agree to bite me. When he finally revealed himself to me, he laughed and told my faeling self that we would one day meet again, and that my request of him would be much different.

I smiled back at its thorny grin. "So the time has finally come for us to meet again has it?"

His gnarled silver glowing eyes blinked and his body creaked with his deep laughter. "Little shadow, you have grown. Do you still wish to be a wolf, I wonder?"

I shrugged, "As fun as it does sound, I do believe the goddess has different plans in store for me." I hitched my thumb over the unconscious shifter suspended in the air by my shadows.

The weretree's large canopied limbs, full of lush silver leaves stretched over us, and shrouded us from the rest of the forest. "So the trees tell me. But yes, the goddess does have other plans for you, little shadow."

I narrowed my eyes on him. "What do you know?"

His silver eyes flashed. "You will have all your answers soon enough."

I sighed with resignation, "If you won't tell me then at least take this nuisance off my hands. He might be a tasty bite. What do you suppose happens to a shifter when bitten?"

He shook with silent laughter and circular silver spiked leaves fell from his quivering branches. I plucked one from my hair and watched it fall to the canopy floor. The gnomes would appreciate this boon. They particularly loved werewood leaves. Their spikes made the perfect weapons for their tiny war games.

"We don't bite shifters. They are difficult to control during transition and never taste pleasant enough for us to risk it."

I sniffed. "No I suppose not, they are scum after all. It may be easier to just kill him."

More leaves fell from laughter and I brushed them off with mild annoyance. Yes, the gnomes were going to have a field day. I'd have to prepare myself the next time I traveled through these parts.

"Except you have not killed him, unlike the others that met your blade here."

"*Yet*. I have not killed him yet, werewood."

His silver eyes flared knowingly again, "There will be a time where you crave to be with this one more than you crave his death and even your own. In this, you will find it very difficult to kill him." The werewood groaned before a brown leather satchel appeared before me, hanging from one of his great gnarled branches.

"Take this. I have fulfilled my promise to the Golden One and kept it safe. I will give it to you for safekeeping until he awakens."

I raised a brow. I had so many questions but I took the shifter's traveling bag anyway. My fingers twitched to look inside. "You know him then? This Golden One? Who is he and how do I not know of him?"

The thorny mouth of the werewood tree spread into a predator-like smile and his silver eyes glowed with dark humor. "Did I not tell you that you'd ask something much different the next time we met?" His great silver branches groaned loudly as he chuckled, "We will not meet again, little shadow, but I will be watching."

I frowned. "Watching?"

The werewood chuckled mysteriously again, "All of Faerie is watching you, little shadow."

"What is that supposed to mean?" I narrowed my eyes on him.

The great weretree just stared back. Awkward silence filled the eerie Wildwoods and then, in a flash, he was just gone. Dissolving into the darkened woods as quickly as he came.

Gripping the satchels strap with annoyance, I growled, "Do your best not to watch too closely, old friend, you're creepy enough face to face."

In the distance the groans of the werewood could be heard once again...laughing at me.

Slinging, the brown leather bag over my shoulder, its weight remarkably light for someone as big as him traveling, I turned to look at the sleeping shifter floating on a black cloud of shadows. Looking at him now reminded me of a human fairytale I heard once. Except that was a princess and ended with a kiss.

I rolled my eyes again—*humans*.

"Let's get this over with." I waved at the shadows and I steered off into the direction of my hidden cabin.

My shadows rushed to my side, twirling around me playfully in spirals of black smoke and I snickered at their antics only to stop short at a loud thump behind me. Pivoting, I turned to see a dumped shifter sprawled unceremoniously on the forest floor. Remarkably, he was still fast asleep.

I snorted, trying to hold back my amusement and sternly addressed the shadows. "Pick him up you foolish beings. You know he's coming with us. Hopefully he will wake soon and tell us who the goddess he is." Turning away from them, I muttered, "If he doesn't wake up, I'm not kissing him. I have no need for a prince."

Shimmering with laughter they rushed to pick up the shifter again.

I gave them one more glance back to make sure they understood my seriousness. "Be sure not to drop him again," I said sternly. Only seconds passed when I heard another loud thump—this one sounding like the handsome shifter's head slamming into a tree.

A wide smile split across my face, highlighted by the three moons in the dark silvery forest. My shadows were playful tonight.

# CHAPTER 5

A LOW GROWL RUMBLED deep in my chest as I attempted to pry open my eyes, the weight of the chains gone like it was only a bad dream. "Fuck."

Faerie may have healed my body but it still felt like I fell from a cliff, hitting several boulders on my way down.

*"Your foul language really is unseemingly."*

"Sweet goddess, you're still there? And here I really hoped that the torture would at least kill you off, cat," I said in a low snarl to the beast who resided inside of me.

He snarled back with warning, *"Two days, fairy boy."*

I shrugged. "We've been through worse."

The cat snorted again and rolled his eyes inside my head, *"You better shift soon or I will force you to. I am tired of being stuck in this repugnant body of yours. Who knows what those irons did to my coat."*

"It's too risky for us to shift now. Your vanity will have to wait." I was pretty damn recognizable in my shifted form—I'd rather not draw that sort of attention.

"Is talking to yourself a side effect of being tortured or do you do it out of habit?"

I inhaled sharply. That voice. Fuck that sound was the most beautiful thing I ever heard and suddenly I was overwhelmed by a scent—lilies after a fresh night rain, Strong, pure, beautiful.

Her.

I inhaled again, tattooing it deep within my memory for fear of ever losing it again. Groaning, I forced my aching body to sit upright and narrowed my feral gaze on her.

She sat on a tall wooden stool, cross legged on her high perch, her hands relaxed on her knees, with her black shadows floating lazily around her.

One would be a fool to mistake her for anything but deadly this way.

"Why in the Sheol do I feel like my head has been smashed in?" Definitely not the first words I'd thought I'd say to my soulmate after one hundred years of searching for her.

Perfect pink lips peeled back revealing gleaming white teeth. "How am I supposed to know why you feel what you do, shifter?"

I grinned back. The fae didn't lie but we were proficient at our phrasing. This was no different and I approved.

"How long have I been asleep?" I glanced at the window, noticing the sunlight streaming into her small dwelling, highlighting the natural blue in her black hair.

"Five hours." Bright emerald green eyes that I could drown in...wanted to drown in, bored into my own, and my mouth went dry. Beautiful, she was beautiful.

*"Keep your wits, fairy boy,"* my cat practically hissed at me.

*"Fuck off,"* I shot back silently and pushed him in the deep recesses of my mind. A talent my father had taught me as a cub after the beast had taken over my body for two whole weeks during the first time I shifted. It had taken my mothers begging tears for the asshole to change me back to the son she knew and not a confused rampaging beast with his own conscious thought. After that, there was no end to the training my father delivered to strengthen my mental shields.

The shadow fae quirked a dark brow at me like she was considering putting me down like a rabid animal.

I scrubbed at my grown out beard with a frown, hoping to rub some function back to my brain and away from my growing arousal. "To answer your question, I was talking to my beast just now." Honesty was *probably* the best route at the moment...probably.

My cat snorted from the depths of my mind.

She frowned at me and tapped her delicate fingers that could kill a fae in an instant, on her knees. "I wasn't aware that shifter's beasts had their own consciousness."

That's because they fucking didn't. I was *special*–specially cursed. Instead, I retorted, "How many shifters do you really know?"

She blinked and her face returned to the neutral mask she wore so well. I recognized it now. It was the same look on her face when she killed those shifters in the woods. I could smell the violence on her and saw the subtle poise of her posture changing...more erect.

I groaned. *Fuck don't say erect.*

She watched me with more distrust. "Alright, let's skip the small talk, shall we." She rose unfurling her legs to stand with a deadly grace. "You will tell me who you are before I decide to make you dead permanently this time." The shadows swirled, hovering above us like a dark cloud.

I slowly licked my lips and my hands twitched to trace every perfect curve of her dangerous petite frame. She was short stature for a fae, my seven foot frame would tower over her, but that did not deter the burning desire she sparked inside of me. Since discovering her, I had over a century to dream up and fantasize many depraved moments between us but also I dreamed of the quiet ones. The stories she would tell me of her adventures I had only heard from others, the sound of her laughter that was reported to be the sweetest of dark melodies, her eyes full of love staring back at me that was foretold to hold the deepest loyalty and trust that any could ever wish for.

I craved it all.

Clearing my throat, I raked my hand through my hair once more, forcing myself to think with something other than my dick. "They call me Emon."

The silent rise of her dark brows was her only response and I smiled sweetly back at her. I knew what she wanted, she wanted my full name, a sign of trust amongst the fae, but it wasn't about that. Once she knew my name the ward of protection I held would shatter and she would remember just who exactly I was. She wasn't ready for that yet and perhaps neither was I.

"As for killing me, you most certainly can try," I stretched my arms up to the ceiling and cracked my neck back and forth. "Although, I think you'd have a hard time doing so," I purred with approval, feeling her eyes rake over my body.

Her careful facade cracked when her eyes rolled, "You are the second being who has said that to me tonight." She reached behind her and I tensed. "This fact makes me want to kill you even more." She laughed at my stillness, "You're even preparing yourself for it. I wonder why that is?"

I leaned in and growled low, "There's more than one thing reacting to you right now, little umbra, and I can assure you it isn't fear."

Her emerald eyes dipped downward and then snapped back up to mine. I couldn't stop my rumbling chuckle at her discomfort.

Scowling, she snapped at the swirling shadows above us, and from them dropped a leather satchel. My leather satchel. She twirled it teasingly in front of me. "I believe you lost something in the woods, shifter."

"Where did you get that?" I hissed, my heart beating faster at the sight of it. I didn't care about the bag so much as the hidden relic inside. I spent days being tortured to ensure it stayed safe. If Jurin had somehow discovered it...

She pitched my bag straight at my head with a grin, attempting to catch me off guard. "From the weretree."

I snatched it with one hand easily, never taking my gaze off hers, noticing a flicker of admiration in her beautiful green eyes. I smiled, I was a shifter...she'd have to find a different way than speed to get a jump on me.

Slowly, I placed my bag beside me and patted it discreetly, feeling for the contents inside. "Thank you for giving it back to me." My body relaxed deeper into the bed and my heart steadied when I felt the knowing curve of the relic. "The weretree didn't give you any trouble did he?"

She raised a sharp brow, insulted, "You know who I am."

"I do. Which means I have to ask," I smiled, "Did you go through my things?"

The cabin grew quiet while I held her steady gaze. Moments passed before a grin grew on my face. She had expected me to search my bag, revealing its contents without blemishing her sense of honor by her doing it herself. In that case, she was in for disappointment.

"Do you have a shower here?"

Her stare broke and lines furrowed on her forehead. "A what?"

"A shower?" I growled. "I fucking smell like a rotting carcass and I am covered in my *own* blood. I don't relish that."

Her arms crossed firmly over her chest, "I'm not in the business of taking in strays and providing for their mangey needs."

I shrugged, "Now you are. You brought me here."

Anger flashed in her emerald eyes. "What makes you think that you're some sort of guest, shifter? That these amenities are even available to you."

Chuckling, I stood. My hands grazed the ceiling of her small cabin while I stretched out my soreness before I slung my bag over my bare blood crusted chest. Her eyes dragged up my body and before tilting her head to scowl up at me. With curling lips, her shadows snapped threateningly in front of me.

Reaching steadily outward, I tickled them on their underside, treating them like any protective animal guarding their master. I was no threat to her. I never would be. Sensing this the shadows melted to a black puddle at our feet.

Remnant inhaled subtly, staring down at her shadows, and I could smell her shock.

"You're *the* last shadow fae, on the run, charged with destruction of the City of Light and the slaughtering of the thousands of fae that resided there, along with their beloved queen." I couldn't refrain from sneering at that last part. She continued to stare down at her shadows but I could see her jaw clench hard and her fists tightening crossed over her chest. "You had the upper hand bringing me here and yet I'm not in irons even though you suspect my power rivals yours. Goddess, you could have even left me out in the woods for your little warring gnomes," I nodded to the window. The stale stench of gnomes was prominent outside this cabin. She was smart to have them here...no fae in their right mind fucked with the gnomes. "I'd say that I am the closest to a guest anyone is ever going to get with you."

She looked up then, her eyes narrowing.

I sighed and reached my hand out again to the shadows puddled at my feet. They rose up and curled around my arm, their cool darkness brushing against my hot skin with affection. "I am not a threat to you, little umbra," I whispered gently.

"So you think you know me, shifter." She released her arms and stepped back, the shadows following her and spreading. The cabin was suddenly pitched in black and the sunlight from the window completely disappeared. "Your power is no threat to mine. You are not in irons because I don't need irons, and you were not left in the woods because your company is not good enough even for my gnomes. You're only alive because I haven't decided to kill you yet."

Her eyes glowed in the darkness and all I could think about was what secrets they held, what I could unlock within them. Images of her spread out under me, her gasps of pleasure, the caress of her smooth pale skin against my own. "Beautiful." My whispered words echoed through the darkened void.

She blinked, the deadly shadows creeping back towards her, revealing the sunlit cabin once more. "Who in the goddess are you really?"

I grinned and puffed out my chest, "I told you already. My name is Emon, shifter of The West Isles, and I have been searching for you, Remnant Ezra Solaire Dark, for the past one hundred years." I nodded to the shadows all around us. "It's time to step out of the shadows and live again." When she took an angry step towards me, I held out my hand and watched the dried blood flake off with a grimace. "Now if you don't mind, I'll take that fucking shower now."

# Chapter 6

Emon

I SHOULD HAVE BEEN ashamed.

But I wasn't.

Panting and throwing my head back, I barely suppressed my groan of pleasure as I jerked off in the shadow fae's shower. Heavy streams of cum were instantly washed away by the running hot water, finally giving me the release I needed in order to function.

The downside of being a shifter.

The more powerful you were, the more basic your animal instincts drove you. Finding your mate and the intense need to claim them is almost impossible to fully ignore, and unfortunately, I had to do just that.

Remnant wasn't ready for two life changing events in one day. Her anger towards me was a testament to that. She was one step away from losing control.

"*You were the same once,*" the beast growled, "*she needs a purpose for her anger, a target to unleash it on. Fortunately for me, it has become you. I am thoroughly amused.*"

I dropped my head to the shower wall, enjoying the warmth of the water raining down on me, and huffed out a long sigh, "I hate you, you know."

"*Your mind has been racing since we got here. Seeking out an answer to get her to leave this place. I just gave you your answer, daft fairy boy. You should be thanking me.*"

I lifted my head from the water pouring over me and scrubbed it from my beard. "You're suggesting I become her next purpose...her next target?"

"*You seem to enjoy playing the sacrificial bait. Why change now?*" He drawled, his voice slinking further and further away from my consciousness.

"Well shit," I growled low and waved the shower off, shaking the water violently from my hair and rubbed myself down with a towel until my skin was red. Snarling, I threw it in the corner of the shower and stepped in front of the sink where an ornate gold mirror hung on the wall.

My brows lowered in my reflection. This mirror didn't belong here, not in this cabin.

It was way too fine of a piece for such a simple rustic place. This cabin was designed to provide shelter and safety, it thrummed with power to provide all the basics a fae would need...especially for a lonely shadow fae on the run.

A basic shower that turned water on and off when needed, a toilet that magically disappeared when not in use, and a sink bowl below the mirror. But the mirror itself—it was *brought* here and judging by the power behind the craftsmanship, I knew it had come from the palace of Faerie's capital.

My frown deepened when I studied myself further in the incongruous mirror. My beard was much more grown out than usual and even the sides of my head needed a fresh shave. Scowling, I braided back my hair and tied it off. I was a goddess damn mess.

My muscles rippled while I examined every inch of my smooth tan skin. The stab wounds were gone but I could still feel the slide of the knife puncturing my flesh like I was made of butter. That fuckers death was far too short for all the trouble he had caused me. I certainly underestimated his level of insanity.

My reflection shimmered suddenly and I blinked hard, studying the smooth surface of the mirror. "Cat. Did you just see that?" I growled low.

*"The mirror is enchanted,"* he yawned.

"Enchanted to do what?"

Before he could answer the mirror flared and I felt my entire conscious self plunging into its cold glassy reflection. The mirror's power penetrated my mind, making me shiver with disgust as snapshots of time whirled by me. Glimpses of fae I had never seen before swirled in and out of my vision before it stopped.

*Remnant knelt with bright red slashes across her face and her emerald eyes shimmered with tears. They fell heavily, mingling with the blood that had dripped over her pale skin. Skin that had been seared off on one side. Her armor clinked when a violent shudder ran through her body before her head threw back into a piercing scream.*

*My chest tightened at the unfiltered anguish that rattled against the walls. Her hands threaded into her blue black hair, forcefully gripping it, and fueling the sound of heartbreak.*

*I gasped and fell heavily to my knees when I felt the shatter of her soul. Pure power exploded out from her, and at the same time cold numbness iced her heart...my heart.*

*I crawled towards her, gritting my teeth against her crushing grief while the vengeful shadows enveloped us both into infinite darkness.*

"Fuck!" I roared, wrenching myself away from the mirror, falling hard on my ass.

*"Foolish, imbecilic fairy! It's a soul mirror—why do you never heed me! I said it was enchanted!"* The cat snarled at me.

I rubbed at the tightness in my chest, steadying my erratic breathing. Pushing up from the floor, I snarled. "Saying something is enchanted is totally different than telling me it's a fucking soul mirror," I growled back, wiping the tears from my face angrily with the back of my arm—Remnant's tears.

*"A soul mirror will force you to witness any fae's memory that has scarred their soul but also to feel every single emotion they had while their soul broke,"* my beast explained, seeing me stare at the dampness on my arm.

Intense sorrow filled me. "Morta. That was Morta," I murmured. "We just witnessed Remnant destroying the City of Light." My fangs lengthened while my lips peeled back. "Why?" I snarled. "Why the fuck would she keep something like this?"

*"Penance."* The cat responded with a solemn heaviness I had never heard from him before. As if he understood everything she had gone through.

"A penance she never needed to serve anyway," I glared past my reflection, seeing fully the depravity of the soul mirror.

Fuck that. This ended now.

My fist slammed hard into the mirror's shimmering depths. It rippled in defense but in the end could not defend itself against brute shifter strength. The mirror gave, shattering into silver dust. Its foul remains fell, gathered by the sink below.

No more penance.

No more hiding.

No more being lost.

It was time for Remnant Ezra Solaire Dark to live again.

It was time to unleash her.

It was time...for me to be bait.

My cat snickered.

# CHAPTER 7

## Remnant

"**T**OOK YOU LONG ENOUGH," I half scowled, half thirsted at the beads of water still kissing the shifter's bronze skin while he sat smugly in my favorite chair. Couldn't he have put a shirt on at least?

The shifter gazed up at me through his lashes, not uttering a single word in his defense.

My lips pressed into a thin line. This shifter knew what he was doing and could likely scent the spike of desire my treacherous body was feeling. "Too comfortable to talk?" I snapped.

I blinked against the radiant smile he beamed at me. "Very. Thank you." He scratched at his bare chest with a sheepish look and I tracked the movement, my eyes roaming over the hard ridges of his sculpted muscle. "I broke your mirror..."

My eyes glared back at his handsome face. "You broke my mirror—"

He grunted again, "More like I destroyed it purposefully."

My cheeks burned red with simmering anger. "You destroyed my mirror."

The shifter leaned forward, his elbows resting on his knees while he gazed at me with the same intensity. "I didn't like what I saw."

"You're not supposed to! It's a goddess damn soul mirror!" I snapped. "I suppose you just make it a habit to destroy things you don't like!"

His brow cocked sardonically, "You don't?"

I laughed coldly and reached out to the shadows that snaked around my arm, following my tattoos with flawless precision. "Objects? No. Fae? Yes."

He chuckled and leaned back, his smile showing fang, "We all have our hobbies."

"I suppose we do. How about you tell me why your *hobby* was looking for me since all your needs have now been met."

He released another deep knowing chuckle and I suppressed the shiver that sensuous sound created. "Trust me, little umbra, not *all* my needs have been met."

I snuffed the shadows out with my hand. "Stop calling me that." Umbra was old fae for shadow and this was the third time he had used it. It reminded me too much of my previous life...a dead life. "You're flirting your way out of my questioning."

He inhaled deeply and his golden eyes sparkled, "You like my flirting."

"I like a lot of things...I also dislike a lot of things. Your evasiveness of my questions being one of them," I snarled through my teeth, unable to resist leaning in towards him. Whether it was from anger or desire I did not know. In fact, I could not remember any other fae affecting me so wholly, not even my former love. "Start talking, shifter."

His fingers tapped on the arm of the chair before he spoke with a calculating air. "Alright then. How well do you know the Sanguine?"

I reared back and my heated anger turned to ice. "Enough to know that it is not to be talked about. Ever!" I narrowed my eyes on him. "The people of the Sanguine...the blood fae, were destroyed by the wrath of the goddess when I was very young. Their terrible power, the Sanguine itself, was destroyed with them."

He leaned in with a growl, "Except such power could never be truly destroyed. Blood is an essence of life just like the water, the elements, the darkness, the light. As long as there's life, the Sanguine will continue to live on. The true question is, were all those who could truly wield it destroyed?"

My sentient shadows popped in and hissed silently at the shifter. "If you think I can wield the Sanguine you have the wrong fae, shifter. There's the door." I turned and walked towards the one thing I wanted him to walk out of.

"I know you don't but someone you once cared deeply for had the possibility to," he growled low, "Deirdre. The former Queen of Faerie."

My steps faltered and my hand trembled on the door latch. I snapped it back to my chest. "The Queen of Faerie is dead. Or did you forget I was the one who killed her over one hundred years ago?" My voice held steady even while acidic grief burned my throat and my heart thundered inside of my chest. The sound of it caused me to stumble to the side and I steadied myself on the window sill as a growing panic seized my body.

The flutter of violet wisps outside caught my eye and I turned my focus on them. Willing my breathing to follow their rhythmic fluttering, I watched as the gnomes scampered about the clearing with their new weretree weapons, jumping and stabbing at the glowing butterflies that left trails of glitter in their wake. One was pissing on my flowers and more than a few were choking on glitter dust, tearing the wings off the very butterflies they had been chasing with their needled teeth.

A soft trilling sound shifted my gaze to a flock of chickadees singing happily in the berry bushes nearby. I fixated on that sound. A sound from my childhood. It was a memory, a whisper, *my little chickadee,* and I clung to it. Allowing it to unwind the tightness in my chest.

I stiffened when I heard the shifter take a cautious step towards me. Somewhere in my panic he had risen from his comfortable seat. "I am sorry. Is there anything I can do? Some way I can help you?"

I continued to focus on the melodies of the chickadees outside. "Yes. Tell me what I need to say in order for you to leave me and this place in peace?"

He sighed, "Are you truly at peace here?"

I snorted. "Peace doesn't exist, shifter. But I try to seek it anyway. Ask your questions."

A low rumble of agitation sounded behind me but I paid it no heed. Silence hung between us before he spoke slowly and cautiously.

"You were the closest to her. The general to the queen as well as...her partner." I didn't miss the catch in his voice at his last words. The shifter race hated the former Queen of Faerie for what she did to their people. I didn't blame him for his distaste at our intimate relationship.

A dry laugh escaped me, "*Close*... yeah...I suppose you could call it that."

"Did she ever speak to you about the Sanguine? About harnessing its power?" He pressed.

"No. She never spoke of such things," I hissed, but she had used it, at least I suspected as much. "Besides, even if Deirdre did have intentions of harboring the Sanguine, *she is dead*!" Uncontrolled shadows exploded all around me and I heard the shifter curse with surprise. "It's time for you to leave now." I rubbed at my temples.

He growled threateningly and I heard his heavy step forward. "I cannot leave here without you. I need you to prove to me that she is dead. That she is no longer a threat to our world because..." his voice faltered and then he inhaled deeply, " because I believe that not only did you fail your people that day, but you failed them twice by not killing her."

"*What!*" I spun back around so fast my hair whipped across my face and my shadows sprung forth to wrap around his neck. "What did you just say to me?"

His golden gaze held mine even while the shadows constricted tighter around his throat. He reached up and instead of pulling them off him, he ran his hand over his braided hair. "Faerie is *dying*, Remnant. The Sanguine is here and I know Deirdre is at the center of it all."

I snorted and snapped the shadows away from him. "All worlds die at some point. I fail to see how the other two are connected to such an event," I hissed back even though that soft whisper of doubt infiltrated my resolve.

The shifter rubbed at his neck and pressed his lips thinly together. "Not in this way."

I narrowed my eyes on him. "I haven't seen signs of such death."

Emon sighed, "You haven't left these woods in a long time. There are places outside of here that have completely succumbed to the Sanguine. It is now lifeless earth and the diseased decay spreads with each passing day. It destroys all, it kills all," he snarled hard, his eyes unfocused, lost in a memory. "There are creatures that haunt the deadlands. Lifeless beings that kill anything they come across. I have lost a few of my friends by their soulless kind." His golden gaze refocused on me with such an intensity that I had to force myself not to rear back. "*Everything* points to the Sanguine resurfacing," he continued in earnest, "Faerie needs *you*, Remnant. You have the power to stop this."

I crossed my arms in front of my chest. "Why? Why the need to save Faerie at all? The fae are already heading for extinction, this just speeds up our timeline," I snorted. "Surely it's not for your disgusting people back in The West Isles with your parricidal king." I arched a brow at him when he flinched. "In fact the only *problem* I see is that your kind are in my woods, unwelcomed."

Hurt flashed in his eyes and then was gone, a predator glared back at me. "You know nothing of my kind little umbra...and you know nothing of the world you choose to exist in but not live in." His lip raised in a small snarl, "You are duty bound still to protect these lands. I know your vows. That kind of sworn fealty doesn't wear off, especially if the ruler you made it to is still alive."

Rage burned within me. "Fuck you, shifter, I am protecting it...from the worst thing that could ever happen to it...me!" I hissed, sidestepping to the door and wrenching it open. "Now, I do believe your kind belongs outdoors—"

His nose twitched and then he was launching himself towards me. The heavy wooden door slammed shut and I gasped as I was forcibly pressed against its cool wooden planks and the heat of his hard muscular body.

"Do not move." A vicious warning growl ripped deep from his throat. Slowly angling his body sideways with his lips peeled back over lengthening canines he peered out the window.

I heeded his warning, only because I knew the look of an animal that was threatened. Of course, it had nothing to do with the delicious heat pouring off of him that felt comforting and safe. I inhaled deep and waited for the panic to grip my monstrous soul. Seconds passed and so did my growing desire...not panic.

Angry at my treacherous body for responding the exact way it should, I drew my shadow sword from the void and laid it across his throat. "Step away from me." The chill in my voice thankfully did not reflect the desirous fire running hot inside. My shadows along with the dormant ones gathered, darkening the room, highlighting my anger, and the immensity of my own power.

The shifter Emon paid no attention to my blade, instead his gold eyes peeled away from the window and slowly perused my face. "Fuck," he whispered, swallowing hard. "You're so beautiful." Raising up his hand, he cupped my cheek, his thumb stroking against my skin softly. "As much as I enjoy this, little umbra. We do have company and I don't believe you're an exhibitionist," he murmured low, sliding that cursed thumb down over the bottom of my lip before he dropped it, stepping away from my blade. "Take a look, carefully."

Irritated, I pressed my lips in a thin line and glared hard at him before dropping my sword and sliding with whispered steps to look out the window.

"No," I whispered with disbelief. The sunlight was no more and the clearing was now replaced with an unnatural gray mist. It rolled over blackened decayed grass that was once green and choked the berry bushes to a pile of ash. Stiff and void of life, my chickadees lay on top of them—soundless.

Desperately, I searched the clearing for my gnomes, only to find them just as unrecognizable. Distinguished only by their sharp pointed teeth sticking up from their shriveled forms like tiny pincushions. Scattered among them were butterfly wings, fluttering stiffly in the sinister mist.

A tingling sense of alarm made me look beyond the rot towards the tree line that was slowly losing its vibrant silver shimmer. And in the middle of it all, black hooded figures floated eerily amongst it, dripping with dark red blood staining the decaying ground.

Spinning back to the shifter, I raised my sword threateningly, "You did this!"

Indignation flashed in Emon's feral gold eyes. "Goddess help me, I know the former War General of Faerie isn't this stupid. You know the stories. It's the Sanguine," he hissed.

Past the point of reasoning, I thrusted my blade towards him and matched his same hissing snarl. "You will tell me what *they* are right now and how to kill them...and when I've finished that task then maybe I will consider sparing your life."

The shifter shook his head and moved so fast, I barely had time to drop my blade, nearly puncturing him through the chest as he yanked me farther from the window. Bowing low he snarled in my ear, "Not a chance, little umbra. What those fuckers are...are a fight for another day. I am not letting you go out there to get yourself killed. Besides, I want my fucking proof that Deirdre is really dead, as you so adamantly swear by."

The shadows deepened and my hand shook from not striking him down. It would be too easy to slide this blade straight through his toned bronze body. "*This* is my home, *those* were my flower pissing gnomes. I don't owe you anything and I am not leaving!"

Again, with very little fear for his own life, he gripped my shoulders, and spun me towards the far side of the room. Further away from the abominations hovering unsuspectedly of the events happening here. Ducking away from him, I twisted my blade and sliced his arm with a controlled precise warning. "Touch me again and I will kill you," I hissed.

Breathing heavily he stared hard at me, not even glancing down at the blood that ran in small rivulets over his forearm and splattered on the wood floor. "I don't fucking believe you'll kill me because unlike those abominations out there, I don't send a chill of fear running down your spine. What I do send down your spine is much more pleasurable. Isn't that right, little umbra?"

I narrowed my eyes and my hand tightened on the hilt of my sword.

He scrubbed his hand over his hair. "We don't have time for this." His eyes clashed with mine, the ferocity and fire there made me take a small step back. "I swear to you Remnant Dark and the fucking goddess herself, we will get your revenge for your pee pollinating gnomes." Snarling through his sharp canines, he tipped his strong chin towards me, "Now, pack a bag or your void of darkness shadow shit. We *are* leaving."

I snarled back at him.

His lips turned up with amusement. "That's more like it. Now where is your escape tunnel? I know you have one. I can smell the stale air creeping from its depths."

# CHAPTER 8

*Remnant*

I GLARED AT THE tanned muscular back of Emon who was setting a quick pace south towards the Balsam Plains, the southernmost point of the Wildwoods. He had easily sniffed out the cabin's escape route and then proceeded to remind me of all my failures, taunting me to follow him.

My jaw clenched and my hands curled at my sides. I knew what he was doing, making himself a target so I would give chase. The problem was...it was goddess damn working!

If Deirdre was alive...

No. She was dead and I would prove it.

My eyes tracked his powerful stride, his toned ass taunting me with each prowling step. Only to be made worse by his bag slapping quietly against his side. Another taunt. I should have pilfered the contents...my damned honor was the only thing that had prevented me from doing it.

Why in the goddess would a werewood tree hide a bag for him?

Who in the goddess was he really?

"It's unusual for a shifter to travel alone. Do your people hate you as much as your little gang in the woods did?"

Amused gold eyes flashed back at me. "The opposite in fact. They adore me. It's me that prefers solitude. I am sure my friends will be more than displeased that I didn't allow them to tag along on this journey." He shot me a smile. "I have a feeling they'd love you though. Most shifters do, you know."

My steps faltered and I narrowed my eyes on him. "I'd say you're lying if that was even possible for us."

He shrugged and danced around a patch of red dragon plants that were ready to snap his balls off.

*Damn,* I was hoping I had distracted him enough to at least see that happen. He gave me a knowing look.

"That's exactly my point," he waved at the plants, "they would have laughed their asses off seeing you distract me enough to step into that kind of trouble." The affection for his friends in his warm growling tone was evident. He raked a hand over his hair. "I do miss them. I have been gone too long."

I tickled the dragon plants under their thorny chins with my shadows and they slumped to the ground in slumber. "How long have you been gone?" I ignored his surprised look at the vicious sleeping plants and stepped gingerly over a pod of mushroom caps.

He quickly caught up to me. "Over the past one hundred years, I've checked in off and on but not long enough to ease their concern." He gave me a small smirk. "You have been difficult to find."

"That was the point," I drawled, "I did not and still do not want to be found."

Would my gnomes have died had he not found me?

He shook his head, reading my thoughts. "My presence had nothing to do with your cabin being discovered," he said softly.

My hand twitched for my sword but I continued walk-ing—fleeing more like it. Was that who I was now? The former general that hid, that ran? A monster following a goddess damn shifter of all things?

Emon started to hum an old tune from my childhood and I found myself glaring at his back again while my traitorous shadows danced to his sultry song. They hadn't left me since he had come and I could not tell if that was because they were infatuated with the shifter or worried for me. In the end, it didn't matter. My shadows were loyal, the only thing I could trust in this world.

Unlike Deirdre...

Her name was like a ghost that haunted my soul. Once the Queen of Faerie, she was the most powerful fae elemental to have existed. Harnessing all the elements and spirit, she was a beautiful and deadly creature...and I loved her for it. We were drawn passionately to each other from the isolation that came with tremendous power.

I hadn't even allowed myself to think her name let alone speak it since Morta and I hated that the very sound of it made my heart fracture—that I still had love for her evil soul.

"Are you okay?" Concerned gold eyes peered back over a deliciously defined shoulder.

I *hated* that shoulder. "I'm Faerie fantastic."

"We will be at the Balsam Plains soon." I could hear the laughter in his deep voice. "Then we can find shelter for the night. It won't be safe to travel in the dark."

Flipping my hair over my shoulder I smirked, "I have no fear of that, shifter. In case you haven't noticed, I am the dark-ness."

He chuckled deeply, "Oh I have noticed, little umbra. How could I not when all its sinful secrets are wrapped up into one beautiful fae?" Casually he launched himself on one hand over a large fallen tree. His entire body planking sideways with graceful ease and then disappearing from sight.

I snorted and rolled my eyes. Waving my hand behind me, shadow wings sprouted at my back and instantly raised me above the ground. Emon was waiting on the other side with his arms crossed and a smug smile plastered on his face. When he glanced up and saw me flying not only over the tree but over his head as well, that smile split into a wide admiring grin.

Landing softly on the ground in front of him, my wings dissolved and I shot him a smug look of my own.

He prowled towards me, "I'm impressed."

I flipped my long black hair again and turned to give him an assessing look. "That only makes one of us."

His deep sensuous chuckle made my stomach flutter and made me walk further away from him.

We were close to the southern ridge-line of the Wildwoods now anyway and I found myself looking forward to the waves of prickling green valleys and thick gnarly brambles of the Balsam Plains. Jackalopes would be out at this time of day, wreaking havoc in the underbrush and disturbing the white flowered fairy rings that beckoned any traveler to its sinful revelry.

As I stepped out of the woods, I faltered, the sun blinding me. Raising my hand to shield its powerful rays, my sight adjusted and I inhaled sharply.

The bright evergreens I expected to see laid charred and broken for miles. Black ash littered the ground with what looked like hundreds of jackalope horns adorning the bleak landscape—a warning to any who came here.

In the distance, I could just make out the faint outline of a fairy ring, except no white flowers encircled it...no powers of seduction called to me to dance my life away inside it...because there was absolutely no life left to do so.

The sun settled behind the clouds and I watched as a dark foreboding shadow fell upon the haunted lands. Forcing myself to step forward onto the dusty black dirt, an eerie black mist curled up around my leathered boot and charred branches broke beneath their thick soles. I could feel the sickening disease leaking from the land, attempting to latch on...clawing desperately for the essence of life within me.

"No," I whispered when my eyes caught sight of large bones protruding from the dead valley. Rushing over, my hands reached out reverently to the towering ribs that arched over my head. My fingers trailed along the smooth surface while tears formed in my eyes.

"I know these bones," I whispered brokenly, feeling, rather than hearing the shifter standing stoically behind me. Stooping down, my vision blurred when I touched the smaller carcass that had been lovingly guarded in its final moments. "This was a cù-sìth mother and her pup." My eyes closed and tears fell. "I saved this pup once. Did you know it takes five hundred years for a pup to mature into a full adult? Its mother never leaves their side until then."

"A loving and honorable devotion that most of us will never be able to experience," he added softly.

Rising, I turned to him. "The fae are not deserving of such a gift."

Emon's eyes froze on the tears running down my pale cheeks. The turmoil inside of me was burning quickly to anger.

"You will tell me everything you know."

"Yes," he choked gruffly and I stilled when he reached to wipe a tear from my face. His touch seared my flesh while he studied the wetness on his fingertips. Growling, he looked back up at me. "I will tell you all of what you need to know, little umbra."

# CHAPTER 9

Emon

"ALLOW ME TO ASSIST you," I pleaded for the third time tonight watching my soulmate dig through the dead earth. Her bare hands had long ago split, bleeding with each clawing pass she made for the shallow graves of the cù-sìth mother and pup.

Every once in a while a tear would fall from those beautiful emerald eyes and soften the earth to ease the way.

"I do not wish for your help, shifter."

Growling, I dropped to my knees and unleashed my claws. Scraping into the diseased ash alongside her with more efficiency than her blunt fingertips.

"I do not care what you wish for, little umbra. This is how I wish to pay my respects as well."

Her bowed head full of black and blue hair snapped up and the three moons lit up the beauty of her features. Her lips pulled back in a sneer and her cheeks were rosy with grief and anger. The delicate swirls of ink on her tattooed arms flexed threateningly and her dirty fists curled in the shallow grave.

I held her stare. She was beautiful even in her threatening pose and I could not help but be awed by the way she mourned Faerie's beastly creatures almost more than her own species.

Emotion burned in the back of my throat. Guilt, shame, and pain seared my insides for not being able to soothe this pain. The way a mate should. But if I unmasked our soulmate bond now, I risked her safety and I needed her far away from here before I could ever allow myself the hope of chancing it.

Seeing my resolve, she huffed out an irritated sigh and her eyes dropped to the ground. She blinked then, seeing what I had seen thirty minutes ago but knew she needed longer to grieve. The grave was ready. "I think this will be enough."

"In shifter customs, when a mother and faeling pass together, the child is placed on top, closest to the sun. It is seen as the mother's final way of making sure their offspring will always walk in the light even in Sheol," I said softly, leaning back on my heels.

Remnant looked over at the bones with a vacant expression. "Yes, I believe that will be appropriate."

Withdrawing my claws, I reached for her healing hand. "Please allow me to do this for you, little umbra."

Her brow puckered, staring at our conjoined hands. "I will do this alone." She pulled away from me and I ignored the sharp sting the action caused.

I grunted and rose, dusting off my leathers, unable to meet her penetrating stare for fear she'd see the lingering pain there. "I'll set camp and then come back to help you cover them."

Setting camp took me little more than a few moments. Her shadows supplying bed rolls and dried meats from their void for the both of us. When Remnant was ready, we silently covered the bones and as I had suggested, the pup was placed tenderly on top of the mother, the last remains to disappear in the ash covered ground.

"Do your shifter customs have a prayer for these circum-stances as well?" Her voice wavered in the dark night as we stood on either side of the shallow grave.

"Hold out your hand," I said gruffly.

She did not hesitate this time and I placed my palm to meet hers, our fingertips brushing against each other's wrists. Our gazes locked.

"To the life given and the life taken too soon, the goddess take you with her golden light to live freely within our hearts where the devoted and young never die."

She pursed her lips and nodded her satisfaction. When I went to drop my hand, her fingers clutched my wrist tightly. I raised my brows in surprise.

Ignoring my inquiry, she added to the prayer, "To the life given and the life taken too soon, the darkness will avenge you so that you may soar through Sheol's doors free at last."

Faerie's winds blew, acknowledging her prayer before she released my hand and walked away without another passing glance at the hallowed ground still wet with her tears.

I followed her, like I always would, to our small camp. The need to whisk her away from this place and let this world come to its tragic end was stronger than ever.

*"Well that would be an imbecilic act fairy, where would you live then?"* My beast commented dryly.

*"There are other worlds,"* I said silently back.

*"We are born to our world for a reason, fairy boy."*

*"Speaking from experience, cat? What goddess damned world did you fall from that has me stuck with you for eternity?"*

I snorted as the soft padding of the cat's retreat was my only answer.

Sitting down in front of her and smoothing out the wrinkles in my bed roll, I felt my soulmate's eyes dissect every inch of me. I was facing the War General of Faerie now and not the fae back in the woods, alive and soaring on feathered shadow wings.

"How long?" Her tone was emotionless, wrapped in layers of steel and ice.

Her strength only ensnared me more. She was a fae misunderstood but I saw through her...I saw her for what she really was...blindingly faithful, pure, and strong.

Faerie never deserved her...and it had destroyed her.

"Since Morta," I responded.

"Morta—" she laughed dryly, tilting her head to the side, "Why doesn't it bother you, I wonder? Why do you not hate me for what I have done."

I shrugged, "I'm a shifter of The West Isles. The City of Light was the home of my enemy and from what I heard, it was already corrupt beyond saving. Your own people sacrificed you to their mad queen on a silver platter."

Remnant snickered coldly. "Fear of death will make even the most loyal waver."

I growled low, "Not all of us. Not you."

She gave me a small sinister smile. "No...but I have never feared death, shifter."

"What do you fear then, little umbra?"

"My fears have already come to pass. Now I have given you enough of my own answers. It is time you start giving me yours."

I gritted my teeth against the sharpness of her cold tone. Every instinct in me wanted to see her fire...her life. "The land is diseased and it is not just confined here. Half of Faerie has succumbed to its infestation and it continues to spread," I growled. "Most of The West Isles have been lost." Thank the goddess for our ancient healer. His powerful wards spared our most precious and treasured city, Finlandia.

"Is that why shifters are in the east?" She hummed and stroked the shadows that drifted lazily into her lap like a purring kitten.

Oh to be *them* right now.

I shook my head. "Shifters don't relish the thought of setting foot in these lands. Your mountains are puny and the wrong color." I winked before leaning forwards growling low, "Those shifters you killed were traitors to their own kind. I was hunting them for the crown."

"You're not a very good hunter then."

The cat inside me roared with laughter.

I ignored him and purred, "Perhaps I was hunting more than one thing."

She quirked a brow at me, understanding flashing in her eyes. "Am I supposed to believe that you used yourself as bait to draw me out? Almost getting killed in the process?"

"I would risk death every fucking day if it meant I would still be in your presence for one more minute of it." I was not ashamed to admit it, it was the truth and the fae did not lie.

Dark brows furrowed over her moonlit eyes. "You don't know me, shifter, not really."

"Don't I?" I spoke softly. From the moment our soulmate bond clicked into place I had made it my life's purpose to know everything there was about her. I investigated every whispered story, searched through every dusty tome, traveled through the lands she had left her mark on, spoke with the beasts she loved, and worst of all, sought the advice of the swordmaster that trained her. I knew her—I understood her, probably better than she understood herself.

She shook her head. "Those shifters in the woods wanted something from you. What was it?"

Raking my hand through my hair, I carefully crafted my answer. "They wanted the location to a lost gateway."

Her hand stilled from petting the shadows. "That information would be useless to them. Only those who hold the crown may open a gateway and they have all been closed forever." Her eyes narrowed. "Why would *you* know the location of a lost gateway?"

I shrugged. "Unfortunate circumstances of my existence I suppose."

Her gaze dropped down to my satchel sitting on the ground next to me. "Your bag. That is why you stored it with the weretree." She sniffed with approval. "Clever, but again risky. He could have just as easily bit you instead."

I smiled wide, not bothering to correct her. What I carried in my bag was far more precious than any gateway location. "I'm a shifter...being cursed in a wolf form isn't far from the curse I already carry with my own beast. Besides, they don't like the taste of us."

*"Fairies are especially revolting. I do not blame the weretree,"* my cat purred back.

*"I wonder if weretrees would enjoy cat chow instead?"* I mused back to him.

I leaned forward, "The real question you should be asking yourself is how those bastards could have even known about the gateway...there's only one other fae I know from these lands that knew of its location. The one fae you claim is dead."

My senses piqued while I specifically avoided Deirdre's name, a trigger for her panic back in the woods. Watching for her eyes to dilate, listening for her breathing to increase, smelling the sour sharpness of pain—all signs of panic that I was familiar with since it plagued me many nights as well.

Instead, I scented the piercing iciness of her anger. "I'll play," she hissed. "If I were to believe that she is truly alive, then everything you spoke of...those creatures, the diseased land, this lost gateway is all part of her grand scheme. To what purpose?"

I inhaled sharply. For a moment, her scent changed. The normal floral scent intensified as she spoke of the long dead Queen of

Faerie and I knew then... no matter how much Remnant despised her, I would still be competing with the ghost of a tainted love to win over her heart.

"Those creatures are called blood wraiths...a product from the Sanguine. That information we know for a fact, it was verified by one of our ancients in The West Isles who fought them in the Blood Wars." I tore into the dried beef the shadows had dumped on my bed roll. "I believe her aim is still the same as it has always been. Look around you, what do you see?"

"I don't need to look to see, shifter," she snapped, "it is the absence of life. The absence of the goddesses light."

I nodded. "Exactly." I ripped into another bite of beef with my fang and watched the blush of her anger drain to white.

"You believe she is attempting to create life again...using the Sanguine," she whispered.

The growl released from me was guttural. "Yes."

Her jaw clenched. "All based on a hunch that she is alive of course. There is nothing definitive that you have told me that proves that."

Humming, I dug my claws into the dead earth, scooping up the lifeless ash and letting it fall between us. I needed to tread carefully here. If I said too much she would piece together who I truly was and I needed her safe in The West Isles before then. "Those shifters you disposed of, do you know who their leader is, who they take orders from?"

She watched the crumbled ash float to the ground before answering. "No, but I am sure you are about to tell me."

"Falcon," I spat, tasting the foulness just uttering that name created.

Remnant's spine straightened and the moon-casted shadows darkened around us. "Impossible. Must be an imposter. A copycat," she hissed with brutal vehemence.

"I know enough about you that you don't prescribe to coincidences nor do you leave loose ends. Are you willing to risk the possibility that the bastard is still alive?"

She looked away, her blue black hair falling in a curtain over her shoulder and shielding her just like the shadows. "No. I would not." Her voice whispered across the deadlands, the air carrying it across the loose ash. "It took two days for the dust to finally settle when my city was destroyed. Two days I stood vigilant. Waiting. Just waiting for signs of life." She swept her hair back and glared at me. "It never came and yet...I am to somehow trust the words of a shifter I do not know? Trust you when you say that the two fae that deserved to die that day, should have died, did not?"

I inhaled deep. She needed a truth and I would give her one. "The lost gateway...it is to the Sanguine. I know where it is and I can open it. Prove me wrong..." I swallowed hard, "prove that they are dead and then you can walk away from me...from this, from Faerie forever."

# CHAPTER 10

MY SOULMATE ARCHED A brow at me suspiciously. "Your words make you sound desperate and I want to know why." She held up her hand. "It's not that this world is dying. It's something else."

I leaned back on my arms and sighed. "I wish it was desperation, little umbra. This isn't desperation. This is confidence. You're just going to have to learn to trust me."

Her lips pulled back in a sneer. "Trust? I trust no one...you should never trust the fae—even if you are one."

I tilted back my head and laughed deeply, "I'd almost forgotten you were Bane's protege. If you're living your life by that swordmaster's code then you're not fucking living at all."

"You know Bane?" Her eyes flared with interest.

"Of course I know him," I said through gritted teeth, hating the admiration for the bastard in her eyes. "He was the one that insisted I should find you. He never once believed the lies your queen spread about you. Said that your loyalty and heart would never allow it." I leaned in, softening my tone. "That's the only thing we have ever agreed upon."

Remnant pursed her lips and started to stroke the shadows still slumbering in her lap. "Where is he?"

"The West Isles."

"Where is the Sanguine?"

"The West Isles," I growled low, my senses picking up her growing agitation.

"And this information you know...that you carry?" Her eyes glanced down at my bag again.

"I will tell you everything once we are in The West Isles." I tapped the bag. "If you attempt to steal it from me, what I carry is enchanted to self-destruct if it is not given freely. I'd recommend against it."

"Why hide it then?"

"Because I made a vow to deliver it personally and if ever lost," I shrugged and looked away, "then I may as well kill its owner myself. They would have nothing to live for anymore and we all need some sort of hope in our lives...no matter how brief."

Remnant laughed, her head was thrown back to the night sky and I couldn't stop myself from hungrily raking over the perfect pale column of her neck. My desire to lick and bite that skin had quickly dissolved any melancholy I was feeling.

Her eyes glittered dangerously at me. "This is just all wrapped up in a nice little package for you, isn't it shifter? Say we get to The West Isles without being killed crossing the seas. I'm still a shadow fae, prohibited to walk your shores...I'm still the one who slaughtered many of your kind on the queen's bidding. Your king will never allow me to take a second breath let alone a second step within his lands."

I raised an eyebrow at her. "You don't know shifters well do you? We are people who value strength, power, and loyalty—but most importantly we love to gossip. Did you really think it went unnoticed that you spared more of our blood than you ever took? Defying your very queen to do so." I gave her a sad smile. "You are not hated where I come from, little umbra. It is quite the opposite really and I can assure you, our king feels the same."

She flinched and her lips pressed into a thin line. "Then they are fools, including your king."

I snarled and leaned in close to her, "You do not wish to trust me, so trust in this. I, Emon, vow to you, Remnant, on our very goddess and all of Faerie, that no harm will befall you from the fae of The West Isles nor from its king."

Her eyes widened. "You know the king personally then, to give such a vow."

I pulled away. "I do."

The cat snorted. *"Digging another grave, fairy boy?"*

*"My grave is your grave, cat,"* I purred back.

We both sat straighter when the soft song of a chickadee called out into the night, neither one of us daring to interrupt its warning call.

She sighed when its song ended and all that could be heard were the soft fluttering of wings flying far away from this place. "Alright. I'll go with you to The West Isles but," she turned towards me, " but I want to speak with Bane when we get there. Vow or not, I do not trust you but I do trust Bane."

I couldn't hold back my growl of annoyance. "Fair enough. Get some sleep. We have a long journey ahead of us."

She rolled her beautiful green eyes. "Faerie may have healed you, shifter but you still spent two days chained to a tree for gutting practice. You need rest and I need to be alone."

I winked at her. "It almost sounds like you care."

"What I care about is traveling with someone who is competent, not live bait."

I chuckled, "Being live bait is worth it if it means I catch you every time."

She stared while I watched the blush steal across her pale porcelain skin. "There is something wrong with you."

Contentedly, I stretched out on my bed roll, feeling her eyes rake over my heated skin. "How do I know you won't just leave the moment I close my eyes or worse take advantage of me?"

She laughed softly, "You're just going to have to learn to trust me, shifter."

Basking in the three moons glow, I huffed. "Using my own words against me, little umbra."

"If need be."

I inhaled deeply, her scent of lilies getting stronger. "Are you sure that's all you need from me then, my trust?"

She shifted uncomfortably. "You'll never be able to give me all that I *need*, shifter. No one can. So stop trying."

I lifted my head up and our eyes locked in the darkness. "Never." All flirtation gone. "You are worth it. You are worth every single obstacle, scar, and heartache I may incur so that you have more than just what you need."

Sadness bled through the green in her eyes. "You will fail," she whispered.

I chuckled low and lowered my head back down gazing at the shimmering stars. "Failing is nothing more than trying multiple times until you get it right and one day—I will get it right and you'll have nowhere to hide."

Silence befell us, drawing my focus back to her delicious scent, so strong that it teased me with its seductive undertones. There was no way I was going to fucking sleep tonight.

# CHAPTER 11

## Remnant

I WATCHED EMON'S BODY relax, sinking heavier into the ground, and couldn't help but smile at the small twitch in his booted foot signaling that he was finally asleep. A strong arm was thrown over his eyes to shield the three moons' glow and annoyingly it highlighted every beautiful inch of his bronzed torso.

Soft growling snores broke the eerie silence of the dead Balsam Plains and I was happy for it. Years of solitude had me craving more of his deep gruff voice no matter how much he pissed me off.

Staring at my dust covered hands, I curled them into tight fists, admitting what I did not want to. I liked the bastard. He was gorgeous, yes, more than pleasing to look at, and those passionate gold eyes felt like they could strip you bare in a heartbeat. Beastly and dangerous, his power was like that of the sun, bright and burning so hot that I barely noticed I was engulfed in the flames.

It made me feel *alive* again.

But the moment his knees fell into this dead earth to dig the grave of a beast that all fae feared, I knew he was more than just something pretty to lust over. There were depths within this shifter. Depths that if I looked closer at, would capture me more wholly than those gold eyes ever could.

Goddess damn him to Sheol, I didn't even want to be here, didn't even want to admit the tale he spun, and I definitely didn't want to develop any deeper feelings for a shifter of all things.

A soft whimper broke the stillness of the night and my head whipped up to see Emon starting to thrash in his sleep.

"Please, no more," he begged, growling and thrashing in the night. "I'll give it to you..I'll give it to you."

He was dreaming...a dream that seemed more like a nightmare. A glistening sheen of sweat broke out across his torso that hadn't been there moments before.

"Just stop. Please, please stop—."

Moving quickly in a crouch, I eased around his sheathed claws that tore at the ground beneath him and knelt at the crown of his head. His face was contorted with pain and his eyes rolled rapidly beneath his closed lids. Tears stained his bronze skin and wetted the bearded scruff along his strong jawline.

Concerned, I tentatively reached out and smoothed back his hair. "This is a dream, Emon. You are safe. Safe here with me, Remnant." My shadows hovered beside me and I looked at them. "Blanket him but do not restrain him," I whispered. By the way he was thrashing, it already appeared he was fighting against bindings in this nightmare.

"Please make it stop, please, please, please—" he begged.

I ran my hands gently through his hair that had fallen loose from his tie. "Shhhh. It has stopped Emon. It has already passed." I smoothed my fingertips over the scrunched lines of his forehead.

"Remnant," he murmured.

Wiping the tears from this formidable fae's cheeks and feeling as if I had intruded on a private moment he did not want to share, I continued to soothe him. "Shhhh. It's over now. Rest. Rest Emon. I will be here when you wake."

A rattling sigh escaped his chest with a few more unintelligible, whimpered murmurs before he finally eased, sinking into his bedroll once more. Pulling my hands back, I rested them in my lap, and watched the steady rise and fall of his sculpted chest...a telling sign that the nightmare had passed.

For two hours, I stayed vigilant over his resting form, watching for any more signs of the terror that had gripped him so violently. Finally, feeling confident that he would be okay, I peered out over the darkness that seemed to have also penetrated our very souls. Tonight, I had seen his...I had looked deeper, goddess damn me, and I knew now that whatever scars he bore, they were similar to mine.

I was not alone. Something I'd never felt would be possible, not after what had been done to me.

Trailing my hands through the black lifeless dirt, I pursed my lips. Irritatingly, Emon was right. This place was tainted, sick, evil—everything about it suggested the Sanguine.

I had been young when the blood wars took place, sheltered away, but I did recall my mothers tales...about the lifeless lands and the ravenous monsters. About the blood fae who wielded a great power that seemed to erase life itself.

The birth of my brother Kade had been the only light for my mother who had lost many loved ones during the war. He was one of the last fae to be born before infertility spread through our people like a slow plague.

A plague that Deirdre had been desperate to eradicate...at any cost. Her decision to ally with the humans on Earth had been the beginning of the end for her.

Bile filled my mouth and I swallowed it back, frantically looking towards the treeline as my breathing began to rapidly increase with panic.

I needed to leave.

I could go back, face the blood wraiths, and reclaim my cabin.

Except it was too late. Gripping the earth harder, the memories took over and I released a soft sob, barely audible over the loud pounding of my heart.

***

*"Why?" I screamed at the elegantly beautiful fae before me with pain and fury. "How could you do this to me?"*

*Deirdre. The Queen of Faerie. My friend. My lover. My everything...watched me with cold hatred and disgust in her exquisite turquoise eyes. It was the same look she had given me the last three months while they raped and tortured me on her orders.*

*"So beautiful and so broken," she crooned softly watching me cling to the cold sterile table I had woken up on.*

*Standing half naked with nothing but a blood soaked shirt to cover me, I was vulnerable and weak. The burns around my wrists ached fiercely from the iron chains that had once bound me, and my right wrist was mottled with deep blue bruises. I glanced down at the completely fractured iron cuff. It should have been impossible for any fae to break but someone had, hammering the abhorrent metal until it gave...eventually freeing me.*

*My bruises were an easy price to pay for the heroic act but who could have done such a thing?*

*I shook my head, focusing on Deirdre. "What have you done to me?" I whispered.*

*"This is all your doing, Remi darling," she purred.*

*"A coward's answer," I spat and spied the flickering of the shadows beneath us—my strength was returning. "You left me here, imprisoned in irons to be used for three months while I begged you to end it." I narrowed my eyes, rage burning my entire being. "You should have killed me."*

*She laughed. A beautiful cold sound that used to make my heart stutter. "Yes, you beg so prettily, Remi darling. It was wholly amusing but very much a waste of your energy. You could have at least tried to enjoy yourself."*

*My jaw clenched. "Like how you enjoyed watching, De."*

*Her eyes flickered over my naked legs and then back to my face. "Yes," she purred.*

*Snarling, I donned my armor from the shadow void. Covering myself in its sleek white silver plates. Deirdre sneered at the sight. After all, it had been a gift from her—a lover's gift.*

*Yet, from the way she was looking at me now, it was hard to believe that she ever held even the smallest ounce of love for me.*

*"You had my loyalty, my life, and my heart. Why was that not enough for you? Why did you take it this far?"*

*"Do not speak to me of your loyalty and love!" She hissed, stepping toward me angrily. "For years you defied me. Sparing the shifters and granting their disgusting kind safe passage in my lands. Protecting those giant lizard beasts while they destroyed our peoples homes." She laughed then. "Let us not forget your little rebel-*

*lion—did you honestly believe you could have stopped me? The Queen of Faerie, chosen by the goddess herself?"*

*My chin rose. "I will stop you."*

*Her smile glittered dangerously in the light. "Oh Remi darling, it is cute that you still think that." She arched a silvered brow. "They have all been hunted down and executed, you know. Their bodies hang on the city's gates as we speak and I made sure every single one of them knew their deaths were because of you. Your captains Xi and Riley especially."*

*I forced my knees to lock before they buckled under me from crushing grief. "Are there any lines left that you have not yet crossed, De?"*

*"You should have known, Remi darling. That I will do anything to ensure the survival of our people."*

*I shook my head sadly at the beautiful deranged fae before me. "This isn't about survival anymore. It is an obsession, a madness. I know you want your own child...to have again what you once lost. But this isn't the way."*

*"You know nothing—" She screeched and furious gusts whipped around me, stinging my face like a winter wind. "You don't know because you never had it! But I did. My sweet perfect baby boy was mine. He was mine and the goddess took him from me."*

*"Deirdre..." I took a step towards her, my heart breaking for the pain that swirled in her stunning turquoise eyes.*

*She snarled at me and I was slapped forcefully with more of her elemental winds. My nails clawed into the metal table to hold myself steady. "I don't need your sympathy! I don't need anything from you. Not anymore! The fae will have what we lost and I will be celebrated once again!" She shrieked.*

*My shadows darkened much like my heart. "What do you mean not anymore?"*

*"It means that you have finally served some true purpose. After all these years, I will at last get what I want out of you." She crooned and smoothed her hands over the curves of her fitted white dress. "I should thank you really."*

*"Thank me for what?" I said through clenched teeth while my heart thundered wildly in my chest.*

*A purely sadistic smile spread across her face and she slowly circled me. I turned with her, following the way she stalked me with analytical precision. The shift of her weight, the limited movement the dress caused her, her hands where she weaved deadly elemental* power from. "Did you know that the shadow fae are fertile?" She laughed at the shocked look on my face. "Yes. These humans...for all their insipid savage ways do at least have some intelligence within them. They have discovered that your females are fertile with one tiny caveat."

She paused when the shadows crept along the floor, under her slippered feet, and towards me. Darkening as they gathered.

Her smile widened and she responded to the darkness with miniature tornados that stirred the sleek silver hair around her as they took form. Their size made them look innocent enough...until they were shoved down the throat of her enemies or used to rip the very flesh off their face, piece by piece—all of which I had seen her do.

"Your females can only be bred with only one lucky male...one male that I have you to thank for discovering."

Memories of someone else roaring flashed before me and then was gone. I shook away the sense of foreboding that seemed to cling like the blood soaked shirt I still wore under my armor. "Who?"

Deirdre clicked her tongue. "For all that you do see...sometimes you really are blind, Remi darling," she tutted and then swirled her finger through one of her tornados. Tiny embers of fire sparked within them showcasing her mastery of the elements. "It does not matter who anymore. The human scientists tell me that harvesting your eggs was successful and will now allow a new generation of fae to be born. Except that simply wasn't enough for me. Why stop with one shadow fae when I can have them all?"

She smirked when the blood drained from my face. Inside my heart stuttered to a halt.

"What have you done?" I whispered.

"Saving our people, Remi darling. Consider your vow to the throne of Faerie now fulfilled my love. The blood of your shadow fae a small price to pay for the many who will graciously live on."

"You were wrong, my love," I spat. The endearment now bitter on my tongue. I let go of the metal table and rose to my full height. "I am not broken but you soon will be." My shadows had been cut off from me for three long torturous months, but now they exploded back into existence, and shot straight towards the Queen of Faerie...the betrayer of my heart.

***

*Deirdre reacted quickly, shielding herself with a gust of air and sending the shadows into a splatter of glittering black dust. For a brief moment, we watched the deadly display rain down on us before our eyes locked over the remaining dust, a small trickle of fear flashing in my lover's eyes.*

*"Whatever is the matter, De, my love," I mocked. "You look worried." This time it was me who stalked her slowly, the shadows trailing lazily behind me.*

*"Worried?" She started laughing and more mini tornados grew around her, their speed intensifying. "It is you who should be worried, you are now worthless to everyone. Not even your body is of use to me anymore."*

*I sneered. "You don't have the power to defeat me or the shadow fae."*

*She chuckled. "You have no idea what kind of power I can wield."*

*She flung her tornados at me in succession, one after another. Defensively my shadows whipped out against her torrent of power absorbing the air greedily and countering. A wall of searing fire rose, burning the attacking shadows in a sizzling blaze, and sending back cannonballs of molten hot earth. Twirling, I manipulated the dormant shadows of the room to swallow up the molten earth, leaving behind nothing but a smoke filled hiss.*

*Seeing her attack so easily dismantled, she glowered at the shadows rising around me.*

*"Disgusting shadows. I am thankful that the humans can manipulate any future offspring to repress your shadow fae genes. They call it genetic engineering. Isn't that fascinating?" Laughing at my horrified expression she threw another small tornado in my direction and I batted it away with a snap of shadow.*

*Toying. She was toying with me.*

*Snarling, the room filled with darkness, swallowing her remaining tornados in its wake. Glowing turquoise eyes narrowed in the dark before a vicious stream of fire lit up the room and roared straight towards me. Dodging it, the shadows snapped around it with a whining hiss, returning the light to the room once more, while they puddled at my feet.*

*She grinned. "Your shadows still fear my light...how sad for you, Remi darling." Wielding both air and fire she thrusted more of her power outward, circling it around the room and forcing it to funnel closer and closer to me.*

*The shadows shrunk, clawing up my legs, and then layering me in their darkness. Completely blocking the light of my armor.*

*"We. Fear. Nothing."*

*Light whispers, barely audible over Deirdre's converging powers, seemed to speak directly in my ear.*

*"Did you just speak to me?" I whispered back to the shadows with awe, not once had I ever heard a sound from them before.*

*"Destroy. Her. Destroy." Simultaneous whispers ordered me.*

*"I—" I choked on my own emotions, the harsh truth escaping from my unwilling lips. "I don't think I can."*

*"Then. We. Will. We. Will. We. Will."*

*I gasped when more power pulsed through me and fed into the dark layers around my body. Suctioning off the inherent power inside me, I realized I was nothing but a conduit for their dark purpose.*

*I was no longer in control.*

*Seeing my power accelerate uncontrollably, Deirdre's turquoise eyes flashed with fearful alarm before she screamed out her own rage, releasing the power she had built up around me.*

*Wind, fire, and earth rocketed in a winding stream of chaotic elements for a killing blow. I gasped when more power was sucked from me and added to the dark shadows encapsulating my body. Lassos of their black swirling smoke struck out rapidly at the earth, fire, and wind. Treating the attack like it was nothing more than an annoying insect to be batted away.*

*Extending their void and encroaching on the queen, I could hear their excited whispers in the darkness. Her power flickered for a split second and then completely sputtered out when the shadows enveloped her. The darkness peeled away from me and I stared in awe as witness to the shadow's immense power.*

*Deirdre screamed out her fury when their tendrils latched onto her wrists and ankles, bending her backward so that her eyes were forced to look upon the plume of shadow looming above her, gathering like an executioner's ax, ready to fall.*

*Our eyes connected from across the room and I searched desperately for any redemption left of the fae I loved.*

*And I had loved her. Cherished her. For hundreds of years she had been my companion, my best friend, my lover. The one I worshiped in the middle of night and basked naked next to in the glory of the sunrise. We shared memories of tears and laughter, moments in front of the fire kissing and licking every inch of each* other's delicious skin, moments in a battle covered in blood, holding hands in reassurance that we would live to see each other one more day.

It was as if time stopped when her scared voice pleaded out to me over the roaring darkness, as if she could see every memory reflecting in my eyes. "Remi..."

"Stop!" I cried and ripped back the shadow power controlling me. Hissing they retracted, just seconds before they kissed the delicate skin of the Queen of Faerie.

Snapping back towards me they whispered in multiple hissing voices. "Mistake. Take. She will take more."

Their cryptic words fell on deaf ears. "What in the goddess?" I whispered, staring in awe at the sunlit marbled throne room of the City of Light. We were back in Faerie.

"No!" Cried Deirdre, reaching out to the gateway that snapped shut and shattered before us in a collective array of shimmering dust.

"Sealed." My shadows whispered in chorus. "Sealed forever."

***

Deirdre spun towards me, fire lighting up her eyes. "You! You have doomed us forever!" She screamed at the same time fire spewed from her eyes and mouth.

"Shit," I snarled and summoned the casted shadows from the sun. They were weakened by the light but were enough to defend me from the roaring torrent of her fire.

A crazed laugh bursted from Deirdre's lips and her earth power joined in her attack. The walls shook around us and I ran, leaping away from the cracking marble beneath my feet and layering shadows between the cracks to prevent the total collapse of the room.

Sliding down a pitched floor, I attacked, firing off bolts of shadow that swallowed up her fire and forced Deirdre's control on her earth elements to falter.

"Enough! You will bring this whole place down on both of us!" I cried out, pulling more split marble back together with the shadows.

"I will bring this whole place down on you and you alone! I will make sure you die here and every court will know that you are the cause of the extinction of all fae!"

Wind, earth, and fire assaulted me on all fronts, shooting out from Deirdre with such power that for any lesser fae it would have destroyed them instantly.

Decades of hardened training came to life and I danced against death's deadly call. My feet sliding on the crumbled marble, my body flowing with the assault, my shadows tiptoeing closer and closer to the source of power being used against us.

Finally face to face, I stood my ground while she poured her full power down onto me. With my shadows shielding me on all fronts, I gazed through the waterfall of her power, holding her crazed desperate look.

"I will let our people decide your fate, my queen. Death by my hands would have been kinder. The courts will show no mercy for you."

Deirdre screamed with rage. Raising my hands with tears pooling in my eyes, I summoned the iron bindings from the shadow void that would silence her power forever.

"Forgive me," I whispered through gritted teeth, holding my shadow shields while the irons slowly circled around her wrists.

A piercing bird-like cry caused my head to snap up and sharp talons sliced deeply across my unprotected face.

Falcon.

The force of the queen's pet shifter sent me sprawling backwards and my control on the shadows faltered.

Rolling, I scrambled to my feet right before Deirdre's full power slammed into me, causing me to howl with pain. A wall of scorching hot fire circled around the three of us, extending from floor to ceiling. Its light cut me off from my shadows and blood dripped down my face—trailing beneath the plates of armor I wore.

Icy winds hit me next, forcing me to gasp and dropping me to my knees. My wrists were forced back moments later, bound by frigid air and sawing into my exposed skin.

A sudden flash from the bird that had landed on Deirdre's shoulder revealed a tall dark fae standing at her side.

"Falcon," I hissed.

The shifter stood in all his false glory, a silver tongued deceiver that had wormed his way into Diredre's inner circle. His eyes and skin were so midnight black that they melded together, making him look more like my shadows than fae. His cruel white smile gleamed as he cocked his head to the side much like the bird he was.

"*Shadow bitch. How ever did you escape your cage, I wonder?*" *He clucked.*

*I shrugged in my bindings, my chin rose high despite my subservient position. "It's not worth explaining to you. Your tiny bird brain would not be able to comprehend it, shifter scum."*

*"I can assure you, nothing about me is tiny. Your lover enjoyed everything big about me last night." He stroked a finger over Deirdre's smirking face as she watched for my reaction with sadistic anticipation. I gave her none while Falcon continued to caress her. "Does it bother you, Remi darling? That I can please your lover more than you ever could?"*

*I threw my head back and laughed. "So that explains her visit to my room late last night." I tilted my head to the side in thought. "I bet your little birdy cries of pleasure were too shrill for the queen's delicate ears." I smiled cruelly at him. "Your twitching birdy cock has no idea how to pleasure a queen. That much was evident when Deirdre spent herself completely with me last night." I licked the blood from my lips, turning my gaze on my lover and purred at her mockingly. "What was it you said to me while I was delirious and still chained, unwilling while you took your own pleasure with my body...oh yes. I recall it now." Deirdre's eyes both dilated with lust and rage. Disgusted, I snarled at her, "You said that you would never taste anyone as delicious as me while you rode my face to completion."*

*Falcon stepped towards me angrily but Deirdre's maniacal laugh drew both of our attentions back to her. "I see I haven't fully broken you, Remi darling." Deirdre turned to Falcon and purred, "I'll allow you to tell her. I want to watch her face when she breaks."*

*Falcon's jealous rage simmered with an evil smile. Those cruel black eyes sparkling with the reflection of the roaring fire. "Congratulations, shadow bitch, you're now the last shadow fae alive in Faerie. Every last of your kind is being gutted as we speak. The crown thanks you for this sacrifice in your name."*

*I stiffened in my bindings. "No," I whispered, horror draining the last bit of fight left in me.*

*Deirdre cackled and stepped closer to me. "Oh yes, I did enjoy that just now." She leaned down and gripped my face harshly, her tongue snaked out and licked the blood from my cheek. Numb, I barely registered her touch. "Almost as much as I enjoyed myself last night. Alas, I shall have to be content with just the memory of you."*

*She rose and I wavered, staring through her. My family, my people—slaughtered. I couldn't save them. I didn't save them.*

*A powerful slap echoed through the room and I half realized that she had struck me. I knew the power behind it had stripped the flesh from my face but I felt nothing. Nothing. There was nothing left for me here.*

*A bubble of insane laughter tore from deep within me. "It bothers you. That the memories won't be enough..." I shook my head sadly at her.*

*"Bitch!" she screeched and then something struck me, the like I had never felt before. An unseen power burrowed inside of me, pulsating, draining. It reeked of death but I was too broken to care. "Your people have been eradicated from Faerie! Your mother, your brother...they are all dead. You are the last shadow fae and you are all alone," she spat.*

*"Alone," I slurred, having control of only one side of my mouth. Her slap had broken my jaw.*

*I started to shake and I could not prevent the power rising up inside me. Agonizing screams of pain left my bruised battered lips. Shadows from all over the room, the city, and the whole fucking world of Faerie were drawn towards me, as if my pain was the center of a massive black hole and nothing could escape it. The air bindings broke around my wrist and the throbbing power burrowed inside of me disappeared. Bowing, my hands wrenched into my dark greasy hair and my screams continued.*

*Memories flashed upon their dark destructive canvas.*

*My baby brother Kade toddled towards me.*

*"Come on Kadey Kins. You can do this."*

*"Rem, Rem, Rem." He babbled at me and fell into my outstretched arms.*

*I tucked him close to my body. Inhaling his sweetness, the last of the fae children to be born since the war. "I'll always be here for you Kadey Kins. You are never alone," I whispered into his curly blue hair.*

*I felt the warmth of my mother's hand on my shoulder and looked towards her to see her smiling sadly. "We all fall sometimes, my beautiful Remnant, sometimes there isn't always someone there to stop it." She plucked my little brother out of my arms. His chubby hands reached for her face and she nuzzled her nose into them. Her grace and beauty had always been breathtaking. "So we must train to be strong. Because one day we will be alone and will need to get back up again. Please remember, my love, even in the infinite darkness we can still find the light."*

*Get back up.*

*Find the light.*

*Get back up.*

*Find the light.*

*Alone. I was so alone.*

*A lone figure stood on the black stoned streets of the City of Night. His head bowed over a fae's body, claws dripping with blood extended from his fingertips.*

*Sensing me watching, he looked up into my grief stricken stare.*

*Gold eyes bore into me. "No!" I whispered.*

# Chapter 12

Emon

"Remnant!" I shook the shadow fae hard, frantic to pull her from the nightmare that held her hostage and caused pain to etch permanently into her gorgeous face. "Please, wake up, my little umbra."

Her screams, the exact replica of the ones I heard while in the soul mirror, had alerted me that something was wrong.

The moment I got to her side, shadows exploded violently and hit me with such force that it had knocked me out for several hours. When I woke, I was sprawled out on my ass with a whimpering unconscious Remnant curled into my side, and the night had passed into midday.

Worse than that, we were no longer in the Balsam Plains, her shadows were missing, and so was my goddess damn satchel.

I shook her harder this time her lashes fluttering against her pale cheeks. "For the love of the Goddess, please, please wake up. I need to see those beautiful emerald eyes open for me." Brushing back her hair tenderly, I added, "One day of your glaring at me wasn't enough. I want to see them sparkle when you laugh, the fire in them when you find your pleasure, the death in them when you take your vengeance—" My forehead dropped to hers and my voice broke, "come back to me..."

*"Her shadows have transported us near water,"* my beast growled and the hairs on the back of my neck stood on end. *"And we are no longer alone."*

"Fuck," I snarled. Never mind the fact the shadows could transport...we had bigger problems. I pulled away, regretting my choices while I was making them. "Time to wake up, Remnant Dark. The water fae are here." Before I could change my mind, I raked my knuckles hard against her sternum. Hoping the sudden jolt of pain would be enough to wake her.

But she only groaned loudly and I watched in horror when a lone tear slid down her pale face.

"Goddess damn it!" I snarled, shaking her again.

*"Unmask your bond and use it to wake her before it's too late. They cannot discover she's alive,"* my beast commanded harshly. He was prowling with agitation inside my mind.

"Piss off cat," I growled back at him, "you know I can't do that. I vowed I would give her the choice when the time came. I refuse to be added to the list of things taken from her."

*"Irrational. What choices she has won't matter when you're both dead. It is unsafe here,"* the cat snarled at me.

I looked over my shoulder and could see a new waterway forming, its crystal depths swirling ominously towards us. I was not well versed in the waterways of Faerie but I knew this river had not been on the maps I studied. Scooping up Remnant, I tucked her protectively into my chest. "We might still have time to get away," I muttered.

*"You're a fool. That waterway has changed in seconds. There is no place to hide now. I can smell their rotten stench even with your meager fairy senses,"* he warned me.

Before I could respond, a sultry coo came from behind me. "You aren't leaving, are you handsome?" The siren-like voice was a soft caress on my skin that made my stomach curdle where I stood.

"Fuck me," I sighed and tilted my head up to the cloudless sky, mouthing a worthless prayer...more like a plea to a goddess that never listened.

"That can be arranged," the siren voice purred again.

Shielding Remnant with my arms I turned around. "I'll pass this time, Kira," I said cooly to the naked water fae standing within the banks of the small river. Like all water fae, Kira was exceptionally beautiful.

Her skin glittered like the water she waded in. Long waves of pink hair covered her breasts and flowed over her toned naked legs, and down into the water around her. Red lips smirked at my perusal and her jeweled rose colored eyes blinked innocently back at me through dark lashes. Water droplets fell from them like crystals into the swirling water, alluring in her sexual innocence that broke the strongest of mind into mindless desire.

Except Kira was anything but innocent. She was a powerful water fae, taking over leadership of her people when their precious Atlantis fell. Her selfishness made any alliance with her a tremulous affair, one that I appealed to stay far far away from.

Recognition crossed her face while she attempted to peek at what I was guarding. "Emon! How delightful that we have crossed paths yet again. Searching for your way back home now? I can take you there," she said huskily, indicating the water around her.

I held back a snort at her clever attempt to discover my homeland. There was a reason the water fae could not travel the waterways to Finlandia and it had everything to do with their conniving leader.

"One would think that our paths are crossing purposefully," I finally said wryly.

Her rose colored eyes sparkled. "Perhaps it's fate." Delicate feminine hands trailed over her seductive form and I felt her siren power flex against my own. "Perhaps we are soulmates and your body yearns for pleasure only I can give."

I swallowed back a gag. "Cut the shit, Kira. Your allure didn't work on me the first time we met and it definitely won't now. I was just leaving, so if there is nothing else?"

Red lips formed into a perfect pout and her eyes drifted lazily downward. "What...no who are you hiding?" She leaned forward for a closer look.

I gripped Remnant harder and pulled away but it was too late.

"Goddess bless us," she gasped, the water splashing unceremoniously upon the beach shores as she stumbled closer. "Is that who I think it is?"

"Don't take another step closer," I snarled, stalking slowly back with a growl rumbling deep in my chest.

Kira's reaching hand snapped back sharply and her eyes glared. "Remove your filthy shifter hands from her and give her to me."

"Touch her and I will kill you." I bared my growing fangs with a hiss and curled my extending claws protectively around my soulmate.

Kira scowled and retreated further back into the water but I was no fool—she wasn't going to give up this easily and the water was the source of all her power.

When her sparkling skin rippled, my entire body tensed at her metamorphosis into a creature of the deep. Thick black layered scales now covered her entire body leaving behind her luscious pink hair and sultry rose colored eyes, the only characteristic left of her land fae form.

I snarled again when miniature whirlpools revealed a score of water fae rising up from its turbulent surface. True to water fae fashion, every warrior flanking their leader was female, covered in the same black scales with an array of matching brightly colored hair and eyes. In unison, multiple spears of bone with sharp poisoned tips descended in my direction.

Kira smiled maliciously with her needled teeth.

"You have a choice, shifter," Kira purred at me, despite my warning growls growing louder, "Give her to me and you won't die this day or fight and die anyway. Either way, she is coming with me."

My cat roared inside me. *"Do not trust the water snake, fairy boy!"*

*"Believe me when I say this cat, I trust the water fae as much as I trust your golden hide."* I held Remnant tighter to me. *"I cannot risk her life fighting them."*

*"This is a mistake, let me out so I can have fish for dinner,"* the beast barked.

I looked back up at Kira, not fully believing what I was about to say. "She stays with me. We go together."

She rolled her eyes. "These are not negotiations, shifter."

My lips peeled back in a silent snarl. "Yet even with your warriors, you cannot risk fighting me for her."

Nervously, a violet haired water fae shifted, their spear dropping unknowingly towards my soulmate. Lunging, a guttural roar ripped from my throat and my claws instantly embedded deep within their skull, their shocked expression the last to form on their face as their spear dropped to the raging river below and the goddess's light left their eyes. Dropping into a snarling crouch, I watched the guard fall backwards into the water, their bright red blood swirling around the remaining warriors.

Curling as much of my body over my unconscious soulmate, I braced for their retaliation, more spears falling towards me while I reached for my golden power trembling just below the surface.

"Hold!" Kira shrieked, diverting their threat and sending their weapons crashing back into the river. Shocked, her guard scrambled back, more fearful of her wrath than my murderous claws.

Growling low, I slowly backed away from the shores, dragging Remnant with me. "Like I said, Kira. You cannot risk it."

Kira looked down at her dead guard floating in the water and cocked her head. "How interesting," she whispered before her eyes snapped back up to me to reveal a manipulative gleam. "I do believe you are correct, shifter. You go together."

Narrowing my eyes, I stood cautiously. "She stays with me."

Kira laughed, a cold shallow sound, and then waved towards the water. "Yes, yes. As you have already said. Shall we then?"

The cat roared at me furiously, *"You can't be this stupid, it's a risk following those water snakes!"*

*"I must,"* I sighed to him, controlling the snarling beast attempting to rip down my barriers and take control.

My foot dragged as I stepped towards the water and then faltered completely when Remnant released a loud gasp, her blazing emerald green eyes snapping open full of renewed hatred...towards me.

I was too relieved to care.

# CHAPTER 13

"**T**HANK THE FUCKING GODDESS," I sighed and brushed my nose against hers, purring gratefully.

She stiffened in my arms and I pulled away quickly realizing my mistake. Shifters naturally demonstrated their emotions through touch...except my soulmate wasn't a shifter. She was a shadow fae and she had no idea who I truly was to her even if our bond struck me to my knees one hundred years ago.

"Put me down, shifter," she hissed coldly.

Reading the violence within her and *liking it*, I reluctantly lowered her gingerly to the ground. Brushing my lips against the soft outer ridge of her ear, I growled softly, "We have a situation."

She tilted her head sideways, her eyes flickering to the watching water fae and then back to me. "I don't trust you," she murmured, her hand trailed down the front of my chest.

I gripped it tightly and brought it to my lips, whispering against the soft pale skin of her fingertips, "Trust in them less then.

There was no waterway here moments ago and I have already killed one of them for getting too close to you."

Remnant shivered then and pushed away from me. The loss of having her so protectively within reach felt like a punch in the gut but she hardly noticed. Instead, her chin tilted high, her spine snapped to attention, and it felt as if she commanded the air we breathed...one could almost mistake her for an air elemental. Seconds, it took only seconds for her to transform from a helpless unconscious fae into the hardened war general that all the legendary stories were made of.

"Kira," Remnant barked, "Is this how you would greet your oldest friend Solaire?"

My brows rose. *Solaire?* Was she really taking my advice and trusting them less? Somehow that was hard to believe.

Something was *wrong* and it stunk with the lingering fear of the nightmare that still clung to her, no matter the flawless performance that said otherwise.

Kira's siren laughter filled the static tension between us. "Oldest friend indeed. You've been getting us into trouble ever since we were little fries, *Solaire*." Her voice curled around Remnant's name with mocking amusement. "I'd ask what kind of trouble you've gotten *yourself* into this time? But it's hard to ignore the disgusting, gigantic shifter next to you."

Remnant shrugged with a sparkling gleam of mischief to her smile. "Beasts have always been drawn to me, unfortunately, shifter scum included."

I cracked a vicious smile and inhaled deeply with a purr, "It's your scent that draws me, Solaire. My beastly nature just cannot get enough."

The cat chuckled mockingly. *"You're a poor excuse for a shifter, fairy boy. Smell harder because I know prey when they want to run and your little soulmate...she reeks of running."*

My body tensed with panic. *"You laugh but if she goes with the fish bitch so will I, even if it's as a goddess damn prisoner. She's not leaving my sight ever again."*

*"I'm not going anywhere near that goddess forsaken water, fairy boy,"* snarled the cat. *"It's not my problem your soulmate wants nothing to do with you. I can understand the feeling."*

The water around Kira had not stopped swirling in its threatening manner when I noticed they were both staring at me. "You sure your new little pet is well, Solaire? He looks a bit sick in the head."

I licked at my fangs and hissed. Several of her guards averted their eyes.

Kira snickered and shook her head. "I'm not so sure I want a deranged shifter loose in The Under after he so..." she looked down at her dead guard still floating in a circle around her, caught in the whirlpools, "murderously accepted invitations to my realm."

"An invitation you say?" Remnant flipped her hair over her shoulder, her body swaying in such a way that it drew the gazes of all around her. My eyes trailed down the delicious curves wrapped in leather...and fuck me, so did Kira's. I had almost forgotten that water fae joined in pods. One male for multiple females. Their males were more like toys to them. Pets...tools to be used for reproduction. Since the fae's infertility, the male water fae's status had fallen even lower. "I hadn't realized invites were delivered with a full platoon of warriors and with your full powers on display, Kira."

Kira giggled. "Oh Solaire darling, you know I love a good entrance. Besides, we have so much to catch up on. Much has changed since you have been away," she waved a webbed hand towards me dismissively, "especially with shifter scum roaming these lands."

I smirked her way. "Awe. Do I make you nervous Kira?" I purred.

Remnant didn't bother to glance in my direction. "Surely a single shifter in these free lands is no threat to you, Kira. A waste of your newfound talent." She waved to the newly created waterway.

Crossing my arms smugly, I waited for the next pathetic excuse that would coo from Kira's siren lips.

She smiled secretly. "You flatter, Solaire. I wonder, would you like to see the rest of my talents?" She ran a clawed hand down the front of her scales.

Remnant rested her hand on her hip with an amused smile gracing her lips. "A fine temptation, perhaps, I wouldn't mind exploring."

Kira smiled brightly and shot a look of triumph my way.

Fearfully, my hand halted Remnant before she even took a step towards the waters. "You're running and I want to know why?

You must know we can not trust them," I said lowly enough for only her to hear.

Remnant glanced down at my hand and the sharp sour scent of her sudden hatred instinctively made me release her with shock.

"There is no we, shifter."

I inhaled deeply, stealing myself before she even took another step away from me. "We had a deal," I graveled out.

Remnant raised a haughty brow. "And I will fulfill it, eventually." She stepped into the water and peered back over her shoulder with a challenging smirk. "Follow if you must, my *little* pet beast."

My eyes narrowed when she turned her back on me and I shook to refrain from dragging her back to safety. Kira giggled and covered her mouth with a webbed hand to hide her victorious smile.

Gnashing my teeth, I hissed before following Remnant like the loyal little pet beast I was. "Challenge accepted," I growled out, watching her body stiffen before stepping into Kira's welcoming arms.

Kira's eyes met mine and I tensed from the urge to rip them clear out of her head. But first I would start with her leering webbed hands that were trailing lower and lower down the sides of my soulmate.

Remnant grasped onto Kira's salacious hands and pulled them from her body. Grumbling, I stepped into the water next to them both, purposefully stomping on the dead water fae still floating freely, and shoving its prone body into the submerged murky sands below.

My cat groaned. *"You're going to get us killed again, aren't you?"*

*"Undoubtedly,"* I answered back.

Turning towards Remnant and ignoring the scathing glare the water fae leader gave me, I spoke truthfully, knowing what she saw in my eyes right now would scare her. "I will always be here for you. If that means I must play the role of your *little* pet beast and follow, then I will obey. Nothing will ever harm you again, not on my watch." With emphasis, I snapped the spine of the submerged dead fae with my waterlogged boot.

The others stiffened with vengeful fury but I paid them no heed. I studied my soulmate intimately. Her green eyes shuttered closed, hiding the pain my words created, and then opened with the same iced coldness as before. "So be it, shifter."

Kira laughed cruelly, the scent of her anger not so easily hidden from my senses. "They are so cute when they are desperate aren't they Solaire?" Kira snapped her fingers and another water fae guard with orange hair stepped forward holding something akin to black tar in her webbed hands while keeping her spear pointed far away from my soulmate.

I flashed a brief smile of appreciation in her direction and lifted my boot from her dead comrade. Allowing the mangled body to rise to the surface and float away from us. My thanks for her caution around my soulmate.

Remnant's lip curled up in disgust at the sludge, paying no attention to my games. "You think after all these years, you'd at least find a way to make this process a bit more pleasant."

The water fae leader laughed again. "Where would the fun in that be? Besides then everyone would come to our lands. The Under is ours and we don't share it. Nay, the sludge will always be the only way to transform into a water fae to explore our world."

That was the truth, the water fae kept their secrets in their own watery depths. Much of their culture was unknown and even those whom I befriended, who were no longer loyal to the deep, never gave up their buried secrets.

Remnant took the sludge from the orange haired warrior, scowling. "Unfortunate that. Bottoms up." Swallowing it with a shudder, she plunged elegantly below the glittering crystal surface of the river just moments before her pale skin transformed with black scales.

Kira's satisfied smile sent a foreboding chill down my spine before it turned on me.

"Well *little pet shifter*? Are you loyal enough to follow? Males usually can never be trusted in this manner," she said flippantly, brushing her long pink hair away.

A deep guttural growl escaped me. "Give it to me."

# CHAPTER 14

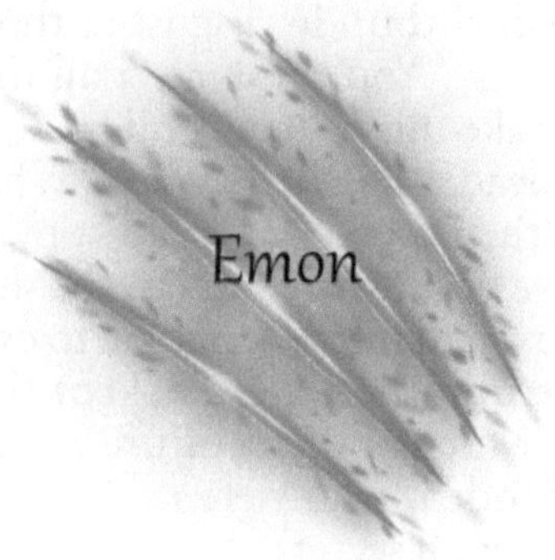



MY EYES HELD KIRAS when her guard extended a trembling hand in my direction. The sour scent of the fae's fear and rage didn't even come close to the foul smell of the sludge she presented. It reminded me of a rotting maggot filled corpse left out in the blistering sun for far too long.

*"I'd rather eat the rotting corpse,"* my beast hacked.

Whether he meant it or not, his utter disgust was enough to motivate me forward and I choked down the sludge with a grimace. It tasted the same as its revolting scent.

I felt the change immediately. The fluttering of gills could be heard at the side of my neck and they beckoned for the swirling pools of water I stumbled toward.

Plunging into its cold depths, I gasped for oxygen while my body transformed into a cascading array of black scales.

I was now a water fae.

My beast gagged.

I blinked rapidly, adjusting to my new magnified sight before realizing I was no longer in the river waters but an expansive body of water reaching far beyond what even my enhanced vision could reveal.

We were in The Under.

Residual growls rattled in my chest as I continued to orient myself to my new environment. The platoon of water fae I had encountered above the surface laughed while swimming beneath me looking like a submerged rainbow, their brightly colored hair waving fluidly in the water.

Not a single one had blue black hair.

"Where is she!" I growled to Kira, sensing the water fae leader at my side. My normal speech slurring in a series of surprising stochastic clicks that I somehow still understood. Kira giggled in return. "It's always so fun to hear a land fae speak within the waves." She cocked her head assessing me, her hair flowing around her in a variable pink cloud.

"Fuck off Kira and just tell me where she is." Panic was bubbling to the surface along with a power I normally held tight control over. This fish would fry if I didn't find Remnant soon.

"Relax, shifter. *Solaire*..." she drawled amusingly, "has been to The Under many times, although it was of course before the blood wars, we were just faelings then. Even at that age she was a fast and skillful swimmer. A talent, it seems, she has not lost." Her small webbed hand pointed further below us where a water fae was racing, twirling, and dodging through the water with limitless ease. Flanking her were two water fae guards. "There, you see?"

I did see and I stared. She was like a beautiful nymph in the water, her speed and acrobatics combined into a sensual and playful show. The joy radiating off her was infectious and even made her guards smile.

Kira sighed wistfully, "She has ensnared you, as she does with all that cross her path. Always excelling at stealing fae's hearts without even trying...she is just so—."

"Fae," I breathed. A gorgeous, resilient, fierce, pure, un-apologetic fae.

Kira hummed. "Come along little pet. Let us see if you can measure up to the female you think your disgusting shifter hide can win over. May the best fae win."

Then she shot through the water like a torpedo, leaving me biting at the water after her. Kira was going to be lucky if she lived through the night.

*"I'm not opposed to some water fae sushi,"* growled the beast, *"let's make it take out though. I despise the decor and the ambiance is all wrong."*

I choked back a laugh, swimming downward. *"As opposed to what, cat?"*

*"Mountains,"* he said longingly and I had the feeling he didn't know he was still speaking to me. *"Where the only tolerable water is from the crystal falls that cut through the towering trees, teeming with flowers and the melodious echoes of the zhar birds...their golden glow lighting up the canopies like stars."*

I paused abruptly in my pathetic floundering of a swim. The vision my beast described was so vivid that I could practically feel the scenery. *"Is this...one of your memories?"*

Never had the beast shared something so intimate with me and we had been together for thousands of years.

The image quickly disappeared. *"I do not know,"* he hissed.

Shaking my head, I continued swimming, and I pushed away the disappointed sadness that came with our complicated relationship. We needed each other symbiotically to exist, that was all, and nothing would ever change that.

I inhaled deeply when over a bend, the staggering views of The Under came into focus. The multi-colored city glowed in the open ocean. Its rainbow spiral towers jutted upwards like the mountains on land. Each one adorned by gold and silver that burned with an enchanting light making the city shine brightly in the deep. Even the luminescent algae, perfectly manicured along the city streets, lit up its darkest corners.

I darted around the sealife, both predator and prey, swimming lazily above the water fae city. The fae here paid no attention to us newcomers, focused only on their own concerns. A show of superiority that was a common trait of their race.

Except, I could scent the stench of their hidden unease, desperation, and rotting disease permeating the water. My predator senses were acutely aware that the city itself was over-populated, overcrowded, and these fae had nowhere else to go. This was the last of their court.

I rubbed at my chest, thinking of home. The shifters were much like these fae. Our dying lands had forced our people reluctantly from their homes and into our capital city, Finlandia.

"Welcome to The Under," Kira interrupted my thoughts with her sharp clicking tones, "the most enchanting place in all of Faerie."

I scowled, Kira's willful blindness knew no boundaries. While the city was beautiful, something obviously festered on the inside. The stench was getting stronger the closer we approached its luminescent depths.

"They used to say the same about Atlantis, I understand. Until the water fae destroyed it with their own greed," I said dismissively.

Kira shot in front of me with her razor teeth bared. "Tread carefully, shifter. You are in my territory now."

My canines lengthened. Despite my playing dress up, my shifter powers remained intact. "Put your pathetic teeth away, Kira. My words are true and there's nothing here worth treading on."

*"We don't even have feet to do so,"* the cat hissed at me, peeking his head out in my consciousness, *"but the talking sushi is correct. Watch yourself, fairy boy, she does have the advantage here."*

Snarling inwardly, I shoved past Kira to dive deeper. *"The water is making you a chatty cat. If I didn't know you better, I'd believe you're nervous for me."*

*"Of course I am, fairy boy. No highly evolved being would ever voluntarily swim with sharks in the water. You fairies are all imbeciles."*

I rolled my eyes. *"There are no sharks in Faerie, cat. And even if there were, I doubt you'd be fearful of one."*

*"I do not speak of the imbecilic sharks you seem to love so much from the human world, fairy boy. I speak only of the sharks that hide behind the facade of civilized beings."*

*"Are you warning me against yourself then?"* I snapped.

*"Finally you are getting it, daft fairy boy."*

Before I could answer, a sudden jolt pulled me down in front of the beautiful fae my entire focus had been on. My webbed fins landed harshly onto a bejeweled pathway, sending my arms careening while I cursed profusely, striving to find my balance.

Remnant's lips twitched with humor. "The pathways are enchanted." She explained when I attempted to lift my mutated feet. "It's to anchor you, so you don't have to swim all the time."

Snarling, I looked towards her and whatever I was about to say stopped in a gurgle at the back of my throat. Her emerald eyes were so vividly bright here...the same brightness I saw in the Wildwoods, when she flew on shadow wings, that I was at a loss for words.

She was alive here.

Kira shouldered past me and with no ability to move my feet, my arms flailed again to regain my balance.

"You still swim so beautifully, Solaire," Kira cooed, hugging my soulmate tightly to her.

"More than beautiful," I added, exhaling with relief when my balance became stable. "You swim like a goddess. Bewitching everyone."

They parted to stare at me and Remnant crossed her arms in front of her. "So you followed then."

I bowed and smirked. "I am your loyal pet after all, mistress." Then I rose, my voice dropping low. "I will follow you into Sheol itself if I must. Although, for a shifter...Sheol would be better than this place."

Kira's musical laughter broke the crackling tension between us. "Is your cat squirming inside, *little pet shifter*?" I glared back at her and she swirled the water around her hand. "Males are so dramatic." Kira smiled at Remnant. "Please allow my people to take you to freshen up, Solaire darling. I'll have some fun with your shifter while you get ready."

Remnant's scaled brow furrowed. "Ready? Ready for what?"

Kira's eyes widened. "Have you forgotten what today is? You are a creature of the dark after all."

Recollection flashed in her emerald eyes. "Of course! The Three Moon Solstice is this day."

I frowned. "Three Moon Solstice?"

"*Savages,*" my beast piped in.

Remnant sighed and her scaled black hands fell to her sides. "It is a festival where the water fae celebrate the three moons of Faerie that control the tides. It is also the brightest night of the year, when the moons' glow reaches The Under's spiral towers and regenerates the light you see coming off them now." She turned to her friend. "Must I attend?"

Kira swatted her with a black webbed hand. "Of course you must!" She smiled seductively at Remnant. "Besides, I know how much you enjoyed the last one you attended."

Remnant laughed dryly, "I had just come of age. I was…curious."

Kira giggled and wrapped her arms around her. "I cannot wait to see how curious you get tonight."

A possessive growl emitted from me, one I could not control. Kira's constant touching of my soulmate sent me over the edge. "Festival or not, I'm not going anywhere without you." I ignored the simmering water fae still clinging to her. "Where you go, I go."

Remnant glared at me but untangled herself from Kira's arms slowly as I huffed.

"Males are not allowed in the House of Fem unless they have their own pod and Solaire has no pod." Kira tilted her head towards the ostentatious swirling tower of gold before us. "You're practically smothering her, little pet. Allow me to show you the city, while she freshens up. Then you may join her for the festivities later."

My eyes darted back and forth between them before landing on my soulmate, a low rumble escaping from me. "This is what you truly wish?"

Her chin tilted upwards, with the sharp sourness of her hatred back again. "It is."

I ran my webbed hand through my free floating hair. "Then let's get this shit over with." I gave her a withering look. "I hope you know what you are doing."

Snarling, she turned her back on me. A true insult to a predatory shifter like me.

My barking laughter soon followed, "Challenge accepted, little umbra."

Hissing over her shoulder, Remnant darted into the hidden depths of the House of Fem and away from me. Misery seeped deep into my bones when she disappeared from my sight.

Kira saddled against my side and clutched at my arm. "Ouch, that had to have stung." Her scales scraped against my own. "Shall we?"

I looked down at her arm and resisted the urge to rip it to shreds.

How did it come to this? Me trapped with an asshole beast, a revolting water fae, and a soulmate that hated me.

Surprisingly, I had been through much worse…

*"And we survived it, fairy boy, and we will again. Of course, that was and will be, because of me,"* the beast preened.

# CHAPTER 15

*Remnant*

**G**OLD.

The word itself repeated over and over in my head. It had sent me retreating into the water fae realm and still followed me into the deep.

Gold...Emon's eyes were gold. The sudden memory of his eyes opened up other haunted areas of my soul—ones I could no longer ignore, like the sound of distant roaring, someone in pain, unable to be saved, just like me. A sound I had never forgotten, from a time I wished I could forget.

Screaming, I punched the fluorescent coral wall in front of me. My outburst caused the coral to disintegrate into dust that floated openly out the window of the spiral tower I was kept in. Breathing heavily, I paused to watch the debris descend, my eyes falling on the busy city below, catching on a peculiar sight.

A small water fae pod moved cautiously through the bustling city. Despite their arrogant air, they seemed distraught. Their gills fluttered, their eyes darted erratically, and the black shine to their scales seemed extremely dull...muted even.

They weren't the only ones.

A growing sense of foreboding pitted in my stomach and I closed my eyes, letting go of my senses to open up my aura sight.

When they opened, I gasped. A burgundy haze surrounded the water fae populace, muting their aura, and draining the life from their scales.

Instinctively, I reached for my shadows but halted, snapping my hand back with a scowl. It was important that they remained hidden, something I had purposefully done. I knew Kira had been watching me closely, looking for the power that once instilled fear in all fae alike. If she thought I had lost them during Morta then she was more likely to become emboldened...more likely to let her guard down because the shifter was right, Kira could not be trusted.

I glanced back to the pod with realization and frowned. "The darker the haze, the more muted the scales," I whispered and then inhaled sharply. "It's parasitic. Feeding off them."

Slowly, I raised my hands up and exhaled, bubbles following its wake. All that glowed around me was my normal deep purple aura and black shining scales beneath.

Whatever this burgundy power was, it hadn't affected me...yet.

The water shimmered and drew my attention to the entryway where a water fae cautiously peeked her head in. Her electric blue hair waved gently around her narrow face, matching her vibrant blue eyes, and the same burgundy film saturated her aura.

"Apologies for the interruption my Lady Solaire but I have come to prepare you for the Three Moon Solstice. May I come in?"

"Yes, of course," I waved her in and attempted an inviting smile. "What kind of preparations are needed from me?"

She approached timidly, her slender frame, holding up a tray full of shells that I had failed to see her carrying. "Do you not remember? The queen said you had attended before. It is tradition for us females to paint our scales to shine in the light of the three moons." She opened one shell to show me an array of neon colored...paints. If you could call it that, it was the same consistency as the nasty sludge that transformed me to a water fae.

My emerald green eyes narrowed and I studied the burgundy haze around her. It seemed complacent enough with its host. "Queen?"

There was only ever one queen amongst the fae and she was dead. There was nothing but an empty throne, in a crumbled ghost city, to rule over a species that was on the verge of extinction.

The water fae's eyes widened and seemed to take up her entire face. Her gills gulped frantically. "Yes my lady. Queen Kira of the water fae."

I withheld a snort. If Kira was vying for the throne of Faerie by claiming herself queen here then she was a fool, but it would be like her to attempt such a thing.

"Of course. Apologies, not sure what I was thinking." Satisfied the burgundy haze around her aura was not contagious, I dropped my sight. "What do we need to do next?"

The water fae's fear dissolved within the fluid waters we floated on and she smiled widely back. Her needled teeth not at all frightening on her petite frame. "To allow me to paint your scales."

"How long will this take?" I eyed the paint like it would cause my certain death.

She regarded me with something akin to mirth. "About two hours my lady. I will also be tending to your hair." She waved towards the black and blue strands that floated around me.

I glanced up at the tangled mess. "Looks like this will take some time. What is your name?"

"Bay." She responded and then looked up after finally sorting her paints with a gentle smile. "Shall we get started, Lady Solaire?"

I smiled back through gritted teeth. How hard could a little bit of primping be?

# CHAPTER 16

## Remnant

"Of course our queen is keeping us safe from the dying lands," Bay chatted, flitting around me with her little brushes, painting my scales with intense scrutiny. Something she had been doing for the past *three* hours.

I unclenched my hands from wanting to strangle her for the hundredth time and sat straighter. "Dying lands?"

She nodded sadly. "Yes, some of the most bountiful parts of The Under have been rotting from within. Several smaller cities of ours have now been lost forever to this death. It is the other reason why our city is so busy aside from the festival of course."

"How has your queen been keeping you safe?"

Bay smiled, lost in her art, while she ran her webbed claws through my tangled hair. "She has found a way to enhance her power and grow stronger. They say she has the power to bring back Atlantis. Sadly most of us don't even remember our great city of old, we are content with just saving The Under. Of course our queen sacrifices much for it. I assume that taking care of the young fry utilizes much of her time but I am told that it is the source of her power."

Quickly, I snatched Bay's arm and gripped it hard. Startled, she attempted to pull away from me.

"A fry? As in a faeling? That's not possible."

Bay's black scales turned gray and her lip trembled. "Oh goddess! Please forget I ever said such a thing! We aren't supposed to know about her. The queen keeps her hidden but my—my cousin is one of the guards and she told...she wasn't supposed to know! Oh goddess, my lady...please I beg you. Do not tell my queen! I swear I have not said a word to anyone else!"

I stared into her panicked eyes, resisting the urge to snap her arm in half to squeeze every last drop of information she had.

Goddess. A child? It wasn't possible!

Slowly, I peeled my clenched fingers from her frail arm and patted it with a reassuring smile. "Apologies Bay. Of course I understand. We will not speak of it." I picked up her paints and held them outwards to her. "Please, let's continue?"

Bubbles blew out from Bay in a sigh of relief and then a beaming smile full of razored teeth spread across her face as she took my apologetic offering, closing the shell. "Thank you, my lady. But there is no need for me to continue. You are finished!" Gripping my shoulders, she spun me to a reflective opal mirror set in a monstrous oyster shell. "What do you think?"

My eyes grew wide with shock at my appearance.

From the tip of my webbed feet to the top of my head, my entire black scaled body was delicately painted with various shades of green scrollwork that reminded me much of my brands in my land form. It was intricate, detailed, and meticulously placed.

Bay was an exquisite artist with her paints and I—I was her masterpiece.

My gaze traveled up to my hair which was tied halfway back into a braided knot at the base of my skull, the rest flowing freely around me in the water and thankfully away from my face. On top of my head was a sparkling silver headpiece that was draped like a delicate net over my hair weighing down the floating strands. Hanging along its delicate chains were teardrop emeralds, the exact same color as my eyes. I reached up to delicately touch the one resting between my brows, realizing they were still arched with complete shock.

"Thank you Bay," I said softly, dropping my arm and turning slightly in the mirror to admire the rest.

"I am pleased you approve, my Lady Solaire." She clapped her webbed hands enthusiastically. "Come! The festivities will be starting soon and I must make sure you are not late."

I felt her water power gently caress my body and urge me out the door. The touch of it was just as warm and graceful as the fae wielding it.

"And what of your queen? Will she not meet us here?"

Bay shook her head. "My instructions were to take you to the festivities and Queen Kira will meet you there. It takes much more talent than my humble paintings to get the queen ready."

"Bay." My hand grazed the young fae's shoulder and she turned mid-swim with wide eyes, much too big for her head. "Your paintings are truly the most beautiful work I have ever seen because they are humble. I am honored to be a part of it and it is only the beginning of the masterpieces you will one day achieve."

Bay flung herself towards me, arms stretched wide to grip me in a fierce hug, before crying out. "Oh I mustn't mess up your paint!" She reared back and then gently reached her hand out to cup my face instead. "Thank you my lady, for your kind words."

I took her hand in my own and nodded. "You are welcome, Bay." I nodded to the open ocean. "Shall we?"

The young fae smiled wide and then spun back around, pulling me forward. Her hand never left mine as she pulled me along and I resisted the urge to free myself from the possessive touch. Instead, I took solace in the tenuous friendship budding between us.

Following Bay out of the city, I tried to ignore the growing feeling of unease. Even without my aura sight, I could still feel the presence of that unnatural burgundy power growing stronger the further we traveled. When a sea of flowing grass and white sand appeared before us, Bay finally released my hand. Other painted water fae began to join us. Their excited tones trilled and clicked within the shallow water. No males were here yet. They would come later if I remembered correctly—without being painted.

I turned my head up to the blurred light of the three moons shining in the shallow underwater grasslands. I inhaled their energy and light, preparing myself against the sinister power crawling beneath my webbed feet.

Switching back to my aura sight, I found the ground saturated deep red, with tendrils of power oozing upwards and hungrily latching onto every water fae here.

Seeing my concern and mistaking it, Bay leaned in towards me whispering, "Do not worry my Lady Solaire. You are the most beautiful one here, aside from the Queen of course, I made sure of that."

I gave her a sad smile, watching the muted burgundy haze of her aura and the leeching tendrils twining up from the white sand towards her petite frame. "Thank you Bay." I gently pulled her away from the parasitic power, closer to me. The burgundy strands paused, repelled by my presence. "But in your dedication to me, you have totally forgotten about yourself." I waved my hand down her body.

Bay's eyes widened and her webbed hand covered her mouth. "Oh my goddess. I was so excited to show you the festival, I forgot about my own paint!" she cried.

I gave her a reassuring pat and gently pushed her away. "Go, quickly. You should still have time before the festivities begin. The queen will find me soon. I will not be alone for long."

Bay looked at me sincerely with those electric blue eyes. "You are sure?"

"Of course."

I stiffened when she wrapped her arms around me for the second time this night. "Thank you, my lady!" Pulling away from me she flashed a bright needled smile.

Smiling back, I jutted my chin outward. "Go on. I'm sure this festival will be one you'll never forget. You must look the part!"

She nodded and then in a graceful flip, she shot back through the water. I watched the burgundy power keenly as it recoiled back to the white sands.

Bubbles burst from me, Bay would be safe for now. It wouldn't protect her indefinitely, the haze was already strong around her, but maybe I could buy her more time. Whatever this power was, it had deeply infiltrated The Under and was growing.

I turned back towards the amassing soiree and narrowed my eyes. I just needed to figure out why.

# CHAPTER 17

"**C**OME ON. ALL I want to know is where the Sheol does your cock go when you are in your water form."

My guard's jaw ticked at my immature question.

My beast snorted and rolled his eyes.

Kira had left me with this silent orange haired bastard to prepare for the festival. He was actually the first male I had seen in The Under since being here and I was thankful to be away from Kira's repulsive touch and insufferable prattling. A moment longer in her company would have ended up with her as ceviche for dinner.

*"How clever,"* the cat drawled.

Ignoring him, I widened my legs and pointed to where my dick used to be. "I mean come on man, where does it go? Do you not have one? Is that why your females prefer one another? I mean it's not like the fae can procreate these days...what good are you if you don't have a dick?"

The male guard glared at me—his matching orange eyes looking more and more like fire.

Laughter surrounded us and the guard's gaze immediately shot forward, his spine straightening.

"Oh how wicked you are, shifter! If you wanted to see Cyrus's cock all you had to do was ask me. He is after all mine to play with. Are you not my pet?" Kira cooed at her male lover, sidling up against him, her hand trailing down his torso to the junction between his legs.

I glared at the water fae leader who was painted like a goddess damned rainbow. The paint accented every detail of her body, from her perky breasts, to the curve of her ass, and womanly bits. An atrocious clacking noise came from shell adorned braids of her pink hair while she stroked the guard in front of me.

Manipulative rose colored eyes twinkled over his shoulder at me. "Cyrus's magnificent cock grows outward whenever it is needed. Doesn't it, baby?" Kira cooed. "Be a good boy and show the shifter what a magnificent cock you have darling."

Cyrus' eyes closed in a shudder at her dominating touch and his scales parted for a growing black cock to protrude forth, settling heavily in her webbed hand.

Groaning, the guard hung his head in shame. Kira giggled and started to pump him quickly, whispering words of encouragement as her guard's arousal grew.

I crossed my arms hard over my chest, my own claws digging into my scales to stop them from ripping Kira's head off. I knew this abuse all too well, I had fucking lived it.

"I'm surprised you even know what to do with a cock Kira." I waved my hand towards the guard, "Release him. You have proven your point and I have zero tolerance for this spectacle."

She smiled sadistically at me. "I don't think I will," she hissed and pumped the guard faster.

*"Let's just kill her now. What are we waiting for? We can rip her rapist's hands off first. Then stuff them down her throat just before we rip her head off too."*

I agreed with him. Sometimes, we were more alike than I realized but now wasn't the time for rash decisions.

Cyrus groaned loudly and his head tilted back just before streams of black cum shot into the crystal waters of the ocean depths. His entire body shook and then slumped into his leader.

Growling, I lunged forward, my webbed hand shooting outward and wrapping around Kira's neck. I slammed her back hard into the rocky coral wall away from the shocked guard. "I said I had zero tolerance," I snarled, inches away from her startled face.

Kira's shock wore off quickly and she brushed up against me laughing, "I didn't know you liked it rough, Emon. You sure you truly want Solaire instead of me?"

I leaned forward menacingly. I was close enough to see the fear swirling in her pink eyes. "Know this, water fae cunt. You're not *strong enough* nor *important enough* to play games with me. You're better off playing tiddly sticks with your little fishies. Fucking do that in front of me again and I. Will. Kill. You."

Cyrus seemed to have recovered because I felt the sharp pointed tip of his spear piercing into my exposed back. Water churned around the three of us and Kira laughed harder.

"Tsk, tsk, shifter. That sounded like a real threat. Your dumb animal brain does remember where you are, correct?" Weaving the water between us she shoved me further onto the spear at my back but my hand held firm around her neck. The familiar searing burn of my flesh being pierced beneath my scales only forced more adrenaline to pump into me.

I smiled dangerously at her even as I tasted the tang of my own blood on the water. "I know exactly where I am—and it doesn't fucking matter." My own power infiltrated my words as my cat roared inside of me, hungry for a kill. His need to bathe in blood was strong.

True to her cowardly nature, Kira pasted a flirtatious smile upon her face, giggling once more. "Poor shifter, let's not quarrel. Solaire would just hate to see it and she is waiting for us. We wouldn't want anything to happen to her, all alone. She has been through enough tragedy, has she not?"

I hissed at her, tightening my grip around her neck, and ignored the pain of Cyrus' spear sinking deeper into my back. "This is a game you don't want to play, Kira," I warned her.

Sniffing, she spat, "Males are so dramatic. Stand down Cyrus, you fool." Water pulsed around us and I hissed as the spear was violently yanked from my body before the water rushed forcefully between us, releasing my grip around Kira's throat, and slamming me straight into the guard at my back. "Heal the shifter. I don't want him bleeding out before his time." She glared at us both before swimming away.

"Yes, my queen," Cyrus murmured stiffly, shoving me away from him.

Burning pain lit up my insides as water burrowed roughly inside my wound and I clenched my teeth to prevent the snarl that threatened to escape me.

"Thank you," I said seconds later, when the pain subsided, and blood no longer tinged the water. "For what it is worth, I never wanted that to happen."

"Fuck off, shifter. Touch my queen again and I won't hesitate to run you through next time," he spat and jerked his head to the side. "Get moving."

*"You deserved that, fairy boy."*

I shook my head regrettably. *"But he didn't, cat. The poor bastard thinks that's how he should be treated. This whole city has succumbed to her sickening influence."*

*"We can't save everyone."*

Sighing, I swam towards Kira. Her pink braids and rainbow fluorescent body art like a gaudy light in the water. *"She is up to something, if we can just figure it out, perhaps we can. But if not, all that matters is Remnant gets out of here alive, even if that means the destruction of the entire water fae race."*

*"We are in agreement, fairy boy,"* snarled the beast.

# CHAPTER 18

I HISSED AT THE growing stench of death permeating the pristine waters around us. Even in this beautiful white sandy clearing, with the moonlight shining down on the colorful water fae, it festered below the surface.

I scented Remnant before I saw her. She was the only one that the stench didn't cling to like a second skin. I followed the scent of pure and potent lilies in a midnight rain to her stunning silhouette.

There was no comparison to her in the crowd.

As if the goddess agreed, a moonbeam shone brightly down upon her like a spotlight, the star's reflections glittering in the water around her, highlighting the delicate green art someone had tastefully painted on her black scales. Heavy teardrop emeralds hung from her thick blue black hair and down the middle of her forehead. She was striking, even with her brow furrowed slightly as she watched the festivities.

"Solaire!" Kira called out to her.

When Remnant turned, the worried expression instantly replaced with joy for her *friend* swimming towards her.

If anyone ever doubted how she survived the queen's court within the capital, they would need to look no further than this moment. She was a mirage. Remarkably convincing in her role to play.

But I knew different. I could smell it on her.

"Kira!" Remnant beamed and gave me a pointed look.

I nodded but remained quiet. I would follow her lead.

A calculating gleam flashed in her emerald green eyes but was gone when she turned back to her friend. "I had almost forgotten about the traditional paints. How do they look?" Remnant asked, twirling in the water.

"Beautiful as always! Bay does exquisite work. It was hard parting with her but I knew tonight had to be perfect for you," Kira exclaimed. "What do you think of my look?" She spun.

Remnant smiled knowingly. "Like a queen," she purred, leaning into her friend intimately.

I perked up at Remnant's statement. The orange haired guard Cyrus had called Kira the same but I had thought it to be some sort of sickening bed play. There was only one queen allowed to be crowned in Faerie and she was dead. Ladies and lords ruled the courts of fae but the Queen of Faerie presided over them all.

If Kira was making a play for the throne then she was getting help from somewhere...or from someone.

I pretended to watch this spectacle of a festival play out with my body half turned away from the chattering friends. Listening closely to any other information Remnant unwittingly fed me.

Sudden cheers muffled their conversation when across the shallow waters a grouping of eager males, holding trays of globulous pearls, joined the soiree.

"Drinks! Drinks for my friends!" Kira ordered and snatched a cluster of drinks that looked like fish eggs from a stumbling fool who stared at his declared queen with simpering adoration.

"What the fuck is it?" I growled when Kira shoved the slimy pile of gelatinous pearls into my hands.

Kira laughed. "Ambrosia pearls of course. They are a water fae specialty. Shifters are so unsophisticated." Her razor teeth smiled brightly at me.

"You call slimy ball sacks sophisticated," I said dryly.

Remnant snorted and rolled her eyes. "What a wee scaredy little pet you are, shifter." Then shot me a wink before she downed her pile with one swig.

I gnashed my teeth together, staring down at them and forced my stomach not to revolt.

*"Not again, fairy boy. I absolutely refuse this time,"* the cat snarled.

Kira giggled and threw back her own slimy ball sacks in one go. "I'll see you later darling," Kira said huskily, leaning in to kiss Remnant's cheek while her rainbow painted hand trailed down her body. "Save me a dance, Solaire," she cooed seductively.

I barely restrained my protective growl when I scented Remnant's fear and anxiety at the water fae's unwanted touch.

Moving to intervene, Remnant flashed me a warning look, stopping my assault. I growled, fisting my hands at my sides while I watched her smirk at Kira and shove her playfully away. "Get going you uncontrollable flirt!"

Kira giggled with a wink before blowing her a kiss and swimming away. Remnant caught it with a smile while her scent was sharp with disgust.

Nauseated with the display, I threw back the pearls to keep the guttural snarl from escaping my clenched jaw.

"Fuck the goddess to Sheol and back!" I gagged on a burp.

Remnant spun around and scowled, "Why exactly did you follow me here, shifter? You clearly know nothing of water fae customs. It's a miracle you're even still alive!"

I peeked out through one eye while another burp escaped me. "I've been known to have many lives."

I did have a cat beast.

Remnant's lips pulled back with disgust.

I straightened, pulling in the tainted air to ease my stomach. "Besides, the real question is why did you come here? We had an agreement, remember? You come with me to The West Isles. Not the fucking Under. What in the Goddess happened to change that? What did you see when you were unconscious?"

Her gills flared. "I don't need to share my reasons with you."

My beast met her ire and I snarled in her face, "You jumped head first into a den of goddess damn water snakes and I am owed a reason why, little—"

Remnants hand snapped over my mouth. Her touch sent a tingling warmth down my spine.

"I've asked you to stop calling me that, shifter. No one recognizes me here and the water amplifies many sounds." Pulling her hand back, she bared her teeth at me. "I am no faeling, shifter. I know exactly what I am doing and I am as safe here as I am anywhere else."

I inhaled her familiar scent and the pleasurable tingling continued. Shaking my head to gain some clarity, I growled, "That's not true and you know it. I'll admit, your act is almost flawless..." I moved closer, dipping my head down to speak low. "But you can't hide your worry and fear from me. I'm a shifter, remember? If I can't see it, then I sure as fuck can smell it."

"Please refrain from sniffing me out, shifter. It's repugnant on so many levels."

I hissed. "How can I not? This place reeks of death and you know Kira cannot be trusted. She has something planned. What in the goddess were you thinking drinking that shit with her?"

Remnant's eyes flashed with fury and she opened her mouth to respond but her words were abruptly lost when a low thrum rippled through the moonlit water. The tingling already in my scales responded to the vibrations pleasurably.

"What now?" I moaned.

*"We never should have come here, fairy boy,"* my cat whined deep within my subconscious.

The water fae cheered and collectively moaned when another series of sounds rippled around us. This time more forceful and louder. The waves and excitement pushed Remnant into my arms and I groaned, tucking her petite frame tightly into me. A fierce need rose and my hands gripped her hips tightly to stop them from roaming all over her delicious body.

Another series of vibrations pulsed and this time a rhythmic beat started and drummed sinfully against my scales.

Scouting for the source, I saw multiple water fae on a dais waving their arms in a flowing pattern as water churned around them.

"What are they doing?" My hands tightened even more on my soulmate to prevent myself from molesting her.

She shoved my hands off her hips and faced me, rolling her eyes. "They are manipulating the entire ocean to create sound. What you are experiencing is the music of the water fae, shifter."

A grin split across my face. "You're telling me we are at a fucking wave rave right now!?"

# CHAPTER 19

I WAS ABOUT TO roar with laughter when another throbbing wave hit me and sent me to my knees. I blinked up at Remnant, my entire being overwhelmed with uncontrollable lust.

What. The. Goddess. Fuck.

Remnant paid no attention to me, watching the cheering and moaning crowd with unease. "Yes. That's exactly what this is. But you are right about one thing, shifter, Kira cannot be trusted. There is death here when there shouldn't be. This is a celebration of life but it is tainted—by what I am unsure of. I've never seen anything like it." Worried emerald green eyes settled back on me just as I forced myself upright.

Her words should have alarmed me but all they did was add to the seductive pleasure of the vibrating water. Another soft caress, this time by strong hands, forced a gasp from my parted lips and I leaned into the touch. My eyes hooded with desire and a snarl ripped from me when they became bolder, gripping my ass hard from behind.

It was wrong and unwanted but felt way too damn good for me to fight against the rampage of lust flaring to life inside me.

Remnant's beautiful face blurred in my vision but I could tell her eyes were wide abhorrence. It didn't matter, all that did were the continuous fondling touches, and scraping of scales rubbing against me. Instead of being repelled, I wanted more. So much more.

"Goddess don't stop touching me like that," I slurred.

"Get your hands off him!" Remnant snarled and I groaned as the vicious sound caressed my scales more. My arms opened wide as she came rushing forward, my heart pounding with excitement in my chest. My soulmate, finally in my arms. My beautiful soulmate—.

Suddenly I was spinning in the water, away from the erotic touches and I whimpered at the loss.

"He is an unclaimed male."

The silky siren voice ran a shiver of pleasure down my spine. "Will you not allow us to pleasure him?"

Peering over Remnant, I saw a pod of violet haired water fae. Their leader purred seductively at me. I licked my lips and brushed up against Remnant's back.

Dipping my mouth to her cheek, I kissed it softly and growled low to her. "Let us join them. Share me. While they pleasure me, I can pleasure you."

Remnant tilted her head to me and she hissed, "Too dangerous, now shut up and follow my lead." She snarled back at the pod of females moving erotically in the water, beckoning us. "He was mine first. I claim him."

My head dropped to Remnant's shoulder at her proclamation, bringing a moment of clarity back into me and I sighed heavily. Both joy and sadness warmed my heart. Remnant had no idea what she had just done. Fae could not lie.

"*Cat?*" I called out desperately. The lust had already taken hold of me again.

"*I am here. I know what you ask of me. It will be harder to mask your bond now that she has accepted it,*" he snarled. Then I felt the void where our connection had already been dimmed completely snuff out to darkness. "*It is done.*"

My lips trailed over the scales of her shoulder, my lucidity already gone the moment her exotic taste burst to life on my lips. "*Thank you.*"

"*You're an idiot, fairy boy. I will enjoy your misery once you fully comprehend your own stupidity this night.*"

I groaned out again as another heavy wave hit us. Whatever biting remark I had was lost by the fast paced vibration generating an undulating rhythm. A rhythm I could not help but move with even when Remnant stiffened against me.

"Are you sure?" The water fae pressured, her gaze dropping down to my crotch with hunger. "You have no pod and he is a male that will require more than one lover by the looks of him."

"Fuck," I groaned, seeing what the others now saw—my fully engorged dick protruding proudly from my scales, eagerly awaiting a partner.

Remnant snarled viciously, baring her needle teeth at the pod of yearning females that all leaned in to get a better look. "He. Is. Mine. And I don't share. I'll not repeat it again."

"As you wish. There are plenty of other fish in the sea," the violet siren scowled back, her entire pod turning and moving in unison together.

I whimpered, feeling their abandonment just as much as the waters throbbing around my exposed cock.

"Need—I need." I gasped against Remnant's scales, humping into the water and gripping her tightly. "You feel so good, little umbra."

Remnant's hand grabbed mine and with a swift move twisted it hard as she spun to face me. The only awareness I had of the splintering of bones in my wrist was the sickening sound of it snapping. The absolute lust masking any pain it may have caused.

"Goddess damn it, shifter, you drank the ambrosia, didn't you? What is wrong with you?" Remnant cursed in my face.

I licked my lips and my non-broken hand dropped to my shaft. "So...beautiful...when angry," I groaned, stroking my cock in front of her.

Her gaze dropped to my movement before shaking her head hard and releasing even more colorful curses.

"Yes. Keep talking dirty to me," I said lewdly while inside I roared against my lack of control.

"Are you really this daft! Those pearls are aphrodisiacs! I assumed the very name would have tipped you off. How could you not see me toss mine? You're a shifter for goddess sake!"

The beast chuckled in my head. *"She is growing on me, this soulmate of yours."*

I could not comprehend her words. I was a slave to the erotic water music pounding all around me. Her anger and dark beauty only added to the thrall.

I needed her...needed her to fucking feel alive.

I barely saw her webbed foot swing outwards as it made crushing contact with my dick and fractured my other wrist.

My beast roared with laughter.

I roared shrilly from pain and it radiated up my spine and keeled me over onto the rippling white sand. Vomit ripped violently upwards from my stomach and I spewed out whatever remained of the grotesque ambrosia pearls.

I clawed at the sands, despite my broken wrists like a wild beast, the only outlet I had to the wracking pain caused by my crushed member retreating back up inside me.

Gulping oxygen back into my system, I blinked up at my soulmate through watery eyes, and ignored the continuous laughter of my cat inside my head.

"I can't—" I gasped. Then shook my head hard before growling out. "I can't fucking believe you did that."

Several of the sex enthralled water fae who had been watching our display moved further away, disgusted by the vomit floating towards them.

"It was necessary," she said dryly, crossing her arms and looking pointedly down on me with the same disgust as the water fae who just left us. "Are you done now?"

"It was *not* necessary," I snarled. The cat's roaring laughter was reaching new heights inside my head to the point that I could barely hear myself speak.

Remnant snorted hard and her emerald eyes blazed. "Do you still feel the need to fuck anything and everything in sight?" She watched me grimace and snorted again. "That's what I thought."

"How did you know that would work?" I groaned out, bracing on my hands and knees to gain some composure.

She shrugged and extended her hand. "I didn't."

I released a stream of curses that would have had my father fucking blushing, and begrudgingly accepted her assistance to stand.

Remnant snickered and patted my shoulder with mock sympathy. "There there, shifter. You are stronger now for it, little pet."

I barely paid her jab any attention, assessing the water fae around us with astonishment. "Just to be clear, I am seeing this correctly...this isn't still the pearls working?"

Remnant followed my gaze to a grouping of painted sapphic water fae erotically pleasuring one another. The subservient male of their pod was being shared in a frenzy of lust while being sodomized at the hands of his female counterparts.

Everywhere I looked, water fae were succumbing to the pleasures of flesh, gyrating to the hypnotic beat in an all out orgy.

Remnant's lips pursed with amusement. "Welcome to the Three Moon Festival. That," she pointed to a lone poor male humping at anything he could find, "was exactly what you looked like a short while ago."

I ran my webbed hands through my hair. "Thanks for sparing me the shameful act, but I had better still have a functioning dick when we get the Sheol out of here."

Remnant smirked before shaking her head. "I still don't understand why in the goddess you drank it, shifter."

I gave her a glare. "Because I thought you had!" I growled and shook my head. "I wanted to make sure that—" I stopped myself. "Forget it. What exactly is your plan here?"

Ignoring my question, her eyes narrowed on me. "You wanted to make sure of what exactly?"

*"Yes, what did you want to make sure, fairy boy? That you were as stupid as we all thought?"* The cat chuckled, his laughter now subdued to smug amusement.

I ran my webbed hand through my hair again, irritated as fuck. "To give you my trust," I snarled at my open confession before sighing. "You don't have to do any of this alone. I will always be here for you, little umbra."

The cat's amusement died and was replaced by something I never felt from him before. Sympathy. My hands fisted at my side, I didn't fucking need him to feel sorry for me.

My confession, however, had the opposite effect on Remnant.

"You!" She seethed and pointed her webbed finger at me. "You don't get to say those words to me! Ever! I barely know who you are, *Emon!*"

My chest puffed indignantly and I seethed back at her. "I can tell you that I'm not your fucking enemy. I am on your side, unlike that water fae bitch, and I am not leaving you in this place to go at it alone!"

Remnant bared her razor sharp teeth at me. "You don't get to decide that for me."

My head snapped back as if she had slapped me. Her words sliced deeper than I thought was even possible. The whole reason why I hid our bond was for her to have a choice. A choice to choose me...regardless of some bond.

She snarled at the broken expression I failed to hide and pushed off of me to swim up and over the raging orgy surrounding us.

Unprepared, I tumbled backwards in the water, unable to stop my momentum until I landed into a group of moaning painted females. They latched onto me like starved piranhas.

I pushed away from them frantically, reaching up towards Remnant who was swimming further away from me. "Wait! Please. Wait!" I called out.

When a water fae licked up my chest, I swore and shoved her aside. Looking back up I saw nothing but the glow of the moonlight mocking me.

Remnant was gone.

Growling I disentangled myself from the humping females and darted upwards.

"Fuck!" I growled and spun in the water sniffing out her scent. With so much sex in the air and the continued smell of death there was no way of me tracking her.

*"This is becoming a habit,"* the cat growled. *"Can't we just put a leash on her and be done with it."*

I snarled. "We have to find her."

"I'm afraid I can't allow that, little pet."

I stiffened and I turned to find myself confronted by armed guards. Their weapons were drawn and one of them sported orange hair with matching fiery eyes.

Cyrus. And with him, the gaudy rainbow water fae leader.

"Kira," I growled, ignoring the guards circling around me.

"Emon," Kira grinned and twirled a pink braid around her finger coyly.

I narrowed my eyes on her.

"What is the meaning of this?" I growled.

Kira smiled sweetly and waved her free hand in the water. "This—" she closed her fist and immediately my gills slammed shut. My supply of oxygen effectively cut off. "This is me playing the game and winning, little pet." She released her other hand from her pink braids and waved it around her, my legs and arms shot backwards by a forceful rush of water, binding me thoroughly.

"Child's play," I hissed between my lips.

Kira's rose colored eyes regarded me with sadistic mirth. "I'd save whatever precious oxygen you have left Emon. Suffocation, I have always felt, would be the worst way to die."

"Original," I wheezed back.

Tinkling laughter made me want to claw out her throat so that she could never make that sound again. "Don't worry, shifter. I am not going to kill you. Someone else has reserved that right."

A deep rumble of laughter emanated from my gut. "Must piss you off," I gasped, using the last of my air to antagonize her more. "A pawn in your own game, someone else calling shots." I tilted my head to the side and my eyes narrowed against the black spots dotting my vision. "You haven't won anything."

Kira hissed through her razored teeth and for a moment I thought she was going to attack me. Instead, she waved her hand and my gills opened once more. Beautiful oxygen filtered through me as I greedily sucked it in.

Kira pouted. "I thought I would at least get to see you humbled as you fucked one of my fae. I knew Solaire would be too smart to fall for my tricks, but you...you are so easily distracted by a pair of tits, and you are desperate to prove yourself. Here's a tip, shifter, you'll never be able to prove yourself to Solaire, no one can."

Another dark chuckle. "So that's what this is about. Tit jealousy. A secret yearning for a fae that wants nothing to do with you."

The cat groaned inside of me and rolled his eyes. *"You are definitely going to get us killed this time, fairy boy."*

Kira smiled wide but her pink eyes blazed with fury. "I am going to enjoy serving you to your death, *golden one.*" She snapped at Cyrus. "Get him up and moving. We have a timeline we must stick to and I need this filth taken care of before then."

I kept quiet this time, I may have had a death wish, as my cat had so lovingly reminded me, but I also had a very good reason to live.

I scented the air one more time, but there was no smell of lilies anywhere, nor was their any sight of my soulmate. The only thing I could see were the water fae fucking. Like captivated starving beasts, they thrusted steadily to the pulsating beat of the waters while their *queen* looked on with greedy pleasure.

# CHAPTER 20

Remnant

*You don't have to do this alone. I'll always be here for you, little umbra.*

Emon's voice overlapped with echoes from the past, words I once said to my brother now paired with flashes of shifter's lethal claws dripping with blood.

*I'm not the fucking enemy,* he said.

I believed him. Deep down in my gut, in my soul, I knew he was not my enemy. So why did it feel like my heart was breaking from what I had seen?

I shook my head and dragged my fingers through my floating hair, raking out the tangles with irritation. "I can't possibly trust him...can I?" The shadows twitched nearby. "Come. It is safe for now but be vigilant. We can't let them know you still exist."

Immediately they appeared along the ocean floor.

"Deirdre is a part of this," I murmured. "The power that is draining these water fae is the same she used during Morta."

The shadows enveloped me in a cocoon of darkness and a red tear floated into the water. Water fae didn't shed just tears, they shed tears of blood.

"It was a mistake to stop you from killing her," I sighed, allowing my anger and sadness to disappear with the gentle tide.

I shouldn't have left Emon there, especially with Kira. Her hatred of males was a known fact and with him tied to me, that hatred was likely very powerful.

"I need to go back."

The shadows unfolded from me when I turned and then stilled.

"Sweet goddess." I gasped out loud at the death of the ocean lands where murky gray waters mixed with a thick oozing sludge rising from the it's floor. A graveyard of bones and dead plant life stretched with no end in sight.

I reached out tentatively to the murky water and felt nothing but the frigid coldness of death.

Instinctively, I switched to my aura sight, immediately seeing the deep burgundy tendrils rising up through the gloomy depths, hungrily vying for anything with life to feed upon just like it did at the festival grounds.

Bay had practically gushed about Kira's ability to keep them all safe but this death was not contained...it was growing.

"My mother says it's because the goddess has abandoned us."

A small child-like voice jolted me from my horrified stupor and I spun towards the sound, willing my shadows to hide below me.

There was a soft giggle, a small tinkling that made my heart skip a beat. "I'm over here."

I spun one more time and then I stiffened with shock. Awe consumed me at the petite creature paddling her feet energetically, sitting perfectly perched upon a large bed of rock.

I gasped. "You are—are you." My voice wavered. "You're a child."

A tiny giggle escaped her again...a child's giggle. "You're funny, but mother calls me a fry."

I stared.

The last time I had seen any child was my brother and that was shortly after the blood wars and yet here she sat, no more than eight summers, with black scales, and muddy pink hair. Her eyes swirled with a contrast of color, never settling on one in particular.

When my aura sight kicked in, it was immediately repelled by a very powerful shielding around the girl. Someone did not want her true nature to be discovered.

"What—" My voice came out in a whisper, tears filling my eyes at the miracle before me. "What is your name?" I asked, swimming towards her enthralled by her presence.

The child stiffened and her muti-hued eyes darted towards the city where the festival could still be heard.

I stopped. "Please don't go. You needn't be afraid of me." I held my webbed hands out apologetically. "My name is Remnant, Remnant Ezra Solaire Dark."

The child's eyes widened. "You gave me your full name! I don't even know mother's full name." She nodded to herself thoughtfully and then looked back towards me. "I will not abuse it and I will stay for a little while. I am called Mariella but I like Riella better."

My heart thumped hard in my chest. Impossible! I knew that name...Mariella was Kira's middle name, it came from a long family line dating back to the creation of Atlantis itself.

"I like Riella too," I said softly and with sincerity. "It is beautiful and you have made your name your own. That is important."

The faeling beamed at me and it was like having sunlight shoot into every dark crevice of my tainted soul. She pointed her webbed hand behind me curiously. "What are those?"

I glanced at my shadows who had peeked over my shoulder to investigate this astonishing creature. I smiled at their silliness and the faeling's bold curiosity.

"I am shadow fae. These are my shadows." I tilted my head with thought. "Would you like to meet them?"

Riella nodded enthusiastically. "Oh yes! May I?"

The shadows did not wait for my answer and morphed instantly into a playful pod of black dolphins. They jumped over and around the faeling in a spirited manner that drew giggles of laughter in their wake.

She clapped with encouragement and then beamed at me. "What else can they do?"

I swam a little bit closer, still keeping a safe trusting distance between us, and settled my body to the murky ocean floor. I rested my hands on my scaled knees, crossing my feet in front of me, and smiled back.

"They are their own beings. Ask them yourself, little chick-adee." The endearment escaped my lips without thought, echoing from a buried past.

Riella gazed up at the shadows excitedly while they flitted around her, still playing dolphins in the water. "Would you please show me what unicorns look like?"

I smirked despite myself. Every little girl loved unicorns, even I did in my younger years. I once had been very determined to ride one through the Balsam Plains, only to learn that they were stubborn beasts—with a tendency to bite.

The shadows shifted into a small unicorn in front of her and nuzzled her cherub face. Riella's arms wrapped around them instantly. "I love you," she hummed and then looked at them. "What is a chickadee? Can you show me?"

I inhaled sharply and a deep ache tightened in my chest.

The shadows morphed into the little bird that had always been my guide in life, and Riella stretched out her hand towards it. The shadowed chickadee flitted into her hand, settling into it lovingly. Black hearts chirped out from its tiny beak and popped against Riella's black scales like little bubble kisses.

Tears pooled in my eyes. I had almost forgotten that such a sweet innocence could exist amongst the fae. But here it was, gently stroking a shadow bird as if it was a living creature that deserved to be loved.

"How old are you, Riella?" Awe echoing my gentle words.

She looked up. "I'm seven." Her eyes shifted to the city nervously. "I have to go. I'm not really supposed to be here. Mother will be angry."

I nodded and floated upright in the water, the shadows snapped back to my side. "I'll take you home."

Riella pouted and her hands twisted nervously in her lap. "But I don't want to go back there." Her eyes swirled and then she looked up at me with mischief. "Want to know a secret?"

I nodded eagerly, adoring the impish look on her innocent face. "I love secrets."

She leaned in and raised her scaled brow. "I know a dragon."

I played along, while knowing that the chance of her meeting a real water dragon was highly unlikely. Water dragons were extremely rare. "A dragon, really?"

She nodded enthusiastically. "Uh huh. He says I don't belong here, that I am meant to be above, with the land fae. He told me all about unicorns." She peered up at me with wide eyes. "Maybe you could take me? I could see a real unicorn then...and a chickadee."

Hiding both my surprise and alarm, I leaned down to her eye level. "I'd love to meet your dragon, Riella."

She beamed at me. "Really?"

An ear splitting screech echoed violently through the water before I could answer her. Turning with alarm and shielding the child from the direction of the sound, I peered out into the murky depths of the ocean's deadlands.

Emon. I needed to find him!

"Riella, I—" My words died in my throat when I turned back to her. The little faeling was gone.

# CHAPTER 21

## Remnant

"Find her, keep her safe!" I commanded my shadows. Terror seizing me for a brief moment before I shook it off with a hiss. "Nothing happens to her, you hear me? Nothing! I'll look for Emon."

The shadows swirled once before popping out of existence and my eyes narrowed on my new destination. Pushing off the seafloor, I raced through the water, this time forgoing the acrobatics and tightening down my scales to reduce any drag that may have slowed me down—my time here while I was a faeling finally coming to fruition, no doubt manipulated by my mother. She knew I would need it one day.

If I was lucky the shifter was unable to escape the seductive sirens of the sea and would still be tangled in the arms of impassioned females. He was a tasty morsel compared to the lean water fae males here and many would have fought for his attention. It was foolish for me to leave him there all alone with no defense against their seductive nature.

Something heavy pitted in my stomach and for a moment I slowed to analyze it. Goddess, did I actually care what this shifter did and who he did it with? Shaking my head, I sped back up, stretching in the water and flattening my scales more. I had no time to think about such things...nor did I deserve them.

"Remi, darling!"

I reared at the sudden appearance of my friend, somersaulting backwards to stop myself from crashing into her.

"Kira!" I gasped and then gave her a wide fake smile. "I've been looking for my pet beast. Have you seen him?" I eased the fluttering of my gills and the pounding of my heart. *Relax, stay relaxed.*

Kira's rose colored eyes flashed with irritation and jealousy. "Trust me Remi, your *pet* is being well taken care of." Her voice was coated with her siren power and I felt the intense need to believe her.

I shrugged off her call with more effort than I usually needed. Something was amiss.

Engaging my sight, I wavered calmly in the water while alarm heightened all my senses at the burgundy shadows swirling viciously through her— feeding her.

I arched my brow. "If that is so, then you wouldn't mind taking me to him. He is mine and we must take care of our pets. You of all fae would agree and want the same, I'm sure."

Kira pouted, anger simmering beneath the surface, seen only by the intense flutter of her gills. "I was hoping to have some time alone with you but of course I can take you to him." She clapped her hands together. "I have a perfect idea. On the way, I want to show you something I know you'll be surprised by!"

Playing, she was playing me. "Lead the way then, old friend." I waved my hand, indicating I would follow her.

"You won't regret seeing this. I know it," she grinned and swam forward, back towards where I had just come.

I took one last glance at the festival before following her. Music still amplifying the water in the distance. The shifter, although incompetent at being a water fae, was very powerful. I prayed it would be enough to keep him alive this time.

Following Kira, I half listened to her prattling about her city and reminiscing about our faeling days while I cataloged my surroundings, searched for shadows, exits, creatures of the deep, knowing that we both were playing a foolish game the further we got from the city...the further we went *alone*.

"Remi darling! Aren't you listening?" She cuddled into me, stroking my arm.

I resisted the urge to shake off her cold manipulative touch, I could feel the disease of that burgundy power clinging to her.

It was the opposite of Emon's, who always felt warm and safe.

"I apologize. I am unused to and unpracticed at socializing."

She nodded. "Almost a hundred years, Remi. Where have you been all this time? Why did you not come to me?" Her fingers tightened on my arm.

I squeezed them back but did not answer, recognizing the looming darkness in front of us. "Shen's Wall!" I breathed and pulled away from her, gazing at the monstrous mountains that split the entire ocean in half.

"I was hoping you'd remember." Her voice sounded almost hopeful.

"Of course! A wall that is not a wall. A true mirage created by the ancient water dragon Shen. It splits the entire ocean in two, dividing us from The West Isles. So powerful that many who cross it are never the same again. How could I forget such a thing?"

Kira laughed coldly. "You *would* remember it that way. Nothing but history and a wall. But I think of it much differently."

My gaze darted towards her stoney expression, hurt flashing in her pink eyes before disappearing completely.

I frowned.

Kira snickered at my confusion, "You never cared about me, did you Remi? If you did, you would have remembered what this place truly was for us."

My eyes widened, fully understanding now. "This was where we shared our first kiss." I looked around, remembering how we sat beneath the looming wall, two friends separated by land and sea but inseparable all the same. I shook my head. "Kira, we were young, curious, and exploring the world together. Just because I never pursued you in that manner, did not mean I never cared for you."

"You always do that!" She cried and pointed her finger at me. "Acting innocent, never taking responsibility for your actions, the fae you hurt around you! Like Morta, like me! But this is the last time I will allow that to happen! I gave you your chance to remember...to remember us."

My back straightened and I flexed my powers. Thankful for the wall casting hundreds of shadows around me. I narrowed my eyes on my former friend. "That sounded like a threat, Kira."

Kira's pink braids jostled while she laughed again. "Oh it is Remi. It is." She waved her hands and water swept in front of me, uncovering a still form buried beneath the sands. Electric blue hair beckoned me from the lifeless being.

"Bay!" I crouched down, sweeping her hair back from her petite face, my hands stilling at her large deadened eyes staring blankly at nothing.

She was gone.

Rage, rather than sadness, trembled deep inside of me and my hands shook as I closed her beautiful electric blue eyes forever.

I breathed deep, schooling my face. "You killed her?"

She leaned in with a scowl. "I didn't kill her, Remi. You did. Because of you, she was sacrificed. For this!" Snatching her hand up, a red crystal shot through the water and Kira caught it quickly. The burgundy power around her brightened.

Swimming up to meet her at eye level, I scrutinized her. "That's a blood crystal." Glancing down at Bay, the pieces fell into place. "You drained her life force with it to use it, didn't you?"

"I am merely the repercussions of your actions. You forced my hand. Bay's death and the crystal."

I shook my head. "You sound just like her. Are you working with Deirdre, is that what this is all about?"

Kira laughed and she flexed her power, the crystal pulsed in her hand. "You would think that wouldn't you? You think so lowly of me and my abilities that you cannot fathom that this plan is all my own."

I crossed my arms, gathering the shadows below me. "You told the queen the crystals were destroyed with Atlantis."

Kira giggled, "Yes, some of them were but not all. And I did not say *all*, Remi darling. You are not the only clever fae around."

"You should have left it where you found it. They were stolen from Sanguine lands, Kira. Only the blood fae knew how to use them properly without causing death. The last time a water fae attempted to unlock its power, Atlantis was lost and fae were killed, including your family!"

She smirked maliciously at me, "You would know how that feels now, wouldn't you?"

I reared back and pulled the shadows up from the ocean floor, they crawled upwards like ink spreading in the water. "Careful Kira...."

Kira snorted at my display and circled me. "Tell me, was your vengeance for your family sweet? Was it exhilarating? Destroying our capital, killing our queen, murdering thousands of fae all to avenge *your* family." She smiled at me dreamily. "I myself have dreamed about such deeds, yet never to the capacity that you achieved. No, I only blamed one person for my family's deaths, not thousands."

Clenching my teeth, I growled, "My mother had nothing to do with your family's deaths, Kira. They were greedy, they wanted to use the blood crystals for their own gain as well as the war...it destroyed them."

Deep crimson anger burned into Kira's eyes. "It was on your mothers orders that they stole them in the first place! You know...I rejoiced at hearing of her demise at first, then quickly realized that she still won. Stealing my revenge by dying!" she screamed shrilly. The burgundy power pulsed faster around her, excited by her anger. "So I thought to myself, what would be the next best thing? Imagine my surprise when the *golden one* shifter practically delivered you at my doorstep! It was then that I knew. You! Your death would be the revenge I need, the revenge thousands of us need now!"

Thrusting her arms up and out, a barrage of water and burgundy power rose to strike. My shadows took the assault, shielding me from the worst of her attack despite the water sending me spiraling through its depths.

Gasping, I dropped low, thrusting shadows outward, cutting through the water and slamming harshly into the burgundy power she shielded with. The blast sizzled against the deep red power and started to grow in size around her.

"The best thing about all of this is that with your death, the fae will rejoice in my accomplishment in killing you. I will be their hero!" she screamed out, hurling an enormous amount of power at me. "And awarded the throne in return!"

I laughed incredulously. Dodging the blast that crashed in a thundering boom to the ocean floor, I slung myself from splintered rock to splintered rock, gathering shadows in my wake and hurtling them back towards her. "To rule over what exactly? A pile of rubble and a dying species?"

Her dark burgundy power cleared and revealed a cruel smile. "Oh no, Remi darling. That is where you are wrong. The fae will be reborn again and I will be their heroine queen that saved us all!"

I gathered more shadows to me, my gills opening wide and breathing in deep. "And where does Deirdre fit in all this, oh mighty Queen Kira? I know she is behind all of it, it practically stinks of her rot." I laughed again. "Do you honestly think the former Queen of Faerie will idly sit by and watch you take her throne!"

Kira giggled. "It's amazing how much you don't know. But then again that is what happens to cowards who hide in exile from their failures! You are so pathetic. Deirdre doesn't care about the throne of Faerie any more. She is the blood witch now and no longer bound by a meager desire to rule over the fae when she can rule over worlds...universes even!"

My heart thundered at Kira's words...worlds...universes. *"Do not come back here!"* I silently screamed to my shadows. *"Find the shifter and take him to the child. She is the key to all of this and must be protected at all costs!"*

I just hoped I wasn't too late...a lock of blue hair floated in the distance...like I was too late for Bay.

I fed the shadows with the looming darkness of the wall, I was on my own now, equipped with only the shadow power every one of my kind possessed...what I was born with. Shadow was darkness and darkness was infinite. The first and the last, the beginning and the end—of all life and I knew how to use it well.

Kira watched the shadows gathering with a twinkle of mirth in her pink eyes. "Only your innate shadows have come to the rescue have they?" She twirled a pink braid, confidence oozing from her vicious smile. "I've been waiting, watching, listening. But the rumors are true, aren't they? You lost your powers the day of Morta. Your sentient shadows have truly abandoned you."

I raised my brows and snaked the dormant shadows up my arms, a shield and sword molding in front of me. "I don't need them to take you on Kira, I never did." I gave her a pointed look. "Are you sure you want to do this? You can just give me the shifter now and we will leave this place." And...taking Riella with me.

"It's too late, *Remi darling*. You and the shifter are now part of the deal, your lives forfeit." She shrugged, "not that I needed a deal to want to kill you." She held up the blood crystal. "And with this, there is nothing you can do to stop me."

I gave her a taunting smile. "If that truly is the case, then I have a confession." I licked at my needled teeth and watched her eyes spark with desire despite her resolve to kill me. Water fae were such sensual beings. "My little pet shifter kisses better than you ever did, in fact every fae I kissed after you was infinitely better than your slimy fish lips."

Taking advantage of her shock, I whipped forth a lasso of shadow from my formed sword and snapped the blood crystal straight out of her clenched hand. From behind, another round of shadows pummeled into her back, shooting her towards me with no time to react. Dodging to the side as she whizzed past me, my shadow sword slashed outwards and scraped harshly across her gut drawing first blood.

"Bitch!" she screamed, surprising me by sealing her wound instantly with her newfound power.

The water bubbled angrily around me and I narrowed my eyes at the thousands of ice shards suspended and poised to impale.

They shot through the water, a whistling hum the only indicator of their storm. Spinning, I weaved numerous shadow shields, deflecting every shard and sending them straight back to their owner.

She responded by melting them one by one back into the ocean and smiled widely at me, untouched. "Too easy, *Remi darling*."

Wielding a thin fog of shadows, I created an impenetrable bubble barrier around my head just moments before I felt the water stir my hair.

She screamed with rage, her attempt to cut off my water supply denied.

I grinned and blew a kiss back at her.

Screaming again, the ocean heaved in response to her shrilling voice and I thrusted my shadows deep in the sand, deeper still into the rocks below. Preparing and bracing for the tsunami of water that threatened to crush me.

I swallowed down my cry of pain, feeling my shoulders dislocate under the harsh grip of the shadows anchoring me against the storm. A glint of red caught my periphery through the crushing ocean waters. It was the blood crystal tumbling rapidly across the sand towards me.

Dropping my anchors, I weaved shadow to scoop up the blood crystal at the same time as Kira wielded the waters to do the same. The two locked in a deadly game of tug of war.

Burgundy power crawled over the crystal and along my shadows that shuddered at the tainted power before snapping away. Desperately, I clawed at the rocky ocean floor to stop another surge of water from crushing me to certain death.

I screamed when my spine snapped horribly against an unforgiving surface. Shen's wall crumbled beneath my body, groaning and creaking while I was being forcefully embedded into its rocky mirage. Pink tinged the water in the shadow bubble when my head slammed harshly backwards, splitting open my skull. Additional debris sliced open my scales, and I raised my torn webbed hands in a pathetic attempt to shield myself.

Chipped green paint on my hands blurred in and out of focus. Lovingly and thoughtfully put there by a vibrant water fae I barely knew but was dead for meeting me all the same.

I blinked hard against the cruel fate of darkness and the sunburst pattern of the brightly lit burgundy power in the distance. Showcased in the center and laughing cruelly was Kira's silhouette...a small shadow casted over her face by the tainted luminous glow.

I smiled and flicked my hand. The crazed laughter cut short by a loud slap of shadow across Kira's face, snapping her head to the side and cutting open her black lips.

I choked on my own blood sniggering. "You never did master the art of silence. Consider this a review."

Kira's head turned slowly back to me, touching her lip with disbelief, the power of the crystal burning brighter in her eyes. "I...will...kill...you."

There was no stopping the force of her power slamming deep into me, burrowing harshly into my body. A scream ripped from my throat and my body contorted against the wall, attempting to find a way to escape the pulsating burgundy power sucking my life essence from me just like it had before—one hundred years ago.

Only this time, the power of the Sanguine wasn't being wielded by the queen, but a mere pawn of a fae that would die just like all the others who played Deirdre's games.

"Enough!" I roared and drew the remaining shadows around my entire body, wrapping myself layer by layer into darkness, cutting off the burrowing of the Sanguine power.

"You won't be able to beat it *Remi darling*!" Kira cooed loudly.

I grunted against the savage power slamming repeatedly into my shield of shadow. Weakening and stripping them layer by layer. I breathed in the darkness and closed my eyes, a lone tear escaping into the swirling ocean waters. I was going to die here...and for the first time in a long time—I didn't want to.

"I'm sorry I wasn't enough." My apology was a broken whisper from my cracked bleeding lips and then...my shadows shattered.

Breathing in my final breath, I opened my eyes to see the remaining shards of shadow being swept away by the violent seas only to be replaced by thousands of burgundy tendrils ravenously tunneling straight for my tortured soul.

# CHAPTER 22

"*I* KNEW YOU WERE *going to get us killed,*" my beast growled irritably.

I grunted, my shifter side tingling with a warning that had nothing to do with the wall of churning water at my back nor the armada of water fae ready to impale me beyond that.

No, it had everything to do with what was in front of me.

A lifeless ocean with murky gray waters and the putrid stench of disease. A large lochness carcass could be seen mere feet away, its rib bones protruding out of the black rotting sand—a warning from its shallow grave.

Remnant would have tried to bury the poor creature if she were here to see it.

I snarled at the deep ache growing inside me. The longer she was absent, the more irritated I became. Shaking out my claws, I glared at the direction Kira had gone, where I knew my soulmate would be.

A place I was unable to go.

Instead, I prowled the water, hissing and snarling, sheathing and unsheathing my claws. A fucking sitting duck—prey. I was prey.

*"Ducks don't live under the water, fairy boy and I don't plan on letting these foul water fae execute me. Get it. Fowl."* The cat chuckled deeply.

I stilled, groaning. *"I should just shift and let you drown for that. Your humor will surely make me go feral one of these days."*

*"You were feral before me, fairy boy."*

I grinned. Therein lay the truth, my crooked nose more than a testament to that.

"Cyrus." I shot back to the orange haired guard who helped escort me to my death. "Does the same thing happen when you need to take a shit as it does for your dick? Again, I'm asking for a friend." The distraction was necessary for my nerves.

"Fuck you, you shifter prick," the water fae snarled back.

My chest rumbled, easing some of the tension building inside me. "I am going to assume that is a yes."

*"It comes."* My beast prowled agitatedly inside my head.

A piercing scream came with his warning and it rattled my scales.

My eyes widened. I knew that sound.

"Ah, shit. Who in the goddess let that asshole out!" I bared my teeth, narrowing my eyes on the gigantic domineering creature slowly crawling out of the pit from which it came, only growing in size.

"Time to die, shifter prick," orange hair called out to me. The faint laughter of the other water fae around him penetrated the darkness.

I cursed under my breath when eight tentacles, with suckers puckering in fluttering ticks, stretched out of the murky waters. Each one of them curled out widely, pulling along the massive lumbering creature attached to them. A molten smell of rot that rivaled the sludge of the decayed ocean floor hit me like a tidal wave.

Damn my shifter senses.

"Cronin." I bared my teeth and folded my arms across my chest. "The last time I saw your ugly kraken ass was when I imprisoned you five hundred years ago for crimes against the shifter crown!" I heard the faint whispers of disbelief from the water fae guards and I smirked—the poor idiots had no idea who they were fucking with.

Cronin's massive black kraken head turned my way. Clusters of red beady eyes zeroed in on my floating frame and then his black beak clicked agitatedly. "Well, well, well, if it isn't the golden prick of the family," his voice boomed in the murky water.

I peered down at my glinting claws and tested their sharpness. "Still obsessed with my dick I see. You'd think after a few centuries you'd move on."

More agitated clicking, grew louder this time. "I'm going to enjoy eating you, Emon...slowly, savoring your bones as they break. Five hundred years has made me more than ravenous for my revenge!"

I chuckled and shook my head. "Same words you said last time and look where that got you, oh guardian of the deadlands." Pointing one sharp claw his way, I growled low. "I'll make you a deal, kraken. I'll spare your life, albeit you're still going back to your prison, for the name of the fae who released you."

Cronin chortled and I gagged on the stench permeating the water from his molten mouth.

"You are in my territory now, Emon. Your puny water fae body is no match for me. I will make no such deal. My vengeance is all I need."

*"Refrain from pissing off the giant sea insect more, fairy boy,"* the cat hissed.

I grinned. "Your moronic simple mind couldn't even come up with any other goals besides killing me, could it?" I purred at him. "I'm flattered, you have been thinking so much about me. Here I thought having eight appendages would assist you in preoccupying your time more pleasurably." Crudely, I cupped my hand and stroked it in the water, winking at the kraken.

The beast sighed. *"And there it is..."*

Thoughtless in his own anger, Cronin torpedoed towards me, his globulous head morphing into an arrow, jetting through the sea.

Smirking, I waited. "Three, two, one."

Darting quickly to the side, a thunderous boom vibrated the gloomy waters and laughter exploded deep from my chest at the sight of the kraken splattering against the water barrier of a wall Kira trapped me in. The water fae guard behind it cried out in their terror, dropping their weapons and scuttling away in fear.

*"I'm assuming that this little stunt was to break down the water barrier?"*

I chuffed, my laughter dying down. *"It was worth a shot."* Dark waters curled up around my scaled legs and I shivered. *"Guess I am alone now. With a kraken...in a dead ocean."*

*"You're never alone, fairy boy,"* my beast hissed at me, like he was offended. *"WE, need no one...we are MORE."*

I sighed exasperatedly. *"I really don't have time for your cryptic bullshit, cat. You've been saying that since I was a faeling and never explain it any further."*

Cronin slid as he peeled himself from the invisible water barrier. His massive frame shook with rage.

"Emon!" he roared.

I roared back. "Here I am, you ugly fuck!"

A thick tentacle whizzed through the waters and I turned, dragging my claws through his rubbery flesh with dark satisfaction.

Jolting from the injury, Cronin's appendage flung me outward and I shuddered just moments before slimy sludge sands and rotting corpses became my new safe haven. My black water fae body camouflaged perfectly in the darkness.

I needed a plan.

*"Get on with it then, it's not like you listen to me anyway,"* the cat grumbled.

I chuckled softly, my beast wasn't going to like this.

"Here kitty kitty kitty!" A laugh from Cronin vibrated the waters. Powerful enough to send me tumbling sideways.

"Here fishy fishy," I hissed back, my eyes glowing with power in the darkness.

# CHAPTER 23

## Remnant



*"Time to wake, cousin."*

I moaned at the sharp commanding tone splitting my skull in half. Every single inch of me was riddled with pain. Death, I had been waiting on death.

*"He will not be coming this day, although it would make for an interesting reunion."*

Gasping, a jolt of power coursed through my body, wrenching me from the darkness. Shivering from the intrusion, my pain subsided, and I slowly blinked my eyes open.

A pair of large orbs, cerulean blue, came into focus.

I blinked again, inhaling sharply.

*"I hadn't realized my cousins had become this dense."*

"Water dragon." I rose slowly, hands raised and cautiously floated backwards from his patronizing gaze.

*"As you see."*

I winced at the invasion of his voice booming inside my head and attempted not to stare stupidly while I gazed upon his beastly beauty.

His cerulean blue eyes were ferocious, housed in a gigantic square shaped head decorated with sharp white fangs extending well past his thick leathered lips. Two long whiskers, alongside his monstrous jaw, floated elegantly in the static water. Wide, round nostrils, the size of my own head, flared much like the gills on a fish and the creature's scales were nothing short of awe inspiring, a wondrous array of purples, greens, and indigo that constantly changed with his movement and trailed over his serpentine body that was coiled neatly on a bed of white rock. Waving lazily and reaching into the waters were webbed spiked fins, like the sails of a boat, changing color with each flutter.

He was magnificent.

I breathed deep, steadying my racing heart. Beasts like him detected weakness and if you were weak, you were prey...something I didn't want to be.

"Where are we?"

He tilted his head indicating the white rock around us with a snort. *"We are within my wall."*

My gills fluttered. "You are Shen, the great mirage water dragon."

The dragon's deep chuckle unsettled me and I braced against his laughter. *"As you see."*

"Sweet goddess," I breathed. "No one has seen you since the dawn of our time."

The dragon curved his head around so that one beautiful blue eye blinked at me head on. *"Is Faerie sweet now? Last time I spoke to her she said my wall was a blight upon her grand design and demanded I remove it. She was rather presumptuous and arrogant, if you ask me. There is no greater masterpiece in this world than my wall dividing an entire ocean."*

I gave him a sympathetic smile that was cloyingly sweet. "Your wall is widely known and is admired by many."

The water dragon's webbed spikes fluttered in the water and he bared his sharp teeth in a ferocious smile. *"I'll take your flattery even if it is purposefully done to appease me. Now tell me. Why do you look like those pests? You are not water fae. What is your business here with them?"*

I spread my hands wide. "Can't a fae enjoy a dip from time to time."

Shen hissed softly. His body uncoiling from its resting perch and circling around me, his massive head inching closer and his tongue flickering out with an air of distaste. *"I'll ask one more time, cousin. Why do you look like a water fae? What have you come here for?"*

I frowned. "You call me cousin, why?"

His eyes rolled and then brought one serpentine eye closer, narrowing vertically on my person. *"Typical fae, avoiding questions and asking your own,"* he huffed, disturbing the calm waters and forcing me to collide with his body coiled around me. *"Yes, we are cousins by nature. The shadow fae were the first fae created along with water dragons—our souls very much crafted from similar origins. For with light there must be darkness. What are they teaching you young ones these days if you are not privy to that knowledge?"*

"I apologize for my ignorance." Sardonic words for a bold dragon.

Shen blinked his vertical slitted eye at me twice, recognizing my lack of sincerity before he retracted away. The sudden movement caused me to spin like a top. When I finally slowed, he was back in his coiled resting position, his head settled with a raised purple brow.

*"Now speak, cousin. Answer the questions I seek now that your curiosity has been satisfied."*

He was a moody beast, much like my shifter. "I spoke the truth, I do enjoy a nice swim from time to time." A long blink demonstrated the dragon's vexation and I sighed. "We were cornered. By Kira. Her demand was that we come to The Under as guests for the Three Moon Festival. When we arrived we quickly realized something was not right and stayed to investigate."

Shen snorted again, blasting me with a shower of bubbly sea water. *"Your investigation did not end well, cousin."*

I crossed my arms and tapped my bicep with my long nails. "I'd say, it went well enough, seeing how I am alive, reunited with a lost family member, and no longer being impaled by the Sanguine."

A forked tongue snaked out as if he was testing the water before his booming voice echoed inside of me. *"An old power rises as the fair one weakens—"*

I could not stop the flood of words from escaping me. "Golden becomes the one true beacon, blood will run on the darkened moons, run child run, I will see you soon."

The great water dragon nodded. *"Yes, that is correct, cousin."*

Bubbles escaped at my exasperated sigh. "Mother."

The water vibrated with a deep chuckle. "Ah yes, mothers do have a curious way of warning their children it seems. To give them just enough information so as not to spark the excitement of an adventure but also just enough to warn them of a future danger. This was especially the case with Eve, although it could have just been her prophetic nature."

My head snapped up. "You knew my mother?"

*"I did. I see much of her in you, although your father's side is much more forthcoming. Especially the snark."*

My heart pounded. "Impossible. No one remembers who he was. Not even my mother."

The dragon chuckled and the water vibrated with his laughter again. *"Everyone has a father do they not? Your mother will remember him again, I'm sure. And also remember how much of an asshole he is."*

Sadness, like a deep ache that could not heal, stilled my racing heart. "You are mistaken. The shadow fae are no more, my mother is dead."

*"You dare question me, cousin? Have you not met one of my kind before?"*

"Land dragons yes, water dragons no," I said cautiously.

He snickered knowingly. *"Tell me, cousin, how do I compare to my land brethren?"*

I tilted my head, choosing my words carefully. "I hardly know you well enough to compare but if I must then I would say the land dragons in the south...have a tendency for battle that does not make them great conversationalists. At times, their wars with the Roc eagles spilled over the mountain ranges and into the heart of Faerie. Where I was often sent to intervene."

*"Intervene...interesting choice of words, cousin. What you mean is that you were sent to slaughter them."* He chuckled out loud when he saw my guarded expression. *"I would not have cared if you did kill my air flapping brethren. Unsophisticated beasts of the sky as they are except—"* He eyed me with interest. *"You never did kill them. You ignored the orders of your queen, made it look like you*

*did your duty but in fact, you saved them. What I want to know is why?"*

I narrowed my eyes. Only two beings ever knew my defiance of those specific orders and they perished at Morta. "I do not know where you get your information from, dragon."

Shen smiled viciously. *"You returned with burns and wounds severe enough to require healers and to make most believe you accomplished such a terrible massacre. But I know otherwise, what I don't know is why?"*

My hands fisted at my sides in anger and the shadows darkened in the white carven. "I do not need to explain my unwillingness to end an entire species on behalf of some inconsequential skirmish that could be contained with a bit of diplomacy and time."

Shen's tongue snaked out and grazed across my cheek. *"Diplomacy. Is that what you call battling dragons for dominance...forcing their submission under your control, Natrix Drakaina?"*

I inhaled sharply. "If you know all that, then you also know that title is only in name. The dragons still rule themselves." I bared my teeth. "All life should be cherished, I do not slaughter innocents. I did what I had to do to save them."

*"Except...you have slaughtered innocents, Remnant Ezra Solaire Dark, thousands of them. You furthered the extinction of your own people. You wished once to end your own life...how is that cherishing the life the goddess granted you?"*

I stared in anger. "I do not deny what I have done. Let me amend my statement. I take no pleasure in murdering others. Life is precious...no matter what form they come in. From the smallest of flowers, to the gnomes that battle, and the chickadees that soar, all the way to the dragons that bellow...even queens that go mad. We all are needed in this world." I swallowed down the emotional pain rising within me. "But what this world never needed was me. I would forfeit my life easily if it meant I could undo the wrongs I have made."

The dragon continued to study me before he spoke with a sad tone. *"It is a shame you place no value upon your own life while you hold others in such high regard."*

"When you are a monster you do not have the right to hold such value."

*"Have you ever considered the fact that the world needs monsters then...to protect the lives that do matter?"* Shen cooed at me, wrapping his body closer around my person.

I stiffened with alarm. When had the dragon started coiling around me? "Speak plainly, dragon. Speak your purpose."

Shen's eye beamed at me, the cerulean blue swirling inside his vertical slits. *"Cousin, I find that I am in need of a monster that places the life of another above her own. Your debt to me for saving your life from those water fae pests will be fulfilled should you agree."*

I glared into the dragons' fierce single eye, stating slow and clear. "No."

# CHAPTER 24

Remnant

S HEN HISSED, HIS TONGUE flicking out and grazing my exposed cheek but my glare never wavered. *"So brave but so foolish. Bartering with a dragon never ends well for the barterer, cousin, and I can see that clever gleam in your eyes. Speak your terms at your own risk."*

I raised my chin. "Give me and my companion safe passage to The West Isles and I will complete your task."

Shen's great head lifted away from me, admiration and knowing twinkling in his eyes. *"I will give only you and one other safe passage from here and it is not your shifter. He must stay. His fate is one that even I will not intervene on."*

I stilled. "What do you mean?"

Shen hummed. *"He is goddess blessed. I cannot intervene in his fate."*

My hands fisted at my side. "Then I cannot help you. Kill me or show me the way out of here."

A fierce flood of bubbles blew from flared nostrils. *"You will do neither, we are out of time and the child nears."*

Riella's sweet little voice whispered in my thoughts...*I know a dragon.* Feigning shock, I reared back. "A child in Faerie? I do hope you haven't conjured up such a blasphemous mirage to fool me into helping you!"

The dragon's deep chuckle stirred my free floating hair, the emerald hair piece that had held it down lost forever...just like Bay.

*"I would not be surprised if the goddess gifted you mirage powers, Remnant Dark. You may drop your contrived performance, such an act does not work on me. The ocean knows many things and is quite the gossiper. Do you honestly believe it would not tell me that you have met the faeling?"*

I crossed my arms over my chest, thumbing at the remaining green paint. "What of her mother? She nearly killed me. I cannot fight against the enhanced power she wields and protect the faeling at the same time." I narrowed my eyes at the winning grin forming on his beastly head as I spoke. "I have not agreed to help you, dragon."

Shen lowered his great head so that it was just inches from me. *"You cannot fight your nature, cousin, no fae would leave a child alone to fend for herself with monsters worse than the one they already keep. And that pest—that parasite, is no mother to the girl just as I am not her father. The blood witch's influence grows and she will come for the child. It is no longer safe for her here."*

I glared. "You know more than what you have told me. Arm me with knowledge if I am to be her guardian."

He scoffed and flicked his tongue out at me again and I batted it away with a growl. My action only made him chuckle with amusement. *"Cousin, you have been fighting with what you do not know since the day of your birth. Will you protect her or not, General Remnant Ezra Solaire Dark? The Last Shadow Fae. Slayer of the Faerie Queen. Murderer of Morta. Monster That Values Life. Keeper of the Golden One. Cousin of the Greatest Legendary Water Dragon That Has Ever Lived?"*

I hissed through my teeth. "Any other title you'd like to bestow upon me?"

"None that I would repeat in front of my little seaflower. Come forth child! I know you are there."

I practically collapsed at the sound of his true voice as it boomed inside the cavern no longer inside my head.

"Dragon...do we need to have a talk about proper etiquette?" I tapped a webbed finger to my temple, cutting him with a knowing glare.

*"Etiquette? When it was you who cracked my wall? I think not, cousin. Do not feign vulnerability with me."* Then his great head turned. "Come. It is safe here, I promise you, my treasure."

Muddy pink hair swirled around a tiny black scaled body as she peeked through the white illusionary walls. Multi-faceted eyes twinkled with delight, darting from me to the dragon before rushing forward to embrace him.

The size of her was the equivalent of one single scale on his serpentine form and I had to shove away my instinct to pull her away from the fearsome creature. Cautiously, I moved forward.

"Riella. It is so good to see you again. Apologies for finding your dragon before you were able to bring me to him yourself."

Shen huffed, water blasted in my direction and purposefully sent my body careening away from the girl.

"Shen Shen!" Riella admonished. "Be nice!"

Gritting my teeth, I flipped away from the rushing current sent by the possessive dragon.

"Yes Shen Shen, do—." My next words seized in the back of my throat.

The water dragon's body was now curled lovingly around the little faeling and nuzzling gently into her. His fin sails swayed back and away from her and his teeth were no longer bared—both carefully placed so as to not harm the vulnerable little fae with his monstrous form.

"I will do it," I choked out instead of my cutting remark.

The dragon's eyes turned on me, unashamed by the sadness echoing in their depths. *"I had no doubt you would, cousin."*

I raised my chin. *"If anything happens to the shifter, I will hold you personally responsible and nothing will stop me from coming after you, dragon,"* I spoke back to him silently. If Emon was to die, I would make sure it was by my own hand. Till then, I had a deal to uphold and it required the shifter to stay alive. I would have to trust that the shadows could make it to him in time and that he would not be too angry at my leaving him behind.

I snorted...the goddess knew that wasn't likely.

Shen's eyes narrowed on me. *"As will I if anything happens to my treasure, cousin."*

*"May our future paths cross then on good terms,"* I glared back.

Shen grunted and slowly pulled away from the faeling. "Little seaflower, remember when I told you there would be a time that you would need to be brave and leave this place for good?"

"But I don't want to leave you!" She cried, flinging herself back into his scales, rubbing her cheek against him. "And... and what about mother, she will be so angry! She will come after me!" Red tears stained the water, disappearing into the muddy pink hair floating around her.

"We will see each other again my little seaflower," the water dragon purred, "and the next time your mother sees you, I promise she will not be angry. She will be unequivocally awed by your greatness."

I swallowed back the bitterness pinging in the back of my throat. To be loved in such a way was something to never take for granted. How was it that Kira had not treasured this miracle more, why was it that the girl was afraid of her?

Clearing my throat, I addressed them both. "You said our time was short."

Shen uncoiled his great body while still keeping in contact with his treasured seaflower. "General Remnant is correct. It is time for you both to leave this place." He gave me a warning look. "The sludge you ingested to turn into a water fae will wear off soon and with it will come more danger. Best you be on dry land before that happens."

I bared my teeth. "This is an example of the knowledge I was talking about and the cryptic lack thereof."

"I have no doubts that you will succeed, cousin. You have all that you need."

"You would do well to not place such faith in a fae that has failed her people and Faerie already!"

The dragon swung his head closer to me, his whiskers trailing up around him, and his tongue flickered. "What is failure but the stepping stone to success. Your only fault, cousin, is believing that your story has ended."

I reared back, my hair whipping across my face. Snatching it away, I opened my mouth only to snap it shut at the sight of the faeling perched atop the crest of the water dragon's head, his whiskers too large for her to fully grasp.

Riella giggled at my stare. "Shen, Shen. Be nice to my new friend. You have broken her."

"She is only in awe of your bravery, little seaflower. Give her a moment," Shen commented, tilting his head fondly back towards her.

My gills flared but my voice was soft. "Indeed, you are very brave, Riella."

Her eyes widened and the colors in them swirled before a wide grin spread across her face. "Want to learn how to ride?"

Glancing at Shen who nodded his assent, I swam up to her perched body, my webbed hand touching her scaled cheek reverently. "I would love that, little one."

The warmth of her happiness radiated from her tiny frame and I gently seated myself behind her.

Riella turned to look up at me. "You can hold onto me. Shen says it is better to lay low to his body when he starts and then move with his form, not against it. That way the water will not pull us off him." Biting her lip, she peered sheepishly at me. "Shen Shen says there are other dragons that fly in the air above the surface. Have you met one? Do you ride them similarly?"

I swallowed back the tears threatening to form and spoke softly, nothing but reverence in my tone. "I have met them, yes. Riding an air dragon takes a bit more force than the graceful movement of a water dragon I would imagine."

Shen growled, "Uncultured beasts, the lot of them."

Riella's swirling eyes studied me while she chewed on her bottom lip with her tiny needled teeth. "When we get to the surface. I will ride one." She released her lip with a pop and nodded once to herself before turning forward. "I have decided I also will ride a unicorn."

I laughed and wrapped my arms around her to give her a gentle squeeze. "Deal. You show me how to ride a water dragon and I will show you how to ride both an air dragon and a unicorn."

Shen snorted and then shot forward. Riella instantly leaned inward as did I, covering her petite form with my body. Muddy pink hair tickled my face and the faeling trembled with excitement.

I smiled into her hair.

A miracle.

She was a goddess blessed miracle.

My chest constricted involuntarily and I circled my arms more tightly around her. The tears I had been holding back spilled into the water rushing quickly past us, finally recognizing the emotion

I had been swallowing down since the moment I met her...one I thought I'd never feel again.
Hope.
Riella was hope.

# CHAPTER 25

"Got any other brilliant *ideas?*" my beast mocked.

I rolled my eyes where I was hiding in the murky black waters that had been concealing me.

Another tentacle came hurtling down through the inky darkness and sent me skittering across the ocean floor like a damn leaf. "*This is all according to plan.*" I grunted when a large rock jabbed into my hip.

The cat all but yawned. "*Is it indeed?*"

"*Are you taking a cat nap? Why don't you just choke on a fur ball instead while you're at it.*" Dry words...serious words.

"*What would you have me do? I'm bored and you're scurrying around on the seafloor like that jackalope I ate a week ago,*" he said haughtily. "*Which reminds me. I'm famished.*"

"*Who in the fuck says famished?*"

153

*"Cultured beings...unlike that disgusting Kraken you seem to be playing with."* He yawned again. *"I told you not to trust that water fae bitch."*

Another tentacle sweep barely missed my head, sending me further along the ocean floor along with the muck. Only stopping when my back bumped into something slender and hard.

A grin spread across my face. *"Did you just say bitch?"*

The beast stilled, blissfully quiet for a moment. *"Apologies, all this water is getting to me."*

I chuckled evilly, *"Perhaps, I'll make The Under my next vacation home."*

No response.

"Cowardly pussy!" Cronin yelled in frustration after another attempt to crush me using his blubbery arms. "Falcon, was right to turn on you."

*Falcon.* I gripped the hard slender objects, baring my teeth in the darkness, and my heart thundered with rage.

Unlike my shifter brethren, natural bloodlust was never the cause of lost control for me...it was the blazing golden power inside that I feared.

*"You're welcome,"* the beast yawned again.

Ignoring him, I breathed in the bloodlust. Embraced it. Seized it. I was fucking hungry for it. Hungry for blood. The price of my one hundred year old revenge.

*"Oh yes, I like this way of thinking,"* the cat perked up.

*"Playtime is over."* My claws extended and my fangs lengthened.

With a loud wrench I yanked off the rib bone of the lochness carcass I had been gripping. Sending a sickening crack through the still waters.

"There you are, kitty cat," Cronin roared, clumsily attacking my position.

A feral grin etched across my face and I roared back, thrusting the lochness rib upwards into the darkness and straight into the rubber appendage of Cronin's tentacles.

Muscling over the curved portion of the rib, Cronin wrenched his appendage back with a painful wail. Suddenly, I was catapulted out of the darkness and into the light.

*"Poetry,"* purred the cat.

I smirked. Whether it was at the cat's sarcastic wit or the grotesque widening of Cronin's red eyes in seeing me dangling like a worm on a hook in front of him, I didn't know.

I tilted my head. "You know Cronin, whenever we see each other, I can never decide which cluster of eyes I should look at," I snickered before I sliced my makeshift weapon downward, flaying his tentacle in two.

Cronin roared with pain, his split limb flailing uselessly in the water, releasing bits of white blubber and bright red blood into the soft flowing ocean.

Satisfied, I brandished the lochness rib and hissed with my fangs. "I thought you'd look better with nine thingys rather than eight." I wiggled my claws at him. "Mistake that, you're still fucking ugly as ever."

I didn't have a death wish but my life was filled with nothing but.

*"And it's just the beginning,"* the cat snorted.

I didn't move when one of Cronin's functional appendages snapped outward and curled around me in a crushing grip.

I braced against the pain of the mounting pressure—my arms were still free, Cronin's biggest mistake that I had bet on.

"I could snap you like a fucking twig and destroy you, you golden prick," Cronin spat, molting gray skin flaking off of him with each agitated movement of his bird-like beak.

"How uneventful." I leaned back into my free arms, the rib bone still clutched firmly in my grip and gritted against the painful squeezing of his tentacle.

"You're right, I like the idea of eating you alive—listening to your screams while I do."

"Oh goddess, not that," I wiggled and thrashed against his grip, my eyes widening with mock terror.

*"If that's acting then I'm a mangey dog,"* the cat snorted.

Cronin's laughter stirred the ocean current.

*"Nah, you just have to know your audience."* I brought my hands together, the rib bone pleading with me. "Please, please don't eat me!"

Cronin's laughter continued, amused by my begging. "As if I would grant such a request! I stopped following you blindly long ago, you golden prick. Looks like it's going to be cat for dinner!"

I couldn't hold back the gag from his rancid breath as I was brought to the underbelly of the kraken beast. His beak opened and closed rapidly while multiple rows of tiny razor sharp teeth gnashed back and forth in anticipation of their meal.

My grin grew the closer I came to the ominous clicking and sawing of teeth. Raising the lochness spear high above my head I stabbed downward with a vicious roar, my beast's voice echoing within, and Cronin's sharp wails joining shortly after. Ripping the makeshift weapon out, I repeatedly stabbed at the tentacle until it started to unravel away from me.

Fully free, I pumped my legs hard, the rib raised high, launching myself straight into serrated jaws of doom.

*"This was your plan?"* the cat drawled.

*"Did you expect anything less!"* I roared back at him and braced before entering the kraken's lethal mouth. Streamlining my body, I clenched my jaw against the cracking of my scales from his sawing teeth, and gripped the lochness bone harder. Roaring one more time, I entered into the darkness, pumping all my strength into my legs to shoot through his body like a knife through butter.

*"I may not have thought this all the way through,"* I choked on the hot viscous guts pouring out around me.

The beast snorted. *"Clearly."*

Snarling, a final push popped me through to the other side of his blubbery body.

Spinning, I took my first fresh breath of clean water, listening to Cronin keen in pain while a trail of his thick dark blood oozed from his punctured body.

When I caught sight of movement in the water below, I narrowed my eyes and raised the rib bone defensively up in front of me. Tracking its movements, I chuckled darkly when it sprung into my view.

"Hello, my little fiends." I lowered my makeshift weapon.

Deadly dark shadows split through the blood tinged water and brushed happily against my scales. I laughed as they rustled my hair playfully and then dove back down, swallowing part of the kraken in their wake.

*"I tried telling you that help was coming. Instead you decided to be swallowed by a kraken. I seriously hope you do not come up with any other brilliant plans,"* the beast rattled.

I barely heard him, searching for the familiar scent or stunning vision of my soulmate that never came.

*"She has survived this long without us. We will find her again,"* my beast attempted to reassure me.

*"Remnant shouldn't have to survive anymore,"* I growled back, *"she should be living."*

Looking past the feasting shadows, towards the hidden lochness remains, I thoughtfully held up its rib bone before me. "To the life given and the life taken too soon, the darkness will avenge you." Releasing the bone, I allowed it to sink heavily back down into the murky water, passing by the shadows taking chunk after chunk out of the kraken like a school of flesh eating piranhas, to find some sort of peace within this forsaken place.

Glancing back at Cronin, I watched death glaze over his red beady eyes right before they were completely swallowed up by the shadows dark abyss.

"Well done, umbras," I purred towards them and grinned when they rushed to entwine around my legs before flipping off of me in an acrobatic show of terrifying shadow.

"I assume your beautiful master sent you and that since you're still here, she is not in any immediate danger."

They swirled around me playfully in response, then coiled up my arm once more.

"I will take that as a yes," I chuckled and stroked their shadowy form, cradling them in my arms like a baby cub. "What would you say to a little dessert, my beautiful little fiends?"

Darkness embraced me—only to be enhanced by the echo of my baleful laughter.

# CHAPTER 26

Remnant

Instinctively, I tightened my hold on Riella as together we weaved through the hidden tunnels of Shen's great wall, our hair trailing behind us while the majestic waters rippled soothingly against our scales. But beneath us, I could feel the tension of the great dragon's body, vibrating with something more than exertion, a worry that had his body coiling tightly around corners and his scales shifting with each deep dive.

I frowned. *"Your wall runs north and south, cutting our oceans in half, this is not the way to The West Isles. Where do you take us?"*

*"Look and you shall see why,"* Shen hissed softly in my mind.

I squinted in front of us. An eerie underwater grave of a great city appeared on our horizon. I shivered at its ghostly golden glow. "Atlantis."

Shen boomed out loud. "Indeed! The bridge between worlds. Welcoming both humankind and land fae to join in worship with the mythical fae of the water." He snorted.

The dragon shook his head, slithering to a floating stop just in front of the distinguished craftsmanship of the golden gates. It was as if neither water nor time had impacted its exalted yet looming presence.

My lips pressed into a thin line and I released Riella. "I was there when the city fell." I dismounted the dragon, sinking slowly with my eyes trained on the gates. "My mother was still fighting in the frontlines during the blood wars, she sent me here for safety. I was young, too young." I shook my head. "I had no understanding of my full powers then. I could do nothing to stop it."

I closed my eyes against the distant memory. The roaring of the ocean, the cries of the people being swallowed whole into a watery grave...

"Another failure," I whispered.

Blinking back the tears, I looked down when a soft touch of a webbed hand joined mine. Riella's colorful swirling eyes, echoing my own sadness, peered up at me.

Shen hummed. "It is my understanding that you dove in and saved many trapped inside before it was completely lost."

I squeezed Riella's hand and peered beyond the gates to the grand white marble columns. Kira had been one of them.... "It made very little difference in the end." I tilted my head when I felt a trace pull beckoning me forward. "The city's siren song still calls." I turned to Shen, "why have you not returned Atlantis to the water fae?"

Shen hissed, "The water fae are selfish beings...they did not deserve this beautiful city then and they do not deserve it now. It was my greatest treasure once." The dragon gave Riella a toothy smile, his giant orb eyes glowing with love. "It is my seaflower's now."

The faeling smiled wide and reached up to pat the array of purple-blue scales upon his great head. "Shen Shen's mirage has kept it hidden," she boasted, proud of her dragon.

My brows drew together and I crossed my arms suspiciously. "For a dragon, you give up your treasure easily."

A frightening smile of teeth and fang descended upon me. "Do I, cousin?" Then he pulled away quickly, his nostrils flared and his sails stiffened. "The blood witch knows. You must go now! Within the city at the innermost sanctum you will find the whirlpools—"

My arms fell to my sides. "The whirlpool portals are still active? After all this time!"

"Yes!" Shen hissed back.

"What is a whirlpool portal?" Riella asked with an eager gleam in her swirling colored eyes, ignorant of the dragon's growing concern.

I glanced down at her. "They are a way to travel great distances, even between worlds. It was how humankind from Earth discovered Atlantis. They even named their ocean after it and told great stories about your people, the sirens of the sea." I bared my teeth back at Shen. "They even have folklore about great water serpents that sank ships to feast on their bones."

The dragon bristled and puffed out a breath of annoyance. "Humans are hardly worth the effort nor the calories, but they did have other interesting cargo."

I snickered. "Where does this whirlpool lead, dragon?"

Shen snarled, bearing his sharp fangs at me again. "It is time you learned to trust, or at the very least have some manners. Trust me when I say, I do not risk what is mine...ever." He turned back towards the tiny fae child. "Seaflower—"

"No!" Riella rushed upwards and clung to her dragon.

I stiffened at the droplets of red tears trailing in her wake.

"Hush now, seaflower, you must stay with Remnant," Shen hummed. "She and one other are the only ones I trust to protect you well enough."

My head snapped up. "What *other* do you speak of, dragon?"

Shen ignored me and nuzzled against Riella more. "You will leave this place together and you both will need each other to survive what is to come. Will you promise me you'll stay with Remnant, my treasured seaflower?"

"Yes," she hiccuped and gripped the dragon tighter, her tiny body shaking with silent sobs.

The water dragon bowed his great head into her distraught form, his cerulean blue orbs peered directly at me, unashamed of the pooled tears silently being washed away by the now gentle current, as if the ocean also mourned with him.

I turned away, leaving him to his grief and swallowed down the bitter bite of my own. It burned in my throat as I buried it deep.

"You are my greatest treasure, little seaflower. I wish for you to have this. Something to remember me by."

Turning back around at the sudden glow in the water, I raised my arm and squinted through the brightness glowing around the dragon. My eyes widened as I watched an ombre scale of purple-blue placed delicately on a silver chain floating through the ocean, to gracefully fall around the faeling's small neck.

Riella's bottom lip trembled and she clutched the purple-blue scale tightly. Without warning she reached to her side and with gritted teeth, wrenched a tiny black scale from her body, holding it proudly upwards while her body bled from her self inflicted wound before quickly healing.

"For you Shen Shen." She said with love shining in her colorful swirling eyes.

Instantly, the scale left her hand and I dropped my arm, narrowing my eyes on the dragon's new adornment—a spec of scale hanging with a silver chain around his neck, directly over where Riella had seated herself. It was barely noticeable unless one was looking for it.

Shen's voice was gravelly when he finally spoke. "This gift shall never leave me, my little seaflower. Never." Then he sighed deeply, bubbles trailing out past the haunting golden gates, before he nudged Riella back towards me.

Still clutching her scale closer to her, the faeling reached for me with her free hand. I swallowed again only hesitating a moment before instinctively pulling her close to my side.

My chin rose high. "I will look after her as if she is my own treasure, dragon."

Shen hummed. "You have no idea how true those words will become, cousin. Prepare yourself, I have told you all that I can. Get to the portal quickly and you will live another day."

"Nothing to it," I half laughed and then looked down to smooth back Riella's muddy pink hair. "Let's protect each other shall we?"

I smiled when she raised her chin high, an exact mimic of me moments before. Flourishing my hand, my gaze never leaving the determined faeling, I materialized a long black spear out of the dormant shadows from the hallowed city. Perfectly crafted for her petite size.

She took the spear eagerly without hesitation.

"Do not wait to stab and kill anything that comes for you," I said sternly.

She nodded, taking it within her grasp and thrusting it forward. "Die!"

Holding back my laughter, I grinned encouragingly. "Very good. Except make sure your power comes from here and here." I placed my hand against her narrow torso front to back. "Your arms are your guide. But true power comes from your core. Try again."

She thrusted one more time, her lips pressed into a concentrated line.

I nodded and rose. "Much better, now it's my turn." Arms raised I tilted my head back, shadows swirled and then draped over me, melding into a belt of black throwing knives that cinched around my waist.

Riella frowned at them. "What happened to the other shadows? The ones that could change on their own without you?"

I smiled. "You noticed that—" I glanced up at the ever watchful dragon and then back to her. "They were sent on another task for me. We will have to make do with these for now."

Tiny features scrunched further into lines of worry. "Will they come back?"

For a moment, Emon's stubbornly fierce golden eyes flashed before me. "Yes—they will come back."

Determinedly, she nodded, trading the hardened grip on her scale for my own hand. Setting the spear at her side, she faced the golden gates. "I'm ready."

I stared. Goddess help me. I did not deserve this kind of trust from such a little miracle. I was the monster in this story.

*"Behind every monster was once a beautiful creature worth loving, one day you will realize this, cousin of mine, and learn to accept both sides of your nature. Keep my seaflower safe."*

Shen's voice was a gentle whisper in my mind and when I looked to see if he was still there, I peered back at nothing but an endless ocean and a white wall that pierced both ocean and skies.

"He is gone," Riella sniffed.

My heart ached for her and I squeezed her tiny webbed hand. "I have no doubt you will meet your dragon again, little one." Blowing out a breath of bubbles, I looked back at the haunted city and the memories of my past. "Are you still ready for this?"

Riella blew out her own sigh of bubbles. "I am ready. I made a promise to Shen."

I blinked down at her, watching those swirling eyes stare out at the city as if she were prepared for battle. For the briefest of moments, it was as if I was staring down at my own young self.

# CHAPTER 27

*Remnant*

"DO YOU KNOW?" RIELLA asked, breaking the eerie silence around us. Her hand had been steadily squeezing mine since we started.

I gazed around me wearily, pulling shadows away from side streets I didn't recognize. "Know what?"

"What actually caused Atlantis to fall? All Shen Shen ever tells me is that it was from greed," Riella whispered.

"Stay back." Pushing her behind me, I hissed at the bright green toad-horse creature, slightly larger than Riella, charging us from the darkness. Bulbous black eyes clouded by a thick film blinked once before swerving quickly into a new crevice of darkness.

My lip curled in distaste. "Kelpies." I tugged Riella forward. "We better get moving into the main palace. He will be back with some friends if we don't hurry along." I refrained from telling her that Kira was quite capable of finding us through creatures of the water. Most water fae could communicate with the beasts of the sea.

The faeling giggled nervously. "They are so funny looking don't you think?"

I looked down at her anxious face. "They are," I said, smiling faintly. "Their eyes are much too large for their body, like bubbles that need to be popped."

I felt her small frame relax next to me as she smiled eagerly. "Exactly! I have always thought that too."

I gave her hand a small squeeze and then nodded to an alcove beside the main palace doors. "There ahead. That side entrance will take us deep into the palace where the water portals should be. We will be less exposed taking that route."

Pulling Riella along, we ducked into the shadowy alcove of the side entrance. The siren song of Atlantis was stronger here and if we were not careful we could easily become trapped within the golden maze of her palace walls.

Except my long stays as a child here were exactly what we needed to get through the perfectly preserved hallways. My eyes trailed over the ostentatious wealth, barely tarnished by the ghostly waters of the sea, with disgust. The water fae's greedy nature was something I never truly understood.

"It's a dead end!" Riella gasped.

I pressed my lips into a thin line at the statue that blocked our path. "It is not."

Reaching up and controlling the trembling in my hand, I traced the face of my former lover, sweeping my hand up over her brow and trailing it down over the back of her ear. If I closed my eyes I could still feel the silky caress of her silver hair as I tucked it away from her face.

"I have never been in this area of the city before, who is she?" Riella whispered in the dark to me.

"Her name was Deirdre, the former queen of Faerie." My fingers caught the latch behind her ear and I smiled.

"She was very beautiful."

I turned my head and scanned the little faeling's adoring wonder, the same worship that many fae had when they gazed upon the Queen.

"Sometimes beauty is a mask that hides many things, Riella. Always see with your instincts, sometimes your heart, but never—never with your eyes." I pulled the latch and shifted back.

Riella gasped when the wall shook. The statue of the queen shifted and bubbles boiled up from beneath while she slowly lowered into the floor, revealing a passageway suddenly pulsating with blood crystals.

My hand gripped Riella's shoulder and I lowered myself to her level, brushing back a floating lock of muted pink hair lit by the Sanguine power.

"Little one, this passageway is very dangerous but it is the quickest way for us to get to the whirlpools. No matter what, do not touch the red crystals." My webbed hand brushed against her anxious face. The existence of her still shocking. "Before, you asked me what caused the downfall of Atlantis—those red crystals are the reason. It is a power that only the blood fae understood how to use...it was a mistake for the water fae to think they could use it against them without a price. Blood power will always require a sacrifice. Remember that."

Riella's eyes widened and her lip trembled. "But, mother has one of those." Her eyes filled with red tears and she swallowed hard. "She was going to take me somewhere with it, I heard her talking to a fae through one of those crystals...mother called her the blood witch."

I inhaled sharply, Deirdre wanted the girl. The water dragon knew this.

"Little one—" A shrilling screech cut off my next words and I tugged Riella harshly behind me, backing her slowly towards the open passageway.

"Riella, kelpies haven't suddenly developed vocal chords in the past few hundred years have they?" I whispered softly over my shoulder.

Her muddy pink hair tickled my scales while she shook her head quickly back and forth. "No," she squeaked.

I narrowed my eyes on the open corridor and backed us further into the red glowing tunnel. From the end of the hallway a dark hooded creature crept around the corner, then another and another.

*A fight for another day,* Emon's growling voice whispered like echoes in my mind and I shivered.

Grinding my teeth and cursing inwardly, I narrowed my eyes on their mindless hunting. They lacked direction as if they were waiting for orders.

Deirdre.

"Riella, when I say swim, I want you to swim as hard as you can and don't stop for anything. This passageway will take you straight to the whirlpools."

"What about you?" Her voice shook.

I reached back and squeezed her hand, tracking the creatures' unhurried movement and whispered firmly. "I'll be right behind you. Don't look back."

My chest splintered into a million pieces as the distance between us grew, her hand falling away from mine.

A slight tilt of a hood, then several more. A slow turn, the current froze. Fifty sightless gazes turned on me.

"Swim Riella! Swim now!" I hissed forcefully. Shoving her hard with my shadows while hundreds of others floated in the water awaiting my command.

# CHAPTER 28

Remnant

THE SHIFTING WATER WAS the only indication that told me Riella had fled as ordered.

The creatures' shrilling screeches forced me to wince, the sound rupturing my sensitive water fae hearing, leaving my ears ringing with pain.

Cutting my arms through the water, I sent my knives sailing. Directing them towards as many hooded depths as I could muster while they shot through the water with renewed vigor.

Deirdre was eager.

Lunging, I reached below into the cavernous hole where Deirdre's statue had disappeared.

"Come on, come on," I snarled, looking up only to throw more shadow knives at the hooded beings barreling towards me. Several fell, slowing down the many others. "Always a stubborn bitch, aren't you?" I snarled, groping the top of the statue's head, fumbling for the lever behind her ear.

The click was loud when I finally wrenched it upwards and her marbled being started to rise. Snapping my head up, I grabbed the shadow knives around my belt. One of the phantom creatures was only ten feet from me—too goddess damn close. Throwing my knife, I weaved the shadow to embed into whatever lay beneath the tattered robes, then sliced my hand through the water, ripping off the screaming abominations head forever.

*"Dimittis." Release,* I commanded and threw seven more shadow knives, each one finding its mark with deadly decapitation, except for the seventh, which had plunged into the back of the marbled queen's crowned head. "That's for being such a bitch," I snorted, feeling the relief of the passageway being sealed, leaving behind the hideous creatures and buying us more time.

I pushed off the statue's perfectly carved ass, knowing full well she had made sure it was molded that way, and shot through the illuminated passageway, careful to avoid the blood crystals as I went.

Riella had made good progress and it was a few moments before I was able to reach her. She cried out, swimming harder, feeling my presence and driven by fear to escape me.

"It's me, little one! But don't stop and don't look back!"

A sob of relief escaped her tiny lips and my heart lurched to provide her comfort. Reaching for the shadows, I molded a herd of unicorns to gallop alongside her. Her giggle in the sinister red glow of the tunnel was enough for me to not dwell on the fact that my power was now waning.

Just a little further.

I felt the power release just moments before it hit us. Sending us both crashing into the walls of the tunnel with the crystals pulsating in a blaze of red light. Riella screamed and my stomach rolled at the sickening sound of her body cracking against the walls. The shadow unicorns beside her torn to shreds by glaring red light.

Rolling through the attack, I caught her tiny body as it began to slide down the wall. "Shh, I have you little one." I soothed, smiling at the spear still clutched tightly in her webbed hand while she blinked up at me. "I have you."

Red tears spilled out of her multi-hued eyes. "What is happening?"

I wiped her eyes, my hand cupping her face. "The crystals feel our presence. They want us." A veiled truth...the powerful burst was directed right at me. I could feel the change in my gifted water fae body. I had run out of time. "We are close but we must continue quickly. Wrap your arms around my neck and I will swim us both there. Can you continue to be brave for me?"

Riella swallowed hard and nodded.

I smiled reassuringly down at her. "You are a true warrior fae, Riella, tamer of dragons. Shen would be so proud to see you now. Climb on and we shall leave this place in no time." Riella darted around me and clung to my back, her arms and legs wrapping tightly around my torso.

"Shen Shen says you are the greatest warrior of all the fae. I do not think I am like you," she whispered into my ear.

My chest tightened. "No Riella, you are not like me," I felt her stiffen and patted her leg. "You are better than me...you are something I never can be. You must believe in yourself, like Shen Shen believes in *you*...like I believe in you."

She squeezed me tighter, the tiniest whisper of her voice brushed against the scales of my neck and my heart splintered. "I believe in *you* too, even if you don't."

"Hold on," I whispered brokenly.

Grasping onto any flickers of shadow in the passageway, I used them to propel us forward, moving faster and faster towards the inner sanctum. Riella molded to my body, streamlining us further, just like she had onboard her water dragon.

I breathed a sigh of relief when the torrent of water could be heard and the current started moving us faster along. "We are almost there." I called over my shoulder. "The whirlpool portals are still dangerous. You must not fight their current if we get separated. Just allow it to take you and I will be with you eventually. Do you understand me?"

"Yes," she nodded against my scales.

The crystals flashed again, even brighter this time and I reared back in both pain and shock. The taste of salt was strong on my tongue and I thrashed violently when water started to fill my lungs.

"Remnant!" cried Riella, attempting to soothe me.

I screamed when the painful pressure in my head ruptured my ears. My cries forced the water filling my lungs outward and I used it to my advantage. Closing my mouth I forced my chest to expand. The ocean felt like a vice squeezing my body, making the task difficult.

I raised my hands, my eyes burning in the salted water and pointed towards the whirlpools, waving Riella to continue onward. My reflection in her terrified eyes confirmed that I had fully transformed back to my normal self.

"No! Not without you!" she cried and frantically grabbed my arms to pull me forward.

Spasms wracked my entire body and I frantically waved her onward but she stubbornly refused. Pulling along my crushed body with pure determination.

Closing my eyes, I focused, sensing the soft dormant shadows around me. With one last burst of energy, I sent them careening outward like a lasso, searching for the portals.

Seconds seemed like hours before a tug wrenched us both forward and I flung my arms around the faeling's body right before the shadow line violently launched us through the rest of the tunnel. Riella's clawed hands pierced my skin, fighting to hold onto me while my own began to slip and my vision darkened.

Our salvation was swift and violent. The water swirled into a darkened chamber, the portal suctioning us into an uncontrollable spin. Down, down, down we spun...the echoes of Riella screaming my name was the last thing I heard before everything went frighteningly silent.

# CHAPTER 29

## Remnant

I BLINKED AGAINST THE blinding rays of a hot sun and a chickadee perched delicately on my chest. Its head tilted side to side for a brief moment before it released a single chirp and launched itself up into a lavender lit sky. Crusted sand fell from my confused fluttering lashes...where was I?

Groaning, I rolled away from the harsh sun, feeling more sand flake away from my body and stared blankly at the faeling laying beside me.

Another slow blink before...

"Riella!" I cried.

Scrambling to her side, my battered body was quickly forgotten while I searched for her beating pulse. It fluttered beneath my shaking fingertips and I exhaled a sigh of relief.

"Wake for me, little one," I whispered, brushing back her hair and giving her tiny body a firm shake.

After a few moments of attempting to wake her without success, I sighed, sitting back on my heels to peel away the wet hair plastered from my face and ponder the new lands before me.

The whirlpools had delivered us to a white sandy coastline that stretched for miles to the right and left. The ocean lapped softly at our backs and a gentle breeze blew the tall green grasses lying just beyond the sandy beach in front of us. My eyes trailed up to the skyline and I inhaled sharply at the large dark red mountains protruding from the earth in the distance. So tall, that even from here, they disappeared into the white puffy clouds of the lavender lit sky.

Only one mountain formation rose that high and was stained that particular red...and it wasn't in Faerie lands—it was in The West Isles. Home of the shifters and their beloved Red Cap Peaks.

A dry laugh escaped me. My vow to the shifter was fulfilled but my free ticket into these lands was still nowhere to be found and I was absolutely positive I needed it right the goddess now.

I was not alone. We were in danger.

By shifter law, our immediate deaths were imminent for trespassing these lands without permission of the shifter king. A king known for his cruel and barbaric ways. I was a fool for believing Emon when he vowed us safe passage here.

A vow that meant nothing and everything for the miracle lying before me.

Cursing, I glared up at the hot sun, mocking and baking our naked bodies. Unfortunately, the transition into land form did not provide clothing and with my sentient shadows still gone, I had no access to the void for my provisions.

A soft whimper from the tiny faeling, drew my gaze back down to her and I fully took in her child-like features for the first time without scales. Like all fae children, she was innocently beautiful, so much so that it physically hurt to look upon her for too long.

She had traded her black scales for bronze skin that shimmered in the sun despite the white sand caking her. Black lashes fluttered against rosy cheeks and caught in a tangle of wet hair. Brushing it away again, my hand stilled when the color began to change. The muddy pink strands were quickly fading into dark raven locks, seeping like spilled ink from her roots down to the very tips.

"What in the goddess?" Water fae hair never changed during a transition, nor did their eyes. It was their one permanent feature that always stayed in both their water and landforms.

Riella released another murmur of discomfort and her innocent face crinkled as if in pain.

"Shhh," I cooed. "It is okay, little one. You're safe."

Reilla shivered and her lashes fluttered but still she did not wake. Instead, tiny droplets bubbled on the surface of her brow.

Frowning, I placed my hand to her forehead only to feel a searing heat that was hotter than the sun glaring down on us.

I swore viciously. "You're burning up!"

My head snapped up when another chickadee called in the distance and my eyes instantly went to the tall grasses. Our voyeurs had crept closer, making their presence known. Discreetly, I slid the dragon scale off Riella's chest and tucked it up into my wet stringy hair, tying it behind my back, hidden behind my wet ponytail.

Standing slowly, I shifted in front of Riella and molded my own casting shadow to protect her feverish body.

It was more than what I could do for myself.

Even the wet gritty sand could not hide the fact that I was now standing nude, poised to fight without a weapon, with the scorching West Isle sun blazing down on me—mocking me in its hot spotlight.

The soft lapping of the ocean was the only distinguishable sound in the thick silence. Blinking, I used my aura sight to peer into the thick grass revealing three glowing auras. One violet—a leader. One a deep blue—a healer. And one, a rainbow—a free spirit, a visionary in a stagnant world.

A perfect trio for a scouting party.

"I won't presume to know your intentions here so either come out and explain or move along. Either way, do not waste my time being a voyeur." I flicked sand from my tattooed forearms. It was nice to see my brands again, instead of the heavy black scales.

I arched a brow at the snarling leopard that leapt from the grasses onto the sandy beach. Yellow-green eyes fiercely clashing with my own.

I snorted at the display. "How terribly rude of me. I'm afraid I don't speak cat, shifter." I waved my hand flippantly. "Your other two companions should just join you. I know they are there."

The leopard hissed at me, whiskers drawing back to the side of its fur lined face, but must have heeded my words because I watched two more of the same stalk from the reeds. Both flanked their leader, watching me with their powerful tails flicking back and forth lazily.

I sighed, wiping more sand from my naked body. "I told you already, I don't speak cat. Shift or get lost," I addressed their leader with the violet aura.

A brief flash was the only warning I had before the leopard transformed into a beautiful female fae with long flowing blonde hair that grazed the sand as it swayed in the gentle sea breeze. She wore a green body suit like a second skin, outlining every curvature of her lean body and the skin that was exposed was darker than the Night Court's midnights.

"You dare!" she growled low at me.

I snorted. "Don't flatter yourself, shifter. I dare with any-one...that right isn't just reserved for you."

She hissed and her gaze narrowed with distaste. "You kind doesn't belong here."

I choked on a laugh and mocked her, trailing my hand sen-suously down my nude form. "You mean to tell me this isn't the nude beach Andromeda?"

The shifter's eyes followed my hand and froze at my sandy tits once she realized what she was doing.

I gave her a wide knowing smile.

"No. It is not," she snarled, her yellow-green eyes striking in their glare against her dark skin.

I brushed more sand off my chest where her gaze had lingered. "Bet you wish it was now, don't you shifter," I smiled sweetly.

I was met with another snarl. "What I wish is for you to tell me who the goddess fuck you are, what your purpose is here, and...what you're protecting behind you." She nodded towards Riella's still form.

I flicked more sand. Goddess it was everywhere. "I'm not your Faerie godmother, shifter. I don't fucking grant wishes." Her attention angrily shifted back to me and away from my ward. Time enough for me to shift subtly, casting a new shadow over the unconscious faeling.

"Goddess' tits!" A new voice called out excitedly. "It's you! You're her! Sweet Sheol, I don't believe my fucking shifter eyes!"

# CHAPTER 30

Remnant

I RAISED A BROW at the second leopard to shift into their fae form. A transition so flawless that I hadn't detected it. Instinctively, I knew this newcomer was the one with the rainbow aura and she was...dangerous.

Physically, she was very different from her leader. Shorter and more athletically built. Her skin reminded me of a rich chocolate, rather than a black night of her companion, and it was exotically accented by a flowing white dress. Her dark hair was shaved closely to her scalp and delicate gold rings pierced her brows, nose, lips, and ears.

Even more gold jewelry sparkled when she waved her hands excitedly, quickly approaching me with soulful brown eyes riddled with enthusiasm. "I can't believe it!" she voiced again.

I arched my brow, calculating her movement. The weak spots in her gait, the subtle way her right shoulder tilted, and how she left her delicate neck exposed.

"Do I know you?"

Her leader, seeing a fellow hunter, snapped her arm out to stop her companion. "Stay where you are," she hissed to the enthusiastic fae.

"Oh my goddess, yes I see it fully now! Just wow!" she exclaimed again, pushing her leader's arm off her.

"Penina," their leader growled low.

"Oh shove off, Eshe. You have no clue who that is, do you?" The young shifter's eyes grew even wider and she turned towards me. "You're exactly how he described you! You wielded those shadows. It has to be you!"

"Penina, when will you listen!" A bright flash revealed the third leopard transforming into a handsome lean fae with bright blue eyes and tidy blonde hair tied back away from his face. His high cheekbones were a characteristic of a descendant of an ancient fae, blushing subtly as he met my assessing gaze.

Their leader *Eshe* scowled at both of them. "Be silent both of you or I will make sure the king gets a full report of your continued insubordination. I will deal with this washed up trash."

The one named Penina snorted and rolled her eyes before pointing at me. "If you had any idea who she was, you'd be giving her far more respect than you are now. How dense can you be?"

My lips twitched with amusement. "It's also not nice to point," I stated dryly.

No one heard me as the growling and shouting continued. This was a dysfunctional unit. The previous shifter king would have never tolerated such behavior.

"This isn't the way Penina!" hissed the handsome blue eyed fae.

"Oh shut up, Quinn! You're only taking Eshe's side because you want in her pants. I'm the only one who is making sure we don't all die today from your foolishness! She is exactly who we have been looking for!" Her pointing continued amid the shouting.

"Again with the pointing," I stated exasperatedly. They were looking for me? Did they know Emon? Did he somehow make it here before I did?

Eshe crossed her arms in front of her chest. Her midnight skin darkened with rage and her yellow-green eyes flashed like daggers.

"Enough!" she snarled and knocked Penina's hand down. "Fall back in line before I make you. Both of you!"

Penina's eyes flashed with defiance but stepped back with her comrade who had already cast his eyes downward in submission.

"Nice to see that you are able to keep some sense of order around here," I drawled out in the silence.

Their leader turned her scowl on me. "Since my companion is so adamant that she knows who you are, I'll give you the chance to identify yourself, sea scum."

I gave her a wide grin that was more threatening than welcoming in nature. "My name is Remnant Ezra Solaire Dark."

The winds shifted, the grasses rustled, and a chickadee tweeted in the distance at the sound of my name.

The one named Penina grinned with self satisfaction while their leader inhaled sharply, and Quinn's eyes widened, suddenly too big for the handsome sharp angles of his face.

Then Riella screamed an ear splitting cry that stopped my heart in my chest. I spun. Not caring about my exposed back to a dangerous enemy. The pain in her cries was visceral and I responded, smoothing away the beads of sweat that pooled on her delicate bronze brow. Beneath my hands, her body began to shake, and I wrapped the thin veiled shadows tighter around her. My poor attempt to calm the tremors wracking her body.

Her cries drew in the three shifters and I greedily snatched their casted shadows that lengthened towards me on their approach. Using them, I shielded Riella and myself from them, spikes growing threateningly from the shadow barrier. At full power, they were capable of impaling any enemy, but with the sun high they were more an illusionary threat than a real one.

"If you value your lives you will not come a step closer," I snarled over my shoulder.

"Goddess bless us—is that a child? A fae child?" The leader, Eshe, gasped, ignoring my warning.

Turning I narrowed my eyes on the male shifter who was staring openly at my naked form hovering over Riella. "Your name is Quinn? You are a healer. That makes you honor bound to protect all fae children. Heal her and I will gladly hand myself over to your crown as long as the faeling stays healthy and safe while in these lands."

Quinn's eyes grew wide and he glanced over to his leader. Eshe hissed. "Do it."

Quinn nodded. "I have no idea how you knew I was a healer but I feel obligated to warn you I am novice at best. Do you still agree to hand yourself over knowing this?"

The small shifter named Penina stepped forward. "This is foolishness! She is *the* General Dark for goddess sake! He will not take kindly to you imprisoning her even if it is agreed upon."

I hid my shock. Mercy among the shifters?

Eshe snarled. "You will do as ordered, Penina." She turned to the healer barking, "Get the faeling stable as soon as you're able. Then we move." Her eyes narrowed on me. "Call off your shadows or I will rescind our deal."

Nodding, I waved off the shadows allowing them to flutter gently down to the faeling, covering her in soft darkness.

Withdrawing them from her face, I wiped her brow scrunched up in pain. "Hold on, little one. I'm here with you and I will make sure you feel better soon."

# CHAPTER 31

Remnant



"**Y**OU'LL BE NEEDING THIS."

I blinked up at the small shifter, Penina, holding a white garment with a small smile on her pierced lips.

It widened at my questioning look. "Not that it bothers me. You're like goddess hot but I do believe it will help Quinn focus on the faeling rather than your tits. It's putting Eshe on edge," she shrugged non-committedly, further explaining, "Shifters are complicated."

Quinn cursed. "For goddess sake, Penina." His eyes suddenly focused hard on his work, a subtle blush rising over his sharp cheekbones.

I snorted and then glanced over at the leader of the shifters, in her leopard form, pacing the length of the beach.

"Thank you." I took the white material in hand and quickly dressed. The white cloth flowed over my body with perfection. An asymmetrical strap hung over one of my shoulders and the rest draped down my side with two long slits to give my legs room to move. I gave the small shifter a speculative look. "A remarkable fit."

She winked, her gold piercing glinting in the sunlight. "It's one of my talents, shifting things. Designing clothes is always my favorite." She waved down at her person with a sense of pride, the scraps she had modified from my outfit into her own. A white sash covered her small breasts and a short skirt wrapped around her hips exposing her navel that was also pierced with multiple gold rings.

The healer cleared his throat, drawing our attention back to him.

"What is it?"

Brilliant blue eyes stared hard at me. "Can you tell me how she got this way? I may be able to stabilize her fever but she is going to need more than what my novice powers can give. We need to move her out of this heat and —" He looked up at his leader who was still pacing agitatedly. "We will need to take her to the city."

Eshe snarled, overhearing Quinn's assessment but otherwise continued her pacing.

I licked my lips, forming my words carefully. "She is water fae, we came from The Under, through their last remaining whirlpool portal."

Quinn's blonde brows raised upwards with disbelief. "Was this her first shift from her water fae form."

I shook my head slowly and answered honestly. "I do not know."

He sighed and studied the girl once more. The energy around us shifted and Riella sighed softly in her fevered sleep. "This should help her get to the city. There she will need to see the master healer. There is a strange power surrounding her, one I have never seen, almost as if something is blocking her transformation and it's causing her to—."

I gave him a hard look. "If she dies, there will be no saving you or your people from me, healer. Morta will look like child's play."

Riella somehow had replaced the cold dark hole in my heart the moment she took my hand in hers. I would show this world no mercy if she was ever taken away from me.

Quinn inclined his head, understanding rather than fear flashing in his eyes. "Then we should move quickly."

Eshe shifted, her long blonde hair swaying freely in the subtle breeze and her features grim. "Penina. Go ahead of us and prepare the master healer for our arrival. Inform our general that Remnant Dark will be entering the city.”

I snorted. “Yes. Let him know the lost shadow fae betrayer is paying his city a little visit.”

Penina sent me an apologetic look. “It’ll be alright, you’ll see.” Then leaned in, her lips brushing against my ear. “Don’t fall for her shit,” she whispered before shifting, disappearing into the high grasses before I could even blink.

I turned to see the remaining two shifters watching me warily. I sighed. “I will honor our agreement,” I reassured them, “so long as she lives,” I added.

“I won’t take any chances with my people. Even you can understand that, shadow fae.” Eshe’s yellow-green eyes pierced me with malice. “The child can ride with me.” She frowned. “I assume you can use your shadows to anchor her securely to me?”

“No,” I said firmly, meeting her stare of malevolence with my own. “I will carry her myself.”

Eshe’s eyes narrowed. “Despite our shifter strength you cannot both ride with one of us.”

“That was never my intention,” I shot back.

Quinn’s bright blue eyes widened with understanding. “Mistress Dark. The quickest way to our city is for you to ride. The trek is difficult and the child needs every minute we may gain by doing so.”

I flashed a confident smile towards him. “I can keep up with your leopard pace.”

“That’s foolishness! No fae can run as far and as long as our beasts. Barefoot no less!” Eshe spat, waving down at my bare feet. “You will only end up putting the child in more jeopardy and with less time for our healer to work.”

I shrugged and wiggled my naked toes with amusement. “I assure you I am no fool. I can and will keep up, *carrying* Riella. This child is in my protection and quite frankly I don’t fucking trust you. But, should I fall behind, my pride will not stop me from asking for your assistance...then and only then will I ask you for it.”

A strange sort of gurgle emitted from the shifter leader before she turned to releasing a growl of curses that even I admired.

Quinn watched Eshe wearily before he spoke. “I see we cannot deter you Mistress Dark. Prepare yourself. We must leave soon if we are to give the faeling enough time.”

I nodded and wrapped the shadows around Riella in a body suit of armor. I slung her with ease over my shoulder and I clasped her legs close to my body dispersing her weight evenly. My opposite arm remaining free to defend and wield shadows as needed.

Cracking my neck side to side, I sent one final glare to the sun. It was the true enemy here, weakening my powers and always mocking me during circumstances of fate.

"Listen up little one," I whispered to Riella from the corner of my mouth, watching the two shifters hissing angrily at each other. "I need you to fight and stay with me. I will be here for you, always." I choked on my last words, the same words I used to say to my baby brother. "I won't fail you like I did him, you'll live, even if I have to fight the death god himself."

Hidden deep in the grasses a lone chickadee chirped, acknowledging my words.

# CHAPTER 32

## Remnant

I SPRINTED, HOT ON the flanks of the shifter leader with a miracle slung over my shoulders like a sack of potatoes. The leopard shifters excelled at strength and agility meant for these hilly grassy plains...a powerful, evolutionary physique I would never have.

Never mind I had yet to fully recover from The Under.

But I loved to defy the odds so I ran harder. Bounding past their leader, I laughed maniacally into the rushing wind of the plains. I knew my white dress clung to me like second skin, my feet were a bloody numb mess, my legs burned in a fiery rage but all I felt was pure euphoria.

Free and untamed in a new land I now craved to explore.

The valleys we traveled through were rich with life. The green grasses were vibrant with clusters of white flowers dancing in the wind, their white petals swirling around us like snow. Occasionally, I spotted sparkling streams snaking through the land where nymphs splashed playfully in the crystal waters. And finishing this wondrous masterpiece were striking lavender blue skies and the menacing red mountaintops—their looming peaks hidden by marshmallow-like clouds.

Faerie's creatures frolicked about, unhindered by our presence, and between my rhythmic breaths, I described them in every last detail to the faeling I carried, including the majestic beauty of the unicorns. The vain creatures somehow hearing my whispered words, displayed themselves openly with their ostentatious pride that forced a wide grin on my face.

Gnomes and pixies stood on alert to watch our traveling brigade, dazzling butterflies and great horned jackalopes raced along our path, and even a fiery phoenix screeched from above, striking the air with fire, whether in encouragement or in defiance to our peculiar group I could not tell.

It was the most ridiculous sight...the last shadow fae, an unconscious water fae child, and two leopard shifters running in tandem together. If I closed my eyes, I could almost hear the laughter of my closest friend, ruminating about this new tale in their *Remnant Archives*.

I wiped the tears that escaped at the memory of them. I hadn't allowed myself to think about the captains of my legion, my closest friends, since they perished in Morta.

A small flash of light, forced me to skid to a halt, my only warning before Eshe shifted with a leap in front of me. Her long blonde hair flowed out from behind her as the winds of the plains kicked up over the hill we stood upon. Hardened yellow-green eyes bored into me with reluctant acceptance.

"I must say. I am impressed, shadow fae. You did, for the most part, keep up." Her lip curled up distastefully.

I took a deep powerful breath, adjusting Riella on my shoulder subtly, and ignored the quaking protest in my body. "Why have we stopped, shifter?"

Eshe tilted her head to the side. "Because we are here."

I looked outwards into the deep valley where a large sparkling river circled its perimeter. The river itself teemed with wildlife. Flying fish and small water nymphs played within it's flowing stream, another herd of unicorns were leisurely basking in the sun. Their gleaming white bodies and various rainbow manes striking against the backdrop.

Riella would have absolutely loved the sight of it.

I frowned, searching the horizon. "I see no city."

Eshe smirked. "That's because you need this."

I had no defense against the sudden bright blue dust Eshe blew directly into my face. But I was able to reach for the shadows that were plentiful from the hills of the valley. Deeper and stronger here beneath the cloudy skies, they responded instantly to my calling. First to further protect Riella in my sightless vision, second to remind this spiteful shifter exactly who I was.

"Stop! Please!" Quinn called out with alarm, having shifted back at some point beside me. "Eshe!"

Hissing, I frantically wiped the blue dust from my eyes, blinking hard against the intrusive glitter enhanced by the glowing sun. I raised my brows in surprise to see the gentle healer turn to predator as he snarled in my face.

"Call off your shadows! She meant you no harm!" he roared at me.

I roared back, shoving him to the side with my shadows that snaked around my arms. "Be still healer, or she will suffer more!"

Turning, I calmly gazed down at his leader who was pinned to the ground by black shadows, fighting against the way she sunk forcibly into the hardened earth, her eyes trained on me with terror.

I narrowed my eyes on her, ignoring the furious snarls. "You keep making mistakes, shifter. I have no doubt this was your backhanded way of trying to prove you have the upper hand." I stepped over her. Fearful yellow-green eyes met mine. "Mark my words. When it comes to you and I, you will never have it...even if I stood before you in iron chains the result would be the same. I'm the true predator here, the monster, and that will always make you..." I waved my hand at her, "prey."

"Please! Release her!" The healer pleaded, standing between us once more, as she sunk lower into a shallow grave. "You don't understand. The dust was necessary for you to see and enter our city!" His hand shot outward frantically as dirt started to cover his friend. "Look for yourself if you don't believe me!"

Narrowing my eyes at him, I allowed myself to look back towards the waterways that carved out the valley. My brows rose at the sight of a sprawling white city, alive with the bustling of fae inside.

"Concealing wards," I hummed. "What a clever king you have. No wonder the queen could never find Finlandia." With a flippant wave, I dismissed the shadows from the shifter, not taking my eyes off the grand city before me.

Quinn scrambled to dig her out of the hollow ground, brushing dirt off her while she growled up at me. "I could have you...imprisoned...for that."

A small smile broke across my face while I gazed in wonder at the city before us. "That was always your intention anyway. But know this, there is nothing you could ever do to me that hasn't already been done before, shifter. Even your worst nightmares can't even come close to what I have survived."

I felt their shocked scrutiny like irons burning into my back.

Carefully releasing Riella from my shoulders and cradling her in my arms, I rolled my neck to ease the tension. Looking down at her, I pressed my lips into a thin line, her bronze complexion ashen in the sunlight.

She was worsening.

My head snapped up at the soft chirps of a flock of chickadees flying above me, twirling in the lavender sky towards the city. I took one step towards them...one step and suddenly the fate of the faeling's future was placed directly into my enemy's embrace. Walking forwards, I glanced back over my shoulder to the two cagey shifters, "Shall we?"

# CHAPTER 33

Remnant

"WELCOME TO FINLANDIA." QUINN'S eyes glowed brighter taking in his city.

I watched the bustling fae around me, some starring openly at the small bundle I held in my arms only to quickly glance away at the violence they saw on my face from their open stare.

"You have protected it well. It appears untouched by the corruption of our world," I observed, draping more shadow to shield Riella from the rooftops above.

Quinn grunted. "Finlandia wasn't always our central home. Shifters used to live within the Red Cap Mountains but we were forced to leave during the blood wars. Our king has done a fine job building the city for the needs of our people." He gave me a sideways glance. "And keeping it out of the hands of the Faerie Queen."

My lips thinned. "Indeed. Your kings have been cunning, yet fae blood was still spilled to make it so."

Quinn shook his head. "It would have never been that way had the Faerie queen not executed Queen Skyler."

I hummed. The day Queen Skyler Strider of The West Isles and soulmate of the former king, was murdered, was the day of no return for both our courts.

"Your queen had a beautiful soul, her death was a great loss." I gave Quinn a hard look. "One your previous king made up for ten fold with his relentless thirst for vengeance. Innocent fae ripped to pieces, their heads placed on pikes to cull his unabating bloodlust. A grieving vengeance that turned into a thirsty desire for more and more slaughter of my people. Peaceful fae that had nothing to do with their queen's schemes."

Quinn looked away. "Those were dark days for the shifters too. I can promise you that."

Surveying the city, I sighed. "As they were for all of us. I remember the day I was called from the southern lands of Faerie. The carnage I witnessed on my way to the front lines." I shook my head, clearing the images from the forefront of my mind. "Despite his madness, King Asher was the most formidable foe I ever had the honor of battling against. Faerie was our chess board and we controlled the pieces."

Quinn sighed. "And how is that any different than your queen playing her games?"

"It isn't. Life is a game, healer. Play or be played. You're looking at a fae who has unfortunately survived both." I waved my hand at the richness of the city. "Your own prince played his own game too. Killing his own father to selfishly take over the shifter throne. To rule over the city you're so proud of with blood staining his hands."

Quinn looked away from me, sadness flooding his eyes. "It is not what you think," he whispered.

"No?" I quirked a brow at him. "Look, healer. My point is, we thrive on the sacrifices made by others. Sometimes you win, sometimes you lose. I was marked a traitor by the very queen I served and then destroyed the lands I loved. Your king took advantage of a vulnerable throne by killing his father and remade the shifter kingdom. And the pawns...they either pay or benefit from the games of power. Your kind benefitted. Mine paid."

Swallowing, I looked away before I betrayed the pain that honest confession had cost me. I stared at a winged sign reading

Griffin Gateau, a lovely building with delicious looking pastries displayed in the window.

The healer's hand gently touched my shoulder and then waved towards one of the many white stone shops lining the street we walked down. "Look further, Mistress Dark," he said softly.

I frowned at the white stucco building again where colorful fabrics covered the breezeways, blocking out the sun where shadows hid in waiting. They beckoned to me. I had already analyzed every exit and escape route, this shop in particular had a courtyard in the back.

I shifted my gaze to the golden haired fae standing just outside its doorway, harnessing a soft glow of light that lit up her exotic features. She fed it into an energy reservoir that powered light in the interior of the building.

Something only an elemental fae could do!

Quickly, I searched across the cobblestone streets for the lively music being played. Amongst the flower gardens that flanked the path, rich with green moss and sparkling pixie dust, fae danced in front of a smiling elemental fae weaving air to play his rich melodies.

Bright yellow hair and a matching pair of eyes caught my attention within the foray. Silently, I watched as he weaved water into aquifers that drained into the many pipes lining the buildings. As we passed, he spun mini clouds of rain showers for baby water nymphs that ventured from the river banks to roll around in the soft green grasses of the city.

My dark brows drew together while my thoughts raced.

Quinn gave a friendly wave to another fae elemental blasting pixies out of his shop with balls of fire shooting from his fingertips. Distracted by the greeting, one fireball missed its target and shot straight for Riella's bundled form.

With quick ease, I snuffed out the blaze with a snap of inky shadow. As their darkness dispersed, the surprised look of a fire elemental came to view.

My eyes narrowed with recognition. "Lieutenant Onette?"

The elemental's face immediately turned white, his eyes bugging even further out of his head.

"Gen—General Dark. I am...my apologies!" He sputtered, bowing and running back into his shop. The door slammed behind him before I could even speak.

Whispers broke out all around us. My name escaping their lips like a fearful prayer.

I turned towards the healer who was watching me with keen interest. "That fae's name is Caval Anu Onette, he was a lieutenant that served in the queen's armies. He is a fire elemental that unfortunately set one of our camps on fire during the war."

Quinn's grin widened and his eyes sparkled. "Did he now? Caval does, at times, still set things on fire, but now his talent serves a much better purpose." He nodded to the sign above the shop.

"Stone fire bread." I read it aloud and then gave the healer a hard stare. "You offered fae sent here mercy, didn't you? To lay down their weapons and join you." I pointed to the others I had noticed. "That one there is a water fae, an air elemental, another fire elemental...living among shifters."

Quinn's chest puffed out, his blue eyes shining with pride. "Not I...our king. He despised seeing good fae die as pawns...when there are so little of us now as it is. A chance to live a new life in prosperity...to lay down hate and to turn to a new way of living."

"A bold move. Hate doesn't die so easily," I said dryly. I gave the shop one final glance before moving onward, winking at the impatient Eshe who had been leading the way.

She rolled her eyes and turned quickly to march forward.

The quick shuffle of the healer's feet told me he had caught up with us. "The fae courts were never meant to live in segregation." He continued with his boastful pride. "We need each other, like the lands need the rain and the plants need the sun."

I pursed my lips, shifting Riella away from a group of fae bustling by. "And the sun? What does the sun need?"

The healer hummed next to me. "Easy. Darkness. So its brightness can be seen."

I smiled sadly. "A novel thought but it ends there healer. Darkness does not need the light, it is infinite and undying. It needs nothing."

He stumbled next to me. "Surely, darkness relies on something."

"It does not," I murmured while looking down at Riella's ashen and feverish face. I pursed my lips and tightened my grip on her tiny body, hearing my words and realizing I wasn't so sure if that was exactly true anymore.

# CHAPTER 34

Remnant

"HERE WE ARE." QUINN said quietly, no longer holding the boastful pride from moments ago.

Looking up, I scrutinized the moderate sized white building that sprawled in similar width and height as all the others.

There was no fanfare about the building itself. Indeed, it looked much like all the other buildings we had passed. Large breezeways, colorful gold shimmering fabrics in the open windows, vines growing from a garden rooftop, and directly in front of us, the entrance of a large scaled oval teak door.

"The king lives here?"

Eshe huffed in front of us and motioned me to follow with an irritated wave, the large oval door swung open. "The king has no need for extravagance. I am sure this is difficult for your kind to understand but our king lives amongst his court. Not above them in a pretentious palace."

"How magnanimous of him," I said dryly, responding the whispers of dormant shadows beckoning me to step inside. Instant relief from Finlandia's brutal heat flooded through me as I stepped into the lair of my enemy and I shivered at the cool air kissing my overheated skin.

Despite the many shadows that lay in waiting here, eager for my call, I felt vulnerable entering the shifter king's home, and it was distastefully humbling. Two things I utterly disliked but was more than willing to feel so long as it meant Riella stayed safe.

I bit at my lip, if I told them I knew the so-called *golden one*, would these shifters accept me or immediately slap me in irons and refuse to help Riella in the process?

Scowling and releasing my lip, I realized even if I did tell them, I had no way of reassuring them if he was alive or dead. No—Riella would be much better off if I held my tongue. Which meant I had to rely on my impeccable charming personality and dishonorable general status.

My scowl deepened.

"This is the reception hall," Quinn said softly next to me sensing my displeasure. "The king is not in at the moment or he would have been here to welcome you to Finlandia."

Damn shifter senses picked up everything I was feeling even if it was interpreted wrong.

I snorted. "Of course he would...*welcome me*." My lip curled up with silent humor and I tilted my head at the large room holding little to no decor. Colorful rugs, the only warmth to the otherwise white interior, designated sitting areas where large comfortable looking leather chairs sat.

Five corridors flanked around us—my exits. Three in front of me and one on either side...I had no idea where those closed doors led but they were heavy with dark shadows. I flexed my power, watching the room darken, and smiling when I heard Quinn inhale sharply next to me.

Eshe was not as startled and she sent me a growl letting me know exactly what she thought of my power play. "Cease your power games shadow fae and come along. You're lucky you're not in chains for your stunt earlier." She waved me on to follow her up a flight of stone steps. "The master healer is this way."

"You were already planning on putting me in chains anyway, shifter." I looked down at Riella and swallowed back any other retort as I followed Eshe up the stone steps. It didn't matter what the shifter said or did as long as Riella received the care she needed.

"Master Riss!" Eshe called out.

"Quit your hollering and stop standing there like a numpty Eshe. Send Mistress Dark and the faeling in at once! There is no time to waste!" Came a deep enchanting voice down the hall.

I didn't even bother to wait for Eshe's approval and smiled at her sweetly as I passed. "In case you didn't know, shifter, numpties are defined as stupid and ineffectual beings. Seems fitting to me." I gave her my back and stepped into a warm sunlit filled room with a vaulted ceiling accented with large wooden beams.

Sprouting from the walls were several large roots that outlined a row of oval shaped beds adorned with pillowy fabrics that looked like soft clouds. Shelves above them were of the purest of glass I had ever seen and encased within were various supplies, from herbs to tools, and even more of the soft cloud-like linens.

And *there*...in the center of the room, standing majestically tall and otherworldly handsome was the master healer. Intelligent sky blue eyes matched exactly with the flowing robes he wore. They narrowed in a catlike slant marking him as an ancient, one of the first fae created by the goddess' hand. Which meant his calm, studious demeanor was only the surface layer to the extremely dangerous power he held at bay inside. Despite this, his presence was that of a warm embrace and my shattered soul calmed within his healing chambers.

Cautiously he approached me, his eyes glittering intimately and with purposeful calculation.

"Mistress Dark," he nodded his blonde head towards me, causing his long unbound hair to cascade around the sharp angles of his ancient face. "I am Master Riss, the king's healer to Finlandia. But above all I am a healer to all fae, the goddess has always willed it so. Please bring the faeling forth and place her on one of the beds. You both will be safe here. I promise."

Guided by instinct and the calming power from the tree root bed closest to the window of a sun filled alcove, I laid Riella down on the pillowy fabrics. The roots immediately shifted to incubate around her petite stature and despite my wariness, I trusted this power more than I did my own. There was something indigenous to its source. Pure and cleansing.

I drew up the cloud linen over her, the softness like a warm caress on my skin, and then released the shadows that shielded her naked body.

Needle-like pain shot through my arms the moment I released her, having gone numb from carrying her for so long. Cradling them to my body, I gritted my teeth at the sudden discomfort.

When a large hand grazed my skin I jolted back, shocked to see the healer standing before me, having not seen nor hear him move.

Blue eyes stared at me with empathy. "You have carried her a long way. Allow me to relieve you of the pain that you have shouldered."

Nodding slowly my assent, I felt the healer's power surge through me instantly and it was like being blanketed by a warm cloak smothering any pain that had wracked my body since coming here.

I licked at my dry lips. "Thank you."

He hummed and handed me a glass of water that instantly appeared in his hand. Taking it, I drank it down deeply before handing the glass back.

He smiled at me and then nodded at the faeling. "A good choice, this bed. Those roots are called Prime. They were cut from the Source. The first tree of Faerie."

I nodded, understanding why the power felt so familiar. A prime tree also grew within the shadow fae lands. "You grew up within the groves, where the ancients rest, as my mother did."

He moved silently to set the glass down on his desk and turned back to me. "I did. Although, I most likely will never see it again in this lifetime. Eve was an exceptional fae and leader. I am sorry for your loss of her and for your people."

I inhaled sharply. I had never had anyone recognize the loss of my mother or my people. I buried that pain and stared straight into the healer's kind sky blue eyes. "They are dead and nothing can change that but Riella is not. I intend to make sure she does not share the same fate. Will you help her? The faeling? I do not have the ability to pay you for services, but I can offer you a life debt and services of my own."

Master Riss raised an elegant blonde brow. "I am an ancient fae, Remnant Ezra Solaire Dark, daughter of Eve, I know your worth more than any other alive. A life debt from you is a grand gesture." He shook his head as if disappointed. "But I highly doubt a trained warrior and killer is of any use to me nor should you be bound to me in such a way."

I shrugged, attempting to shake off the unease his words created. "I am what I am."

He smiled brightly then, his primal beauty difficult to bear. "Yes, a lesson to be had then. I do hope you learn to believe in those words. There is no need for such a life debt, *forta*. Of course I will help the faeling, as is my duty but also my calling." His brow arched again. "But also, I will help you as a friend. Goddess knows you need one. I pray that your services will never be needed by me but know that, seeing how you are my friend now, you will assist me should that day come. Today is not that day, fortunately. Now sit, *forta*, before you spout more nonsense from that elegant mouth of yours."

My eyes widened at his endearment. *Forta* meant brave girl in ancient fae.

His smile widened. "Sit *forta*." A branch extended towards me from the bedside.

Slowly I sat down. "Her name is Riella." I smoothed my hands over the dirty white fabric of my dress.

The master healer nodded and billowed out his robes before sitting himself lower on a similar branch on the other side of the prime root bed.

"Yes, I caught that. A beautiful name." He placed his hands gently on Riella's forehead and chest. The fluttering of her dark lashes were the only indication that she registered his touch. "Quinn did well treating her symptoms."

A throat cleared from the doorway and I gritted my teeth seeing the shifter Quinn standing there. "Thank you, Master Riss."

"I said this because I knew you were there *and*...I am proud of you. You have something to tell me. Come over and speak then." The master healer's studious gaze stayed on the faeling, not bothering to look up as he evaluated her with his power.

"Yes of course," Quinn cleared his throat again before walking over to us and bending to speak quietly into the healer's ear.

I narrowed my eyes at them both, unable to make out the soft whispered tones.

The ancient hummed and nodded in agreement, then closed his eyes. "Quinn tells me he believes there is something blocking the child from fully transforming out of her water fae form. He is...halfway correct. There are powerful wards here, power the likes of which I haven't seen in a very long time. They are blocking a *transformation*...of what I do not know yet. Do you have any information about why that is *forta?*"

I kept my stare steady on Master Riss. "No, I do not know *why.*" I chose my words carefully. I didn't know why Riella had wards upon her but I did suspect that they were Sanguine in nature.

The healer grunted. "So be it then. I will have to break them to fully heal her. I am not sure what the repercussions will be once I do. Do you still wish to proceed?"

I scooped up Riella's small hand and squeezed it. Shocked to find it clammy and cold. "Will it harm her?"

The master healer shook his head, eyes still closed and focused. "I do not know but as an experienced healer I will do my best for her to be as comfortable as possible during the process."

I bent, my hair falling over my face like a dark curtain, shielding me as I kissed the child's small hand and whispered a prayer on her ashen skin. Rising, I chewed on my bottom lip. "I am not entirely sure this is my decision to make. What if we do nothing?"

Master Riss hummed again. His slanted blue eyes opened and slammed directly into my own. I felt it like a vice squeezing my chest.

"She will fade and then die."

Sucking in a sharp breath, I managed to meet the healer's intense gaze. "Then do what you need to save her."

The ancient tilted his head in thought...after a long pause he nodded to himself. "Let us begin."

# CHAPTER 35

## Remnant

"**D**O YOU HAVE ANY need of me?" Quinn fidgeted with his sleeve and glanced nervously over at me.

Master Riss frowned deeply, tarnishing his ancient beauty with worry. "Our time has run out," he whispered and then waved Quinn closer. "Yes, you will need to stay, my boy. This will be a power you have not yet experienced as a healer and I have an unsettling feeling it will not be your last. Link with me."

Quinn's jaw tightened, grunting his assent and reaching out to the ancient fae's shoulder.

The hairs on my skin stood on end when the air shifted and an influx of warmth pulsed through the room. Curious, I shifted to my aura sight and was awed by the vibrant shades of blues molding together into a perfectly balanced power of unity. Auras only reacted that way with family lineage or with soulmates!

My sight switched back to stare at the blonde features of the two fae before me. Their build, the bright blue of their eyes....

"Quinn is your son!"

Master Riss's twinkling blues smiled up at me and then back down again. "That he is, *forta*."

"You could have told me." I shot Quinn with an accusing glare.

The healer's son gave me a small apologetic smile. "Apologies, Mistress—"

"No time for that, my boy! Pay attention! Do you see?"

A slight blush stained Quinn's face before his thoughts turned inward, pinching with concentration. "What in the goddess above is that?" he gasped.

"A power I hoped to never see again. It is the Sanguine, Quinn."

I looked away, my jaw tightening. Of course an ancient fae would recognize the Sanguine power! It was likely he once knew the extinct blood fae at the dawn of their creation and it was very likely he fought in the blood wars against them, just like my mother had.

This time Quinn shot me a look of accusation. "How is that even possible? That power was eradicated."

Master Riss shook his head gravely. "The people were, not the power. But what I do not understand is why it has been used on this poor child—look here boy!" The healer said waving to some invisible thing over Riella's chest I could not see. "Do you feel this here?"

Quinn pursed his lips as he focused. "I feel it, father."

"Follow what I do and *only* exactly what I do."

My hands clenched and unclenched in my lap at the long pause in the room. I exhaled slowly. "Is there anything I can assist with?"

Master Riss did not look up from Riella while he focused. "I do not need anyone threatened or killed right now but thank you, *forta*. What you need to do for yourself is rest. You have had a trying journey and you look half dead sitting there, not to mention you smell like..." He wrinkled his nose with distaste. "Cat shit."

I snorted. The healer had confirmed what I had already known. During my trek here, Eshe had deliberately led me through scat dropped in the grasslands to satisfy her petty urge to dominate me.

"Ah Penina, perfect timing as always," hummed the master healer.

My head jerked up to see the petite shifter leaning casually against the door frame staring at me with a wide grin on her face. "Told you not to fall for her shit, general."

My eyes narrowed but a small smile graced my lips. "Indeed, you did say that."

The Master healer tsked. "Penina, please show Mistress Dark to her rooms to freshen up, then have the cook bring some food up for all of us. I am sure that our shadow fae *friend* and *guest* will want to stay with the child."

Penina sighed. "Eshe had other orders." Then she wiggled her brows at me suggestively, her gold piercings glinting in the sunlight.

I grinned darkly. I could only imagine what *those* orders were.

"I'm sure she did." The healer responded evenly back, ignoring the two of us. "Please do as I say. This will be a long night for everyone. No need to add even more discomfort to what is already brought upon us. Now be off!" Then he growled low, "Slowly my boy, you must not untangle the ward too quickly! Feel this here, now do exactly what I am doing."

Sighing, I stood, my dismissal obvious. "Thank you again, Master Riss. Send for me if there are any changes."

"What the goddess fuck did you do to my creation?" Penina exclaimed, gaping in horror at my desecrated attire

I shrugged. "Went for a run."

Quinn snorted roughly. "A run? She out sprinted Eshe's leopard for miles—."

"Pay attention boy!" snapped the master healer.

"Sorry father," Quinn muttered.

Penina practically bounced on her feet with excitement as I approached her. "In that case, let's get you cleaned up! I have the perfect outfit for you to try!" She gave me a reassuring smile and looped her arm within mine to guide me out of the room. "On my honor, the faeling will be okay. Master Riss is the best healer in The West Isles...in all of Faerie really."

I glanced back at Riella's sweet face. "For your sake and the people that live here, you better pray to the goddess that is true, shifter."

The shifter's steps faltered. "It's easy to forget," she stated simply.

I frowned. "Forget what?"

"How dangerous you really are," she whispered and then smiled, tucking me in closer. "It's going to be so much fun having you here!"

# CHAPTER 36

Remnant

M Y EYES SNAPPED OPEN...KNOWING two things immediately.

I was being *watched* and my shadows were back.

Checking on Riella who rested peacefully next to me, I watched her tiny chest rise and fall without labor. After a long night of unraveling the wards that prevented her from her true transformation, the master healer had finally declared her free of the Sanguine bonds, but she would need additional healing sleep for a full recovery.

Slowly, I peeled away from my protective curl around her and sat up to shove my long dark hair away from my face to peer into the shrouded darkness where a single moonbeam streamed in hiding whatever was within.

Shifting to my aura sight, I braced against the sudden blazing white gold outline of a shifter's aura, feeling my heart skip a beat along with unexpected relief knowing he was alive.

"So you are alive...how fortunate for you...again." The shadows curled eagerly into my lap and I caressed them, feeling the sharp void of their absence diminishing inside of me and using them as a distraction from the flutter in my stomach. "I missed you too, my loves," I whispered down at them as they twirled between my fingertips.

The shifter Emon chuckled as he stepped into the moonlight, his stunning bronze skin glowing like his aura. Still shirtless, his muscles rippled with his stealthy movement and under the cover of the darkness, I took advantage of admiring him fully. It wasn't until our eyes met that I realized he was devouring me with his own gaze as well.

"You don't sound happy nor surprised about my survival, little umbra." Emon's eyes trailed searchingly over my face before he crossed his arms in front of him. "At least I brought your shadows back to you."

I suppressed a carnal shiver at the combination of his husky whisper and bulging muscle flexing in front of his chest. That infuriating pull towards the shifter was back, stronger now than it ever was in the Wildwoods and he knew it too—his smile spreading cockily across his face.

I blinked.

For the briefest of moments, I could almost forget his connection to the slaughtering of the shadow court and my family. I needed the truth. There could be nothing between us until I learned it.

"They would have come back to me even despite you doing so," I shrugged.

"I have no doubt of their devotion to you, little umbra." Frowning, his hand raked through his messy brown hair. "Speaking of, I thought we had an understanding to help one another? What happened? That night I could not wake you? Why did you run?"

I shoved away the memories threatening to resurface from that night. "You seem to be under the impression that we are friends. I owe you no allegiance nor insight to my own personal actions." My voice sounded hollow, like someone else was saying them. "In fact, I do believe it is you who owes me..." I raised one finger and then a second, "twice."

He gave a heavy snort. "Truthfully, Faerie did the life saving in the Wildwoods. You just took care of some maggots that I should have squashed long before then besides I had things more than handled in The Under."

"If you had things handled it would not have taken you a whole day to return from those infernal depths. You and I both know my shadows saved your life in The Under, although from *what*, I can only imagine," I purred at him evilly. "It's too bad that I was not there to witness it."

His beautiful eyes flashed with pleasure and my stomach flipped. "You were keeping track of how long I was gone."

I reared back denying him with my actions even if my words could not. "I was keeping track of my shadows, yes."

He chuckled, seeing through me easily. "You're underestimation of me is wounding, little umbra. We just got a bit delayed but it was fruitful. The shadows made cleaning up easy."

I laughed and gave him a wide grin. "Swallowing enemies whole is their speciality."

A predator smirked back at me and my grin faltered. "Do that again," he purred.

My mouth went dry and I licked my lips. "Do what, exactly?"

"Laugh," he growled low, taking another step towards me. "You are so fucking beautiful when you laugh," he whispered reverently. "I never dared to dream this moment even though I wished for it desperately...of having you here in my home, with my people—dressed in my colors no less." He waved a hand at the gold dress I wore, one of Penina's choices—she had winked knowingly when I put it on. "I could have never conjured up a dream that would have been the equivalent of you here, right now. You are breathtaking, Remnant Ezra Solaire Dark."

The reverence in his voice came out like a dark confession and I felt it, deep in my soul. The shattered remains of it clicking back into place.

"You cannot mean that." I denied it, my soul could not possibly be saved.

His stare did not waver. "Fae do not lie."

Hissing, I threw myself from the bed and stood before him. Anger and confusion clouding every ounce of decorum I should have had. "How dare you? After all that you have done!" My shadows swarmed around me, mimicking my misplaced anger while I tugged at the layers of fabric I wore for emphasis. "It must be goddess damn nice to have your people around for them to wear any color of your kingdoms! Something, I wouldn't know, since you were the one who murdered mine."

He jerked back as if my words struck him, his voice a dark warning rumble while he watched my anger ripple through me. "Explain."

"You were there!" I whispered, taking a step towards him menacingly.

Everything was at war inside me. I wanted him. I hated him. I needed him. I denied him.

"You want to know why I ran from you? Why you couldn't wake me? Because I *remembered*. I relived every second of the days leading up to Morta. Right up to the time where my shadows exploded from me when I was shown the shifter that was responsible for destroying my people. A shifter that looked exactly like you—covered with my people's blood."

Emon's eyes trailed over my furious face and the horrifying grief I exposed there before tilting his head to the ceiling with a quiet curse. "This is what you think of me?"

I stepped closer, my sword materializing in my hand. My shadows had returned and with it the void where I kept all my possessions. "You don't deny it then?"

He made no move to defend himself but his voice was cold. The coldest I had ever heard it and part of me hated that I was the cause of it. My grip tightened, my knuckles turning white, I was a mess but I would see this through.

He shook his head. "You fucking thought I was seeking you out to what? Finish the job? To finish *you*? The last shadow fae." He growled with disgust. "You are that convinced I would commit such a heinous atrocity?"

Centuries of training had my sword laid against the steady pulse of his neck before he could detect it. Just like that, I switched off my emotions, the connection to him, and became what I really was—a monster, a killer. "I saw it, I saw you there." I pressed the blade in, making a shallow cut and watched with satisfaction when the blood trickled over his pretty bronze skin and ran down the muscular valleys of his smooth chest.

Emon exposed his neck further but his eyes blazed down at me so fiercely they were almost white. "If you truly believe this, then fucking end me. I do not want to ever live in a world where you look at me the way you are now."

Tears pricked my eyes and my sword arm shook but I pressed the blade harder against his flesh anyway, making more blood flow. "Give me your answer! The Goddess showed me the vision of you, standing in the City of Night. Blood was on your hands when I begged her for the truth. Begged her to tell me that my people were still alive even knowing what my queen had ordered." I did not fear the furious golden power pulsing off him with my shaking words. My darkness was just as deadly and I would use it if I had to. "So I'll ask you one more time...do you deny it?"

Emon blinked slowly and I watched the anger in his eyes become a kaleidoscope of emotions. Pain, sadness, and then...a scornful smile split across his face and he *laughed*.

# CHAPTER 37

I FUCKING *LAUGHED*. IT was a condescending sound, cutting through the cold burn of Remnant's emerald green eyes that were flooding with tears. What I said to her was fucking true. I could not...*would not ever*, live in a world where she looked at me in this way—I'd rather die on the cold edge of her sword than endure it a moment longer.

My stomach churned.

Of all the damned scenarios that I imagined when I finally had her safe in my arms, safe in my home...this was not one of them. And I had many, many, years to imagine. Almost a century to be exact.

My soulmate hated me. She thought I was a murderer...a genocidal monster.

Well fuck it.

Fuck her.

Fuck the goddess.

Fuck Faerie.

Fuck this kingdom.

Fuck everyone.

*"That's a lot of fucks that I personally know you don't have the stamina for,"* the beast commented dryly.

*"Real funny cat, are you not the least bit worried for your life right now with her sword drawing our blood,"* I snarled back at him.

The cat huffed. *"Don't be so dramatic, fairy boy. If she was going to kill you, if she even could, you'd be dead already."*

I blinked slowly. The clarity I needed to see past the accusations she lashed upon my soul forthcoming.

The cat snorted. *"Such a dramatic fairy you are but you are welcome."*

This was a Faerie fucking disaster.

"Enough," I growled, wrapping my hand around the shadow blade and giving it a hard shove. Its dark edge sliced deep, but it was nothing against the sharp sting of her incriminations. The cut would heal but the damage being created between us may not.

Recognizing she wouldn't be killing me either she thrusted her blade back into the void of shadow. "Well?" she snapped.

"I have proof that I did not kill the shadow fae." I raised a brow. "I can show you, if you allow me the chance."

"You are insinuating that our own goddess, our creator, lied when she showed me her vision?"

I snorted. "Lied? No." I shook my head, my hair falling over my eyes. "Manipulate? Scheme? A cunning deceit?" I shot her a look of reprove. "You should know this better than even I. Your own queen interpreted her visions incorrectly all the time. It was what led her to imprison you."

Remnant growled lethally and my entire body jolted at the sound, having the opposite effect she intended as arousal stirred deep within me.

"Screw you shifter. How could you possibly know anything about that?"

"Deirdre having the sight was known to all and trust me little umbra—" I instinctively growled back, my lust growing the longer I stood in her presence, just like it had at the cabin in the woods. "I'd like nothing better than for you to *screw* me."

Her dark brows shot upwards before she scowled. "I suddenly feel the need to kick your ass just to remind you who you are talking to."

Stepping stealthily closer to me in a threatening manner, I inhaled her concentrated scent of nighttime lilies. Desirous need thrummed through my body as it penetrated my senses and drew me in. Inhaling again, I breathed deeper this time, fully bathing in everything that made her irresistible.

Goddess, I didn't just want her...I needed her, she was my fucking air.

"Little umbra." A deep guttural growl escaped me.

"Stay away from me," she hissed, recognizing my need and pathetically attempting to shove me away. She had done the same in The Under, except this time I wasn't under the drugged influence of the ambrosia pearls and floating in fucking water. This time I could smell her need just as much as my own, this time I could see the dark dilation in her eyes, this time the killer in her was softening and revealing the passionate female beneath.

She gasped when I captured her hands to my chest and purred deeply at the feel of them on my bare skin. She shuddered then, her eyes burning with desire snapping up to mine.

Unable to resist, I twirled her, enveloping her in my arms where her small body seemed to be swallowed by my large form—safe within my hold. I relished in the feel of her firm back pressed deliciously to my chest and that perfect ass pressed straight into my stiffening cock. Trailing my nose along the soft skin of her neck I realized I didn't just bathe in her scent anymore, I was drowning in it.

Home. She was my home.

All those years of not knowing where I belonged after the darkness I lived through...only to find it was her.

It would always be her.

A deep throaty groan escaped me and Remnant gasped, a seductive sound in the glowing moonlight, and she tilted her head further back, beckoning more from my lips while the raspy words tumbling from her delicious mouth told me the opposite.

"Unhand me shifter or I will kill you before the master healer can even have you thrown out."

I chuckled darkly, creating tiny goosebumps along the flushed surface of her delectable skin. "I'd love to see Jar try to throw me out of my own home, little umbra. Especially since he lives here in service to me."

"Your home, service to you?" she breathed, there was a long pause and I could practically see the pieces falling into place inside her. "*Your* people...*your* colors!" she hissed angrily.

"Yes," I rasped, fingering the elegant gold fabric of her dress at her sides. It looked like Penina's work. "My *royal* colors," I added, gripping her dress and pulling her harder to me.

I could not stop my lips from crashing down onto her pale moonlit skin, giving into the seductive madness that she created inside of me. Hungrily, I ravished her with my mouth, my tongue, and my teeth, groaning when her own wandering hands reached back along my neck, pulling me closer to her with a shiver and a sultry purr.

She moaned, her head fell back against my chest and she reached up to drag her nails through the shaved sides of my head, pulling me even closer.

"Remnant." It was a plea, a prayer, a curse upon my lips.

"Emon." Her breathy hiss stole every function from me. So much that I didn't even notice the way she tensed, the way she gripped my neck, her subtle shift...until it was too late. With the speed of a damned shifter she quickly dropped, pulling my entire body with her before launching me over her shoulder and sending me crashing through the healer quarters. My heavy shifter ass was flying through the air with disbelief before my instincts finally kicked in. Twisting just before my back slammed cruelly into the unforgiving wooden floor, I landed in a perfect plank, my nose just barely kissing its surface that would have otherwise smashed my face in while my arms shook at the sudden deceleration they were forced to control. A small drip of blood splattered onto the pristine wooden planks.

My head snapped upwards and a slow grin spread across my face as she stared glaring down at me. Her anger was just as alluring as her arousal—she was fucking glorious.

I shoved myself upright and prowled back towards her watching me cautiously. "That wasn't very nice, little umbra."

"Oh are we playing nice, shifter?" Remnant spat, her face flushed with lingering lust and anger. Her shadows drew up around her. "Or should I address you as your majesty now? Would that be nice enough for your kingly self?"

I shrugged arrogantly. "It would be courteous but also I am not entirely sure you understand what the meaning of nice is." Then I tilted my head to the side. "Although you may call me whatever you want as long as I am the one making you moan with pleasure."

"You!" She pointed her finger at me furiously. "You're the fucking shifter king of the West Isles!" She barked out an incredulous laugh and mimicked my growling tones. *"I, Emon, vow to you, Remnant, on our very goddess and all of Faerie, that no harm will befall you from the fae of The West Isles nor from its king,"* she spat. "No kidding, you are the goddess damn king!" She wound her hands into her hair. "How could I be this stupid?"

My shit eating grin grew wider. "That is a terrible impersonation of me. If it brings you any solace, I never wanted to be king, nor did I expect it at such a young age."

*"Young?"* The cat chortled.

*"I am surprised you don't have any comments about the shadow fae throwing me across the room."*

*"I attempt to stay as far away from your sexual adventures as I can, fairy boy. Foreplay included."*

I barely restrained my bark of laughter.

"What is the meaning of this!"

We both jumped at the flood of light and a very pissed off master healer standing between us in a fluffy white robe and rainbow unicorn slippers.

# CHAPTER 38

Emon

"**F**UCK JAR, WHERE IN the Sheol did you come from?"

"I could ask you the same thing, your majesty. Alas, I asked you a question first! What exactly is going on here?" Jarquinn's sharp blue eyes darted between the two of us, his unicorn foot tapping with irritation. "Well? I am waiting on an answer from you two! One that warrants disturbing the healing sleep of my patient and effectively my own as well!"

"Good to see you too master healer," I grumbled.

"What was that sire? You do know I can still hear you when you mutter. You may as well say it loud enough for all of us to hear."

Remnant snorted.

Jarquinn's angry blue eyes turned on her. "And you Mistress Dark, I know what to expect from this *cub*," he spat and jerked his thumb in my direction, "but you, I expected better. A royal shadow fae no less."

A blush stole across her pale skin and she crossed her arms defensively. "I had asked him nicely to leave."

Jarquinn raised his brows at her in scrutiny. "An excuse coming from the lips of a shadow fae. I thought I would never see the day! Did this nice request require his blood as well, blood that is currently smeared all over my clean floors?"

Remnant's cheeks turned a darker shade and she pressed her lips firmly together. Her eyes flashing with retribution.

A low rumble of warning escaped me and I took a step towards the healer. No one chastised my soulmate.

Jarquinn's attention snapped back to me with full understanding. "Shove it, Daemon Ash Strider. I expected proper decorum and behavior that is warranted of a king. Let alone some fucking manners of the fae I raised you to be. Do not forget you are not just the damn shifter king of The West Isles but also a grown male that I know I taught better—as did your father and mother."

I rolled my eyes and sniffed, ignoring Remnant's stiffening at my title. "You never fail to remind me, healer, but I cannot take you seriously in those right now..." I waved at his unicorn slippers—the toes were shaped in elegant snouts complete with glittering silver horns and rainbow fabric manes that dusted the floor.

Jarquinn huffed with aggravation. "Do not fuck with my unicorn slippers, your majesty. And if neither of you have answers for me then with all due respect to your station...get the Sheol out of my healing quarters—the both of you. That poor faeling needs her rest and you two are just short of fucking on the goddess damn floor. I may be ancient but I am not a fool."

I froze, his words having the opposite effect on me. "What in the goddess did you just say? Did you just say faeling?"

Slowly I looked back towards the bed Remnant had risen from and I extended my senses to the being laying there. I had been so enthralled by my soulmate that I had failed to recognize the other being in the room.

Jarquinn hummed and rolled his eyes. "Sometimes I worry about you, Daemon."

I waved him off as I stepped towards the small bed. A tiny fae girl with raven hair and the most beautiful cherub face I had ever seen was resting sweetly on a pillow of clouds.

Then the vision of her was gone, replaced by the angry protective stance of my soulmate.

I raised my brows and then peered back over her shoulder afraid I had made up such a vision. But there she was. Bronze skin, dark lashes—the sight of her hit me like a punch in the gut. She was the second most beautiful creature I had ever seen.

"Fucking Goddess above, that is a fae child!" I breathed.

"Goddess, give me patience," Jar groaned.

"What in the Sheol has been going on here since I was away?" Unable to contain myself, I quickly stepped around Remnant to get a closer look.

Remnant's hand gripped my arm. "Stay away from her shifter or I will rip out your insides," she hissed, her teeth bared with her nails digging into my skin.

I looked over at my soulmate and bared my own fangs. Insulted by her insinuation that I'd ever bring harm to a child. A miracle no less. To hurt a child was abhorrent and a line that no fae crossed unless seeking their own death.

Then I saw the tinge of worry in her blazing eyes and my anger disappeared. Remnant was acting like a mother guarding her cub, somehow she had taken on the role of the girl's guardian. Something that was celebrated and honored by shifter customs and that made her even more beautiful.

I placed my hand reassuringly over her harsh grip. "I shall not harm her. She will be protected in my name. This I vow, little umbra."

Remnant snatched her hand back and looked away. "Then your people better hope you never break that vow, your majesty."

The girl sighed then, drawing both our attention back to her frail form. I watched with fascination at the lock of raven hair that fell across her face. My stare fixated on the darkness of it and with a trembling hand, I reached out to brush it away.

The moment my skin touched hers, my heart seared in my chest and I released a slow breath. A new truth slamming hard and deep into my soul.

I now had two beings in this world I would protect with the last dying beat of my heart.

I didn't know what the future held for this little miracle, nor any idea where she came from, but I did know one thing. This tiny beautiful child laying on a bed of soft white was somehow the anchor that would hold this world together or the weapon that would tear it apart.

Questioningly I looked over my shoulder at Jarquinn whose lips pressed into a thin line. He shook his head subtly but I saw what was behind those ancient blue eyes. The master healer had more answers...answers he didn't want to reveal here and now.

My gaze slid over to Remnant, where her shadows swirled behind her, poised to send me to my death if need be. "Be at ease. My need to protect this child runs just as strongly as yours now. She will be welcomed here and so are you." I bowed low in greeting and rose. "Welcome to my home and Finlandia, Remnant Ezra Solaire Dark. The crown is honored to have you here and blessed that you bring such a beautiful miracle with you."

"Riella is *mine* to protect. She is not a boon for your people, *King Strider*."

I flinched at the venom in her use of my title. "Clearly we have some things that we need to discuss."

Remnant snuffed out her shadows. "Clearly."

Jarquinn groaned with exasperation. "Then would you two please leave and discuss your business elsewhere?"

I nodded and stepped back. "Of course."

"Riella will not be waking any time soon, *forta*. She will stay in a healing sleep for now." Jarquinn said kindly to the hesitant shadow fae behind me.

*Riella*—*my* mind rolled over the meaning. *Gift and Strength*. Fitting for the first fae born in centuries!

"How long will she be this way?"

Jarquinn's knowing gaze sparkled with mischief. "As long as it is needed."

I smirked. Clever ancient fae. "Indeed."

Jarquinn grinned then, snatching me into his warm embrace, unable to help himself from smothering me with his obnoxious fluffy robe.

"It's good to have you back, my cub. We have missed you."

I heard the hitch in his voice, the emotional toll that my absence had caused. I buried my face further into the white fluff, squeezing him back.

"I missed you too, Jar."

Jarquinn cleared his throat, pulling away from me with tears filling his sky blue eyes. He winked at Remnant standing silently to the side with a slight frown on her face.

"He's a right pain in the ass, Mistress Dark, but please do try not to kill him. I know first hand that sometimes it seems like an impossible task but we do sort of love him here...the goddess only knows how much I do."

The shadow fae bowed her head respectfully. "He is safe from me for now, master healer."

I chuckled and shook my head. "For now."

She stared flatly back at me. "For now."

"Yes, yes, for now. No killing. Goddess bless you both. Now please just leave!"

I snorted and rolled my eyes before turning towards Remnant. "Ready?"

"Of course, lead the way, *your majesty*." She waved her hand towards the doorway.

I ran my hand through my hair again and released a deep sigh. "How long am I to be punished for not telling you?"

"Likely forever, *your royal shifter highness*," she hissed.

Sighing again, I led her from the room toward my more private chambers.

"Have fun, my cubs!" Jarquinn called out, "I think I'll pray to the goddess that I don't have two more patients before the morning sun rises," he added more quietly, just barely loud enough for my shifter ears to hear.

# CHAPTER 39

## Remnant

I STARED AT EMON—NO, not *Emon*.

King Daemon Ash Strider of The West Isles. Ruler of all shifters!

There was so much there that I should have recognized. Gold eyes, a family trait passed from father to son. The term *golden one*, the prince of shifters was crowned the golden son. Even his goddess damn name, Emon, was a giveaway, even if it was shortened.

Had I just been blinded by his charismatic compassion? The ease at which he had exposed his soul to me? Was it all a ploy to gain my trust and for what gain?

I swallowed back the sudden rising bitterness.

"It's not you, it was never you. I blocked your ability to recognize who I was with personal wards put upon me. The moment you entered Finlandia, they broke."

I frowned. I focused on the one question that mattered. "Why?"

The shifter king looked over his bare shoulder at me sympathetically, pausing before a large wooden door. "Why did I choose to keep the truth from you?" He gave me a sad smile. "Would you believe me if I told you it was because I wished to keep you safe and also selfishly wanted you to get to know the real me and not as the murderous king you already think me to be?"

"That's not good enough." I barely kept the hurt out of my tone. "Knowing you puts no more of a target on my back than the one I already have."

He grunted and pushed the heavy door open. "I wish that were true, little umbra, but knowing me puts you in more danger than you realize." He stepped to the side, sweeping his arm out to beckon me to enter. "I am sorry if I hurt you from my omission."

"No you are not," I spat, irritated that I couldn't say that he did not hurt me. I smoothed down the gold layers of fabric I wore before gliding into a room that looked much like a private study.

Two exits were on the back wall leading out to a large balcony where gauzy gold fabric stirred from the coolness of the night breeze. The exits framed a floor to ceiling black stone fireplace that was roaring with warmth and light. Lavish rugs of all colors were strewn about on the floor, absorbing the warmth from the fireplace and yielding comfort against the otherwise white stone walls.

Two leather chairs faced the fireplace and on the adjacent wall, was an enormously long and elegantly carved live edge desk that looked like a tree had just laid to rest here in this very room. Books lay scattered across its polished grain, some open, as if someone had been frantically looking for answers.

"Even still it was never my intention," he continued.

I looked up to see his imploring concern, the same expression he held the night we buried the cù-sìth together. I gritted my teeth at the annoying way my heart fluttered. Had it not learned its lesson yet?

"Even you can admit you never would have come here knowing who I truly was." He shut the door.

I shrugged indifferently, the opposite of the way I was feeling. "I never did want to come here." Without him...I stopped the words from tumbling from my treacherous mouth.

Emon grunted. "Yet you are here. How? And with a faeling?"

I spun and faced him. "Fate," I said snarkily.

Startled gold eyes searched mine and I held my breath at the shocked silence, recognizing that my words had caused a crack in the barriers I had made to protect myself.

I flicked a finger in his direction, hardening my voice. "Enough of this, it is you that owes me answers, shifter. Not the other way around. Stop asking the questions and start answering them."

Shaking his head, he laughed. "I have not forgotten. Get comfortable and settle in. We are going to need a few drinks for this. At least I do." He turned away towards a bar cart in the far corner of the room.

Instead of taking a seat in one of the large leather chairs near the fireplace, I perused the books scattered on his desk, my fingertips skimming the thick dust covering their pages. With the amount layered here, whoever left it this way was in a hurry, and was gone for a long time.

I glanced at Emon's turned back where he poured a drink, already knowing that fae was him.

Why would he have left his kingdom for so long just to find me?

Frowning, I tilted my head to read the titles. The History of the Blood Wars, The Accounts of the Blood Fae, The Sanguine-Blood Lands, Transformations of Fae, Faerie and Its Creation...my hand stilled on one in particular.

"The Unaccounted Life of the Last Shadow Fae," I read it out loud, my voice hoarse.

A glass of amber appeared in front of me and I took it, glancing at him, noticing he was sipping from his own drink and staring at the book with admiration in his eyes.

"A good read for those who love tales of outlandish adventure and the daredevil risks of the most powerful shadow fae alive."

I looked back down, trailing my hand over the delicate script. "The last shadow fae. This book...it's about me?"

The hairs on the back of my neck stood up feeling his predator-like grin roaming over me. "Yes. You are famous here, little umbra. I told you that. Most shifters see you differently than the fae of Faerie."

"Oh." I had no words.

"I have to know." He stepped closer and took a drink, I could see him watching me intently over the rim of his glass. "Did you really surf the skies upon the wings of the Roc?"

A nervous bubble of laughter escaped me. "The mountain eagles would not appreciate such outlandish tales about them. Surf the skies on their wings? The audacity! Although that would have been a much more pleasant experience." I shook my head, seeing that time of my life very vividly. "It was more like free falling from their fire-lit talons, thousands of feet in the air. I was forced to use my shadows to saddle-break their leader mid-flight while fending off streams of fire, beaks, and flesh tearing talons. It took me three days to heal. In the end, the Roc finally listened to me."

Emon chuckled. "Sounds like a good time to me."

I smiled fondly. "It was." Closing the book, I frowned. "I was unaware there were books written about me." I skimmed the black leather cover. "There is no author."

I could feel Emon's thoughtful gaze at my back. "These are the accounts from all over Faerie. Told by many fae. Most of it was written in my hand but the stories are not my own. Perhaps one day I may be blessed to have my own tales to recite about you."

I pressed my lips together and held back the one glaring question I always had when it came to him.

*Why?*

Except, I was not brave enough to face that answer. Instead, I scanned the wall behind the desk where thousands of volumes were lovingly stacked against it. "May I have access to some of these? There are a few I do not recognize."

Emon grunted beside me. "Of course. What is mine is yours. You do not need permission from me."

Spinning I turned to confront him but he had already walked away, back to the bar cart. I studied him curiously...not understanding him at all.

Feeling my scrutiny he waved towards the leather chairs in front of the onyx fireplace. "Sit. I believe I owe you answers—proof and an explanation."

Following his bidding with gritted teeth I took a seat in the large confines of the leather chair, surprised by the buttery softness holding in the fire's warmth.

Emon settled himself in the other and sighed, dropping his head back, blinking up at the vaulted ceiling, his drink still gripped loosely in his hand on the arm of the chair.

"Ask."

Mesmerized by the beauty of his profile, I barely registered he had spoken. "What?"

He chuckled and slowly turned his head towards me with amusement. "Ask your shadows to return my bag to me. They stole it in Faerie, before Kira discovered us."

I raised my brows at him. "You have an odd habit of trusting other creatures to take care of your things...things that seem to be very important."

Reaching out and feeling my need for them, the dark plumes of shadow appeared in front of Emon, spitting out his leather satchel straight into his lap.

Emon jolted at the impact and then chuckled fondly at them. "Thank you, my little deviants."

A small smile graced my lips, he was just as crazy as I was...talking to shadows.

Waving them aside he set his drink down on the side table between us and flipped open the heavy flap of his bag, reaching inward. He rummaged through the contents with excruciating slowness before pausing. There was a slight tick in his jaw, a stiffening of his body, before he exhaled forcefully and pulled from within an ornate black scroll.

I leaned forward in my chair as did the shadows in the room, drawn in by it. "*Where* did you get that?"

# CHAPTER 40

Remnant

M Y PULSE THUNDERED AS the king placed the scroll slowly on the table between us. Lifting his hands in the air he spoke softly. "Your mother gave this to me, Remnant."

"Why? How?" I could not take a full breath, the shallow rise and fall of my chest falling in rapid succession with the blood pounding in my head.

Emon lowered his hands and gently set his bag to the floor, his eyes never leaving me the entire time. "Before your people were attacked, your mother gave this to me. She said it would one day bring you back to her and then the entire court fled. There was blood spilled that night, yes, but none of it was shadow fae."

"It is a sacred scroll," I breathed and licked at my dry lips. "It can only be given freely to a named receiver by the Lady of Night...my mother."

He grunted. "You also know it will destroy itself should the receiver be unworthy of carrying its secrets."

My drink clanked horribly in the stillness of the room as I set it down on the table. My hand shifted to hover over the onyx scroll laying there, trembling before I snatched it back with a sudden whimper.

"I can't." I gasped for breath, clutching my hand to my chest. "What I saw—." I rocked in my chair as a gripping panic rose inside of me. Splitting my chest into two and leaving me with panting breaths. I could hear that horrible roaring again, as I always did when the panic set in, a tortured sound of someone in pain. I whimpered, rubbing at my wrist frantically and feeling the memory of the burning iron. I would never be free...never. "I can't."

"Shhhh. It's okay, little umbra. You don't have to."

My head snapped up and blinked at the shifter king kneeling at my feet. The roaring intensified.

A broken plea left my lips. "You must get away. Dangerous. Too dangerous." The darkness stirred within and it called to me.

"Just breathe, little umbra. Breathe, Remnant." Emon reached for my hands, pulling them away from my chest and uncurling my clenched fingers to press his palms to mine. "Do it with me, Remnant. Inhale."

A command. I inhaled.

"Exhale," he ordered.

I exhaled.

"Inhale," he purred and started drawing soothing circles against my palms, his gold eyes never leaving my grief stricken face. "Exhale." He repeated. "Again. Inhale."

I began taking deep breaths without his cues, his proximity amplifying the spiced chocolate scent that was uniquely his. My chest opened, my breaths deepened, the pounding pulse eased, and that horrid sound was gone.

"Good," he purred and slowly withdrew to press my glass back into my hands. "Drink."

I looked away. Too deep. I was in too deep with this shifter. "I am fine now, thank you." I took a long swig, ignoring his gaze and allowed the burn of the alcohol to chase away the rest of the panic and the stirring feelings inside of me.

The shifter king sighed and moved swiftly back to his own chair. "Do you wish to talk about it?"

"No." I took another long drink and waited patiently for him to continue.

From my periphery he raked his hands through his hair, frowning at the fire. "I don't know why the goddess only showed me in her vision but the truth is, your mother and I staged the attack, giving her time to flee with her people. I believe that scroll is the location of their new home...your home." His voice wavered slightly.

I did not want to look at the scroll. "You said blood was spilled but not shadow fae. Who was it then?"

Emon took a long drink from his glass, the firelight dancing across his bronze skin. "Falcon sent shifter forces by order of the Queen to destroy the court." Emon bared his teeth. "I was there to rip that fucking bastard to shreds...but he never showed, just like the coward he is. Instead, I ripped apart his followers, fae I grew up with. Ones that I once called friends."

"Shifter blood," I whispered.

He chuckled darkly. "Turns out I am just like my father. I can kill my own people without hesitation too."

I shook my head. "I don't understand. How could you have known about Falcon or the queen's orders?"

His beautiful gaze turned on me searching. "I was already in Faerie. To discuss the treaty terms and to bring my wayward emissary Falcon to heel. Despite what Deirdre had done to my mother and my desperate need to gut that dishonorable cunt, I was so goddess damn tired of the bloodshed that I was willing to hear her out. By the time I stepped onto Faerie shores, word of your betrayal spread and I knew then that if the queen could betray the woman she loved—if she could spread vile, disgusting lies about the most celebrated general in all Faerie, then there was no hope for me and my own."

I flinched and looked away.

"Forgive me, that was tactless." His tone was remorseful.

I stared into the fire. "Do not apologize, shifter, and you needn't fear. I am quite under control. Your city and people are safe for now."

Emon snarled. "I do not fear your lack of control, little umbra. I only meant that I do not wish to cause you any pain and my words were thoughtless—" his voice softened. "I am sorry."

My fingers tapped against my glass. "I do not need your censure nor your concern, your highness."

He snorted and stood. "Another drink then?" He arched a questioning brow.

I swirled the amber liquid. "I will pass, your highness."

Grunting he spun back towards the bar cart. "Did you know that my father and your mother were allies once upon a time." He shot over his shoulder.

"Once upon a time ends with a happily ever after. This is no fairy tale."

He turned, his hip resting against the cart and a new drink in hand. "It could be. We just need to restart once upon a time."

I tilted my head, studying him in all his bronze godliness. "You are still seeking an alliance with me?"

"I am."

"To save your people," I said dryly.

"To save Faerie," he amended. I could see something else in those golden depths, something I'd seen before, something that made me nervous.

"Is it even worth saving anymore?" I muttered.

"If you're in it, then yes. Yes it is."

My eyes met his and the intensity between us caused us both to take in ragged breaths. Alliance or not, in this moment we were ensnared. Irrevocably.

My shadows burst forth and snatched up the scroll when the large wooden doors swung violently open.

Emon turned with a vicious growl, murder in his eyes at the shifter barging forth.

"Sire! You are home at last!"

# CHAPTER 41

I COULD NOT CONTROL the murderous growl that escaped me as the doors flew open even though I knew exactly who had come. From my peripheral Remnant's shadows had snapped up the scroll and she had returned her gaze back on the fire, deciding to ignore me and the newcomer.

I turned to the one fae I had trusted to make sure Finlandia stayed safe while I was gone.

"Eshe, I believe knocking would have sufficed. I may have been gone a long time but I do believe that courtesy still remains despite the fact."

I didn't fail to notice Remnant tensing in her seat.

My steward sauntered in, her long blonde hair swaying with each long stride towards me.

"Forgive me sire." She delivered me an unapologetic grin. "I was eager to see you for myself after learning you have returned."

Her yellow-green eyes shot behind me and she glowered. "I see you have met our *guest*."

Remnant snorted and took another sip of her drink.

Choking back a laugh, I folded my arms over my chest and stared at Eshe ferally until her eyes drifted away from mine.

"I am pleased that I did not find my invited guest and ally in the dungeons, Eshe. I do believe that was your intention."

Her eyes rounded and she glanced back at me, a dark blush stealing over her cheeks. "Sire, had I known—"

"But *you* did know!" My hand sliced through the air. "Her clemency was granted before I even left these lands, Eshe. Not to mention, Penina reported that she warned you."

Eshe's blush deepened. "Your majesty—" she stammered.

I growled and folded my hands over my chest. "I left you in charge because out of all of us you are the most impartial. Rarely have you ever let your emotions override sound decisions. Something this kingdom desperately needed while I was gone. Was I wrong in my judgment, I wonder?"

She inhaled sharply, her eyes snapping up to meet mine with strong resolve. "No your majesty."

"Good. Is there anything else of immediate concern that compelled you to barge into my private quarters?"

Eshe's proud stature slumped and her eyes turned down to the floor. "Forgive me, sire." She licked her lips subtly. "Your majesty, if I may..."

I waved my hand for her to continue.

Squaring her shoulders, she looked up at me. "You state that you value my objective insight, sire. As such, I would ask that you recognize *our guest* is dangerous...not only to our court but to you as well. A guard would be appropriate."

Whatever she saw in my eyes forced her to take a step back. Inhaling, I spoke slowly. "Eshe, I am very happy to see that you are healthy and as always I am indebted to your service in keeping my kingdom running so smoothly. Please let the others know we will resume our morning routine once again. Penina knows already, you need not bother her."

Her jaw clenched. "Yes of course. Thank you."

I softened my tone. "Please make sure no one disturbs me until then. General Dark and I have much to discuss regarding our alliance and the future of this court."

"As you wish, your majesty." Her bow was stiff, her long blonde hair sweeping the floor before she spun quickly from the room, slamming the door behind her.

I groaned, scrubbing my hand over my face.

"Trouble in paradise?" Remnant snickered, having been stoically silent during our exchange.

Lifting my hands away, I watched her stand mesmerized by her stunning beauty. The gold fabric she wore flowed majestically around her, hugging every sinful curve. The swirls of her ink were only more enhanced by the gold color as was her blue-black hair framing a halo of darkness around her heart shaped face. I needed no goddess to worship with her by my side, whether in sight or in heart I would forever be falling to my knees in reverence.

"The only paradise I'm interested in is yours, little umbra." Like a prayer falling from my lips, a deep blush spread across her pale cheeks.

"Stop doing that!" she hissed at me.

"*Doing what*, little umbra?" The corner of my mouth ticked up in amusement at the cloud of embarrassed anger rolling off of her.

She pointed an accusing finger at me. "That. That right there, stop calling me that. Stop trying to flatter your way to this alliance. Just tell me what it is you would have me do for it to occur."

I blinked slowly. "What would I have you do?"

The possibilities were endless...allow me to undress the layers of gold fabric like I would a present. To kiss my way from her shoulder to her fingertips along those tattoo brands. To elicit the sweet gasps of pleasure from those soft lips while I worshiped her on my knees...where I always wanted to be with her.

Roaring need raged inside of me and I was losing my fight in resisting our bond. It called to me like a siren and my fortitude dissolved like the tides it sang upon.

"I'm going for a run," I barked hoarsely, spinning on my heels and hit the balcony in three long strides.

I needed an outlet. A strong, rigorous outlet that would calm this fucking lust and build back the reasons I held her away from me.

The incredulous pitch in her voice pierced me from behind. "A run?"

I grunted. "A run," I croaked and stepped out into the night air. Its coolness doing nothing for the flames of desire burning inside of me. Foolishly I shot over my shoulder. "Care to join me? The city is a spectacular sight at dawn."

And so was she.

I felt her deadly stare trailing over my flesh and I shivered at the feel of it. It wasn't cold enough out here.

"I was under the assumption that you required me to help save the *world, King Daemon*. This is the most inappropriate time for a run." Her sharp, condescending tone only made me more aroused.

"No," I rebuked with a husky snarl. "This is exactly the right time." And even then a run may not even take care of the kind of release I needed. Perhaps a cold shower. A very, very, very cold shower.

"*Amateur,*" my beast growled and rolled his eyes.

"*Shut up, cat.*" He had been silent since we entered the study. I wished he had stayed that way.

Growling, I launched myself up the outside wall to the rooftop deck, there was no need to use the ladder with the pure energy buzzing in my system. I heard Remnant curse me to the deepest, darkest depths of Sheol and I couldn't hold back the feverish laughter rumbling from my chest out into the lingering night.

# CHAPTER 42

I CRACKED MY NECK side to side, surveying my sprawling city. I had been young when my father and I birthed Finlandia. Now, where there was once only a few rooftops, there were hundreds, each one covered in a soft blanket of darkness and each one was getting harder and harder to hide from the Sanguine.

Yet dawn was quick approaching, peeking just slightly over the hills of the valley beyond. Soon the city would light up with a gorgeous glitter of white buildings welcoming The West Isle sun to warm the city's heart.

This was my favorite hour. When the darkness of the night melted into the brightness of day. Surrendering their differences in a stunning colorful array of possibilities.

"This better be worth it," Remnant huffed next to me.

She had cursed herself all the way up the ladder. At me, at herself, at the goddess, and even the death god himself.

My lip lifted amusedly and I turned to her before sputtering in shock. "What is that?"

My arms floundered idiotically at my half naked soulmate's attire. Scraps of black fabric covered her breasts and even smaller black shorts hugged her firm ass like second skin. Creamy pale skin was being kissed by the night, her abdominals bare and flexing as she pulled one arm across her chest to stretch. My eyes danced along the scrolling swirls of ink once again, admiring the tone in the arms that wielded a blade with ease and killed with them even easier.

For goddess sake! If I was struggling before when she was fully clothed in layers then I was damn near exploding looking at her now.

She quirked an eyebrow at me, pulling her hair back in a high ponytail, highlighting the elegant profile of her heart shaped face. "What is wrong with you, shifter? You invited me to go on a run. These are my running clothes." She bent at the waist and stretched to touch her bare wiggling toes. My gaze shot straight to her ass saluting the sky.

I turned away from her swearing under my breath.

I heard her tiny bare feet pad against the wooden deck running in place. "So where are we running? There isn't exactly enough room up here."

There was room enough to fuck though my mind whispered. "You up for a wager?" I said instead.

"First an alliance now a wager?"

I smiled at the horizon, she didn't hide the curiosity in her voice well enough. "Yes, a wager."

"Depends on if you'll tell me the details this time. What is the task and what are we wagering?"

"A kiss." I was a depraved mess.

*"And to think you do it all by yourself, fairy boy,"* the cat snickered.

She blew out a harsh breath. "A kiss..."

I held mine. "Yes, a kiss. If I win you owe me a kiss. If you win then..." I shrugged, "you get to decide if you want to kiss me or not."

She snorted. "That is the worst wager I have ever heard."

I barked out a laugh still looking straight out at the slow rising sun. "You're right. Name your terms then."

"Pastries."

I looked down at her with amused shock but had to immediately pull my gaze back. Staring straight into her exposed cleavage would not assist me right the fuck now.

"Pastries?" I croaked.

I could hear the soft brush of her tongue gliding over her plush lips. *Fuck...me.*

"Yes, pastries, I saw the most amazing bakery when I came through the city yesterday. I want to go there."

I chuckled to hide the shiver her desire for pastries sent through me. "Done."

"Excellent. You win, I kiss you. I win, I get pastries." Remnant bounced side to side, turning towards the horizon. "Now how do I win?"

I leaned down and pointed along the rooftops. "*We* run on the roofs."

A smile spread across her face surveying the city. Excitement blazing in her emerald green eyes.

I chuckled. "So eager to kiss me then?" I teased.

She snorted and glanced up at me. "Fuck no, shifter. But I am hungry."

Booming laughter escaped me and leaned even closer to her. My breath steady on the shell of her ear. "So am I, my little umbra." Remnant stopped her bouncing and inhaled sharply. I straightened to my full height and nodded. "See that building way over there with the purple flags? The garden rooftop?"

She narrowed her eyes. "Yes."

I cracked my neck again. "Race you to it. First one to capture the flag wins."

"No shifting," she snapped.

I barked out another laugh. "No shadows."

She tilted her head and for a brief moment I witnessed the look at the deadly strategist that once was Faerie's most respected war general. "You have undoubtedly done this before and have the advantage. Your shifter speed being one of them."

I snorted and pulled back my own hair in a knot at the crown of my head. "And you are the greatest war general of all Faerie and much smaller than me. That makes you more agile and cunning."

Stories of Remnant's accomplishments were legendary in The West Isles. The book she discovered in my study didn't even touch the surface of it. My hands already ached to write the latest accounts of her story.

Remnant began bouncing again and I really wished she wouldn't. Images of her breasts bouncing as I thrusted into her over and over again was in the forefront of my mind.

"Alright, *your majesty*, let's do this."

The predator in me practically drooled. "I'm going to enjoy every moment of those delicious lips on mine," I taunted.

"Oh Emon." Startled by the sound of my name, I looked down at her. "One more thing." My nostrils flared at her sultry tone that had me leaning in towards her like she was my gravity. The only thing that kept me grounded to this world.

"Yes?"

"You're going to lose," she whispered and I was blinded by the wide smile lighting up her stunning face, right before my ass went flying backwards and slammed to the ground with a booming thud.

I watched stupefied as Remnant launched herself from the roof and onto the next one, running straight for the distant purple flag with her laughter floating through the air behind her.

Seeing Remnant Dark alive again, running through my city was a goddess damn dream and I would be a happy fae if it were to be my last. But I was also greedy and I wanted all the dreams of her, not just one.

Inspired by her mischief, a plan of my own began to form. Springing forth, I was back on my feet and leaping across the building in one bound. Remnant hadn't made it far enough to compete against my shifter speed and I found that I didn't mind the view from here.

"You're going to pay for that!" I roared against the winds.

"Are you just a sore loser, your majesty, or is that your ass talking?" she called back over her shoulder, those green eyes flashing with glee.

I grinned and with three large bounding strides, I leapt onto the next roof ledge, running with perfect balance on its rim while surveying the waking city below.

My city.

I was finally home. I breathed in the morning air, peace filling my soul for the first time in centuries.

It didn't take long for the waking fae to notice their golden king on the rooftops.

Cheers, whistles, and clapping filled the streets. More fae rushed outdoors to watch as the calls grew. Their king was finally home and heart warmingly back to his regular antics.

"Welcome home King Daemon!"

"Better run faster your majesty!"

"Best sunrise I've seen yet!"

"She's got you beat, shifter."

I barked a laugh at that one and I could hear more pealing laughter from Remnant ahead of me. Performing a series of flips and twists she showed off her agility for the crowds above and below. The pure athleticism and warrior strength in her was fully appreciated by the shifter community when more cheers filled the sun kissed streets.

"Show off!" I called out. Then launched forward, landing directly in front of her, flashing her a wide grin over my shoulder, my claws digging into the white stone.

Remnant let out a startled gasp, skittering to prevent herself from crashing into me and then banked in an arc right over the wide street to the building next to us. Tucking herself into a roll she tumbled and then leapt to her feet, up and running again.

"It will take more than that, shifter!" she smiled widely across the street from me, meeting me stride for stride.

My pounding heart stuttered at the radiance of her in the moment. She rivaled the very sun, the light of the stars, and the three moons above. I was never again going to let that light die from her eyes.

I also wasn't about to let her win. My plan was still perfectly in place.

Breathing deep and using my own stamina, I performed my own series of flips with precision and perfect timing.

Her distracted gaze settled on me when more of my court cheered.

Three.

I flipped over the street and landed right next to her, forcing her to stumble and veer away onto another building. The crowd below gasped, some running along the streets with us.

She gave me an annoyed side glance.

Two.

I purred and twisted toward her again. Arching right into her path with a wink. She veered again, leaping onto the building in front of her, her attention fully on me now.

One.

I roared with laughter when she disappeared with a loud splash of water following her wake.

Just as I had planned.

That purple flag was all mine...and so was my kiss.

# CHAPTER 43

## Remnant

ONE MOMENT I WAS running, the next I was fully submerged in the crystal blue depths of a rooftop pool. Choking on the frigid cold water I sprung from the bottom of the pool upwards, sputtering when I broke the surface and swimming towards the edge.

I was going to kill that shifter! King or not.

He knew. Of course he knew. His outlandish flips and constant careening into my path were all part of his strategy to herd me straight into this pit of water. No doubt he had made it to the flag by now. I was only a few roofs away from my victory before landing here.

Sighing, I decided to rest my head and arms on the stone surface of the pool to enjoy the warmth of the morning sunrise while the cold water soothed the tension in my body.

I sighed again with content. Maybe it was worth losing.

A shadow passed over me and blocked the sun.

"I take it you enjoyed your morning swim, little umbra?"

I flipped my wet ponytail off my face to see the smug shifter king waving the purple flag at me.

"You tell me..." I waved my hand and my shadows materialized into existence only to shove the shifter king face first into the pool. "...how it feels, your majesty." I snickered and rested my head back down on my arms.

Sputtering he emerged from the water, shaking his wet body with a reverberating growl. "How...refreshing."

Not bothering to open my eyes, I snorted. "You cheated."

"So did you," he rumbled suddenly next to me.

I peeked open my eyes to see him mirroring my relaxed state. Everything about him was brilliant and vibrant. I felt like I was trapped staring at the sun and if I looked much longer I would be burned by the purity of his soul and—goddess help me, I wanted to burn. I wanted to live in the light of the world he continued to hold open for me.

His smile widened and he leaned in ever so slightly, water glittered on his long lashes like tiny diamonds in the sun. Tapping my nose teasingly, he rumbled. "I'll take my kiss at a later time."

Then he hauled his large god-like body from the pool, the water sluicing down his powerful frame. I wet my suddenly parched lips at the flex of his defined ass, so much more accented by the wet plastered leathers.

I looked away. "I believe on account of cheating our wager is void, your majesty."

Emon crouched low and tilted my chin up to him with a deep purr. "Cheating or not...I'd say we are both ravenous right now." Extending his hand to me, he winked. "For pastries that is...and I can smell them now. Fresh baked from Griffin's Gateau. Drey just pulled some from the oven."

I sniffed at the air excitedly but could smell nothing but pool water. Emon choked with restrained laughter watching me.

"Damn, shifter nose," I grumbled, taking his hand. There was a slight pause and then I threw him over my shoulder back into the pool. Practically drowning again by the enormous splash Emon's unsuspecting body made.

Scrambling out before he could retaliate, I rose, picking up the purple flag on the pool deck and smiling at the sputtering shifter king rising out of the water.

"*Audentes fortuna iuvat.* Fortune favors the bold, shifter," I said in old fae and waved the flag at him, smirking. "You never called the game to an end."

My smile widened when Emon's roaring laughter rattled the lavender lit skies.

# CHAPTER 44

Remnant

D REY, THE BAKER OF Griffins Gateau, turned out to be
the most gigantic shifter I had ever seen with the skittish
nature of a bunny. The terror in his eyes when he saw me was
a reminder that no matter how accepting Emon was of me, I
was still the feared monster to most. I had quickly given the
shifter king my order and excused myself from his shop to wait
outside.

I couldn't hold it against him though. Drey was a goddess
damn good baker—my lips smacked when I sucked the delicious cherry and cream cheese hand pie from my fingertips,
swiveling in the chair that occupied the king's breakfast room.

"Oh to be that pastry right now." Emon's voice was gruff
sitting beside me.

Still living in my own personal dream world, I sucked one
of my fingers teasingly, humming around the digit purposefully.

The shifter king made an indistinguishable noise. Somewhere between a choking sound and a whimper in the back of his throat. "Cruel, little umbra. Very cruel."

I snickered, wiping my hands, and patting my bare happy stomach. "Why are we here? Better yet. Why am I here?"

Emon tilted his head and drummed his strong fingers on the polished wood table. I forced myself to look at his painfully handsome face instead of his sinfully bare chest.

"I'd like the pleasure of introducing you to my inner circle personally, despite you having met most of them already." He seemed deflated by that fact but it did not last. Jumping out of his chair, he peered at the doorway. "Here they come now!"

"Emon!" squealed the young shifter I met yesterday. Penina laughed and ran to slide across the table in an array of pink chiffon and gold jewelry right into the shifter king's waiting arms.

Seizing her, Emon spun her around with a tight hug, before setting her down and smiling grandly.

"Good to see you Nina. Remnant, I'd like to officially introduce you to Penina Sythe. Penina serves as my specialty advisor for all things within the city."

I stood, hiding my surprise at Emon's affection for the young shifter. A genuine affection like this could be exploited and used against him by any other fae. Without uttering the words, it was a reflection of his trust in me.

Penina's eyes trailed down my body and her hand settled on her hip. "Why is it every time we meet you are naked?"

I laughed and waved my hand towards the scraps of black fabric I still wore. "Only half naked this time."

Emon's eyes narrowed and he growled out, "What do you mean every time?"

Penina snickered.

I extended my hand out to her in greeting. "Pleased to formally meet you, Penina Sythe."

Taking a calculated risk, I tugged her towards me, drawing a shadow blade from the darkened corner, and stabbed low towards her exposed side.

She responded *exactly* how I expected her to. Twirling away, Penina slammed her palm down hard on my wrist, forcing me to drop the shadow blade, and I blinked when her dagger fell across my throat.

I smiled, baring my teeth and winking at the shocked shifters. "Advisor you say? I think not...I know an assassin when I see one, your majesty. False truths don't work on me."

The king of shifters grumbled under his breath and shook his head. "Withdraw your knife Penina."

Penina's pearly white smile lit up her face and she flipped her blade away, skillfully hiding it in her pink chiffon clothing. "I hardly know what you mean, General Dark. I advise my king in many ways."

"Remnant will do." I sat down with a swivel. "And you mean you advise him in all things death."

Penina took the chair, next to me, where Emon had been sitting, and propped her bare feet casually on the table. Every single dainty toe was ordained with gold jewelry.

"Perhaps," she grinned.

I grinned back at the seemingly youthful shifter. There was more to her than what she allowed everyone to see. Something mysterious and unknown.

*I liked it.*

Flashbacks of another time forced itself to the front of my mind and I buried it again. Those fae were gone, nothing could bring them back from what I had done.

Emon groaned and scrubbed a hand over his face. "That was my chair."

The *young* shifter wiggled her petite frame deeper into the leather. "And you warmed it up for me. Such a thoughtful king." She reached over and grabbed an apple from an elaborate bowl of fruit decorating the table.

Emon chuckled and shook his head, plopping himself down in the other unoccupied chair next to me.

Penina bit into her apple with a loud crunch and then leaned towards me, her gold pierced brows wiggling comically. "Did you know, when I was a cub I used to pretend that I was the great General Remnant Dark. I would climb the tallest peak of the Red Caps and race along its ridgeline pretending they were the Nocturnes."

The Nocturnes were the snowy mountains of my homeland and wrapped around the giant crescent craters that bordered the City of Night. "That sounds like something I would have done. Perhaps one day we can run the Red Caps together."

She grinned, her bright smile beautiful in contrast to her mocha skin.

"It's a good thing you are not her Nina, or else you'd be a traitor to all of fae kind." I knew that voice. "Your majesty." Eshe flipped her long blonde hair over her bare shoulders showing off a thin crop top covering her midnight skin, paired with a long flowing red skirt.

It was an outfit meant to entice and I knew exactly who it was for.

I glanced over at Emon who was frowning at his steward in confusion.

"I don't believe that," Penina snarled next to me.

Eshe sat with a flourish right across the shifter king. She gave Penina a condescending smile. "The general has a habit of killing whoever gets close to her...I for one would never want to be like that."

My hand snapped up in front of Penina, who I sensed was just short of launching herself across the table.

I stared into Eshe's yellow-green eyes. "I do not deny that I have killed thousands of fae in my lifetime as well as that many in a single day. An atrocity I live with but I am what I am." I placed both my hands on the table and watched the shadows spread across it like spilled ink. Eshe's smug grin fell as she watched the shadow creep towards her. "And who I am is much better than being the ignorant and short minded fae that you have proven yourself to be." I leaned back and the shadows snapped towards me and swirled up my arms. "We all have our faults I suppose."

Penina snickered and crunched into her apple. Chewing very slowly and watching her companion compose herself.

Emon raked a hand through his hair. "Despite what her demeanor has been of late," Emon shot her a warning glare, "Eshe has been and is very loyal to this kingdom as well as the fae within it."

"Thank you, your majesty," she purred.

Emon gave her a pointed look. "You know better. Get over whatever the fuck is hanging you up about having the general here and start acting like the fae I am proud of."

The room stilled and Eshe's face turned a shade of gray.

Penina bit into her apple with another obnoxious crunch.

Then Eshe bowed her head to the shifter king. "Apologies, your majesty."

Another crunch of apple within the awkward silence.

"Who's the new beauty?"

All of us looked up to see a massive shifter sauntering in, his wide shoulders swinging arrogantly. Like the king, he wore no shirt and his body rippled with muscle. Muscle that was a canvas to the inked artwork that covered every single piece of his body that was bare. Even his head, that was completely shaved, was covered in exquisite artwork. Obvious silver bar piercings decorated his tapered ears but neither the piercings nor the tattoos were the most striking feature about him. No, it was his stunning deep purple eyes that glowed bright in the streaming sun.

"Cat got your tongue beauty," he grinned and folded his arms over his chest.

"My name is Remnant Dark, not beauty."

"*General* Remnant Dark," Emon corrected me.

My hands fisted in my lap. "Former," I snapped, not bothering to spare Emon the murderous glare I directed towards his friend. "There is no crown for me to serve anymore."

A deep rumble emitted from the king. "You forget our alliance so easily, General Dark."

Violet eyes of a predator, looked between Emon and I with an amused smirk.

"So it's like that, huh?" he commented dryly, allowing his eyes to trail lazily over my body.

I recognized the look. He was assessing my weaknesses. I had already done the same. He favored his weight to the left, there was a slight decrease in his muscle girth of the right upper chest, but he made up for it in the light way he stood on the balls of his feet. Ready to pounce at moments notice.

He lowered his massive body into a chair at the far end of the table, his eyes never leaving mine, and leaned back stretching his body on full display.

"It is exactly like that," Emon snarled, leaning over me. "Knock it off before I'm forced to kick your ass in front of everyone here."

Bright purple eyes shifted to his king. "You've been gone too long without training, I don't think it would be my ass that would be getting the kicking, your majesty."

Penina grinned, her mouthful of masticated apple on full display.

"I'll be happy to prove it to you later, asshole." Emon's claws snapped open and dug into the table.

Bared fangs responded back. "Dickhead."

"Twinkle Toes."

The newcomer leaned in slowly with a grin. "Pussy."

"Good Morning Mistress Dark." The master healer, Jarquinn Riss, swept inside the room. Emon straightened quickly back into his chair as did his friend. "I have just seen our patient and she is doing very well. Still asleep, clearly, but well." The healer's eyes narrowed on both the shifter king and his friend with reprove, even glancing at Penina who suddenly started to close her mouth while chewing.

"Thank you Master Riss." I inclined my head to his son that had come along with him, "Good morning Quinn."

Quinn smiled. "Good Morning, Mistress Dark, you look well rested this morning." He sat next to the sulking Eshe while the healer took a seat next to the purple eyed shifter.

The room was full. *Too full.* I fisted my hands in my lap, feeling trapped.

Conversations broke out all at once, each one attempting to talk over one another as if they hadn't been in one room together in a long time. While Emon was the center of gravity drawing them together despite their differences.

I fisted my hands in my lap. The buzzing noise of their chatter being replaced by that familiar roaring once again. Fog clouded my vision and a cold sweat broke out across my temple. My chest seized when I attempted to inhale, finding no air to relieve the gripping tightness.

I needed to leave. I didn't belong here. I was better off alone. Always alone.

My legs went numb, trembling beneath the table.

"Breathe." The shifter king leaned towards me whispering low enough that only I could hear him. To anyone else it looked as if he were exchanging secrets about his friends.

"I can't. I can't control it." The soft vulnerable confession barely whispered across my lips.

# Chapter 45

*Remnant*

E MON HUMMED AGAINST MY ear and reached down to my trembling fists, flattening it out with his own like he had done the night before in his study.

"You can control this. Think of the pool. The coolness of the water. The sun on your face. The peaceful weightlessness of your body floating there. Now breathe and picture it."

I focused on the lingering power that resonated from his deep soothing voice even as he leaned back in his chair but never pulled his hand away from mine. His roughened fingertips trailed across my skin with lulling swirls and it reminded me of the cool waters of the pool, caressing over my heated skin.

Inhaling deeply, I felt the vice in my chest ease, then opened my eyes. The fog had been lifted, the buzzing had dimmed even though the shifters in the room were still eating and conversing. No one glanced at me oddly, no one stared at the shifter king's hand in mine, no one noticed the beaded sweat on my temple that I subtly wiped away nor the darkened shadows that had crept across the floor around them.

I let out a relieved sigh that unfortunately drew the violet eyed shifter's attention towards me.

"I hear there was quite the commotion on the rooftops this morning." He winked at Emon and I. "I'm sorry I missed out on all the foreplay before the meeting."

No one saw the master healer's hand until the sound of a loud smack upside the shifter's head echoed in the room.

Penina snickered, tossing her apple core on the table before grabbing another one, her foot bouncing to a beat only she could hear.

"Oww, what the fuck was that for healer?" The violet eyed shifter turned snarling.

"You know what it was for," Jarquinn pointed out. "Now behave and don't make me do it again."

"Don't worry, my friend," Penina cooed through a mouthful of apple. Eshe grimaced across the table. "Your stamina would not have been able to keep up with those two. We all know you're a *short sprinter.*"

"Do not provoke him, Sythe! And get your feet off the table." The master healer's ice blue eyes glowed with purpose but he could not stop the twitching of his lips breaking into a smile.

Laughter seized the room. Penina's comment had been well timed...almost purposefully timed.

The young shifter's brown eyes turned on me knowingly. Glancing down at Emon's hand in mine, she winked.

Emon chuckled next to me, seeing her just as I did and withdrew his hand without anyone noticing.

Penina turned her attention back to her new apple biting into it with an overzealous crunch, her feet still on the table.

When the laughter died down, Emon cleared his throat and sat straighter in his seat. Everyone noticed the subtle shift in power. I knew if I turned on my aura sight now, I would be blinded by his might. "Now that the introductions are done let us move onto more important matters."

The tattooed shifter with piercings and purple eyes growled low in his throat. "Not so fast. Aren't you going to introduce me to beauty?"

The king's eyes widened with mocking shock. "Oh did I forget you twinkle toes? Apologies. General Dark, meet dickhead."

His friend chuckled and shook his head. "I don't need you to introduce me, you self entitled prick." Jarquinn's hand twitched on the table. "I am General Tyr Cloud, leader of the West Isle armies, beauty. Feel free to come to me when you're ready to dust yourself off. I'll take pleasure in being the first to break you in."

Emon snarled softly but I laughed.

"You can't break what's already broken, shifter, but even as a rustic relic you're no match for me." I shrugged. "But if you want pointers in areas that you're *lacking*, I'll be happy to oblige."

His violet eyes twinkled as he stretched his arms out welcoming. "Inspect me anytime, beauty."

Emon lunged into his vision. "There will be no fucking inspecting anyone!" he hissed. "Yet, you wonder why I don't introduce you to anyone."

Tyr grinned, his fangs showing off in the morning sun. "It's because you always find it so hard to share your love for me with any other."

Emon stared at his general for a long moment while everyone held their breath, then he snorted. "If that is what you wish to believe." He scanned his inner circle with a mixture of both love and sternness. "Before I get to why I called you all here, would anyone like to share something of concern to them?"

There was a quiet silence before Penina piped in. "Freya's pastie cart has a new flavor."

Everyone groaned.

"I know it! I hate it when she does that." Quinn looked up from his hands, his crystal blue eyes full of anxiety.

"Aye, son," added Master Riss, "everyone knows her traditional pasties are the best."

Emon stared down the healer's son with concern. "What's the new flavor then?"

My lips pressed together to keep from laughing at the serious way they were discussing a change in menu.

"Lamb and parsnips with tarragon," Quinn groaned.

"Lamb?" Emon frowned then swiveled to Eshe. "What's going on with our beef stock? Did Gain raise the prices again?"

Eshe rolled her eyes exasperatedly. "Of course he did, your majesty. The moment you left actually. I am sure beef pasties will be back on the menu soon enough with word of your return. It's likely Gain saw your morning run this morning and peed his pants knowing what that would mean."

The shifter king grunted. "I'm not giving him reprieve. Put Gain on the community cycle next month. Let him service the very neighbors he has been ripping off."

Eshe nodded. "With pleasure."

"Which reminds me...when is my next rotation?"

I frowned. The king of shifters did community service?

Emon noticed and winked. "Don't look so shocked, how do you think I stay in such good shape?"

Penina gurgled around her apple. "Don't let him fool you. He takes the easiest jobs."

Emon bristled. "There has to be some perk to being king."

Everyone rolled their eyes. I sensed this wasn't their first conversation regarding the manner.

"There is an open spot for nymph duty, your highness." Eshe fluttered her eyelashes and everyone sniggered.

Emon rubbed that scruff of his beard, his lips thinning with a grimace. "Anyone want to trade?"

The room was silent. Even Jarquinn, the *ancient* fae healer, looked disturbed.

I dared to break the stoic silence. "What is nymph duty?"

"Babysitting, beauty," Tyr called down. "Those little demons go wild when they know their parents go away for their great hunts once a month. They fucking terrorize the city."

I raised a comic brow at all of them and bit at my lip. "You are afraid of watching baby nymphs?" I turned towards the king who was rubbing his hands against his pants with nervousness. "Even you?"

Emon flinched. "I'd rather face down a full flight of dragons or better yet your shadows then those little beasts."

I choked. Then snorted. Then a burst of laughter bubbled out from me and once it started it could not stop. I felt tears roll down my cheeks and my stomach pull in my hilarity. Wheezing, I was able to control myself into soft giggles, wiping my eyes with the palm of my hand.

"You do all realize—" I chortled again and then took a deep breath to calm myself. "That baby nymphs naturally go into a deep sleep when their parents hunt in the wild? Their mothers and fathers leave them with siren songs they collect from conch shells. A week long lullaby to keep their little terrors in a deep sleep," I snickered.

Silence. Dead silence. Even Penina's foot stopped bouncing on the table.

"Eshe," Emon said softly, "I want an immediate rush on siren cursed conch shells. The faster the better."

I shook my head, more laughter escaping me.

"Consider it done, your majesty." Eshe nodded with determination set in her eyes.

"And take Quinn with you when you go to see Gain," he added.

Quinn sat straighter in his chair, a hopeful expression crossing his handsome face. I glanced at Eshe next to him who did not seem to share a similar sentiment.

"No need. I can handle Gain."

The king sighed. "I have no doubt you can *handle* him. I am hoping to avoid that."

Eshe pouted. "Of course your majesty."

Emon's authority swept across the table like the cool morning breeze snaking through the windows. "Anything else?"

Across the table the master healer cleared his throat. "General Tyr received word from the Red Cap Mountains requesting your presence when you've returned home," he said softly, giving the king a pointed look.

The air seemed to be sucked from the very room, every shifter in the room inhaling with stiff forms, their expressions solemn.

Emon drummed his fingers on the table and inhaled deeply. "So be it, it seems I will be needing to go there anyway." His stern gaze casted across the room. "If that is all, then I have some very grave news."

# CHAPTER 46

I TOOK A MENTAL picture of the moment. Memorized the faces of my friends with my soulmate at my side, knowing this would likely be the last time we would find ourselves all together like this ever again.

Slowly, I spoke, "Faerie's lands are suffering just like ours and the blood wraiths are becoming bolder. They are attacking outside the deadlands. Their attack on our city will be inevitable, the wards must hold for the safety of our people."

Tyr snarled. "Let them come. I am ready for them."

I shook my head. "This is not a fight we are prepared for my friend. We must make sure that Finlandia is never exposed. It must remain hidden for the sake of the lives living here."

"I will have the elementals strengthen the wards then and push our armies outside the city for their training," Tyr responded evenly.

"Why now?" Quinn said. "Since the first death of the lands, the blood wraiths had always stayed within them. What has changed?"

"Time," I confessed. "It has been almost a hundred years since the gateway to the Sanguine had last opened. It will again, in less than a fortnight."

Remnants head snapped to me.

Eshe frowned. "The Sanguine lands? You are insinuating that the death of our lands and the blood wraiths are of Sanguine power? How long have you known this?"

I challenged the fear swirling in my friend's eyes. "I suspected but did not know for sure. It is my responsibility, as your king, to keep you safe. With that comes the weight of *when and if* I need to share information. Today is that day."

Remnant's breathing increased. She was piecing it together...where Deirdre had been hiding all these years.

"But it was destroyed." Eshe looked around the room to see any confirmation from the others.

I sighed. "I wish it were so. The blood fae were destroyed by the goddess...not the lands. Not the power."

Eshe shook her head. "But who can use it? Only the blood fae could wield the Sanguine and as you said the goddess wiped them out. The water fae attempted it once with the blood crystals and it practically destroyed them."

I turned to Remnant.

Her gaze searched mine worriedly then her chin tilted high and her shoulders squared. "I'm with you."

Holding the courageous strength in those emerald eyes, I delivered the next blow. "There is one who can. Deirdre. The Queen of Faerie."

The room exploded. Curses and conjectures filled the room.

Remnant's eyes never left mine and amid the chaos, she reached her hand across to me. It was then that I noticed that they were trembling.

Her palm flattened against mine before she whispered just audibly for me. "Breathe Emon."

I took a deep breath.

Penina's feet dropped from the table and her hands slammed onto its surface startling everyone into silence. My assassin friend did not often explode with anger and when she did it was best to listen.

"Impossible. She's dead. *They* are dead," she growled viciously towards me.

Remnant turned calmly towards her. "It is not impossible. Emon is right. Deirdre is the only one who would dare wield the Sanguine and I have seen it, felt it. It is her."

My eyes widened realizing now that was what had held Remnant from coming to me in The Under.

*"Idiot,"* the beast prowled inside my head, *"You never asked your soulmate what exactly happened there."*

Shocked. I stared at my soulmate's delicate profile and the way the sun outlined her beauty but it was her strength that ensnared me...the energy it took to hold the scars underneath at bay while calmly confronted her demons.

Gently Remnant added, "I didn't want to believe it either, Penina." She sighed. "Believe me when I say, I want her dead more than any of you do."

"Do you?" Eshe interjected with a fearful snarl. "She was your mate, your lover! How do we even know that you're not working with her, that you didn't lead that bitch straight to us!"

Shadows bursted out from Remnant and I jumped to face them, crouched low on the table, blocking Eshe from their threatening darkness and halting their attack on my foolish friend with a commanding gesture.

Gasps rose around us. I knew what they saw. A shifter controlling the power of the most lethal shadow fae to ever have lived but this wasn't control. It was respect. Respect to not kill their mistress' soulmate but even that was a delicate balance.

Keeping my arm outstretched, I snarled over my shoulder to Eshe.

"Sit back down slowly and refrain from speaking again unless it is helpful." Gentling my voice I gave her a concerned look. "Your fear is driving your actions."

Eshe's eyes were frozen on the fierce shadows that blocked out every bit of sun in the room.

"Eshe," I growled lower. After another long moment, she turned her wide eyes on me. "Sit down Eshe, please."

Turning back, I could not see my soulmate through the cloud of terror but I could scent her anger and her pain. "Go to your mistress," I purred gently to the furious shadows, stalking them slowly across the table until they snapped out of existence, and I could see Remnant's beautiful face once more.

Her chest heaved with a gasping breath as I slid off the table and turned her chair to look at me while everyone stayed stoically silent.

"You are thinking you don't belong here," I murmured, studying the wild emerald light in her eyes. "That you are a danger to us all." I looked out across the table. "The truth is, everyone in this room today has felt that at one time or another. Yet we have all bonded together because of that danger, in spite of that alone feeling we have. Together, we honor the scars we cannot heal." Then I shot them all a hard commanding glare. "I have never asked any of you to follow me nor have I ever expected you to agree with my decisions but what I do expect is the same amount of respect and understanding you have given each other towards General Dark. It takes great strength and vulnerability for her to share with you what she has today. Something you all would do well to remember." I nodded to Penina. "Control your anger." Glancing at Eshe, I said softly. "Conquer your fear." Turning back to Remnant, I said sincerely. "Accept you are not better off alone and we need you here. I need you here."

Her jaw clenched. "Perhaps, for now."

Penina blew out a harsh breath. "I'd still like to hear why you think that bitch is alive?"

I arched a brow at my soulmate. "Would you like to explain, General?"

Remnant sighed, turning towards all of them. "I won't presume to know all of your king's reasons but from what I can piece together is that she used the Sanguine to escape me during Morta and fled to the lands of the blood fae where the gateway was sealed once she entered. She has been biding her time in those lands, gaining more power until the gateway opens again."

Her brow arched at me and I responded with a grunt. "Yes. That is what I believe."

Remnant nodded back and hummed. "Deirdre has the power of spirit at her disposal. A power that allows her to manipulate others through the dream world, and she has mastered the ability to project herself into the bodies of others. I believe this has allowed her to infiltrate the water fae courts even from the other side of the gateway. She has been using their leader in The Under to further feed the Sanguine power with blood crystals...it has been draining life from the ocean and all water fae living there. It feeds off them and becomes stronger each day."

Penina clicked her tongue. "But the blood crystals were lost with the City of Atlantis. The crystals could not be harnessed and were destroyed."

"I'm going to stop you all right there." Everyone turned to look at my general with surprise while his finger pointed straight at me. "You were in The Under?" His teeth flashed with the feral grin he directed at me.

I groaned and wiped my hand down my face. "Now isn't the time for this, Tyr. But yes. Our lovely shadow fae led us into a den of water snakes and a kraken."

"That's what took you so long?" Remnant's brows raised when she looked back at me.

I smirked. "Impressed?"

She snorted and rolled her eyes. "Not at all, shifter. I was too busy dealing with a water dragon."

I gaped at her before I threw my head back and howled with laughter. "Of course you were! I should have known! Never mind that no fae has seen a water dragon since before the goddess left our lands."

"A kraken. Was it him? Was it Cronin?" Penina's eyes flashed with deadly intent, black bleeding into her brown. We had fought to imprison him together, she had wanted to kill him then but I resisted.

"Yes. But he's been taken care of, permanently." My voice was hard and she stiffened at the tone, and I waited for the soft brown to return back to her normally kind eyes.

Tyr rapped his knuckles obnoxiously on the table to pull everyone's attention from our assassin friend, keeping her secret safe. "We are losing focus. Tell me you didn't pussy out?"

I wanted to rip his head off except I knew Tyr. Knew him better than any of the others here. The first time we had met was when we were just young cubs. Unknown to my parents, I had been recklessly exploring the Red Caps during the blood wars and found him paralyzed by the emotional turmoil the mountains contained from the death surrounding us.

It took me a week to pull him out of it and then another week to recover from the punishment my father had delivered upon me when he found us emerging safe onto the mountain's summit. It was the first time I had ever seen pure fear in my father's eyes.

I never uttered a single word that Tyr had been the reason I was gone for so long. And when each lash hit my hide, Tyr's eyes never left mine and in them I saw my pain...the slight flinch in his body, the way his breath held tight with each punishing blow, the tears pooling in his amethyst eyes. All a reflection of me.

That was when I knew...Tyr was an empath, an incredibly strong one.

From that day forward he never left my side. A constant and loyal friend in this fucked up world we lived in and his exterior demeanor, at times most unsavory, was his form of protection from the world's emotions that plagued him everyday. Tyr felt *everything*...and in turn taught himself to feel *nothing*.

And today, there was too much tension in the room for him to handle, he was cutting it down the only way he knew how.

I ran my hand through my hair with aggravation. "Yes."

My friend leaned in excitedly. "And?"

"Growers...hidden beneath their scales." I rubbed the back of my neck sheepishly with heat pooling across my face.

Penina snickered and Quinn gave a quiet chuckle. Eshe and Jarquinn rolled their eyes in annoyance.

It was made worse when Remnant added dryly, "Your king also had the enjoyment of experiencing said *growing* after the fool drank water fae ambrosia."

There was stunned silence and then...Tyr's roaring laughter rattled the walls. Penina giggled next to us, and suddenly...the air in the room lightened.

I playfully scowled down at Remnant, locking my body in my chair to keep from kissing her with pure gratitude. There was no doubt that she was one of us already...she belonged here.

"And I'm still feeling the effects of your remedy to that, General."

Remnant shrugged. "Like I told you, it was necessary."

"There had to be another way," I retorted.

She shrugged again. "Perhaps but it wouldn't have been as satisfying."

I snorted at that.

Tyr pounded the table, rattling the polished wood with his raucous laughter. "I was fucking right! You know what that means."

I did. It had been a boyhood wager...one that was coming back to bite me in the ass.

Tyr winked. "You can pay up later."

"How kind of you," I growled low.

He shook his head, the heavy bar piercings on his tapered ears clinking. "Still can't believe you were in The Under though."

"Afraid of water, shifter. Let me guess—" Remnant tapped her finger to her lips, "you're a wee little kitty cat."

I scrubbed at my face with a groan. These two were going to be a problem.

"Nothing about me is wee, beauty. And I'm not afraid of being wet, I just prefer my females that way."

"For Faerie's sake!" Jar exclaimed and smacked Tyr upside the head again. This time it was hard enough to almost faceplant him into the hard wooden table.

Penina covered for him. "I do believe we have...*got off*...topic." And then winked at Tyr who's head popped up with a grin, his hand extended in an air high five.

Jar rubbed his temples. "Goddess help us all," he muttered.

I snorted and Remnant grinned, shooting me a comical look.

"My question still remains unanswered," Penina continued, propping her bare feet back up on the table, relaxed once again. Jar glared at the tiny gold adorned toes. "How were the blood crystals not destroyed when Atlantis fell?"

Remnant sighed. "The blood crystals did indeed disappear with Atlantis but they were not destroyed. Nor was the city. It was how I was able to come here from The Under."

There was only one way that was possible.

"The whirlpool gateways are still active?" Awe gracing my tone.

"Apparently." She shrugged.

"That may come in handy."

Remnant shook her head. "I've been told that they are only a one way portal now."

Tyr whistled. "Should we expect an armada of angry water fae on our shores?"

"I did some house cleaning before I returned home," I purred. "The water fae have taken a huge blow...I doubt they will be mounting an attack on us anytime soon. Our main focus should be stopping Deirdre from coming through the Sanguine gateway."

Remnant crossed her arms when I ignored her inquisitive look. "I don't know about water fae..." She narrowed her eyes with thought. "But I believe fortifying your shores against blood wraiths if able would be appropriate. There were almost a full score of them inside Atlantis when I escaped there."

"Done," Tyr snapped, no questions asked. I gave him a small smile. He respected her.

Penina cursed. "Do we know if the blood wraiths can use these crystals if they are in The Under?"

My brows furrowed. "Perhaps I may be able to find some answers about that in one of my texts," I attempted to reassure them.

"Your majesty, if I may?" Jar's bright blue eyes were full of unease.

I nodded in earnest.

The master healer stapled his fingers in front of him. "I feel that some truths need to be told behind the Sanguine. Truths that you will not find in the history books you love so much Daemon," he paused, tapping his fingers, drawing our attention further in. "As you all know the Sanguine was more than just a power, it was also a court, the blood fae court."

Nods of understanding came from around the room.

Jarquinn continued, "The blood fae held a tremendous power we now refer to as the Sanguine. With this power came the ability to control any living lifeform through their blood...like a puppet. They were the world's deadliest manipulators and often created mischief with other courts. Except this terrible power came with a terrible price...it drained the blood fae of their own immortality and they aged. Quite unlike the rest of us, who stop aging in our thirtieth year and become fully mature in our centum."

"Let me guess..." Penina drawled. "They didn't like that."

Jar gave her a pointed look. "No. They did not. Nor would you if you had been in their place. Their power destroyed them. Imagine if shifting destroyed you."

Penina's lips thinned. "I get your point, healer."

He nodded. "Be sure that you do, my cub." He looked down at the table to me. "Their resentment of their own power turned onto the rest of us and they quickly found that they could quite literally suck our immortality by drinking our blood. Not only did they become youthful again but their power heightened." Jar visibly shivered as if he were lost in an old memory. "The more powerful the fae they drank from, the longer their youth lasted. They started to become more animal than fae, hunting the ancients first as their favored blood source since our blood was more potent. It was dark times and I lost many loved ones from the blood fae's unquenchable thirst. Including my beloved." He looked sadly over at Quinn. "Your mother was one of them. It was that moment that I turned my attention to healing rather than killing, a path that was too little too late for our family. I am sorry, my son."

"I know you would have saved her if you could have, father," Quinn said quietly.

The healer's blue eyes sparkled with tears. "It wasn't until our most powerful and revered seer from the elemental court was slaughtered that we collectively reached our breaking point. The blood wars were the result of the shifter, elemental, and shadow court joining forces to stop the blood fae once and for all."

"Who was the seer?" Penina twirled a piercing on her furrowed brow.

Jar looked at my soulmate. "Her name was Talgira," he said solemnly.

"Deirdre's mother," Remnant breathed.

Jarquinn nodded. "Yes. Talgira was a wise and kind fae, with very powerful insight. She was able to see blood fae attacks and thwart their plans quite effectively. We all looked to her for safety but that also made her a target. She was sent into hiding, away from her family, with a powerful and brutal ancient shifter fae we all voted for as a guard for her. A shifter king we all know as Daemon's father, Asher Windswift Strider."

I inhaled sharply. "He never told me any of this."

Jar gave me a sympathetic look. "Because to his greatest shame, your father failed although it was never his fault. As I said before, Talgira was a very powerful seer, an ancient like myself, and she was shown a vision. One of our world dying if she stayed in hiding. Those were the words she left behind hastily scrawled out on parchment before she drugged the shifter king into a deep sleep." He bowed his head. "Her drained husk of a body was found a week later on our shores along with her newborn grandson protected tightly in her arms."

Remnant looked out the sunlit window. "Deirdre's son."

"Goddess," whispered Eshe, a hand covering her mouth with horror.

"That is why...that is why the queen hates us so much," Penina whispered. "She blamed the shifters for the death of her mother and her son...killing our queen was her retribution."

Jar slanted eyes closed. "Sadly, yes," he sighed and swept aside his blonde hair. "You all must understand that grief can either form us into something dark and twisted or allow us to grow into something more, it can fuel our vengeance or deliver us peace. It is a choice we make, at times without notice. Deirdre made her choice and never looked back."

I heeded Jar's advice and let go of the deep hurt in my chest from knowing that my mother was killed for misplaced revenge. "But why want the very power that destroyed her own mother and son?"

Jar sighed. "The thirst for power is a vicious cycle and thirst for justice even more so...while searching for it, the lines blur, and we often become the villain in our own story." He looked at me pleadingly. "Be sure to understand, Daemon, that Deirdre led us through the blood wars, without her, many fae would have perished. None of us knew that her grief was festering beneath the strong front she held for all of us during those dark times. If we had...if I had. I would have stopped it."

I gave him a sad smile, knowing the toll it took for Jar to be the cause of one's death and not the preventer of it. "You are like a father to me, Jar. I would never have blamed you even if you had. But thank you for telling me that."

His blue eyes gazed at me thoughtfully and then he sighed. "There is more." Tapping his fingers together he continued. "Deirdre was insistent on destroying the blood fae entirely...like we all were. But without Talgira, we had no way of defending ourselves during their attacks and with each victory of theirs, with each feeding, they got stronger and stronger. So much blood was spilled during that time that the mountains turned red...and stayed that way. Like the vile red cap creatures who soaked their hats in the blood of their kills, the mountains did the same with the blood shed of our people. We call them the Red Cap Mountains now because of that, but they were never that color when I was young."

I glanced at Tyr who sat very still in his chair and I knew he was remembering those caves. There would be no lightening the mood for him. Sometimes we just had to feel...and learn from it.

Jar held our attention when he leaned in and flattened his hands on the smooth polished wood. "That amount of bloodshed drew the ire of our Goddess Faerie and along with her...her two god brothers—"

"I'm sorry but did you say brothers?" We all stared with wide shock when Remnant gasped. "The goddess has brothers?!"

# CHAPTER 47

Emon

J AR'S LIPS THINNED AND then grunted. "Yes, she has brothers. Very few have memories of them, their existence erased from most fae after the blood wars by the Goddess herself."

"How is it you have remembered, father?" Quinn asked, concern etched on his face.

Jarquinn regarded his son thoughtfully. "As a healer, my body continually heals itself with my manifested power. My memories cannot be altered, when they are...my power just heals itself and the memory comes back." He sighed deeply, "It is a curse as much as a blessing. There are many things I'd like to forget but cannot." Then he smiled at Quinn, the love for his son shining bright in his eyes. "But then again, there are many memories that I am blessed to remember so vividly."

I narrowed my eyes on the master healer. My father had told me once, after one of many philosophical lessons from Jarquinn, to not listen to the words the ancient had to say...but the words he did not. That was where the real truth was. "What risk does this put you in, telling us this, if it's something we should not know, Jar?"

He grinned at me. Pride shining in his eyes. "None that I cannot handle, my clever cub. Do not fret, Sheol will not come for me this day."

I growled low, "Be that it will not come ever. We need you Jar."

His slanted blue eyes held mine. "Even you cannot make such a promise, my king."

Snarling, I looked around the room. My need to protect the ancient fae like he was my own father thundered in my blood. "None of this information leaves this room. Vow it now or leave before any more truths are to be told. I will not hold it against you."

"I'm too comfortable to leave at this point." Tyr emphasized his comfort by nestling more into his chair.

Penina wiggled her feet. "Same. I'm in 'til the end of the end."

Jar gave her a thoughtful look and my gaze darted between them. Penina held most of her own secrets close to her heart but every once in a while it was as if she left us clues to find them.

Quinn nodded dutifully but his face was lined with worry. "Of course I am with you my king. I vow it."

"I vow to never share the tale you are about to tell. We love you Jar." Eshe gave the healer a loving smile.

Everyone turned to the stoic shadow fae at my side who was watching Penina intimately just like I had been. She looked up with surprise when the silence was too obvious and her eyes darted around the table.

"Me? You're asking me? Of course I vow it. I've had a damned target on my back since the day of my birth. There is no other way to live for me."

Jarquinn's sky blue eyes gazed at her with the same love he held for all of us. "So be it." He waved his hands around the room, spinning his tale. "In the beginning the Goddess Faerie did not create this world alone. She had help, the help of her two brothers. Shea her older brother, the god of death, and Ichor her youngest brother, the god of blood. While Shea had a realm of his own to rule we often refer to as Sheol, Ichor did not." He chuckled at the surprised looks around the room before he continued, "As an act of gratitude for assisting her in creating Faerie, she granted her two brothers the ability to create two species of their own in their like image, a species she called the fae. Shea's creations were creatures of the night and he bestowed upon them powers to manipulate darkness. He named them the Shadow Fae." The master healer gave Remnant a pointed look before continuing. "The blood fae were Ichor's creation, created in his own image and he gifted them a small fraction of his power we call the Sanguine. Faerie then created the rest of the courts...the shifters, the elementals, and the water fae. And so the era of the fae began. The God Shea returned to his own realm, leaving the shadow fae to live under his sister's rule but the younger brother remained having no realm of his own, he wanted to watch over his creations along with his sister. Faerie indulged him, for she loved her brothers, especially her youngest...even if he always craved for more."

Jarquinn's eyes became distant and Tyr shifted uncomfortably in his seat, wary of the ancient healer lost in forgotten memories.

"When the wars reached their peak," he began again, still distant, "we realized it wasn't just the hunger that drove the blood fae but also the encouraging whisperings of the God Ichor. For he craved the entire world for himself, a world of his own to rule. By the time his sister noticed Ichor's influence had spread, the damage was already done. Their feud clashed in a brutal force of power that even to this day, I hope to never witness again."

Quinn stood abruptly and rushed to his fathers side. Placing his own healing hand on Jar's shoulder. "Father?"

Jar shook his head, murmuring words that even my shifter hearing could not make out. The rest of us stayed deathly silent. It was foolish to provoke an ancient unless it was life or death and since the time I could remember I had always been respectful of the power Jar held at bay. There was a reason he chose the art of healing instead of death.

Blinking back the haunted memories, Jar's hand shook as he placed it over his son's supportive hold. "We were all pawns in the games of war for the gods and Ichor had many years to plan his conquest. Faerie's grip on her brother began to slip." He gave us all a pointed look. "You all must understand that much of her power is utilized to sustain the world she loves, fighting her brother and keeping the lands stable weakened her greatly. So she sent one fae deep into the depths of Sheol to recover her absentee older brother, in hopes that he would agree to turn the tide of the war in her favor."

"Shea," Remnant murmured, her brow furrowed as she listened.

Jarquinn's eyes twinkled. "Yes. Shea, the god of death, initially wanted nothing to do with the battle, seeing it merely a squabbling feud between his two siblings. He had his own realm to rule and it was currently flourishing from the influx of souls the blood war created."

"What convinced him then?" Penina interrupted.

"Not what...but who." Jarquinn's eyes leveled on Remnant and the whole room turned to gawk at her.

She snorted and let out a small laugh. "Really? I hadn't even come into my powers yet and was doing my training in The Under during that time." Remnant cocked her head. "You have an art for story telling, Master Healer, so I'll ask what everyone wants to know. Who was it that Faerie sent?" Remnant inquired.

Jarquinn smiled. "*She* was a stubbornly fierce, intelligent, and beautiful shadow fae named Eve—"

Remnant froze next to me and her shadows sprung upwards, cloaking my soulmate in darkness. "My mother? My mother was the one Faerie sent to Sheol," she whispered, shocked from the information.

I frowned. Either Eve never shared this information with Remnant or rather could not. As Jar had said, all of our minds had been erased of such knowledge.

Jarquinn nodded sadly. "Yes, your mother Eve saved us all really. She convinced the God Shea to join his sister Faerie for the good of our world. Together, God and Goddess defeated the blood fae but at a great cost. As a god of death, Shea was bound by a set of rules, one of them being that he was never to interact with our world. If he did, a price had to be paid."

"Our memories," Eshe whispered.

"Indeed. But I do believe that he suffered a worse punishment for his partaking. We will never know for sure."

I cleared my throat. "What of this brother god, Ichor?"

Jar sighed. "Not having the heart to kill her own brother, Faerie allowed him to flee after she killed the last of his creations but not before bitter Ichor delivered a final crushing blow. In his wake he left a terrible, awful curse. One meant to cruelly torture his sister in the most festering of ways."

My brows arched and I growled, "He made us sterile."

Jar nodded. "Yes, your majesty. Blood is life, as much as Faerie has the power to nourish life and Shea has the power to take it, Ichor has the power to gift it."

I snarled. "He took life from us in the only way he could without the blood fae to manipulate."

"Yes and there has not been a faeling conceived since that day. Those born after the blood wars were already in the womb of their mothers. Until no," he added.

Eshe spoke with a shaky voice, "The faeling. What does it mean then? Has the curse been lifted?" The fragile hope in her eyes was almost painful to see. Like most of us, Eshe longed for a child of her own.

"The faeling is...unique. She was warded with the power of the Sanguine...it was literally altering her life essence...turning her into something she was not born to be."

I growled. "What the fuck does that mean? If she is not water fae then what is she?"

Jarquinn shook his head. "I have no way of knowing yet. Her healing sleep will reveal much but not until she wakes, which won't be for some time now. What I do know is that with the wards lifted, she will become what she was meant to be at birth."

"It doesn't matter what she is. What does matter is that those blood wraiths wanted her in The Under and I will kill anyone who attempts to take her from me," Remnant snarled and the hairs on my arms stood up at the lethal tone of her voice while the mate in me purred with admiration of her protective nature.

I leveled Jar with a stern look. "If the wraiths were after her in The Under then that means she is vital to Deirdre's plans." He nodded and I shifted my gaze to Tyr. "The faeling is under full protection of the crown and this city. We must be even more heavily prepared for any attacks that may come."

"Acknowledged, sire," Tyr growled, then tilted to Remnant snarling, "I will make sure not a fucking thing gets near her, beauty."

Penina tossed the apple she had finished an hour ago onto the table and Eshe sent her a disgusted look.

"To sum this fucking mess up. Our memories were erased about a war between gods that caused us to be cursed with infertility. In the meantime, Faerie is still missing, our lands are dying, blood wraiths are extending past the deadlands, and Deirdre is alive and well—likely to appear in just a few weeks from a gateway that's been closed for one hundred years, and this faeling is the key to unlocking our future." She rolled her tongue along her teeth, a strange light lit in her eyes. "Did I miss anything?"

I watched the expressions on my family's faces and knew it would stay ingrained in my memory forever.

Penina's held conviction, Tyr's eyes glittered with the prospect of battle, Jarquinn looked on solemnly at his son who gave him a reassuring nod, Eshe's lips thinned with stubborn resolve, and a shadow storm was brewing around Remnant—the darkness shifting in her emerald eyes along with the shadows cloaking her.

"Fuck," I snarled.

# CHAPTER 48

Emon

"WHERE ARE YOU TAKING me?" Remnant folded her arms across her chest. She had thrown on her leather vest and boots but still wore her tight black shorts that fit snugly around her shapely ass where her ponytail brushed against it with each aggravated stride. "I should be with Riella."

I stole a glance at her. She was still vexed that the master healer had kicked her out of the healing rooms.

*"An idle shadow fae is never a good omen. There is no work for you to do here right now, forta. I will protect her. Now get out!"*

Then he pushed my soulmate out the door and straight into my arms.

I flexed my hands, still feeling how right it felt holding her. "I thought you had a desire to *inspect* Tyr's armies." I nodded for her to follow as we strolled outside the city to the training yards.

"As I recall, you were not too keen on that concept, your majesty."

I gave her a wry look. "I am always up for seeing Tyr get knocked down a peg or two. I'm sure that is the kind of inspection you're implying, right, little umbra?"

Remnant snorted. "And if I wasn't? He is, after all, quite formidable and handsome."

I stooped to growl low in her ear. "Then I'll simply just have to kill him. I seem to have an abundance of generals around here all of a sudden. Would you like the job?"

Her steps faltered and I steadied her with a guiding hand, laughing.

Ignoring her fierce glare, I added, "Besides the inspection, I have a surprise I want to share with you."

"A surprise? Don't surprises usually come in some form of a gift? Chocolate, flowers, jewelry?"

This time *my steps* faltered and my head snapped down to study her gorgeous smirking face. She was mocking me but I saw something else flash in her eyes—excitement...desire.

"I suppose..." I said slowly...cautiously, "if that male were courting said fae. Would chocolate, flowers, and jewelry please you, little umbra?"

Her cheeks turned pink and she shifted uncomfortably. "Absolutely not."

I released a low chuckle, murmuring, "Perhaps a pet then, something beastly."

She hissed, "You're irritating me."

I chuckled darkly again. "That wasn't a no."

*"I do hope you're not thinking of using me to woo your female, fairy boy. In my day your own prowess was all that was needed to impress a female. You must be lacking in this area."* The beast yawned at me.

I growled low and Remnant looked at me startled. "Something wrong?"

*"Evidently his show of prowess,"* the cat snickered in response.

*"Goddess, I hate you,"* I shot back at him, grateful that Remnant could not hear his pompous ass. I gave Remnant a reassuring smile. "I'm fine, little umbra. General Tyr!" I shouted out to the tiger shifter who just sent one of his warriors sprawling across the dirt and was preparing for a second attack.

Tyr's head snapped up and a slow smile spread across his face. Reaching down he picked up his fallen comrade and dusted him off. Touching his forehead to the trainee's he murmured a few choice words before he shoved him away with a snarl. The trainee scrambled to his feet and then started running like his ass was on fire.

Tyr turned then and sauntered towards us. "Your majesty," he purred, before bowing low. "Twice in one day, what an honor." He winked at me and then looked over at Remnant, puffing out his chest. "General Dark, come for my inspection have you?"

I groaned, regretting bringing her here already. How could she think him *formidable*?

*"Don't forget handsome,"* the cat cooed.

Remnant rolled her eyes. "I'm not interested in whipping out our dicks to start measuring who's bigger, General Tyr. It's a male weakness I appreciate not having."

*"Now that's prowess. Take notes from your soulmate, fairy boy."* The cat chuckled.

Reluctantly I agreed, laughing softly.

Tyr grinned. "Then you're just not using a dick correctly, beauty."

I snorted. "Cut the shit, Tyr. You know why we are here." I shot him a warning glare.

Tyr winked at me, his violet eyes glittered humorously. "This is going to be fun." Then he turned and bellowed, "Elemental twins to me! The rest of you ass-wipes take a hike. Literally. I want a perimeter patrol!"

Remnant's eyes narrowed on my general. The elemental twins were not twins really. Not even fucking close. But they were inseparable, I had never seen them apart since they came here.

Her eyes trailed off of Tyr and then froze. A small gasp leaving her lush lips as two elemental fae came into sight. They halted in front of her, their eyes rounding with just as much shock as Remnant's.

My soulmate stepped forward stumbling with the violent shaking of her body and my hand snapped out to steady her. Her scent was strong with equal amounts of fear and hope.

She brushed off my hand with a growl and I frowned. Perhaps this was a mistake.

"Xi? Riley?" Remnant's head bowed then, her knees collapsing to the ground, and her palms raised outwards to them. "Forgive me. Oh goddess, please forgive me," she sobbed brokenly.

Panic and concern roared to life inside me and I moved to gather the remaining shreds of my broken soulmate in my arms. I was wrong, she wasn't ready for this.

Tyr's heavily tattooed arm shot across my chest, effectively restraining me.

I turned to snarl viciously in his face, "Unhand me, now. That's a fucking order."

Tyr met me head on with his own low whispered snarl, "No. She needs this."

I gnashed my teeth in his face but before I could say another word the cry of the elemental drew my attention back to my bowed soulmate.

"General? Is it really you?" The green haired elemental, Riley Dragoon, rushed towards Remnant, sliding on his knees to wrap her up in his arms. "Goddess save me, it is you! Xi, come quickly, our general has finally returned to us!"

Xi Chin didn't hesitate a moment longer, running towards them both she slid to her knees and shakily tucked her white shoulder length hair back from her face to regard her general with loving adoration.

Shocked, both Tyr and I stared openly at the exposed beauty of Xi's gray eyes shimmering with tears. It was the first time I had ever seen the other half of her face and she was stunning. "The king always knew you were alive, but we had almost lost all hope...I can't believe you are finally here with us!" Her tears fell, staining the olive tones of her skin.

Remnant shook her bowed head. "I failed you. I failed you both so much. Please forgive me. "

The anguish in Remnant's voice nearly undid me and my chest rumbled. My body yearning to prevent the pain I felt radiating off my soulmate. Tyr's arm tightened against my chest but this time I didn't bother retaliating against it. Begrudgingly, I had to admit the bastard was right. Remnant needed this.

"Oh Rem, my general," Xi sobbed, then draped her body over the trembling Remnant and her companion Riley, who still hadn't pulled away. "You have never once failed us. We failed you Rem. We failed to protect *you*."

Riley nodded against Remnant's side, his body trembling with grief. "We are so sorry we could not be there to help you—" he choked, "to save you."

Remnant's head reared up and grasped her friends' shoulders, pushing them away to study them both fully. They smiled sadly back at her, both shedding tears of happiness. "I cannot believe...I cannot hope, it's really you," she whispered.

Xi laughed and swiped her tears away, she gripped Remnant's hand on her shoulder. "Well fucking believe it, general. We are alive. You're alive. Thank the goddess!" She lunged forward, hugging Remnant tightly to her chest.

Riley snickered. "I can see your struggle, Xi revealing her face and giving out free hugs. It is quite unbelievable."

"Shut up Ri," both females mumbled together and without pulling away, tugged him inward. Laughing again, he wrapped his arms tightly around them both like they were the most precious thing in this world.

A gift.

I swallowed hard and looked away. The bond between the three of them was clearly the same as it was for my own strange family.

Tyr's eyes met mine and I knew he felt the same. He cleared his throat and thumped my chest heartedly before dropping his arm from me with a wink.

I grunted back.

"How?" Remnant choked out and I gritted my teeth when she touched Riley's face reverently. "How is this possible?"

The green haired elemental glanced over my soulmate's shoulder towards me and then pulled her hand from his face, cupping it in his own. I raised my brows, he had always been an intelligent little bastard.

Riley gave her a sad smile. "We went south when you disappeared. Hoping to find any trace that would lead us to where you were. We never believed the queen's tales...that you betrayed us all."

Xi finished for him, "When word of Deirdre murdering any fae she thought was associated with you and hanging them on the gates, we knew something went terribly wrong and that we had to return. But we were too late—" Xi choked. "We thought we lost you forever and when the shifter king found us we were prepared to join you in death. Except he offered us a home and the promise that he would find you, that you were alive." She glanced up at me and smiled. "Thank you for delivering on your promise, my king."

My voice rumbled with emotion. "It was my pleasure. Shifters enjoy a good hunt."

*"If you call nearly dying half a dozen times hunting, fairy boy,"* my beast snorted.

Remnant looked over her bare shoulder at me. "If you have been searching for me all this time then when was the last time you were home?"

Tyr raised his hand and shot a glare in my direction. "I can answer that. It's been fifty two years and thirty six days since he was last home. I should know since he tied me up before leaving us all behind...again. Insistent that he would find you on his own."

I flinched but held Remnant's startled expression, the same question rolling in her thoughts that she always had but still hadn't had the courage to ask me yet. *Why?*

Our bond was becoming harder and harder to temper, especially since The Under, when she unintentionally claimed me.

I held her stunned emerald gaze. "Like I said before, little umbra. You're worth it. Every minute of it." I grinned. "You didn't make it easy, though."

Riley's knowing gaze turned on me. "She found you, didn't she?"

I flashed my fangs at him.

"I knew it," he laughed, along with Xi who shook her head with disbelief.

She held my gaze for a moment longer. "I don't understand you, but I am grateful," she said softly and my heart sputtered at the vulnerable sound.

I grunted. "You are most welcome."

She searched my face for another moment before turning back to her friends. "If you were there...then you must know. It was me. I destroyed them...killed them all."

Xi's hair fell back over her face when she shook her head. "We do not blame you for what happened in Morta, Rem. Deirdre did this. The goddess curse her putrid soul. You loved her and she betrayed you, betrayed all of us—the people she was supposed to protect." She touched Remnant's chest with her hand. "We know your soul Rem, that you would have taken their place if given the choice."

Remnant's eyes snapped up and her mood darkened. "Then you don't know what my soul is capable of."

Both Xi and Riley stiffened, as if startled to see the stirring darkness revealed by her but I wasn't. It was a part of her and it made her all the more beautiful. Whatever she was capable of, it would be a masterpiece when released. For the good or for the bad of us all.

At that moment, the sky suddenly turned black and the warm Finlandia sun disappeared.

I snarled, stepping towards the scent of my soulmate in the darkness.

# CHAPTER 49

Remnant

I STOOD QUICKLY BUMPING into Emon's chest as I threw a shield of shadow over Riley and Xi who had stood with me. Drawing my sword from the shadow void, I looked up where the sun should have still been shining. My eyes widened at the massive dark swarm.

"Are those—"

"Spy crows," both Emon and Tyr snarled together, their deadly fangs had extended, claws were unsheathed, and their eyes flashed bright with a predatory gleam.

They were feral shifter gods. One a glowing sculpture of bronze, the other a tattooed masterpiece of muscle, and they flanked me as if I was their sacred honor to protect.

Except I didn't need protection.

Averting my gaze I watched the dark swarm of birds, squawking above us. Up close, spy crows were a medium sized bird, all black, except for their beaks which were bright red with sharp sawing teeth. My nose wrinkled with disgust when the frantic beat of their wings brought with them the stench of rotten earth.

I touched the shifter king's arm, drawing his attention back down to me. "They are searching for the city," I breathed.

He nodded. "Tyr, sound the alarm. Fortify the wards. They shouldn't be able to see the city but I'm not taking any fucking chances!"

Tyr cursed violently before he transformed into a large formidable white tiger and raced towards the city of Finlandia.

Emon hissed next to me. "I haven't seen spycrows since my mother's death."

I narrowed my eyes up at the sky and winced at the chilling squawks. "A death omen. It was Deirdre's favorite way to inform her enemies they were her next mark." Fear filled me. "She must know Riella is here!" I lunged in the same direction as the tiger shifter.

Emon's firm grip caught me and tugged hard at my arm, spinning me back around. "I need you, the best way to protect Riella is to make our stance here. Not to bring them towards her. Deirdre would expect that of you...of us."

Wrenching my arm from his grip, I flashed my teeth at him. "Fine but I don't have to like it."

"Do we need to know who this Riella is?" Xi asked, despite having been quiet up to this point.

I glanced back to see both her and Riley drawing their lethal scimitars. They always did favor those curved blades. My shadows still draped lazily around them and they were at perfect ease with their presence, Xi even patted at them against her shoulder with her free hand.

There was a reason they were once part of the shadow forces.

Without time to explain, I used the one term they would understand. "Chickadee."

Xi hummed and Riley nodded. "Riella equals kill anything that threatens her. My favorite kind of mission."

No questions asked.

"I always knew the chickadees meant something to you," Emon said softly next to me, still watching the swarming spy crows that were drawing nearer.

Tyr appeared just a second later, a subtle flash the only sign that he had shifted back. His purple eyes flashed angrily. "Our forces are on their way and reported incoming wraiths from the south."

Emon cracked his neck to the side. "They can cover all of the West Isles sky and search all of her lands but they will never find our city." He glanced over at me. "She will stay safe."

I twirled my blade in my hand and gave him a hard look. "Good. Now what are *my orders*, your majesty?"

His brows raised.

"You said you needed me here. You wanted this alliance...it seems I still have one monarch left to serve." I flipped my blade across my forearm and laid it out to him. "King Daemon Ash Strider, my blade is yours." Bowing my head low, I waited with baited breath. It felt...right and if he rejected me now...my heart may never survive it.

"I accept," he said gruffly.

Exhaling harshly and rising, I stilled at the fierce blazing intensity radiating from his predatory eyes. Enraptured, I could see every one of his emotions in that moment. Hope, admiration, awe, fear...and something else, something that was the answer to all my whys.

I inhaled sharply, stepping back.

Emon blinked, the bright intensity calming.

Growling, he glanced back up at the sky then back down to me. "I need the umbras to take out the spycrows." The birds screeched down upon us, now flocking in the millions over the valley. "Every. Fucking. One. I don't want a single one of those pests surviving."

I grinned. "Oh is that all, my king? And what will you be doing while I do all the hard work?"

Emon chuckled darkly and stepped closer to me. His hand reached outward and tucked back a loose strand of hair from my face. "Avenging your flower pissing gnomes it would seem. There are wraiths out there and I haven't forgotten my promise."

"In that case, save some blood wraiths for me too please," I said sweetly, leaning into his palm. His touch felt way too goddess damn good.

"It's never good when she uses that tone," Xi whispered.

Riley and Tyr grunted in unison, identical wariness in their expression.

Emon ignored them, his hand caressed over my cheek and skimmed my smile with his roughened fingertips. "What a savage blood thirsty shadow fae you are. Shall I hold them down for you while you gut them too?"

I brushed my lips against his hand. "How kind of you, your majesty."

Emon's chest rumbled and his eyes bled with hunger...hunger that wasn't for killing anymore.

We both jumped back when the shadows snapped up between us impatiently.

Emon chuckled and shook his head. Glancing up at my dumbstruck friends he snarled, "Keep your General safe while she takes care of that feathered shit! Tyr you're with me!"

Tyr growled low. His eyes glittering with excitement looking to the south.

I raised my hand and the shadows slithered up it menacingly then plumed above us. "You should go, your majesty. I'll only be a few."

Riley snickered this time. "It never bodes well for us when she uses *that* tone either."

Stepping forward, Emon suddenly gripped my chin. His touch light, but commanding at the same time. "Be sure that you are just a few, for even a mere second not in your presence is a second too long."

His tone was everything dark and sensual and I shivered at the sound of it. If Emon noticed he didn't point it out, instead he gave me one last lingering look before snarling and spinning away, grabbing onto his general who was grinning smugly at his friend.

I didn't bother to watch him leave. I had a job to do and my stomach flipped with a renewed sense of purpose.

"Time to play my loves," I cooed at the shadows.

Raising my hand upwards they exploded with such a force that I had to brace from stumbling backwards.

I felt Xi's strong hand grip my right shoulder, then the firm grip of Riley's on my other.

"Those eager bastards haven't changed one bit, have they?" Xi murmured.

Regaining my balance, I laughed. "Of course not. Would you expect anything else?" The hardest part was never getting the shadows to obey my commands in battle...it was getting them to stop.

The three of us watched with trepidation as they plumed upwards with racing speed straight towards the swirling cloud of spy crows. Darkness versus darkness, the shadows billowed outward like a massive black hole that had torn open the sky.

Raising my other hand, I drew the resting dormant shadows that had spread from the overcast skies and sent them upward to reinforce their sister shadows.

The shadows started to curl, corralling the panicked shrilling birds further and further into their net of darkness. A thunderous boom rippled across the sky before they snapped inwards disappearing completely, along with millions of spy crows.

Not a single one remained as Finlandia's warm sunny rays glowed down on our upturned faces once again.

Riley cleared his throat and released his hand from my shoulder.

Xi blew out a breath, her white hair billowing out from her half covered face, and dropped her hand as well. "That never fails to creep me the fuck out. Every goddess damn time."

I snickered but knew the shadows weren't quite done. I grinned when another snap signaled the start of black shadow feathers raining down on us like celebratory confetti.

I reached up, trailing my fingers lazily through the shadow feathers with dark amusement. "I was wondering where your flourish was...I love the final touch my loves."

The smoke feathers shimmered around us and then oozed back into one ominous cloud hovering near my feet, satiated after their grand feast.

I giggled down at them like an amused parent.

But our reprieve was short lived when a different kind of piercing wail gathered our attention south. The blood wraiths had arrived.

"I don't suppose there is any beauty under those rags," I commented and tapped my shadow sword at my side in thought, finally seeing them more clearly. They were hooded creatures, draped in black decaying robes that appeared to be soaked with deep red blood dripping from the tattered edges. "Let me take a wild guess. Decapitation?"

Riley twirled his scimitar eagerly, his green hair flopping over his brow. "Of course."

Xi stepped next to him, sighing. "Except those bastards don't allow you to get that close without trying to fry you with their blue fire of death. Don't let it hit you...it will spread once you're hit and it burns like a fucking ice plunge in Nocturnes."

I stretched my neck to the side and started walking forward. Emon and his armies were only a few minutes ahead of us. "Sounds mildly challenging. At least I won't get bored killing them."

"Shit," Xi cursed, following behind me. "I hate it when she gets like this. It always ends with me covered in blood."

Riley chuckled darkly, shuffling with relaxed countenance. "You know you both look good in blood."

"I have white hair Ri."

I felt the earth rumble and I knew Xi was drawing on her elemental powers.

"I'm sure one of the shifters will be more than happy to lick you clean afterwards."

Gusts of wind blew around us, Riley was summoning his elemental air power.

"Not the hair Riley...it's not as if they can lick the stains out of my hair. I'll be looking like a goddess damn pink pixie for the next few days."

The earth beneath us splintered with her agitation.

An unnatural gust, forced me to turn around to look at Riley with surprise. He was twirling air around Xi's head and tying it off in a knot. "There. I call it the h-air shield. Get it. Hair...h-air. No blood will get past the shield of air around your head," he chuckled.

Xi's jaw dropped and she stumbled.

"Ah shit," I snickered and shook my head, facing forward.

Xi hissed menacingly. "How long have you known you could do that? How many battles have we fought? How many times have I complained about blood in my hair?"

Riley's grin faltered and I felt his inquiring gaze on me.

I just shook my head, not bothering to look back at him. "You're on your own, Ri."

Xi snarled at him. "When this is over Riley Dragoon, we will be dying your hair pink for the next month."

Snorting laughter bubbled from my smirking lips.

"Goddess, I missed you both so much," I breathed.

Riley caught up to me and nudged my shoulder. "We missed you too, Rem. Now shall we show these shifters what it's like to fight alongside shadow forces? The real legends of this story?"

Xi caught up to me on my other side and whispered conspiringly in my ear, "He'll be a legend alright. A pink haired one."

# CHAPTER 50

THERE WAS SWEET SILENCE behind me and nothing but ear splitting wails of wraiths in front of me. Remnant had completed her task and now it was time for me to complete mine.

Avenging flower pissing gnomes.

"It is as you said, they are attacking outside the deadlands...in broad daylight," Tyr hissed.

I ran my tongue along my extended fangs. "The gateway is weakening and Deirdre's influence is getting stronger."

I growled grimly at the way the wraiths moved in a lazy, unhurried manner that held no concern for their own lives. Their blood drenched cloaks dripped upon my beloved valley like a bad omen, killing anything it touched. The ghastly stench accompanying them was an offense to my nostrils.

Tyr's eyes narrowed. "By my count there are over two hundred wraiths out there. That damned bitch is measuring our strength and showcasing hers."

I could feel the restlessness of my warriors at my back as we watched the amassing horde. "So it would seem. Let's be done with this," I snarled, "I'd love a good night's worth of sleep for once."

We both turned and faced our armies with ferocious roars.

Tyr's voice rang proudly as he faced them. "Let us make sure none of those abominations live to suffer another fucking day! Show them the might of the shifters, the might of Finlandia, the might of our king, and the might of what it means to *live!*"

Cheers rose up and dozens of flashes sparked across the valley adding snarls, screeches, hisses, growls, and everything else in between. The sound itself rumbled the valley and shook the very lands. The Red Caps trembled in the wake of the battle cries of my people.

*All* of my people. Not just the shifters answered the call of battle, elemental and water fae roared along with them. Equipped with their power and steel, we made a fearsome sight.

An enormous yet soft head nudged my side and I smirked down at Tyr's white bengal tiger who purred against my hand. His long whiskers pulled back over black lips to show off gleaming white razor teeth that were ready to tear into any wraith who dared to approach him. He nudged me harder this time.

I smiled down at him. "I will not be shifting tonight my friend, I'll keep command for you. Enjoy your hunt."

My beast snarled, "*My hunting is by far more superior. That tiger has nothing on me. Let me out.*"

"*Not this time, cat. I need to stay in my fae form for Remnant.*"

He scoffed. "*You're afraid, fairy boy.*" He sauntered to the back of my head. "*It's not my fault that she will find me more interesting than you.*"

The distinct sound of three snarling leopards made me spin to the east and a sinister smile crossed my face. Eshe, Quinn, and Penina had come. Together we could not fail.

Prowling the lines, I stared down my forces. "Not a single fucking wraith shall leave these lands alive!" My power was imbued in every word I spoke, loosening slightly the tight leash I held on its raging inferno ever since I was a child. It seeped into my court, amplifying their power, and bolstering their energies.

Roaring, I charged forward and my court followed. Fae of all races ran alongside me and the rush of our unity spurred me forward, outwardly I challenged the fastest beasts on land and air for win of the first kill.

I scented no fear in my people, just a ferocious need to protect the world we built here, and yet despite our impressive front the wraith's slow advance did not falter. Their own shrill cries called back to us while the night began to descend on the valley, the sun dropping low below the Red Cap Mountains in the distance, casting a great shadow over the lands.

Beneath my feet the earth shook and all around us great fissures of earth revealed large boulders rising upwards from their sedentary rest. Gusts of forceful winds shot several of the massive boulders forward straight into the front flanks of the ascending wraiths. The sound of their shrill cries rose higher when the boulders effectively crushed several wraiths at the same time.

"First kill is on me!" I heard behind me.

I grinned. The elemental twins had arrived.

"I don't think so! That was my earth, my kill!" Xi Chin, the earth elemental, shouted back.

"Throw more pebbles my way Xi and let us see who really is delivering the death blow!" Riley Dragoon hollered back over the wailing wraiths.

My grin widened when the shadows raced beneath my feet, zigzagging through my path, and taunting me to run faster.

"Care to drop in, your majesty!" my soulmate called out to me.

My stride faltered when I looked up to see the raw beauty of Remnant surfing her shadows like it was the high tide waters of the West Isle shores.

Her long black hair had become unbound and it whipped across her face, her sparkling emerald eyes glowing with rejuvenated life. My breath caught and I knew I would never forget the sight of her in this moment. Her solid crouched stance, sword raised high over her head, her other hand grasping a shadow dagger at her hip, and the subtle tilt of her head. An invitation for me to join.

I didn't hesitate again, leaping onto the shadow platform right behind her. The shadows snapped me into place and I was careful of my sharp claws as I gripped onto her hips to steady myself more thoroughly and buried my face in the crook of her neck, inhaling deeply her scent.

"I take it the spy crows are no more," I purred against the pale column of her throat, knowing she could hear me over the stormy winds and the chunks of earth soaring over us like deadly arrows.

"Not a feather left behind," she snickered.

I chuckled darkly and marveled at the power of her shadows. "Hmmm, I could get used to this," I purred against the shell of her ear.

"Get down!" she cried and pulled me to her just as hot blue fire blazed over the top of our heads only to stop short by a tornado of rock and wind. The elemental twins' power ripped through the wraith's bodies with ease and showered us with rags, blood, and bone. Together they were a deadly combination that was a true marvel to behold in battle.

"Fuck!" Remnant cursed, wiping blood from her face and then glared over her shoulder. "I blame you for that one, Xi! I can't help that your hair is white damnit!"

Crazed laughter responded with more air and earth rushing by us.

Reaching with a singular claw I wiped the blood dripping over her brow.  "I think you look good in blood, little umbra."

"Told you!" Riley roared, sliding by us on a landslide of rock, pulling wraiths to him with gale forces and impaling them on his curved blade.

Remnant snickered and then winked back at me. "Better prepare yourself, your majesty! This is our stop!"

I snarled savagely at the oncoming group of wraiths. "I'm ready!"

The shadows reared, slamming us straight into a cluster of screeching wraiths. Flying forward my claws sank into the first one that had the unfortunate fate of being directly in my path. Wrenching my claws from its falling body, I leapt to the side, ripping the head off another that was about to shoot fire at my soulmate who was slashing down wraiths at an accelerated rate.

Shifters, shadows, fire, winds, water, and earth raged across the valley. Wraiths fell only to be replaced by a dozen more. Their blood showered through the air like a hot night rain and I relished in the feeling of satisfaction it brought.

Alongside me, Remnant surfed her shadows through the carnage. When I spun, she twirled. When I jumped she hit low. When I slid, she arc'd over me like the avenging goddess of death she was. Our bodies pulled and pushed, leveraging each of our attacks in tandem. Every move, every fucking breath, every beat of our thundering hearts was one...we didn't just kill. We goddess damn danced while we did it.

A wraith lunged and I swung outward, catching its side shoulder while its blue fire spit at me in desperation to get away. Swinging my other arm around, my claws stabbed into the back of his neck. The snap of its spine audible while I flung it to the side where another wraith Remnant was corralling towards me was fleeing. I roared, slashing in fury, shredding its worthless body in a mess of rags, tissue, and bone.

Remnant brushed against my back, covering my loss of sanity during my killing rage, I could hear the silencing of the shrills as she delivered death stroke after death stroke with shadows and steel.

Snapping my head up, I watched a growling white tiger and three leopards pounce over me pinning wraiths to the ground and mauling them savagely until their screams became silent.

Tyr tossed a decapitated hooded head in my direction with a snarl.

"Didn't your mother tell you not to play with your fucking food!" I teased the tiger and then rolled as more blue fire blasted towards me. The heat of it singeing the back of my head.

Tyr reared, slashing the wraith attacking me down with his deadly claws before turning to hiss at me with bloody fangs.

I snickered. "I know. I know. Be careful. I am the king bullshit." I patted the tiger's head affectionately. "Good kitty cat."

Tyr hissed and a bloody paw, encrusted with tattered cloth and tissue, swiped out for my head. Laughing, I sidestepped him, killing a few more wraiths in my way.

Looking across the valley, I grinned, noticing the numbers were thinning.

"Your highness!" I turned to see Xi pointing in the distance, a few other elementals working with her to control the earth. "They are retreating and we cannot reach them that far!"

My eyes searched for the unruly head of green hair. "Dragoon!" I roared across the battlefield.

# CHAPTER 51

A GREEN HEAD POPPED into view. Riley's hazel eyes burned bright across the battlefield searching for the source of my call.

When our eyes met, I thrust a bloody claw outward, roaring against the continued rushing winds. "Slow those fuckers down and destroy them!" I knew his air had a farther reach than earth.

His shrewd eyes locked on the escaping wraiths the same time his sword thrusted behind him, killing an approaching wraith at his back before sheathing it at his side.

The damn elemental fae was veritably savage and I fucking loved him for it.

"Riley!" Remnant called out.

My heart stuttered to a halt when I caught sight of my soulmate running at a quick pace towards the retreating wraiths.

"Remember chasing Nightmares!" she hollered over her shoulder.

Riley's narrowed eyes widened with understanding and I felt my stomach sink with dread.

Roaring, I lunged forward viciously killing any wraiths in my way as I headed straight for the air elemental. "No! Dragoon, stop now!"

He was about to help her run straight into danger alone.

Riley gave me an apologetic look, watching my advancement with hesitation in his hazel eyes.

"That's an order, Riley Dragoon!" Remnant commanded, sliding through the heavy blood soaked grasses, using shadows to propel her through the carnage.

I heard his hard grunt and soft murmur as he gathered more air around him, "Apologies, your majesty."

"Don't you fucking dare Dragoon!" I bellowed, continuing my race to reach him. "That's my *royal* order!" I shouted out to both of them.

Riley's lips pressed together but his focus never left my soulmate even as I charged him with furious rage. A sudden rush of gale forces bursted from him, heading straight into Remnant's direction and effectively sending me careening sideways through the bloody grasses.

From the ground, I watched as my soulmate leapt into the torrent of air, cocooning herself in the rushing winds. It spun her upwards, her hair whipping around her like a halo of darkness before shooting her across the sky like a deadly black comet—a tail of ominous dark shadows following in her wake.

Growling, I rose and slowly began to circle Dragoon, watching the sheer concentration on his face while he flew my obstinate soulmate across The West Isle sky.

I snarled. "If you fucking drop her, I will rip out your insides and feed them down your fucking throat."

A single bead of sweat dripped down his temple. "If I drop her, I'll do it to my fucking self."

I grunted at that. Fucking bastard *was* indeed a savage. I glanced up at the fleeing wraiths. "She won't get there in time, the closer they get to the deadlands the stronger they become. Pull the wraiths back towards her."

His jaw clenched harder, his other arm thrusting out in front of him. "Yes, your majesty."

I tilted my head and started to circle him again. "You sure you're not a shifter, Dragoon?"

The air elemental smirked at that, still not looking at me. "I've learned from the best...and she's not a shifter, your majesty."

Then, as if conducting an orchestra, he snapped back his hands, pulling them to his chest tightly, and I looked up to see Remnant completely suspended in the night air. The wraiths swirling around her, trapped in Riley's fatal corralling winds.

She didn't hesitate. She lashed out spinning, twirling, and slashing the score of wraiths with effective ease. There was no escaping as Riley delivered them towards her murderous blade.

Below her the shadows spiked up with hungry intent, swallowing wraiths in the infinite void, protecting her blind spots and preventing the cold blue fire from raining down on her.

I felt the others gathering around me, watching the bewitching vengeance Riley and Remnant created. An orchestra of death.

Xi shouldered past them and stepped around me without a passing glance—joining Riley's side and she rested a bloody hand on his shoulder.

He grunted in acknowledgement. "I need you," he whispered. If it wasn't for my shifter ears and being so close to him, I would have never heard his vulnerable confession.

"I know," Xi murmured, "I got you Ri, stay steady."

I stilled when I felt Xi's power flow directly into her partner, feeding him more energy as he continued to fly Remnant through the night sky.

Remnant screamed and we all gasped when she ended the last three wraiths attempting to escape in Riley's cyclone of air with one javelin-like lunge of her sword. They were skewered onto her blade and with a final battle cry she flung them downward straight into the mouth of the eternal abyss hovering below her.

Silence. Pure sweet silence.

I flung my head back and released a victorious roar that rattled the grasslands, my beast's power echoing in my celebration of triumph. My court joined me, the bellows traveling through the world, letting every fucking enemy know that death awaited them here should they dare to ever take a step into these lands.

I pounded the air elemental roughly on the back, grinning at him. "Well done Dragoon. You won't be eviscerated...today."

Riley swallowed hard but smiled back at me. "Thank you, your majesty."

"Now bring her back to me in one piece before I change my mind."

Dragoon barked out a short laugh. "Always, your majesty!"

Nodding to Xi, who smiled at him proudly, he weaved his hands with quick succession. Remnant shot back towards us, spinning, twirling, and tumbling in the star filled darkness before landing crouched in front of me. Slowly she stood, facing me with her chest heaving and her eyes bright with adrenaline.

Riley and Xi stepped quietly away as we continued to stare at one another.

A bright smile beamed across her face as she took in my enthralled stare. Completely covered in blood and her hair a disheveled mess around her, it was as if she stepped out of my dreams.

My hand snapped out, gripping the back of her neck before slamming my hungry lips to hers—need consuming me. I needed to taste that life within her, to feel that she was real, to bask in her glory, and her greatness.

She gave into my kiss, her desire and need matching my own as her fingers clawed into my skin and her hips pressed flush against mine. Lost in carnal hunger, she gasped in my mouth when I lifted her, wrapping her legs around my body, skimming the hemline of her shorts with my fingertips before cupping her ass tightly into me.

She moaned, arching in my arms when my lips trailed over her collar bone.

"Fuck, you're so beautiful," I rasped, licking at her thundering pulse covered in blood.

"Emon," she breathed, the complete rapture on her face highlighted by the stars was my undoing. Growling, I slanted my mouth over hers, claiming her thoroughly as mine—only mine.

A throat cleared behind me but I ignored it, whatever the world wanted from me it could fucking wait.

But Remnant did not, her eyes snapped open and she stiffened in my arms, her inhibitions returned as she gently pressed away from me.

I followed, dropping my forehead to hers, my heavy breathing blowing the loose strands of her hair away from her gorgeous face. I couldn't help but search her eyes for any regret or worse...rejection.

"This isn't over with," I whispered only for her ears.

Remnant's brow furrowed and her eyes searched for the same thing as mine...regret. She wouldn't find it. There was nothing I would ever regret when it came to her.

She exhaled. "It should not have even started, shifter."

"It was inevitable, my little umbra," I softly whispered and brushed a gentle kiss to her forehead. "You owed me that kiss anyway."

Her eyes widened and I grinned, slowly unwrapping her legs from my body and setting her safely onto the ground. Leaning over, I tucked back a strand of her blood soaked hair, watching the emotions war across her face, her soul gluing itself back together, and her heart awakening from the cold shell it had been frozen in.

Another throat clearing. "Your majesty?"

Snarling, I spun. "What the fuck is so goddess damn important that you can't handle it yourself, General Tyr?"

Tyr straightened his large tattooed covered body. His eyes darted to my soulmate before looking back at my angered state. "Apologies my king but it's your protocol to give you a status report after battle, no exceptions."

"Then fucking give it, General," I snarled, more angry at my own damn rules than anything else.

He didn't hesitate. "All our people are accounted for, no losses thank the goddess. A few minor injuries that Quinn has been able to heal, the more seriously injured are being escorted back to the master healer by Penina and Eshe. Not a single wraith survived nor are there any sightings of spycrows." He snickered and winked behind me to Remnant. "Thank you for that, beauty."

I hissed at him. I was in no mood for his flirting with my soulmate.

Remnant snorted. "You're welcome for that, shifter."

Subduing my animalistic nature, I raked my hands through my hair. "Have Penina and Eshe check in on the people within the city afterwards. Our people need to be reassured they are safe in their own homes."

He scowled. "We did well but truth be told, we were not prepared for an attack of this scale. We don't have the numbers for any larger attack, especially with spy crows involved."

"I know."

His lip peeled up in a silent snarl, stretching the silver piercings. "The queen is here for both of them."

My face crinkled. I knew what I had to do. "I know."

My beast read my mind. *"These attacks won't stop and the next one will be larger as the gateway weakens. We must bring the battle to them."*

Tyr growled and shook his shaven head. "If it wasn't for beauty handing them their asses, this could have been much worse."

I turned and looked at the shadow fae who was now caressing her shadows like a pet cat, silently listening to our conversation.

"I know," I said sincerely.

Remnant's dark head raised and her brows arched—she was expecting a different answer but I knew my soulmate's worth even if she did not.

Dragoon and Chin stepped up and cleared their throats.

Remnant turned and flung her arms around them in greeting. Pulling away she gripped their shoulders proudly. "You both were amazing!"

Xi smiled. "And look, no pink hair!"

They laughed and I glanced over at Tyr who just shrugged. I didn't miss the increased attention my friend had looking at Xi's exposed face.

Remnant looked over her shoulder. "Am I dismissed, your majesty?"

I snorted. "You're willing to follow orders now, after directly ignoring them earlier?"

She shrugged back at me and Riley averted his eyes when I turned my stare at him. Xi snickered.

I snorted and waved my hand. "This is an alliance not a service, General Dark. Go. Catch up with your friends, I can manage the rest on my own."

Emerald green eyes hesitated for a moment before she stepped forward and pressed a kiss onto my unsuspecting mouth.

I blinked with shock as she pulled away just as quickly, giving me a small smile. Her eyes twinkled up at me. "Thank you for taking care of my friends, your majesty. Consider that kiss one freely given."

I stared at her back when she turned away with shock. Both Xi and Riley glanced over her shoulder at me with the same surprised expression that I surmised was still on my face.

Tyr snickered next to me. "You look like a damned kelpie, gulping for air."

Snarling I turned and shoved him hard enough to break his balance. "Shut up, asshole."

He chuckled, righting himself and winking at me. "Dickhead."

Rolling my eyes, I tilted my head for him to follow me. Away from the trio that was snickering at our backs.

"I will be leaving the city tomorrow," I said in a low tone.

Tyr sighed. "I could feel that coming. It's been fifty two years—"

"And thirty six days. I know," I cut him off. "That's why you and Penina will be coming with me."

Both of us stomped together on the wraith in our path.

Tyr dug his booted heel harder into its dead mangled body. "Decided not to leave me behind this time?"

I could hear the hurt in his voice. "You and I both know that you were dreading another round on Faerie grounds."

He looked away. "I would have done it for you."

I gripped his shoulder and turned him to me. "I know my friend but you served me better here and you knew that. It's why I got away with tying you up in the first place. Don't think I didn't know that."

Tyr's eyes darted at me and then he snorted, shaking my hand off him.

Peals of Remnant's laughter sounded behind me. I glanced back for a brief moment. Stealing a look at the joy on my soulmate's face. I paused. "Have Dragoon and Chin readied as well."

"And General Dark?"

I faced forward once again. "Remnant will be coming too."

Tyr shook his head as we started to walk once more. "There is no way you'll be able to convince beauty to leave the faeling. Her connection to the girl is strong. You'll have to be pretty fucking convincing to get her to even leave the city."

I hummed. "Pastries."

He glanced at me alarmed. "What?"

I shook my head, "Never mind that."

He shot me a concerned look and then shrugged. "Alright asshole, and where the fuck are we all going then? On a goddess damn picnic? Sightseeing so you can charm her clothes off?"

"To the outpost."

"*It is the right choice,*" my cat purred and then sauntered back into the recesses of my mind.

Tyr's large stride faltered. "Fuck." He swallowed.

"I know."

"I will have everything ready to go at dawn," he said gravely.

Large raucous laughter erupted from the elemental twins. "I don't think I ever heard them laugh," I said.

"That's because they don't." Tyr said, his expression thoughtful when he shot a look behind him. "Until now."

I grunted. Kicking a wraith to the side and watching it fly ten feet from me. Landing in a loud thud. "Mid morning will be fine," I said, my plan still forming. "We all need our rest and I need to speak to Jar before we leave."

"Consider it done," Tyr said seriously, kicking another dead wraith out of the way.

I eyed the distance his wraith had flown and then we both grinned at each other mischievously.

"Whoever kicks the next wraith the farthest buys the other a drink?" I challenged him.

Tyr's eyes gleamed in the dark. "Prepare to lose, you're going to be buying me several, your majesty."

# CHAPTER 52

"DAEMON, THANK YOU FOR coming," Jarquinn called from his worn wooden work desk as I stealthily entered the healing quarters.

I had never been able to sneak up on the ancient fae, even when I was a cub.

Crossing my arms over my chest, I studied him in his predictable light blue robes. His tall frame and sharp lethal grace gave him a dangerous air that one would be foolish to ignore. Jar was like a father to me, especially after the loss of mine, I had never feared him but I did respect him.

"I wanted to have a word with you anyway." I stole a glance at the sleeping faeling on the bed by the window. "I know you organized for Penina and Xi to take Remnant out this morning."

Jar nodded. "Yes, your suggestion of pastries was most helpful, your majesty."

I chuckled remembering the mixture of fury and eagerness as she stormed out the door heading straight towards buttery baked goods at Griffins Gateau.

"The truth is, *Forta* will not find what she needs to heal in here," Jarquinn added, picking at his long sleeve with deft fingers.

*"He's nervous,"* the cat observed.

I narrowed my eyes on his pristine sleeve. "What's going on Jar?" Alarmed, I took a step back towards the door. "Is Remnant in danger?"

Jarquinn was in front of me before I could think about dragging my soulmate back home. His shifter speed and ancient origins made him faster than even me. A testament to the true animal that lurked below, one I had never seen in my lifetime.

"Calm yourself Daemon, my cub. All is well with *forta*. Aside from needing fresh air and exposure to society, she is well. I swear it on the goddess."

I reached up and encased his in my own with concern. "Then why are you so fucking nervous, Jar?"

"Language, cub!" Jarquinn chastised me sternly and then gripped my shoulder with his free hand to guide me further into the room. "It is about the girl," he said quietly, motioning for me to sit on the long prime tree root that extended beside her bed.

"Riella?" I looked down at the sleeping faeling with alarm. Her small tanned face was serene while she slept. Black hair had been braided to the side and it reminded me of my mother in another time, long ago. Fluffy cloud blankets had been carefully and lovingly tucked around her, engulfing her small form. "What is wrong with her?"

"Nothing is wrong with her physically," Jarquinn said slowly, "she is healing well in her induced sleep and she will undoubtedly wake in the next couple of days."

I sighed with relief, tiredly scrubbing at my beard. I had stayed up too late with Tyr. Thank the goddess for fae metabolism or I'd still be stumbling around drunk this morning. "What is it then?"

"It is about the child's origin. She is not water fae—she never was."

My brows furrowed. "We knew this...are you telling me that you have discovered what she is? Is she a shifter?" I looked back down at the innocent child again, my protective nature still calling to me. "The other night, when I came home, she felt *familiar* to me. I know you noticed it too."

*"Be prepared, fairy boy."*

I stiffened. *"What do you know of this cat?"*

Silence.

Growling, I cursed him to Sheol and back.

Jar tensed, his blue eyes wary. "I want you to know that I have gone over my findings multiple times. The end result was the same every time...Daemon, the child *is* shifter fae," the ancient rubbed at his crystal blue eyes, as if he had been up all night as well, "and she is shadow fae."

My brows rose. "That would be almost impossible. Even if we forget the fact that the fae are sterile, the other fae races don't associate with shifters...until Finlandia. And the shadow fae are gone!" I shook my head. "Not to mention, to carry both traits. Our makeup chooses the most dominant side of power, always."

The master healer nodded. "Yes, all of what you say is true...normally. But Riella is no normal faeling. She harbors equal shifter and shadow fae power within her. Her parents are very powerful—very equal beings."

I frowned at her features once more...the sense of familiarity only growing stronger. "If I am to accept this, then who are her parents?"

"I need you to try to stay calm for this Daemon," Jar pleaded. He never pleaded.

My stomach turned, seeing the deeply set worry in his ancient eyes.

I growled low. "Tell me."

"Riella is the daughter of General Remnant Dark."

Rearing back, like his words were a slap to my face, my chest heaved and something fractured deep inside of me, golden power surged forward, pulsing loudly in my skull. I rose when my vision blurred with looming bloodlust in an attempt to control the rising power while the sound of splintering wood and breaking glass filled the room.

I roared when strong arms embraced me, reflexively lashing out viciously with my claws.

"Remnant is mine—my soulmate!" A low eerie keen escaped me. It just couldn't be possible. Whoever this male shifter was...goddess—fuck.

*"Calm yourself!"* My beast's voice rose over the thundering golden power. *"Breathe, Emon. Breathe. You are hurting the healer. Hurting Jar."*

As if I was doused in a bucket of ice cold water, I froze. The red haze cleared and I shook my head holding back the sob that threatened to rip out of me.

"I should have found Remnant sooner...I should have...."

"Daemon," Jarquinn whimpered, pain straining his voice and drawing my attention.

My beast's words finally registered and I blinked at the sight of Jar pinned to the wall by his shoulders with my claws. Blood seeped into his light blue robes and I stared, realizing what I had done.

"Fuck!" I snarled and ripped my hands away, trembling with shame and horror.

Jar exhaled shakily with relief, sliding down the wall and waving his hands over the wounds instantly healing them.

"Forgive me, Jar," I bowed my head, gripping it in anguish.

A wet towel was thrusted under my bowed head and I heard the healer chuckle. "There is nothing to forgive Daemon, I had foreseen this. I am only sorry for the pain it has caused you."

"Do not make excuses for me, master healer," I hissed back, taking the towel and wiping furiously at my bloodied hands. "I am the damned king of The West Isles! I don't lose control, I can't lose control, and I damn well don't attack my own family! I won't be like him!"

Jar shook his head. "You are many things Daemon Ash Strider but you are not your father...your control right now is a testament to that. You've just learned that the fae you love has a daughter." He chuckled and shook his head again. "Your father would have shredded this place to pieces with such knowledge." He gave the splintered prime root that I had ripped off in my rage a forlorn look. Its severed limb was across the room, littered with broken glass, the source of the crash I had heard. "However, I do believe it will be some time before the prime root trusts you again."

I eyed the stump of the ancient tree shamefully. "Apologies, Prime. I was not...myself."

The tree shuttered and Jar chuckled. "Another difference between you. Your father would have never been caught apologizing to a tree."

I cursed and started to pace. "Why hasn't Remnant said anything about this?" I scrutinized the girl and then I saw it. The black hair, the dark lashes, the heart shape of her face. She looked just like her mother...except the faeling's skin was tanned almost bronze—nothing like the flawless pale skin of my soulmate.

Jarquinn pondered my question a moment, tapping a long finger to his pursed lips. "Because...she does not know. Daemon there is more—"

"What?" My head snapped up. "How could she possibly not know?"

"There is more..." He said again slowly.

"Fucking goddess!" My hands could not stop raking through my hair as I prowled agitatedly. "What of the *father*, this fucking shifter fae. Is that the more you need to tell me?" I choked on a growl. How could this fae ever leave Remnant alone with a child? He was below the worst scum of Faerie, I would eviscerate him...then order Jarquinn to heal him before eviscerating him again, repeating the process over and over. "I'm going to kill this asshole."

Jar snorted. "I sincerely hope not. Not unless you plan to kill yourself Daemon."

My pacing paused abruptly. "What?" I snapped.

*"I told you to be prepared."* The cat was solemn.

*"You knew!"* I roared at him. *"You knew and never said a word to me! You're fucking lucky that killing you would kill me too."*

*"Calm yourself, fairy boy. I suspected. That is all Emon. I can detect both your shadow fae's scent and your scent from the child. Of course if you would have shifted I would have known for sure."*

*"Stop! Refrain from using my name! You have lost that privilege if you even had it in the first place. It only solidifies your own guilt,"* I snarled back.

Sliding down to the edge of faeling's bed I stared at the girl. I could see it now. Tanned skin kissed by the sun, the same as mine.

Sorrow and guilt seized me and I struggled to take a deep breath. "How? Why? When?" I whispered.

"I suspect the queen was finally successful in her experiment to create a child, from what you told me of your imprisonment she was able to use you both to accomplish this. It is my theory that the blood wraiths are her failed experiments with using the Sanguine and the deadlands are created from the drain of energy required to sustain their ghastly lives. The Sanguine cannot sustain life like our goddess can, so she has gone straight to the source. Our world." He shook his head. "I do not know how she ended up in The Under. That one is a mystery to me."

My body shook as I attempted to digest the information, but the vivid memories of my imprisonment were starting to take over. "No matter how much I was...we were—" I closed my eyes against the visions of Remnant...those screams. Goddess her screams. "We are not an experiment," I growled, my claws dug into my hands, puncturing my own skin.

Jar's voice broke. "I know this Daemon." He sighed. "My job has always been to protect you, especially since your father was lost to us, but this truth, I'm afraid it is something I cannot protect you from." I opened my eyes to see tears in his. "That day we found you, after being stolen from us for those three long months, I was beside myself with joy. So relieved to know that you were alive and here with us. But you never really returned fully. I know that some nights still plague you, that the scars reopen and you avoid sleeping because of this."

"You take too much responsibility upon yourself Jar." I turned away. I would have been naive to think that he didn't hear me heaving my guts up at night, waking up in a cold sweats barely believing I wasn't in that horrible place anymore.

"Perhaps," he murmured. "There is a part of the story I left out, Daemon."

I looked up through anguished eyes. "What—" I croaked. "What story?"

"Of Faerie and her brothers. The god Ichor did indeed curse the fae...but he failed to curse *all* fae. His malediction only affected Faerie's fae. But the shadow fae...were not created by Faerie. They were born of—"

"Shea," I whispered. "They were created from the God of Death."

He nodded. "Deirdre must have discovered this when she imprisoned General Dark."

My teeth ground together and I hissed. "That was why she wanted the shadow fae."

Jar gave me a sad look. "She did not want just *them*. She wanted to *harvest them*. For their ability to reproduce."

I stared at Jarquinn in horror. "All the experiments they did to Remnant—they were harvesting her?"

Tears filled the master healer's eyes. "Yes, technically you both were. A monstrous and unforgivable violation."

I choked and dropped my head into my hands. "How? How is it that I am her father?"

"Daemon." Jarquinn placed his hand on my shoulder again. "You couldn't have known, my cub. This is not your fault."

"I need to know. If the God Ichor cursed us...then how is it that I can be the girl's father, Jar? I am a product of Faerie. You said it yourself. She created the shifters."

Jarquinn hesitated before he spoke. "You are goddess blessed Daemon. The power you hold within you...that burning, raging power. It is the power of the goddess, the power of Faerie. Your mother and father knew it the moment you first shifted."

*"We are more,"* the beast said within me.

I ignored the cat and looked up at the healer. "In the Wildwoods. I was healed by Faerie's power. You're telling me I did that to myself?"

"I cannot say for sure, but what I do know is that you were blessed with this power even before your capture, quite likely at your birth. You have always been more, Daemon."

I scrubbed my face at the echoed words of my beast. "Fuck. I don't want to be more. I don't want to have to pay for more either." I sent the healer a tortured look. "When is it enough? Why has the goddess abandoned us? How could she allow this to happen?"

*"She is with you Emon,"* the cat whispered softly to me...almost submissively.

*"Do not speak to me. Ever again."* His withholding of information was the deepest of betrayals.

*"You are hurting. I apologize for ever causing you this type of pain."*

*"Do. Not. Speak,"* I ordered harshly.

"Your father once asked me the same question after your mother died. I will tell you what I told him then." Jar's ancient eyes bore into my own. "Our circumstances are a tool that we can use to mold our lives. It is up to you what you decide to create from them. Use it to mold your own peace Daemon, a life for you, *forta*, and the girl...you will not find it from others. Not even our goddess."

"Peace? There will never be peace for me, Jar. Not anymore. Not while that bitch is still out there! Hurting us, hurting my soulmate...my daughter." I choked.

"It is imperative that you do not lose focus on what really matters. You and Remnant have been given a gift, it is up to you on how you receive it. Despite how terrible the queen's purpose was or still is…this child is a miracle, the first shadow shifter, and your daughter."

"Shadow shifter?"

Jarquinn nodded and shot me a small playful smile. "I do hope you give me the credit for naming a new fae race. We won't know how her power manifests but I am sure it will be a combination of you both."

"A combination of us both," I murmured.

The fae coveted power above all else and now my daughter held more power in her small frame than any fae that had ever lived.

I stared at the healer with renewed fear. "How do I keep her safe, Jar? How do I keep *them* safe?"

His eyes widened, not expecting open vulnerability. "Oh Daemon." He kneeled and pulled me into his warm embrace. His healing power washed over me like a warm blanket. "You know what you must do. You must go to *him*, my cub, and then you must tell *forta* the truth. Let her choose the path she will take from there."

I hugged him fiercely, not knowing what I would ever do without him.

"The attack last night forced that decision already anyway. I have plans to leave today," I grumbled.

Jar pulled away with a sad smile. "I have no doubt you will be received well, my cub. Time has a way of healing many wounds and revealing many wrongs."

I looked back down at the faeling. "Time…" I said softly. "We've already lost so much time." I shook my head growling, I wasn't about to let any more go with us apart.

I rose, my chest expanding and my voice clear, "I want you to personally reinforce all the wards around this room. No one is to come in here except myself, you, and Remnant." I glared hard at Jarquinn. "Fucking no one. No exceptions," I growled.

The ancient fae healer nodded. "As you wish, your majesty."

"Thank you," I said sincerely, "Thank you for not being afraid to tell me the truth. Thank you for always watching over me and now my daughter. Thank you for saving her. For caring for Remnant. For loving me."

Jar sighed and smiled happily at me. "Daemon. You were born into this kingdom to be its brightest light but you never needed to shine to be one in mine."

As if his words were the trigger, a sudden force exploded deep inside of me and I gasped at the pure warmth spreading in my chest.

"Sweet goddess, what is that?" I gasped, leaning over and gazing at my daughter, the source of this new strange power.

Jar stared with awe. "She has bonded with you!" He shook his head, his brows raised in surprise. "I would know the feel of that bond anywhere. It is the same I hold with my Quinn. The same your father held with you." He smiled widely at me. "Your daughter will be very powerful indeed if she can bond to you in a healing sleep like this. Although, I wouldn't expect anything less."

"It is beautiful," I said in awe, reaching down and tucking the loose strands from her braid behind her ear. "She is beautiful." I placed a soft kiss upon her delicate forehead. "I claim you Riella, my wee little cub," I whispered, "I will protect you with every ounce of life that is left in me and even when my soul leaves my body it will never stop to ensure your safety. This world will know no fiercer protector for you than me. I swear it, on the Goddess, this world, and the whole universe combined. Nothing shall ever harm you."

# CHAPTER 53

Remnant

S OMEHOW THAT CLEVER MASTER healer manipulated me into leaving Riella's side again with the promise of sweet buttery pastries and I knew just who he got that information from.

Just the thought of Emon, had my heart fluttering with anticipation and admittedly, I was more excited to see him than I was to sink my teeth into a cherry cream cheese hand pie.

Penina's arm snaked through mine suddenly, pulling me closer to her lavender swathed body as she greeted the people of Finlandia with energetic acceptance. Leaving me forced to awkwardly smile or nod to the people she stopped to talk to.

My former captain, Xi, trailed alongside us with a wry smile on her face. Enjoying my utter discomfort at being man-handled by the energetic shifter.

I smacked her with my free arm. "You're enjoying this too much."

She raised her singular brow at me, the other half of her face covered once again. "It is a beautiful day and my friend has returned to me. Yes, I am enjoying myself immensely."

I opened my mouth to tell her just what I thought of her cheeky comment but I was suddenly pressed back into Penina's side, her conspiratory tone low when she whispered to me.

"So you and the king..." Her big brown eyes sparkled and she wiggled her brows, the gold piercings glinting in the sun.

"The rush of battle," I formed my words carefully, resisting the happy sigh that wanted to escape me. Fighting alongside Emon's formidable power was breathtaking. And then that kiss, goddess help me that kiss.

Xi snickered. "Right...I've seen you after battles before and never did you fuck the first fae in sight."

"I did not fuck him!" I punched her hard in the arm.

Uncontrollable giggles bursted from the tiny shifter cuddling against me. The sound catching many frowns as we walked the white stoned paths.

We couldn't get to Griffins Gateau fast enough.

My former captain rolled her visible eye and snorted. "You're both lucky you had clothes on or that's exactly what would have happened."

Penina snickered. "Then, I call that very unlucky." She patted my arm when I scowled fiercely forwards, not daring to meet their eyes. "That's not even the best part though. Did you see the look on Tyr's face?"

Xi laughed outright. "His jaw hung open for almost a whole minute and the bastard actually blushed."

"Now *he was* the lucky one. Lucky he didn't get his head ripped off. I thought Emon was going to rip his head off." Penina's brown eyes widened dramatically.

A slow smile spread across my heated face that had nothing to do with the sun. "You both are incorrigible. Besides, I saw the way Tyr was looking at you, Xi. Care to share with us?"

"We are here," Xi said quickly, turning to the shop and ducking under the shade.

Penina giggled. "I wish you the best of luck in understanding those three."

I gave the shifter a side glance. "Three?"

She hummed. "Riley, Tyr, and Xi, of course. It is quite a conundrum."

I glanced over at my former captain who opened the door, ignoring our low whispers. When the aroma of fresh baked bread, warm spices, and chocolatey sweetness caused my mouth to water, I filed away my intrigue for a later time. Goddess, that smell, it almost smelled like Emon but not *quite* as delicious.

I jumped when Penina released me, supporting herself on her knees as she howled with uncontrollable laughter once more.

Xi's eye was wide on her face and there was a blush spreading across her olive skin.

"Did I miss something?" I frowned with genuine confusion.

"The king…" Penina gasped, her soulful brown eyes sparkling with mirth, "the king smells…" she laughed harder. "…delicious."

This time the blood drained from my face. "No….I didn't say that out loud…please tell me I didn't say it out loud?"

Xi yanked on her white hair to cover more of her heated face. "Rush of battle eh?"

Shadows burst around me. "For goddess sakes! I blame you both for this!" I practically ran into the shop to hide the utter embarrassment I had created for myself.

Penina's laughter lowered. "Shit. She isn't going to kill us is she?" I heard her say behind me.

"Naw, if Rem wanted to kill you, she'd let you know beforehand," Xi said dryly.

"That's a relief," Penina said with genuine consolation.

I silently chuckled and shook my head. Xi wasn't wrong but it still didn't stop the slight sadness I felt that Penina feared me. When I met the eyes of the large baker, Drey cowering on the back wall, I stilled. His eyes were trained on my shadows swarming around me. Waving my hand I snapped them out of existence but the damage was already done. If the baker was afraid of me the first time I arrived in his shop then today he was right terrified.

"I'm so sorry, Drey, I mean you no harm. We just came for the delicious hand pies you sold me yesterday. It was truly the best pastry I have ever had."

His massive frame did not relax. Someone his size could crush a skull with a single hand and yet he kneaded bread instead. His aura was the most beautiful lightest shade of pink. An aura of the heart—tender, kind, sensitive.

"Gggeneral Dark," Drey stammered, wiping his gigantic flour covered hands on his apron nervously, stepping towards the door-wall away from me. "How—" He swallowed. "How can I help you?"

My chest tightened at his obvious fear in his dark eyes, all he saw was a monster, and suddenly I could not take a breath.

"I'm sorry," I choked and stumbled back. The walls of the bakery seemed to shrink around me and I felt the gripping clutches of panic start to take hold.

"Good morning Drey!" Penina rushed past me, bringing the terrified shifter's attention onto her as she hopped the counter and jumped into his flour dusted arms.

Drey laughed nervously and then stammered an apology for getting flour all over her lavender finery.

My hand clutched at my chest and I turned, stumbling again towards the door. I *needed* to leave this place.

Xi was suddenly in front of me. Her hands gripping my shoulders firmly, her voice gentle. "You're safe here Rem." She stooped to draw my panicked gaze to her. "Breathe with me. In and out. In and out. The ground is firm beneath your feet, always steady."

My vision blurred and I felt the trembling in my body start to climb. Then the distant roaring in my ears started again, the same tortured sound of someone in pain. Through wheezing breaths, I rasped. "No...no one is safe—around me." Tears pooled in my eyes and the pressure in my chest felt like it was going to burst.

"Think of the king." She brushed aside the tears. "What does he smell like again? Breathe in that, know that."

I attempted to glare at her but through my tears I saw no humor, just concern and concentration.

"Close your eyes, Rem. Think of him and breathe."

Whimpering, I closed my eyes. Through the thundering of my pulse I could just smell the faintest aroma of spice and chocolate. It wasn't quite as potent as Emon's scent but it was enough to ground myself from the uncontrollable spin my panic had triggered.

I focused on the roughened feel of his fingertips tracing my palm calmly, the gentle timber of his voice when he laid the cù-sìth mother and cub to rest, the way he watched his family with gratitude for the moment he was in, the sound of his chuckle when the shadows played with him, and then the smaller moments. The moments when his golden eyes captured me so thoroughly that the fierce devotion and immeasurable love he coveted for only me was so simple to see.

The *why* I could not face and did not understand.

I took a deep gasping breath and then slowly exhaled.

"Little umbra." The sexy growl of his voice forced my eyes to open and I held myself rigid to not sink with the pure relief his presence brought me.

Concern crinkled at the edges of his eyes as he crouched low to meet my weary stare. A lock of hair fell across his rugged face giving him that boyish charm that I had no defense against.

"Emon," my voice trembled.

"I think we will take five hand pies now that the king has joined us, Drey!" Penina called in the background.

Emon reached down for my fisted hands, his eyes never leaving mine while he unfurled my clenched fingers, and with the pad of his thumb traced soothing circles into them. "You're okay now Remnant. I'll always be here for you, little umbra."

I inhaled at the unguarded look he held just for me. "I believe that now." My fingers curled around his. "I am okay. Thank you," I said softly and then I glanced over at Xi who had taken watch by the window. "Xi. I—"

She gave me a sardonic look. "I had a friend once who reached into the jaws of a basilisk because she noticed that it had a rotten tooth that needed to be removed. That very same basilisk had been terrorizing every small fae town on the coast for months, and yet, instead of killing it, she decided to help it. Its venom could have seared off her arm. Its fire could have burned her body to ash. Its eyes could have turned her to stone. Instead, the damned thing bowed its head in thanks and slithered off back to the deep mountains of its home to never be heard from again. I thought you to be the bravest fae then. Crazy. But brave." Xi's voice broke. "But now, I think you are the most valiant being in this entire universe and not because of what you *can* do but in spite of it. You owe me no explanation, General. You never will."

I blinked back the tears threatening to spill from my eyes.

Emon cleared his throat and pulled me into his side. "Good morning Drey."

The baker looked up from Penina's flirtatious attention and regarded the king, glancing down at his hand still holding mine and then back up at the king himself. "Your majesty...you honor me by coming here not once, but two days in a row. Thank you."

He bowed his large head, the heavy braids of his hair falling over his shoulders.

Emon grinned widely and kissed my hand in front of him. "You have General Dark to thank for that one, Drey. She has proclaimed you the best baker she has ever had the pleasure of meeting and she has a penchant for sweet things, like I do," he purred, winking down at me. "Do you still have that quaint little garden alcove in the back? I do remember it being the best place to cool off on a hot day."

"Yes, of course, your majesty!" Drey beamed at him.

"Lovely." The shifter king smiled. "We will take a tour then."

# CHAPTER 54

*Remnant*

THE LITTLE GARDEN WAS a simple wonder in a small alley, one that was carefully tended, with no doubt in my mind, by the baker himself. Colorful small birds, vibrant butterflies, and shimmering pixies flitted about the glowing floral vines that created a shady canopy over the stone tables and chairs beneath. Little petals fell enchantingly around us as Emon led me to the quaint spot.

Stepping in front of me, he cupped my face, peering deep into my eyes. "Has it fully passed? Is there anything you need?"

I tipped my face into him and nodded. "Yes. It has passed." I pulled his hands gently away from my face and walked past him, allowing my shadows to drape around me as I did. Surprisingly, their comfort this time was not quite the same as being cocooned in Emon's embrace.

There was a long pause then he spoke, his voice a soft timber at my back. "For me. They come at night. Sometimes I wake from these night terrors so fucking vivid it's like I'm still there and I cannot escape. I have a hard time knowing what's real and what isn't and when I finally pull out of it, it takes me hours to recover...to find some semblance of peace in it all." His voice was barely above a whisper. "There are some things that not even an ancient master healer can cure."

I was quiet, remembering the image of Emon thrashing in his sleep in the Balsam plains. The pain etched on his face while trapped in the nightmare. It was the first time where I realized Emon's soul was just as scarred as mine.

"Mine started after Morta...." I confessed. "Sometimes it's just a look of fear, a scream, a smell, or simply just too many fae surrounding me like yesterday in the breakfast room."

"And today, just now?"

"The baker Drey..." I waved my hand towards the building. "He fears me. I can see the terror in his eyes when he looks at me. It's not his fault, he is a gentle soul, but when they trigger, I am so terrified that I will recreate Morta in those moments that I spin out of control even more. That's why isolation was the easiest way. At least then...I wasn't around anyone I could hurt ever again."

"The cabin. That's why you spent so much time there." His soft words were like a caress on the back of my neck.

I pulled the shadows closer around me despite the heat. "Did you know that the cabin was created by the goddess herself, a halfway house for fae who needed solace to heal?"

"Did you? Did you heal, little umbra?"

I shook my head and turned to face him with honesty. "I don't know if I ever will."

"Alright lovebirds," Penina called out, stomping through the doorway. "You two can finish your serious as shit conversation later. I'm starving!"

Emon chuckled. "You're always starving and always eating. I have no idea how you stay so small."

"Calisthenics." She winked at me and chucked a white pastry bag at my face.

I caught it with a snicker, choosing the shady side of the stone table across from her. "Cherry with cream cheese?" I peeked in the bag.

Penina snickered. "Of course. I stayed away from the chocolate spiced croissants. Didn't want you to have a different type of meltdown," she teased.

Emon's brow raised when he sat next to Penina, forcing her to shift over so that he could sit directly in front of me. His knee brushed against mine underneath the table.

Four days ago I wanted to kill this shifter for touching me. Now I was starting to worry I couldn't live in a world without him.

Goddess, who was I now?

What was I now?

The hero or the monster, the vigilante or the avenger?

Broken or more powerful than ever?

The lines blurred so much that it was a wonder I could even distinguish them before now.

"Am I supposed to take the hint that spiced chocolate is your new favorite flavor?" Emon queried seriously, looking at the two of us with a narrowed gaze.

Penina choked on her pastry.

Mortified, I looked at the gagging shifter. "Where is Xi?"

Penina's brown eyes glittered and she pulled out a hot tea from her bag, taking a long sip. "Oh right!" She cleared her throat and then took another bite, before talking through another mouthful of butter and sugar and dough. "Tyr sent a messenger. Something about a scouting mission she was needed for."

I frowned. "Xi has to be the worst scout in Faerie...he should know that."

She shrugged. "That's exactly what we both said." Still talking through the mouthful of pastry, she added, "Who knows with Tyr...he's notorious for saying one thing and then meaning something completely different—all part of the training, he says."

I snorted and unrolled my own pastry. Sticky, buttery, flakey dough laid before me and I practically drooled on it before taking a bite. Moaning my pleasure at the symphony of godly flavors.

Then I watched in disbelief as a bronze hand reached into my space and ripped off a piece of my hand pie without so much as a may I. Following that hand, I dragged my gaze upwards, watching the smirking shifter king slowly place my pastry in his mouth and chew.

Licking his lips, he drew them into a salacious challenging smile that made my shadows curl up around me possessively.

Penina whispered a harsh curse next to us.

"Care to try that again?" My shadows darkened and curled around my arms, following the swirls of my tattooed ink.

Emon raised his brow with a predatory gleam. "If I do?"

I gripped my dagger from my boot and threw it point down into the stone surface of the table—right in front of my pastry and said sweetly. "I didn't promise Jarquinn not to kill you today."

He chuckled darkly and then lunged. His shifter speed was a blur but I also had speed of my own. Another dagger appeared in my hand from the void and I threw it at his advance. Emon's claws slashed outward and the blade ricocheted off them, spinning straight for the youthful shifter munching happily away on her own treat.

Right before it struck, Penina leaned backwards, the blade passing by her nose as she took another bite, humming delightedly to herself before returning to her seated position.

At the same time, my shadows launched forward, pinning the king of shifter's arm to the table while my hand wrapped around the buried dagger between us. The blade spun in my palm until its edge pressed against Emon's exposed throat, my fingers curling around the hilt. Our heavy breaths mingled together while I leaned into his space, and Emon smiled, brushing his nose against mine with a rumbling purr.

"You should look up, little umbra," he teased and I could see his other hand in my periphery waving.

My eyes slid to his waving hand where my damned pastry was skewered on his claws like a dessert barbecue.

"Your move," he whispered, kissing my turned cheek affectionately.

Sliding my gaze back to him, I played his game, returning his affection with a soft kiss on his smiling mouth. "I could just slit your throat and take it," I whispered breathily, watching his eyes dilate with desire.

Emon purred. Somehow leaning closer without actually touching me. "Such a savage, bloodthirsty animal you are, you sure you're not a shifter too?"

The sound of baking paper sliding between us drew my attention. Glancing down, I noted another fresh pastry bag had been placed in front of me along with my wayward dagger.

I snatched the bag, pulling the dagger from the shifter king's throat, and sitting back down with a quizzical look.

Penina winked watching me toss the daggers back into the void. "His majesty is known for pinching pastries, General Dark. I had a feeling you wouldn't appreciate that, knowing your affinity for them. I was prepared." She shrugged and nudged Emon with her elbow. "You should really ask him sometime why his nose remains crooked."

Emon grinned at me and lowered my skewered pastry down to his delectable mouth, eating it straight from his claws, and challenging me with that fierce stare.

I scowled, digging into the bag. "I was wondering why you ordered five of them." I murmured but eyed Penina's anticipatory character suspiciously.

Emon drew my attention by slapping his toned stomach happily, then chuckled. "Do you mind releasing your shadows now?" The three of us glanced down. The shadows were currently snuggling Emon's arm like a damned cat. "They are not so much holding me hostage now as they are cuddling me." He shook his head at them ruefully and reached over to pet them.

"Stop domesticating them," I snapped out and commanded the shadows to release the king. Slowly...almost reluctantly they released him.

Emon chuckled and stretched out his newly freed arm. "Now that we are all fed—"

I interrupted him with a snort and bit with emphasis into my hand pie.

He stared at my mouth as I chewed, then blinked, clearing his throat. "Almost fed. We are leaving for the outposts today, as soon as we finish up here."

"It wasn't Tyr that sent Xi on a mission was it?" Penina's normally cheerful demeanor darkened. I had seen it like this once before...during breakfast yesterday when she learned news that the queen had survived.

Emon spread his feet outward, brushing his legs against mine affectionately. I allowed it. The shifter was quickly becoming my constant grounding force and I craved the security that brought me.

"Technically he did, on my orders though."

"And when you say we?" she questioned darkly.

"Tyr, Xi and Riley, You, Remnant, and I."

"No." The word left my mouth instantly, both shifters turned to me. "I'm not going anywhere where Riella is not. I promised that faeling I would stay with her. I won't break that on your whims."

"It is in her best interest for us to leave," Emon said slowly, watching my reaction attentively, "the blood wraith attack yesterday proved that."

I shifted in my seat and narrowed my eyes. "You think my presence led them here. Why?"

He tracked my movement like startled prey. "They traveled into the Wildwoods, The Under, and now here. As I said before, I don't believe in coincidences and I know you do not either."

"No, I do not," I hissed through gritted teeth. The shadows curled around my arms, sensing my unease.

Emon watched them sadly as if he was disappointed he could not be the one to comfort me. "I assure you, little umbra. Riella will be safe here. I have ordered Jarquinn to triple the wards on the healer quarters and no one is allowed in but you, me, and the master healer himself. Besides...there is someone you demanded to see that resides in the outposts. And I am a fae of my word." His leg brushed against me again, his eyes imploring me to understand.

I arched a brow at him. "Bane."

Penina inhaled sharply and looked away.

"Yes," Emon growled.

I shook my head. "If you tripled the wards then you felt that she was not safe here, all the more reason for me to stay. Send for Bane to come here."

Emon growled and leaned forward, "I tripled the wards as a precaution because we are leaving, not because Riella is not safe here." He cleared his throat when his voice became unsteady and he raked his hands through his hair. "Trust me when I say this, there is absolutely *nothing* in this world, nothing in this goddess forsaken universe even, that I wouldn't do to ensure her safety."

I scrutinized the shifter in front of me. Emon knew something that I did not, it was lying there beneath the surface and clearly he was shaken by it.

Penina turned back, the darkness still prowling in her eyes. "Your majesty, allow me to scout ahead to ensure your safety?"

Emon tilted his head at her and then slowly nodded. "Of course. General Tyr and the others should be already on their way. You will likely catch up to them. Stay with them please and bring your provisions."

I scowled with irritation.

Penina nodded and stood gracefully, smoothing down her lavender outfit. "I will see you there," she said tightly and then spun, walking away with quick silent feet. Right before she disappeared around the corner she threw a warning look at her king. "By the way, your majesty. There is another pastry under your seat. So stop salivating over General Dark's!"

Emon and I both turned towards each other and I quickly reached down, stuffing the remainder of my pastry into my mouth unceremoniously.

"It's mine now, shifter," I cooed, chomping on the sticky cherry dough zealously.

Emon's deep dark chuckle caused me to pause mid chew.

Smiling, he reached across the table to tuck a piece of my hair behind my ear before he poked at my overstuffed cheeks. "It wasn't the pastry I was salivating over my little umbra."

# CHAPTER 55

"W HY WOULD BANE LIVE outside the city?" Remnant mused keeping up with my quick strides without complaint. Her shadows weaved around her happily, dodging direct sunlight, and at times, disappearing altogether to pop back into existence once more.

"It's Bane. Who knows why that asshole does what he does." I avoided the direct answer, she would find out soon enough. "And the outposts are not just outside the city's edge. They are at the base of the Red Cap Mountains and the lands bordering them. It is where the deadlands are."

She paused for a moment, chewing on her lip. "Why do you dislike him?"

I snorted and slowed my pace to keep her from jogging next to me. "Why do *you* not dislike him?"

Remnant smirked up at me, her green eyes flashing. "I never said I liked him, shifter." She flipped her long blue black hair over her shoulder with a huff. "Goddess knows he's beaten the crap out of me enough times during training. I hated him as much as I respected him then. But there is truly no one better with weapons in all of Faerie than him. He's earned the right to be a bastard."

"Even better than you?" I squinted up at the hot sun, cursing. We would have to travel fast to get there before dark.

A quiet snicker left her. "My methods are not...formal enough for Bane. He does not call it mastery." She pursed her lips, the laughter still alight in her emerald eyes and I couldn't help but purposefully pause to remember the look of her in this moment.

"Bane should appreciate a fae using their natural instincts to stay alive in this world," I said, quickly noticing her startled look. I walked faster. "No war was ever won by following the rules."

Remnant laughed, jogging next to me again. "You may keep your reasons for not liking Bane to yourself, but *that is* the exact reason why he would not like you."

I grinned while baring my teeth. "You are correct in saying that. Our dislike for one another is the only thing we have in common, unless it is about you of course."

The city's guards bowed low as we excited into the valley.

Remnant chewed on her lip again and I found myself waiting in anticipation for her next inquisition. I was thoroughly enjoying her openness.

"What is your shifter form?"

My stride faltered with surprise. I looked down at her. "You don't know?"

She shot me a look of annoyance. "If I did I would not have asked, *your majesty*."

I raised a brow. "We are back to that again, are we, little umbra?"

"We never left it," she shrugged.

I chuckled and shook my head, placing my hand on the small of her back to guide her towards the river that surrounded our valley. "I thought it was common knowledge. My shifter form is not like most. It's part of the reason why I never shifted before you knew who I was."

She rolled her eyes. "Forgive me for not subscribing to the history and life of the *golden* prince's fan club."

I stopped abruptly and looked down at her in surprise. The tinge of jealousy there was something I had not expected from her. A gentle wind blew her hair across her aggravated face and I could not resist tucking it back, allowing my fingers to trail down her cheek.

"You should, you know. Subscribe, I mean. You'd be the first and only one in it. Ever."

She arched a brow at me. "I don't believe that for a second, your majesty. I'm sure your city is full of such fan clubs."

"Be that as it may, I only care about one of them and it's the one you are in."

My soulmate huffed but she did not pull away from my touch, if anything she leaned more into it, something she had done more than once today.

"Why are you avoiding my questions?" she murmured.

"I suspect the same reason why you are avoiding telling me if you want to be in my fan club."

"Tell me." She finally pulled away from me and glared.

I dropped my hand, enjoying the commanding tone growled from her delectable lips. "Just like your shadows are different from your own court, my shifter side is different too...the cat's soul is his own...he is not of our world."

*"Thank the Goddess for that."* The beast peeked out from my deep subconscious where he had been sulking.

*"I was wondering when you were going to chime in. I believe that was the longest you have gone,"* I shot back harshly.

The cat huffed. *"You told me not to speak to you."*

Remnant's green eyes studied me for a moment, reading the inner dialogue on my face. "Show me him."

My brows raised up humorously and studied the stubborn set of her jaw. "Are you commanding me again, little umbra?"

"I really wish you'd stop calling me that."

*Little umbra*, little shadow. From the moment I first spoke those words and I heard her deadened heart come stuttering back to life, I knew that I would never go a day without making sure I said it as often as I could.

"I don't think so. Besides, your shadows would be disappointed if I did." On cue, the shadows burst forth, spinning me in their tornado of darkness before releasing me into a dizzying stumble of laughter.

Remnant sniffed and her lip pouted out. "Do not underestimate their loyalty to me just because of their fondness for you."

My smile diminished and I nodded seriously. "I would never question their loyalty to you, Remnant Dark." I stared deep into her eyes. "And know that you are worthy of that loyalty from all of Faerie, not just your shadows."

She broke my stare, looking out over the river with pain in her eyes. "Loyalty to me only gets fae killed, shifter. Like my shadows, you don't know what I am capable of, which is why I don't champion any fan club."

Reaching outwards, I turned her face towards me meeting the blaze in her emerald eyes. Goddess, I could lose myself in her eyes alone. Pledge my entire being with just one look from them.

"I know exactly what you are capable of and more Remnant Dark. I'm not afraid of it. I fucking want to unleash it. But if you cannot be in my fan club...then I will be in yours. Always." I leaned in and planted a soft kiss on her plush mouth before pulling away. "I also find that I cannot deny you anything. So prepare yourself."

She frowned.

*"Your turn, cat,"* I growled low in warning. *"Don't fuck this up."*

# CHAPTER 56

Remnant

IN A BRIGHT FLASH, the breath rushed out of me as I stared up at the shifted towering form of Emon's beast.

A radiant and monstrous *golden* panther.

His fierce feline eyes, rich with the same gold light as Emon, lowered down to peer at me and the power that radiated off of him was terrifying.

Without any self preservation, I took a trembling step forward in awe. If I thought that being around Emon was like being burned by the sun, then his panther's presence was like being burned by all the stars in the sky.

Emon was correct. His beast was not of this world, perhaps not even this universe.

The cat's regal head bowed. *"Finally we meet, princess of the shadows."* His voice was dulcet and cultured, it boomed melodiously inside of my head.

My shadows rushed toward the giant beast the moment he spoke, draping over him like one would a lost friend. For a brief moment, the beast was a true panther in all black and within, there was darkness. A cold calculated killer that lurked beneath the breathtaking shimmer of his mystic self.

"Where is Emon?" I narrowed my gaze on him suspiciously, suddenly worried for the fae that was stealing the shattered pieces of my heart.

*"Fairy boy is more than safe."* His bright eyes blinked slowly. *"He is currently yelling at me to stop scaring you."*

My lips twitched. "Fairy boy." I shook my head. "I am not frightened but merely intrigued."

The panther's great paw swiped at the shadows, peeling them off of him like the shedding of a cloak. *"Forgive me. He said that your look indicated either you were afraid of me or were going to kill me. I didn't believe the latter."* Lowering his body to the ground so that his massive head was only inches from mine, he regarded me thoughtfully. His long golden tail flicked back and forth. *"We are trapped with each other as you see but worry not. He is still here. He's always here. Like an itch I can't scratch. Like a parasite that won't die. Like a disease with no cure."*

I laughed in the face of the universe's ultimate predator. "That is most unfortunate," I said with mock sincerity.

The panther grinned, a terrifying sight of sharp gleaming white teeth that in length were as long as my arms.

"Are there any more like you?" I said breathlessly.

He shook his great golden head, sadness echoing in those mystic glowing eyes before answering. *"I do not know. I cannot remember, princess of shadows."*

"I am sorry to hear that," I said simply.

*"As am I."*

My shadows rubbed against his front legs sympathetically and he turned his head into them purring affectionately before batting them down playfully into the ground. His dangerous black claws slicing through them without harm.

"You seem to know each other?" I watched the shadows curl around his front legs and he nipped at them friskily.

*"Perhaps from a life that has long passed, I believe,"* he rumbled, shaking the shadows off of him, growling. *"Would you do me the honor of allowing me to escort you to the outposts? Fairy boy is most anxious to get there before nightfall."*

I opened my mouth to protest but snapped it closed when the regal panther moved closer, turning one eye on me. I could see my full silhouette in the reflection of his golden gaze and my nervous shifting in the presence of his greatness.

*"I understand that you would prefer not to, but please spare an old cat the torture of listening to the fairy boy complain about it. He is already demanding that I will have to make you see reason."*

I snorted and rolled my eyes. Swallowing down the numerous questions I wanted to ask the panther. "I'll concede then, only to spare you the torture of course. But you will owe me."

The great cat's pink tongue darted out to lick his lethal sharp canine slowly. *"To owe a fae is a dangerous bargain."* He smiled again and I suppressed a shudder. *"But I find I am intrigued and will play this game."*

"May I?" I reached my hand out towards the side of his face, his whiskers brushing coarsely against my bare arms.

The panther inclined his head. *"I am honored princess."*

My hand shook slightly when I tentatively reached out to touch his fur and sunk into his fine silky coat while I marveled at the dreamy texture. The giant of a cat melted under my touch, purring happily when I continued my petting from his neck to shoulder, pausing only to wonder how in the goddess I would ascend such a beast.

The shadows decided for me, wrapping around my middle and suspending me upward until I sat astride the panther's powerful front legs. His body was so massive I was forced to tuck my feet behind me, leaning forward into his enormous frame.

*"Fairy boy insists that you hold on tightly. I am in agreement."* He looked back over his shoulders.

I nodded eagerly and I grasped fistfuls of his silken fur. I exhaled slowly. "I'm ready."

He hummed and I felt his muscle tense before he bounded forward, soaring over the expansive river that bordered Finlandia.

A squeal of delight escaped me, watching the valley and water blur beneath us in more than a twenty foot drop that left me breathless. He raced gracefully through the valley, speeding faster and faster towards the Red Cap Mountains. His powerful body and pace created a strong wind that whipped back my hair and stung my eyes, cooling my body from the burning West Isle sun.

My shadows raced with us. Blasting in front of the panther with their smokey darkness, that in turn he would plunge through with zero fear, transforming his body from black to gold before the shadows rippled away, parachuting behind us to start their game anew.

Laughing, I tilted my head back and released my hands from their tight grip to raise them above my head. Closing my eyes, I breathed as the world passed us by.

"Amazing," I whispered. This...was living.

*"We are both glad you approve, princess of the shadows,"* the panther's voice rumbled beneath me.

Bringing my hands back down, I leaned forward again. "Why do you call me that? I am no more a princess than the blades of grass beneath us. The faerie queen disbanded monarchy within the courts many years ago." It was her way to unite all the fae under one ruler...to bring the courts together.

It was a facade. Deirdre coveted power and saw a chance to take it. Only one court did not follow. The shifters.

*"Like Emon and I. You are more than what you realize."*

I paused, giving his words more thought. Unlike my people, my sentient shadows came the night I was born and never left my side since. My brother and I's biological father was always a mystery to us, one not even our mother could explain or never wanted to.

"What is your name?" I wondered out loud.

*"Cat. Beast. Unseemingly other things the fairy boy calls me that I will not repeat,"* he grumbled inside my mind.

I laughed. "You are much too celestial for me to call you such names," I teased.

He purred. *"I held many names. Many titles. None of which I can remember now."*

"How does one forget their own name?" I stroked his fur sympathetically.

*"Unfortunately, I do not know the answer to that either."* His gold eyes looked over his shoulder at me briefly. *"What name would you choose for me?"*

I frowned at the unusual request. Like all fae, I believed a name held power. For one to know its true form was to have power over you. Bravely, and with more trepidation than I cared to admit, I ran my hands through the panther's silky golden fur once more and turned on my aura sight, something I had been avoiding since meeting him.

I gasped at the blinding infinite shimmer of white gold that stole my vision. His aura blocked out the sky, the sun, the moons, the land before us. I was completely encapsulated within its glow. Its stretch was vast with no ending to its divine light.

The panther was power, he was godly, he was universal, he was supreme, he was—"Ethereal," I whispered, the name escaping from my lips like a soft prayer.

His aura flashed brightly before burning away, returning my normal vision. I blinked at the renewed shimmering sparkle of his golden coat.

*"Yes! That is my name. I remember now. Thank you! Thank you, princess of the shadows!"*

I was stunned. "You're welcome, Ethereal," I said baffled. "You are most welcome."

# CHAPTER 57

I PACED INSIDE THE cat's mind. Livid, shocked, helpless.

Thousands of years I lived with the cat bastard. When I first shifted as a cub I was terrified of him and wanted to know more about the voice in my head, in my teen years I challenged him demanding that he tell me who he was, and now in my adult years I just learned to live with him, never asking again since silence was all that met me when I did.

Yet my soulmate met him for five fucking minutes and had him purring in her hands and with a name to call him by.

I paused my pacing to rage. *"Why in the fuck wouldn't you tell me that you lost your name? After all those years I asked about it, about you. Why?"*

*"I could not nor was it necessary,"* he sounded resigned, despite the delight I could feel burning through him.

*"Not necessary?"* I practically snarled at him within his consciousness. *"Giving a name is bestowing trust. Trust you obviously never deemed me worthy of. We are fucking stuck together... forever...or did you think that someday you'd get rid of me."*

There was a long pause. *"You are more than worthy, Daemon Ash Strider and I would never harm you."*

*"Thats not a fucking apology, Ethereal,"* I snarled out his name.

He sighed. *"There is not much I can tell you, fairy boy. My name was...lost, it has been lost a long time. I am left with very few memories and I did not want you to feel responsible for hunting those down too. When you first came to maturity, there was already so much responsibility on your shoulders. The son of a king, with a legendary beast, and power that rivaled the gods. Then your mother died, you lost your father...it did not seem important anymore."*

I snorted. *"Careful cat, you almost sound like you care about my life. And Remnant, where does she play in all this? What is she to you? Because if you think for one fucking second I'll let you use her like you have used me—"*

The panther snarled at me. *"Enough! Like the fae, I cannot lie. I would never hurt you. Which means I could never possibly harm her. Be at ease, Emon. As I said, I remember very little about my own life but what I do remember was that only your soulmate could ever recover what I had lost."*

*"How convenient for you,"* I snarled, *"So it is her that you will burden with finding your lost memories is it? Well too fucking bad, I won't allow it."*

The panther huffed. *"You do not listen, still young, still hot headed and ignorant to the words you do not wish to hear. I shall repeat it one more time for your fairy brain. None of it is important to me anymore."*

I snapped my teeth at him and paced again.

*"I know you are angry with me, fairy boy. But I am beginning to think our connection is more of a blessing than a curse, as you so wonderfully put it. Call it my redemption if you cannot trust that I care for you, a second chance to do what is right."*

Both our attentions snapped back to the present at the sound of Remnant's voice.

"The deadlands," I heard her gasp.

Normally, the panther's sight was awash with color, each varied tone corresponded with a specific scent that immediately gave him a predatorial edge. But within the deadlands—when he turned his vision to this lifeless void, there was nothing. Just gray bleakness and the putrid stench of decay.

The extent of the Balsam Plains and The Under had nothing on the deadlands of The West Isles. The death stretched for miles without any end. Most of it bordered the long ridgeline of the Red Cap Mountains and deep into the southern valleys.

Despite my deal to Remnant to see the asshole swordmaster Bane Steelhead, I was here for someone else entirely. A being that most of Faerie thought was dead.

A lone roar and a snarl disturbed my inward thoughts and I grinned at the sound. Riley and Xi sat astride Tyr and Penina's large cat forms, racing alongside us.

Remnant shouted a laughing greeting to them while the panther slowed his pace across the dusty lifeless lands to allow the smaller cats to keep up.

*"We are here."* I stared out through the panther's eyes at the outpost with hard resolve. *"My best wishes to you, fairy boy,"* the panther said gently and then slowed into a stalking prowl. *"Know that I do care, Emon. Deeply. I will do everything it takes to keep you and your family alive."*

Then the bastard shifted. Remnant's body slid into my waiting arms and I gripped her to my chest, breathing into a dark cloud of her blue-black hair and with it my new favorite scent of lilies.

She gasped. "Emon." Her head tilted up at me and I swept away the hair from her face. "Your panther is amazing."

My hands slid upwards, tangling into her windswept locks, taking in the exhilarated color on her pale cheeks, the brightness in her eyes, the small vulnerable smile on her soft lips.

I kissed her gently. "The cat does not need more fuel for his ego." Inhaling, I grumbled. "You do not think he is more amazing than me do you?"

She laughed then, pushing me away from her with a deep blush spreading across her cheeks. "You are almost as incorrigible as Penina and Xi."

On cue, our friends shifted and stepped in line beside us as we looked up at the outpost manor.

Remnant placed her hands on her black leather clad hips. "So—this is where the great swordmaster Bane lives."

"Yea, piece of shit if you ask me, beauty," Tyr remarked behind us.

A hard slap of skin echoed off the ridgeline of the Red Caps.

"Owe, what the fuck, Chin? I am still your General here. I could make you pay for that."

I heard Xi snort. "Then don't be an insensitive dickwad."

"Dickwad you say?" Tyr growled low. "You won't be saying that later Chin."

"Quivering with fear, General," Xi said dryly.

I shook my head. I should have thought harder on what it would mean to have Tyr, Xi, and Riley all in one place.

But Tyr was right. This place was in need of some vast improvements. The outpost had once been a gateway manor into the mountain ranges and was flanked by two soaring towers. Standing atop one of those towers, one could overlook Finlandia and even see a bit of the coastline of its white sandy shores.

It was in much worse shape than the last time I was here. A dreadful task that I never wanted to relive again, nor come back to again.

The others were quiet behind us. We were all on a precipice. The moment we stepped forward everything would change. Looking at my soulmate's silhouette backed against the bright red of the mountain ranges, I realized I had been foolish for holding back for so long. She had a right to know.

"Remnant..." She turned, her brow arched. My mouth opened and closed. Where the fuck did I begin?

*"Speak from the heart,"* Ethereal said gently.

"Daemon?"

Remnant spun back around at the sound of the gruff voice coming from the manor's entrance. I dragged my eyes to the source, my gaze sliding over the tall imposing fae that took up most of the doorframe, his eyes the exact replica of my own, wide with alarm.

I straightened and nodded cordially. "Father."

"Goddess, it is you!" he gasped and took a hesitating step forward. "My son."

# CHAPTER 58

Asher Windswift Strider, former king of The West Isles, thought to be killed by my hand five hundred years ago, stood alive and well in the large doorway of the manor.

I knew the stories they told. That he had become a mad king after the death of his wife, my mother, and that I took advantage of his grief and killed him in cold blood for the throne.

And I had let those rumors spread, encouraged them to spread. Fear of the murderous shifter king that killed his own father kept my court safe but also kept my father safe as well, except that wasn't the truth of it.

Even at his most blood thirsty stage, I was devoted to my father. He was my role model, my idol, I wanted to *be* him. I obeyed his orders, sent shifters to their deaths under them and I told myself that it was justice for us, for our family, for my mother. But deep down I knew that she would have never wanted to see innocent fae being slaughtered in her name.

It wasn't until my father commanded our most powerful ancients and master healer to pick up his retired sword, that I knew he had to be stopped. Jarquinn had vowed after his wife died in the blood wars, that he would never kill again but the master healer was also fiercely loyal to my father. When I found Jar unsheathing his blade with tears running down his kind and beautiful face, something in me snapped.

That day was the day that I invoked the ancient and archaic shifter law called Bloodlust Rights. A challenge to death...a law made specifically to protect the shifters when their ruler became lost to bloodlust.

But by doing so, I invoked the rage of another fae...who joined my father in the fight against me. The swordmaster, Bane Steelhead.

Most believed the swordmaster had earned his right to live within shifter lands from sheer skill alone, but that wasn't the true story.

What was true, was that Bane Steelhead had grown up with my mother Skyler, on Inquus Islands, a small grouping of tropical isles off the coast of our mainlands. Bane had been my mother's closest friend growing up and at one time they were even lovers. Except, their time together came to an abrupt end, when my father visited the isles and met my mother for the first time. Their soulmate bond snapped into place immediately and they were inseparable ever since.

Call it unrequited love or just a coveted infatuation, but Bane Steelhead never stopped caring for my mother even then and spent much of his time visiting her after his travels to become the best weapons master Faerie had ever known.

My father, wholly in love with his wife, respected and acknowledged their friendship, and awarded Bane Steelhead the rights to live among the shifters of The West Isles. The first elemental to ever do so.

He was a happier fae then, from what I was told. Until I was born. I was a very glaringly obvious symbol of something he would never have with my mother, even though he loved her fiercely. Just like my father, when my mother was murdered, a piece of Bane did too.

Both of their devotional love for the same woman was almost an unstoppable force the day I fought them both in the arena. I had barely walked away with my life that day but instead of finishing them both off, I banished them. For the sake of my mother's memory and the two fae that loved her so fiercely.

I hadn't been back here since...until now.

My thoughts slipped back into the present as my eyes slid over to Remnant and froze. The mixture of disbelief and betrayal in her stare gutted me.

"Remnant." I took a step forward.

She held up her hand, shaking her head. "How many more secrets, shifter?"

I flinched and pressed my lips together.

She sighed shakily. "Too many then."

I sensed our friend's shift nervously behind me. "Scout the area!" I barked. "I want to know if the deadlands have spread further since the last report and if there are any wraiths nearby."

"Yes, your majesty," they all murmured in unison, quickly moving away from the potential storm brewing.

"He is the other reason we came here," I ran my hand through my hair explaining, "we will need him."

Her jaw tightened. "I suspect you have some plan formulated that you have not told me about then." Her lips pursed and she shook her head. "An alliance means we work together, Emon, not just when you decide if and when it is convenient for you."

I grunted at the verbal blow. "There is more..." I sighed. "Time just has not been on our side for me to explain."

The shadows curled around her arms as she tilted her head, lips still pursed thoughtfully. I held my breath at the silence between us.

"We will have to make time then," she said slowly.

I exhaled harshly. "Deal."

A throat cleared.

"I hope I am not interrupting too much."

We both turned to watch my father's approach, the slight limp in his gait a painful reminder of the day I had stripped him of his crown and banished him to the outposts. Jarquinn was barely able to save his leg when my panther had ripped it off during our fight for the throne. Fae healed from most injuries but a severed limb was difficult to heal fully.

*"He was mad with bloodlust and he would have never stopped his thirst for revenge. Your people were paying the price. We did what we had to do, fairy boy. He would have killed you."*

My jaw clenched, despite his limp, I could still see the dominant and powerful ancient shifter fae I knew him to be. He looked strong, healthy, and above all else...sane.

Shaggy blonde hair trailed over his shoulders, his eyes were slanted like all the ancient fae's were, and he sported a full neatly groomed beard that glinted in the sun. We were both similar in build and height, with the trademark golden eyes of the Strider clan.

"I do believe that it is us interrupting you, father."

Cunning eyes glanced between my soulmate and I. He bent to take a knee before me. "Your majesty. Your presence honors me. How may I be of service?"

"You need not bow for me, father. Are you not well?" I asked with alarm, reaching for him to rise and then staring at the tears that fell down his face. I had never known my father to cry. Not even when we lost my mother.

He smiled sadly, gripping my arm tightly, "Yes, my king. I am well. I am just a father happy to see his son."

I arched my brow. If he was being facetious I could not tell.

"The formal titles are not necessary either, father."

I reached for Remnant. She sidestepped my hand to move next to me. Her avoidance to my touch was guttural. Somehow the distance between us in that moment felt greater than ever, despite her standing shoulder to shoulder with me.

"I'd like to introduce you to General Remnant Dark. Remnant, this is my father, Asher Windswift Strider, former king of The West Isles. I do believe you once begrudgingly respected one another while strategizing ways to kill each other at the same time."

My father's eyes widened on my soulmate. "At last, we meet, General. My son is correct. It is both fortunate and unfortunate that we have not yet met. Even in my madness, I always looked forward to your next move. You are quite the clever strategist...Faerie was lucky to have you." His gold eyes twinkled as he extended out his hand.

"I don't believe they share that sentiment." My soulmate's voice was strong and unwavering as she took my fathers hand. "Your Grace."

My father raised her hand to his lips, kissing it softly. "You have the look of your mother in you, General Dark." His eyes roamed her face, searching.

There was no stopping the warning growl, but a sharp glance and a deep chuckle from my father was enough to tell me it had been a test. And I failed. He knew what she was to me. Remnant snatched her hand back and glared at both of us.

"It seems whether it was intentional or not, I am eternally indebted to you, General Dark, for bringing my son back to me."

"Your son has a way of keeping his intentions to himself, so there is no debt owed, your grace," Remnant stated sharply and I grunted at the blow of her stinging words.

A barking chuckle shook my fathers wide shoulders. "Asher will do just fine, General. My son is the king here, I'm just an old fae who's happy to have company." He smiled at me and I was taken aback by the love I saw there.

No hate. No resentment.

*"Your father has always loved you. He stayed away because you both needed time to heal,"* the panther sighed.

*"I am not sure if I am liking this nice streak, cat."*

*"Apologies, fairy boy. Perhaps it's a momentary lapse in my judgment but I rarely make those kinds of mistakes."*

I couldn't help the snort that escaped, drawing their startled gazes.

"That panther harassing you still son?"

I sighed. "When has there ever been a time where he has not? His name is Ethereal by the way."

My father's blonde brows rose all the way up to his hairline. "That old cat finally told you his name, did he?"

"Fuck no." I looked at Remnant who shot me a smug grin. "He gave General Dark the *permission* to name him."

My father stared for a long moment, before he threw his head back with howling laughter.

I felt my tension ease at the rich sound and I smiled at the pleasure the simple story had given him. My father was exactly the fae I fondly remembered him to be before our family had been ripped apart.

"What is all this goddess damn racket you are making out here Asher? Are you trying to attract every wraith in the five hundred mile radius?!" Bellowed a stern voice from inside the manor.

I growled. Goddess help us all. Bane Steelhead had arrived.

The bastard rushed out like a wailing banshee with his sword swinging, poised to strike down anything within reach. His body itself was honed like a weapon, all sharp angles of lean muscle, he was always vigilant, always ready. His steel blue eyes cut through me and I crossed my arms to watch the foolish spectacle he created.

Sparks flew and I saw his intention before he even moved. His deadly blade rising to cleave me in two.

*"Idiot,"* the panther and I growled simultaneously, ready to take him down.

# CHAPTER 59

Emon

I DIDN'T NEED TO move, I couldn't move.

A shadow fae was in my way, the ringing of her blade blocking the swordmaster's reverberated off the mountains. The sound was so loud that it toned out my father's roars for his friend to cease his attack.

Shadows ricocheted off her parrying blade and darkness rose around her. Standing ready, if she needed them.

Bane's eyes narrowed on my soulmate, and his muscles rippled while he pushed dangerously against the lock of their blades. "So this is how it is to be then, Dark?"

Remnant did not falter under his continued pressure and her voice was without strain. "To what are you referring, swordmaster? You attack without provocation, you are far too old for these kinds of games, Bane."

Bane bared his blunt teeth and pushed harder, sparks flying over his arms...*lightning* sparks. Bane was a fire elemental.

"The boy lives, that's provocation enough. He is no king of mine," he spat.

Remnant shoved his blade upwards and inched closer. "Nor is he mine and you don't see me trying to kill him."

Bane smirked lethally, more white hot electricity crawling up his arms. "Yet."

I remained intelligently quiet. I wasn't about to remind Remnant that she had threatened to kill me just this morning.

Instead, my eyes trailed over her powerful stance, pausing on the round globes of her flexing ass. A delicious sight that was worth the momentary delay.

"Stop staring at my ass, shifter," she hissed, her eyes staying on Bane. To break eye contact now would be submitting to the bastard and I knew enough about my soulmate to recognize that she would never let that happen.

"You can't blame me, little umbra," I groaned, "You are the sexiest fae alive when you are defending me like this."

Sparking steel eyes, bulging with disbelief, cut over her shoulder at me. "Show some damned respect boy."

"Indeed. I'd say the same to you, Steelhead," I snickered and waved my hand through the shadows that curled around her like poisonous smoke. Bane's eyes narrowed, then widened when the shadows danced along my body in their usual playful manner.

Smugly, I hummed, twirling the shadows around my fingers. "Was that enough, little umbra?"

There was a hint of a smile in her tone. "More than enough, your majesty."

Bane swore just before Remnant swept his blade aside and sent a violent kick into his chest. His solid frame flying backwards to land unceremoniously on his arrogant ass.

"At least when you tossed me, I landed on my feet," I remarked dryly.

Remnant's lip twitched and she twirled her ominous shadow blade with a flourish at the swordmaster.

"You're losing your touch, old man. Allowing yourself to get distracted like a faeling and taking your eyes off your opponent. A novice knows better."

My father prowled over to Bane and yanked the stunned swordmaster back to his feet. Leaning forward, he snapped his teeth directly in his face. "Like a goddess damned prick you mean." Shaking Bane, he roared, "Daemon is *my son*! Mine! We live because of him. And I will kill you if you ever try that fucking shit again. Don't fucking test me in this, Bane."

Bane shoved away from my father. "Fuck off Asher, you're a right bastard too just like him. Your asshole son brought with him the most dangerous shadow fae alive, two powerful shifters, and two elementals who were former captains in *her* army. I wonder why they are here." He pointed an accusing finger at Remnant and I growled lunging forward.

Only to be cut short by the blunt of a black blade slapping against my chest. Nostrils flaring, I slowly looked down at the her sword. "Little umbra..."

"Hush, shifter." Remnant didn't even bother to spare me a glance and cocked her head at Bane with a mocking smile. "My, my, my, Bane. You sound paranoid. Although, I do appreciate the fine compliments. Most powerful you say?"

Steel eyes narrowed on the blade restraining me, or rather the reason I had not shoved it away. "Not powerful enough if this is the filth you acquaint yourself with these days."

"The only filth I see is the shit all over your pants from falling on your ass, Bane Steelhead."

I laughed derisively only to be slapped in the chest again by her blade. Bringing my laughter to a whining halt.

"I said hush, shifter. I am still pissed at you too. You brought me here to meet your father under false pretenses, a fae who is supposedly dead, and my former enemy no less? Do you have any idea how messed up this is?"

I tapped her blade with an extended claw. "You wouldn't have come then."

Bane choked on his own laughter.

Remnant glared at him. "Shut up swordmaster. You have no room to talk. You sent this nuisance to track me down."

"I thought you'd be skilled enough to avoid him," Bane shot back and then gave me a look of disgust.

My eyes narrowed but I obeyed my soulmate. Pressing my lips together and gritting my teeth, I made not a sound.

The swordmaster's brows arched mockingly. "So the pup does know how to obey."

"Stop provoking him, Bane," my father and Remnant snapped at the same time.

I grinned wildly at the two of them, silently laughing at the look of horror on Remnant's face and the one of approval on my father's.

Bane shifted his focus from me. "You've gotten much faster, Dark."

She inclined her head towards him in respect. "I once had a great mentor."

Bane's smile was genuine this time but it did not last when he jutted his chin toward her feet. "I take it back. Your stance is all wrong."

Remnant tilted her head, her black and blue hair trailing over her bare tattooed shoulder. "Your eyes are old, they do not see things correctly. Allow me to help you with that."

Releasing her blade from my chest with a flourish she lunged for the swordmaster who grinned in the face of her assault. Raising his blade at the very last second to defend himself, he parried and thrusted back. The sound of their blades echoed in the dimming light.

"She is very good." My father stepped next to me to watch their physical prowess.

"You haven't seen anything yet," I said wryly, "but if he so much as nicks her, his head will be on a pike outside Finlandia gates."

He snorted. "I do not doubt that, my son." He nodded at my arms. "New pets?"

I followed his gaze to the now docile shadows curled in my arm. I hadn't even realized I had been holding them to me like a slumbering cat.

I shook my head, smiling fondly at them. "They seem to have claimed me."

"As much as their owner has it would seem."

I grunted. I knew he had seen the truth the moment he laid eyes on Remnant.

"That series was sloppy Dark!" Bane chastised loudly as he shifted into an offensive attack.

"Don't mistake originality with your stiff regimented forms, Steelhead," she responded casually back.

Remnant wasn't wrong, Bane's movement, while graceful, was carefully placed footwork designed for power and positioning. Remnant's was more fluid and she slid on the terrain, allowing her to use Bane's advances against him. It was an ebb and flow that was simple and beautiful.

Remnant Ezra Solaire Dark danced as she fought.

"A blind person could see how loose that grip is. You're out of shape Dark and you will tire eventually."

She laughed and I savored the sound.

The dead dirt kicked up in a smoky cloud of dust around them as their paces quickened along with the constant clanging of their blades. Remnant's shadows snapped to attention in my arms and then leapt forward, quickly slithering across the deadlands to hover closer to their mistress.

Devoted and ready, just like I was.

My father shook his shaggy head. "I am happy you are here, my son. When should we expect the others to arrive?"

"Before sun down I expect, if the deadlands have not grown since the last report."

"Unfortunately they have but not enough to cause them to be much longer than that. I suppose Penina is one of them."

I flashed a wide feral grin at him mischievously. "Of course."

He grumbled. "That's a dangerous game you play with Bane, my cub. But then again, the sour old goat needs a little unsettling in his life." My father nodded at Bane and Remnant. "Those two look like they will be at this for a while."

"Yes," I said simply.

"You expected that...hoped for it even."

"Yes."

"This sounds like a conversation that requires a seat and a drink," my father remarked before gripping my shoulder, turning me to face him. His blonde brows rose high on his handsome face. "Let's go inside my cub and tell me what weighs so heavily on your heart when it should be light with your soulmate standing just mere feet away from you."

I barked out a short laugh. "I see you haven't lost your power of truth."

He grunted and guided me to the manor. "Sometimes I wish I had. To see beyond the falsehoods of the fae and the words they spin, to see the truth and need in others—it's more like a curse at times."

I couldn't agree more.

# CHAPTER 60

I SNIFFED AT THE drink my father placed on the long worn table between us, and my nostrils flared.

"Bane calls it Dragon's breath. It's his own brew."

Narrowing my eyes, I swirled the glass. "Is it poison?"

My father's strong shoulders shrugged and his eyes sparkled. "Likely but hasn't killed us yet."

Tossing it back with one gulp, I hissed while it slowly burned my insides. I sat down at the long kitchen table and admired the strength of the fae before me.

My father studied me with the same quiet intelligence he possessed most of my life. It had made him a powerful leader before the bloodlust took him. He poured me another drink and waited. The same way he did when I was a cub, silently watching me until I was uncomfortable enough to confess all my secrets...except this time there were so many, I didn't even know where to begin.

I dropped my gaze to my glass and swirled it just like the thoughts running amok inside my head.

The cat was surprisingly quiet. Taking a page from my father's book.

"Daemon," his voice rumbled and I looked up to see a sad smile on his face. "Son, it's been hundreds of years. Let us not waste any more time to speak to one another. What is on your mind, my cub?"

"How did you do it?" I blurted out, just like when I was young. The silence always won. "How did you stand it? When mother died?"

He stiffened and sadness bled into his patient gaze. "You and I both know that I didn't. My own people suffered and I nearly killed my own son—I almost lost everything that I loved, not just her."

My throat burned and it wasn't from Bane's poison. "I am sorry. I'm so very sorry for what I had to do."

Blonde brows fell heavy over his eyes. "My cub...you did the right thing. I would have done the same in your position. There is nothing to apologize for. After your mother—" He released a guttural growl and I tensed, my hands tightened around my glass. "After we lost her, I lost myself. The only thing that made the pain go away was giving into the rage...but it also made me forget. I forgot about everything that I once cherished." He sighed and tilted his head. "You're afraid. Afraid of this happening to you, afraid of your soulmate bond."

"I'm fucking terrified and it's not even complete. The way I feel for her..." I rasped and then bowed my head so he could not see the anguish inside of me. "I won't survive it. You know what is inside of me. Our world won't survive it. If I lose her again...I can't do it."

He was silent for a moment, his lips pressed in a thin line before he barked a short laugh. "You know what your mother would say?"

I spread my hands on the dark worn wood, not daring to look up. "What would mother say?"

"Our greatest strength comes from embracing fear with love." I could hear the sad smile in his tone. "Bond or not, my cub, you love that fae out there. That is a glaringly obvious truth. I don't need my powers to see that."

"She doesn't know," I swallowed, "I've masked the bond."

More silence.

"Why?"

I ran my hand through my hair and stared hard into his concerned eyes. "Deirdre would have used it against us, against Remnant. During my capture, she was already using her against me. She thought it was my own honor she was torturing. If she knew there was a soulmate bond," I shivered, "there's no telling what kind of depraved torture she would have concocted."

My father's gaze was intense and haunted. "Jarquinn was not alone that night he found you. You were barely alive when we tracked you down. When you were stabilized, I returned home. I was worried what my presence would do to your recovery. I should have stayed."

I inhaled sharply. "I did not know. Jar never told me."

He drew a shaky breath and leaned in towards me. "I thought I lost you Daemon, and all I could think was that one day I would be given another chance to be a better father. What Deirdre did to you, seeing her cruelty with my own eyes, the suffering you endured." He choked again and looked away. "I am sorry that you have paid the price for my mistakes Daemon. All of them it would seem."

"My suffering is nothing compared to what that bitch did to my soulmate," I rasped and I reached out to grip his hand. "And that had nothing to do with you. Deirdre was tainted from the beginning."

He gripped my hand and growled fiercely. "Are they all dead? The ones responsible?"

I blinked at the memory of terrified eyes begging for mercy, I had almost forgotten him, the human. I pulled my hand away. "All but one. But you should know it wasn't just humans under Deirdre's influence. It was our own people, father. Shifters, led by Falcon."

"Falcon?" My father hissed, curling his fingers into his palm, no doubt imagining strangling him. "What does that two faced feathered shit have to do with all this?"

I inhaled deeply. "The war between our nations had to stop. No matter how much I wanted to honor mother for you, I could not stand losing one more innocent fae."

My father remained silent...allowing it to spill more secrets.

I snarled and rapped the table with my claws. "It had to stop. The unnecessary death. Our people needed to move on and I could no longer throw the lives of good fae...the only fae left in our world right into Deirdre's heartless clutches."

My father flinched but said nothing.

I took a deep breath and I dug my claws into the table, just like my next words would do to my fathers heart. "So I drew up a peace treaty and sent Falcon with a large contingent of shifters with an offer that would appease her."

I looked away, no longer able to meet his strong gaze. I knew how it sounded but I also knew my mother. She would have done the same.

He glanced down at the table and stared at the deep gouges. "You gave her the gateway to the Sanguine."

I ripped my claws off the table and hissed at him. "Not at first, but I implied it. When Falcon sent word that she would only agree to peace if I came to the City of Light myself, I knew Falcon had betrayed us and the queen would make a play for the Sanguine. What I didn't know was the extent to which Deirdre had imprisoned her own people, Remnant included, and where they had disappeared to. Which was a problem because I had made a vow to a very persuasive swordmaster when he heard that I was traveling to Faerie."

"You got captured on purpose," he growled.

"I did." Picking up my drink, the glass shook in my hand. I swallowed, using the fiery burn to calm the rolling turmoil inside.

"Fuck Daemon."

My hand tightened on the glass. "One day my guard made an unfortunate mistake." I licked my fangs in satisfaction at the memory of slaughtering the bastard. "Even in my rage, I was pulled by an undeniable force straight towards her room instead of escaping. Her torture had driven me mad with the need to protect her and I thought perhaps I could save one soul in that goddess forsaken place, end her misery." My vision swam and I shut my eyes, the screams echoing from the past. The same ones that woke me up in cold sweat most nights. "Our bond snapped into place the moment I touched her...but I wasn't successful in getting her free."

I growled, shaking my head violently against the images, then my eyes snapped open, my power clashing thunderously inside of me and I realized I was shaking, the glass had shattered in my hand and its contents were spilling over the side of the table.

*"We are not there anymore, she is not there anymore. You are safe, fairy boy."* The panther attempted to quiet my turmoil.

I stared at the liquid as it dripped over the edge like the blood in my nightmares. My body trembled, the power burned inside of me, attempting to burst forth. Where was this fucking power when I needed it? Why had it failed me then?

*"Open our bond, Daemon, We need to filter it before it destroys this place!"* The panther growled at me, recognizing the dangerous levels spilling inside.

I stared. Drip, drip.

*"Open the bond now!"* The beast roared.

*"Fuck you,"* I snarled but it was enough. I tore my gaze away from the spilling liquid and opened our connection, allowing the beast's presence to absorb the overwhelming surge of power.

My shoulders sagged and I slumped in my chair, my breathing erratic.

Quietly, my father swept the glass aside and wiped up the liquid staining the table, then set another glass down in front of me. I watched the liquid pour in a daze.

Silence again. I hated the fucking silence.

So I continued. "I begged you know," I confessed, "I begged that fucking bitch to make me a deal. One I knew she couldn't resist. The location of the Sanguine." My head snapped up and I snarled at my father. "And now I have doomed us all and I would do it again too. I'd do anything to keep her safe. I'd barter this very world if I had to. Morta has nothing on the destruction I will bring down on Faerie if anything ever happens to her again. I have been telling myself all this time it was for her, to allow herself the choice to choose me but if I am being truthful with myself. I am fucking terrified to lose her...just like mother."

My father's eyes flashed and then he reached for me, gripping my bloodied hands that had been cut open from the shattered glass.

"What you say is true, Daemon. You are capable and powerful enough to bring this world to its knees. Your mother and I knew that the day you were born." I flinched and he squeezed my bloody hands. "But if you are in search of a truth from me then here it is. Choosing to live a life denying your soulmate the bond is the same as your fear of losing her."

I grunted.

He shook his shaggy blonde head. "As for the Sanguine. You didn't doom us Daemon. Even after the Blood Wars...we all knew that it would be a matter of time. Power like that does not die."

I gripped his hands harder and snarled at him.

"She's alive. Deirdre...Falcon too. They are all alive and they have been using the Sanguine. It is the cause of the deadlands, the wraiths, everything. Yesterday, she attempted to attack Finlandia. Wraiths and spy crows flooded the valley."

My father rocked back in his chair, utter devastation on his face. "Fuck." His eyes narrowed on me and he growled low. "You're going hunting."

A low snarl emitted from my clenched teeth. "Yes."

# CHAPTER 61

Emon

"**I**'M GOING WITH YOU." My father tapped his glass in thought. "You are king now, you do not need me to access the gateway, you also didn't need me to tell you that it's foolish to deny your soulmate bond." He leaned forward. "As happy as I am that you have come, why are you here Daemon?"

Slowly, I licked at my fang. "I have a daughter."

The whole manor suddenly became eerily quiet.

That fucking silence again.

My father blinked with his drink frozen halfway to his mouth. "I don't understand."

"During our travels, Remnant discovered a faeling hidden in The Under with powerful Sanguine wards upon her. Jarquinn was able to break them and the child transformed into her true nature." I gave him a tentative smile despite the complexity of the news. "The girl is mine and...Remnant's."

Shakily, he set the glass down without taking a drink. "How—how is this possible?"

I shook my head sadly. "The reason why Deirdre had been imprisoning fae in the first place. To find a way to procreate. It would seem that she was finally successful with her experiments using Remnant and I."

*"He will not remember the origin of the curse, the story of the goddess's brothers, careful with your words, fairy boy. Remember your promise to the healer."*

"You have a cub? A daughter? I have a granddaughter?" he choked. "Tell me..." I tracked the lone tear that escaped down his stunned features. "Please...tell me about her."

I hesitated and cleared my throat. "You do not care? About how she was made?"

"Care?" he whispered and I closed my eyes, fearful of what I would see there. "Of course I care. I *care* that so much has been taken from my son and his soulmate. I *care* that you have been robbed of everything beautiful and sacred that a soulmate bond can give you, including being able to bring life into this world. I *care* that you are still paying the price of past mistakes."

I opened my eyes to see nothing but love and concern staring back at me. Tears still falling from my fathers eyes and wetting his beard.

"What I *don't* care about are the circumstances in which your daughter came to be...we all have our origin stories. This will be hers." He smiled wide and wiped his face with his large roughened hand. "I mean fuck, I stepped out of a goddess damn grove and just was."

I chuckled, then sniffed, wiping at my eyes.

Clearing his throat he pushed his glass aside and leaned closer toward me. "Please tell me about my granddaughter, Daemon."

I smiled proudly then. "She is no more than seven summers and so very small. She looks like Remnant with her petite features and long raven black hair with just the perfect shade of blue." I said fondly, seeing our daughter so clearly in my mind. "But her coloring is mine...just like mother's. She is in a healing sleep to help her with the new transformation. She does not yet know that Remnant and I are her parents." I paused then. "Remnant also does not know this."

"Son," my father growled in warning, "I saw the look on your soulmate's face when she learned who I was. I heard her tell you that she wants truths to trust you. Do not fuck that up."

I sent him a pleading look. "How the fuck do you tell someone that, father? Oh by the way, I'm your soulmate, we have a daughter together, and also I need you to save the world with me so she has one to live in," I hissed.

My father picked back up his glass. "Sounds about right to me. I recommend a drink though."

I scoffed. "You want to know why I came here...it's because you didn't prepare me for any of this! I don't know how to be the king for my people, a soulmate to Remnant, and most importantly how to be a father to a little girl that has already had the first part of her life taken from her!"

Anguish reflected back at me. "I wish there was some sort of ancient fae advice I could give you Daemon...but the truth is that after two thousand years, I still haven't figured out how to be the father you deserved, I failed at being a king, and I lost my soulmate. There is no right answer. All you can hope for in the end of your days is that you have loved and been loved back. And you are, fiercely. By your friends, your people, your mother and I...and also by that shadow fae outside."

My voice dropped low. "What did you just say?"

My father's gold eyes laughed at me. "Daemon, she is out there right now cursing and knocking Bane on his ass repeatedly because he threatened you. She is as much in love with you as you are in love with her."

My mouth hung open.

He grinned wide, his canines sharp in the light. "Jar sent you, didn't he? He knew you could not see the truth unless it came from me."

I grunted admittedly. "Yes."

"Clever fae," Asher chuckled and then leaned in. "Now tell me. What is my granddaughter's name?"

"Her name is Riella," I smiled wryly. "I am quite certain her eyes will be gold."

My father beamed. "A true Strider shifter."

I shook my head. "Jar says she will be both shifter and shadow fae. The first of her kind and infinitely more powerful," I said proudly.

My fathers brows rose up into his hairline and his lips quirked. "The first shadow shifter?"

I chuckled. "Don't tell Jar you came up with that name, he thinks himself clever and is claiming the ownership of naming a new species of fae."

My father chuffed and then stared at me for a moment before leaning forward across the table to touch his forehead to mine. A traditional shifter greeting. "I have missed you, Daemon. You must know, I love you my cub. And I am so fucking proud of what you have become. You will be a wonderful father. Better than the best, I should know—I can *see* the truth of it."

I pressed back into him and breathed in his calming scent, our volatile bond finally calm. It was...peaceful? I had forgotten the feeling.

"I love you too, Father."

He pulled away smiling. "Stay for dinner?"

I let out a strangled laugh. "Depends on what's on the menu?" I winked.

He arched his brow. "I believe I still remember how to make your favorite dish."

"Done!" I smacked my lips hungrily. "When do we eat?"

I grinned when his roaring laughter rattled the walls.

# CHAPTER 62

Remnant

A FTER CLEANING UP FROM my training with Bane, I stumbled into an aroma filled kitchen with our friends finally back from scouting. They were sitting and chatting away at a large worn kitchen table while two shifter kings, wearing aprons, were cooking pasta...

Goddess damn pasta.

Su Filindeu to be exact.

A sophisticated dish with a light cream sauce that had me licking my fingers clean and setting fire ablaze in Emon's eyes. Sitting there, I started to seriously doubt if Emon's favorite food was even food at all. His eyes stared hungrily at my mouth with each delicate bite I made.

"What did she do next?" Penina said breathlessly.

I had been tuning out Xi's wild tales about me at the dinner table, focusing on my food instead of her stories to save myself the embarrassment of my younger years. A time when I had a world to conquer, shit to prove, and a penchant for dangerous beasts.

I glanced at Emon. The latter I had yet to grow out of.

He had decidedly claimed the chair next to me, warning off any others while he draped his arm around me. He still wore an apron over his naked chest and I eyed it appreciatively. I wasn't ever going to forget the way I had stumbled to a halt walking into the manor seeing his hair tousled over his brow while he bent over a large pot, stirring it in nothing but tight leather pants and that apron barely covering the rippling muscle of his chest.

All my anger and frustration at his secret keeping were quickly forgotten in that moment. If Asher hadn't been there...

Emon caught my admiring look and grinned down at me.

Inhaling, I narrowed my eyes and quickly looked away. Heat spreading across my cheeks.

He chuckled darkly and shifted in his chair.

"General Dark decided that the best thing to do was to hitch a ride." Xi's uncovered eye rolled dramatically.

Tyr barked a laugh and he pinned me with a disbelieving stare across the table. "You rode a cù-sìth and didn't die for it?"

I shrugged. "Obviously."

Emon leaned in to whisper against the shell of my ear, "I'm starting to realize most of your stories involve you *riding beasts*, little umbra." I shuddered at the feel of his warm breath on my skin, and the deep timber of his purr.

Riley shook his head, green hair falling over hazel eyes glazed with memories. "There were fae that literally shit their pants when that beast strolled into our camp."

Everyone laughed. Everyone except Bane, who sat in a shadowed corner sulking.

Emon's father, Asher, sent me an approving look. "I will consider myself lucky that no cù-sìth was sent into my camps, General."

"I was saving it for a later date," I teased.

Asher winked. "I'll be sure to save my dignity and not shit myself when that day comes."

I snorted and noticed Penina and Tyr looking at me like I was a lunatic.

I spread my hands on the table. "Look, Xi is a great storyteller, but the truth is that I was terrified of having a cù-sìth owing me a debt for a couple decades. So I traded in my debt for a ride back to camp." I sobered. At the time, I didn't want such a monstrous hound trailing behind me waiting for its debt to be paid but now I wished I had. Maybe then I would not have had to bury her and her cub in the Balsam Plains.

Emon's arm reached around me, sensing my distress. "I will help you keep your vow even in their deaths, little umbra."

Sighing, I tentatively leaned more into him, allowing my burden to be shared just this once.

"I am starting to feel even more sympathetic for your mother," Bane called out from his darkened corner. "I only had to deal with you for a couple decades. She had a couple thousand."

Emon's arm stiffened around me and instantly I reached to calm him. Gripping his leg under the table to cut his growl short.

Realizing my mistake, I attempted to remove my hand from the new tension I had created but he grabbed it, keeping it pressed firmly to his thigh and swung his eyes to me.

My breath caught at the blazing intensity there...the small moments where I could see everything he hadn't said to me...everything I hadn't asked for but now hopelessly wanted. Something had changed between us since coming here...the shifter was no longer holding back his feelings from me and mine were growing.

Xi tapped the table and I tore my eyes away, watching her white hair fall forward as she leaned in to capture our attention. "The cù-sìth was nothing...wait till you hear about the nightmares."

Emon pulled me even closer to him and his voice rumbled with curiosity. "This is one I haven't heard yet." He turned to me. "One of these days, little umbra, I'd like to hear these stories whispered from your own delectable mouth," he breathed. "You mentioned nightmares when we were fighting the wraiths. Right before your little elemental twin launched you like a fucking star into the sky."

"My name is Riley."

Emon snorted, ignoring him and I was captured by the way his hand stroked mine under the table. "What were you doing around nightmares, my vicious little umbra?"

It had been a long time since I last saw a nightmare...majestic black winged horses who fed on dreams. Flying in fae's homes at night and feasting on all their wicked goodness and replacing it with fear.

"Doesn't every girl dream of wanting a horse?" I said coyly.

My breath caught when a full grin crossed his face. His voice dropped low for only me to hear, "I knew you would want a pet beast for a courting gift over anything else."

Riley interrupted with his own snort. "Only a delusional shadow fae would want a nightmare. Don't let her fool you, she was trying to control the damn thing."

Tyr frowned. "Why in the goddess's tit would you want to control a nightmare?"

I barely saw Asher's hand smack the backside of the tiger shifter's head.

"Owe, what that fuck Asher?" Tyr complained.

Asher snarled softly. "Goddess I do believe I missed doing that...and you know exactly what the fuck Tyr."

I pulled away from Emon. "Why don't we save the stories about me for another time."

Penina pouted, her bottom lip sticking out dramatically. "Awe, please tell us! I really, really, want to know why you wanted to catch a nightmare. It may be helpful...for future references."

Xi laughed. "You don't catch nightmares—no fae can, but you can control them for a short while. Remnant wanted one for her little gnome friends."

I laughed with her. "Hey! That's not fair!" I turned to Penina to explain. "Gnomes are deathly afraid of nightmare hair and there was a gnome infestation in our camp. I was tired of listening to those two faelings over there complaining about them."

Emon chuckled. "You love gnomes," he said thoughtfully.

I jerked back. "I do not."

"She does," both Xi and Riley said together.

I pointed an accusing finger at both of them. "You both are lucky you're no longer under *my* command." The death glare I sent them did nothing but make them both laugh harder. "Gnomes are incredibly useful," I muttered over their outburst.

"Aye, for pollinating flowers with their own piss," Emon grinned at me and everyone laughed.

"That's enough at my expense." I arched a brow at Emon. "When are you going to tell everyone what they are really here for? That we are going to the Sanguine?"

Emon ran his hand through his hair when the room filled with silence. "How did you know?"

I snorted. "An assassin, two warrior kings, two powerful elementals, a tank of a shifter," I eyed Tyr, who grinned smugly, "a weapons master that knows Sanguine lands, and me...an unknown player. Every fae here is someone you trust with your life. If that's not a hunting party I don't know what is and the only place to hunt is through that damn gateway." I shook my head. "You want to bring the fight to her before the gateway opens."

Asher winked at me. "And that is why I could never beat you."

Emon sighed and ran his hand through his hair. "Yes, we leave tomorrow."

I snorted and Bane quickly rose to his feet, his eyes flashing with electric bolts of fire. "Do you even understand what you're doing? Stepping just one foot into those lands is sentencing every single fae in this room to death right alongside you. Are you willing to shoulder that weight?"

Emon's hand tightened on mine, still pinned to his thigh. "This is not a task I can do alone. If I could, I would have done so by now." He looked around the room. "I will not force any of you to come but the invitation is open."

Penina shrugged. "Seems convenient for me. I'm in."

Bane sputtered at her. "Convenient?" he sneered, then turned on Emon's father. "Asher you can't seriously be considering this?"

The former shifter king waved his friend away. "There is no consideration. I have already decided to join my son on his hunt."

"We are in," Xi and Riley called out together.

An odd emotion flickered in Tyr's eyes while he looked at the elemental twins. "You two running amok in the Sanguine without some supervision...I don't think so. Count me in too."

Riley raised his green brows and Xi muttered curses under her breath.

Emon turned to me whispering. "And you, my clever little umbra? The unknown shadow fae." He smirked. "What will you decide?"

My other hand fisted in my lap and I bit at my bottom lip. There was so much more meaning in his simple question than the others realized. I felt my heart flutter with excitement as I peered deep into his patient gaze. "You. I choose to go with you. We will do it together."

Emon's eyes widened and his hand tightened on mine. "Together," he breathed, the awe in his voice sent shivers down my spine.

I swallowed and then nodded.

Asher tapped the table. "You're sure you will be able to get through the gateway before it fully opens Emon?"

Emon nodded confidently, dragging his eyes away from me. "It is weakened. We will be able to enter."

I pursed my lips. "How do we get back out?"

Emon looked grim. "We will have exactly twelve days to find Deirdre, kill her, and make it back through the gateway before it closes for another one hundred years."

I exhaled deeply. "What should we expect on the other side?"

Bane cursed, nevermind no one even questioned that he hadn't vowed to come. "Anything, nothing, everything," he snarled at the table, banging his hand down on it and then glared at Asher who growled in warning. "Don't try me Asher, you know this is a foolish plan. It's been more than two thousand years since we set foot in those lands and there was a reason we left it and never went back. There is no possible way of knowing what the Sanguine is now and very little on what it was like even when we were there last."

"Unless you're me!" Penina snarled.

# CHAPTER 63

*Remnant*

EVERYONE TURNED WITH SHOCK at the sunny carefree shifter whose entire demeanor changed into a wrathful storm. Her eyes bled from brown to black in a matter of seconds.

Bane glared at her condescendingly. "Girl, you were just barely born then. What would you know about the Sanguine?"

The gold piercing of her lip flashed in the dim light at her silent snarl. "You always love to remind me of how old I am, you fucking fossil. But you know my very birth had everything to do with that goddess forbidden land since you were the one who cut me and my twin out of our mother's dead drained body."

My eyes widened and I looked around the table, noticing Emon, Asher, and Tyr were the only ones not shocked by this news.

Bane's eyes narrowed on her, ignoring everyone else shifting uncomfortably. "If I could forget that day, girl, I would. Except *you also love to remind me* of it all the goddess damn time too."

"It should have been you that day." Penina leaned across the table and hissed. "It should've been you drained to a fucking husk by the blood fae. You failed her, you failed the queen, and you failed me!"

Bane flinched and she laughed at his discomfort.

"Go back to your pouting corner, Bane. No one wants you here."

The swordmaster narrowed his eyes, his lips pressed in a thin line. Jerking back a chair from the table he sat down directly across from her with a sullen glare. "I think I'll sit right here, thank you."

Riley and Xi raised their brows and looked over at me. I turned my head to Emon who shook his head slowly at all three of us, but there was a small satisfied smirk on his face. He was enjoying Bane's fury.

Tyr opened his mouth only to be instantly covered by Asher's hand. "Whatever foolishness is about to come out of your mouth, Tyr Cloud, we don't need it. Swallow it down or I will do it for you."

"Penina," I said gently and waited for her to turn those angry black eyes on me, "What can you tell us about the Sanguine?"

She blinked, frowning at me as if she had forgotten we were all still here. "The Sanguine is void of the sun, it is in constant darkness, and a frozen tundra of earth. There is very little plant life, very little water, and temperatures at night drop to unbearable conditions. I've already prepared our gear, it's been ready for years, in anticipation for this day."

I frowned at her. "How is that possible?"

Emon cleared his throat. "Penina has been crossing the gateway each time it has been opened for centuries now, aside from the last, her personal quest has now become an asset."

Penina nodded. "Emon and I had anticipated that it would someday come to this." She turned to the former shifter king. "Apologies, your grace but I don't have supplies for you and fossil over there, should he curse us with his presence." She jerked her thumb at Bane across from her.

The grinding of Bane's teeth was audible but he remained quiet in his glare.

Asher snickered, glancing at his friend. "Not to worry. This place still acts as an outpost for the Red Caps. We have more than enough cold gear of our own."

Humming in the back of my throat, I turned towards Penina. "What kind of threats are we looking at?"

She sucked on one of her gold lip piercings in thought. "Assuming that all the blood fae are truly dead and the lands don't kill us? Bruxa, Dullahan, and Baobahn. Those are the big hitters that I have come across. There are also accounts of red caps, naga, and trows."

The color in Bane's face drained, worry seeping into that hard glare.

"Any chance there are any creatures there that don't want to fucking drink our blood dry?" Tyr asked drily.

"There is one gentle spirit," Bane said gruffly. "Willow O Wisps."

Penina gave him a passing glance. "He is right, the wisps exist there too."

I leaned forward excitedly. "If we consume a wisp then we will not have to worry about the freezing temperatures and may travel undetected within the lands. Our heat will not attract those looking for a blood source."

Xi groaned. "Do I even want to know how you catch a wisp and ask it to sacrifice itself to take on its power?"

I waved my hand towards the void and pulled out a leather sack from it. "Wisps are pure power, the effects of their consumption only lasts for a few weeks before they return to their natural state. Long enough for us to get in and out of there within the timeframe we are under." I unrolled the floppy leather, revealing eight perfectly made throwing knives. "But to answer your first question. We catch them with these." I balanced the tip of the blade on my finger. Unlike a dagger they had no handle, tapered at both ends. "You will all need to practice." Flipping it, the knife fell perfectly vertical into the wooden table.

It was Riley who smirked at me mischievously, "Dodging daggers?"

I nodded enthusiastically, seeing the fond memories in his eyes. "Dodging daggers."

"You want to play a drinking game to practice catching wisps?" Tyr drawled, stretching back in his chair, his tattooed muscular chest on full display.

I smiled. "What else do you have to do?"

Tyr grinned. "I could think of a few things, beauty."

Emon growled low in warning to him.

Asher stroked his beard thoughtfully. "Can someone explain this dodging of daggers?"

Emon sighed. "It's an initiation for new recruits. The new initiate has to throw a dagger at their superior while blindfolded. If they hit them then they are able to ask their superior any truth and become an initiate, if they miss them, then the superior may either deny the initiate to join or ask then for a truth. It's been modified to a drinking game to kill the boredom."

I elbowed him hard and he grunted. "You missed explaining the reasoning." I turned to Asher. "It tells you several things about them." I raised three fingers up, counting down. "One, their weapon skills past sight and aim. Two, their inquisition skills. And three...the most important one of all, if they could ever catch a wisp for you."

"You gotta be shitting me," Xi sputtered through her white hair covering her face, "I've seen you determine those first two within meeting new recruits in seconds. Which means you have been testing all of us this whole goddess damn time to see who can catch a fucking wisp?"

I shrugged with a small smile. "Like gnomes, wisps are incredibly useful. Why do you think you and Riley were promoted so quickly?"

Xi grinned. "My life is a lie."

Riley shook his head next to her chuckling.

Tyr grinned and gave the air a large sniff. "Let's do this. One of you two old timers has a strong-smelling sort of spirit in that cellar. Let's all drink when someone fails, to make this more interesting."

"That would mean all of us will be drinking since one of us is always going to fail," Riley pointed out.

Tyr licked at his fang, grinning. "Exactly."

Penina practically bounced in her seat, her brown eyes as well as her personality back to their normal warmth. "I volunteer to dodge."

I raised a brow at her. "You think you can dodge me, shifter?"

Her brown eyes sparkled with the challenge. "I know I can, shadow fae."

# CHAPTER 64

Remnant

T HE LARGE WOODEN TABLE was shoved to the far wall. Asher
ordered Bane to bring up multiple bottles of spirits he called
Dragon's Breath from the cellar—Bane's own sadistic brew he had
been creating while in exile.

One sniff of it made my eyes water. It wasn't easy for a fae
to get drunk but it seemed Bane found a way to make it possible
and I wondered if it was because of the one shifter in the room he
continued to watch with simmering anger.

I glanced at Penina who stroked the throwing knives on the
table, ignoring Bane's blatant stare. "Why silver?"

I picked one up and raised it in the light. The metal gleamed
and I studied my own reflection within its metallic depths. "Silver is symbolic of feminine tranquility, awareness, and intuition.
Wisps are particularly attracted to these attributes."

I passed her the throwing dagger which she took eagerly, testing its balance in a series of spins and flips.

I continued, "But more importantly silver represents strength, clarity, and persistence, the wisdom of self reflection." I snatched the dagger she tossed mid air and balanced the pointed tip on my finger to hold it at eye level. "Every fae must be able to look at their reflection one day and live with the blood that stains their blades. If you cannot, then you don't deserve the silver you killed with."

"I need a set," she whispered reverently.

I laughed, shaking my head. "Your king has already pointed out that I don't believe in coincidences. I have eight blades. There are eight of us here. One of these has your name on it, Penina Sythe." I reached for her hand and placed the silver knife into it. Curling her fingers around the sharp blade. "May you always accept who you are in your reflection."

I glanced up at Emon and realized that this was what he had done for me. He destroyed the mirror, the horrible reflection of myself that I had defined myself by and then he made it anew. Piece by piece he stole my shattered heart, glued back my soul, and then forced me to look in the mirror again—to see that the darkness was also the most beautiful part of who I was.

I studied those golden eyes so full of warmth while he spoke to his father and I swallowed down the burning gratitude I felt for the shifter that had stolen a piece of me I didn't realize I had left.

Penina's boney elbow shoved into my side and whispered, "Asher is convincing Emon to take you somewhere. I suggest you go with him tonight. You won't get another chance to be alone once we set out for the Sanguine."

Startled, I looked down at her still flipping the blade. "How do you know that?"

She shrugged, her look far away from anything happening in this room. "Shifter hearing."

I hummed, studying her profile with scrutiny. She couldn't fool me. I knew that distant look. I had seen it many times reflected in the turquoise eyes of my last lover. The seer sight had plagued Deirdre too and from Penina's cryptic words and actions, her sight was extremely powerful. She saw timelines...not just glimpses of the future.

I dropped my voice, "Care to take your own advice and make amends with Bane?"

Penina's lost look snapped to me with surprise.

I smiled at her knowingly. "I know my former master well. The colder his eyes, the deeper he cares, the deeper he feels. Feelings make him angry and his eyes have not left you this whole night."

She glanced at the swordmaster who stiffened at her regard, then she turned back to me. "Some things cannot be amended. Especially with that old fossil."

Scrunching my nose, I stated slowly, "I can't believe I am going to say this but...Bane will be an asset in the Sanguine. He is a fire elemental and like you, has also navigated those lands. Plus no one wields lightning like Bane does, nothing flying above us has a shot in Sheol of surviving him."

Penina chewed on her bottom lip, glancing at the moody elemental. "I have not considered that, but you are correct."

Tyr whistled low at us, picking up one of the silver knives. "Damn Beauty, who'd you fuck to get yourself a set of these and can I get in on that?"

Emon's head snapped up and the very air seemed to be sucked out of the room. He took a dark threatening step towards his friend, his eyes bleeding with murderous intent.

Xi beat the king to him and slapped Tyr hard upside the head.

"Idiot," she hissed and walked away, shaking her hand out.

"Goddess damn it, Xi. That's the second time today!" Tyr called but instead of turning angrily towards her, he was looking at Penina with worry in his eyes.

There was pain on her face, pain she masked well but was still there, threatening to surface. Penina was hurting fiercely and Bane was the cause of it.

"Just for that you'll be dodging *my blade* tonight," the tiger shifter grinned widely, now turned towards Xi and pointing the knife at her.

Xi rolled her uncovered eye and started to pour a tall glass of dragon's breath, squinting hard at the three jugs. "There might not be enough of this shit for me."

Sliding a knife out for myself, I spun it in my hand. "Despite what you may think, Tyr, I forged these myself...in the Argenti Caves. There was no fucking involved."

Emon hissed across the room.

Tyr crossed his arms over his chest. "Gaib Castella doesn't allow anyone near those caves."

I arched a brow, rolling the blade over my knuckles. "Gaib Castella had no problem letting *me* in the Argenti Caves. He just wouldn't *let me out* until I forged the perfect blade *exactly* eight times. He was insistent on that number." Winking at Penina, I continued, "Not a single one could be off balance, not a single one could be blemished, not a single one's edge too dull."

The sound of the shifter king prowling towards me captured my attention and my voice trailed off. Licking my lips, I became lost in the way his sculpted body prowled towards me.

When he deftly plucked the blade from my hand and rolled it over his claws I sucked in a ragged breath. Tossing it upwards, he followed its movement before slicing down with his claws, sending it hurtling towards the far wall. It embedded in the stone and the thud echoed around the room.

Fiery eyes turned towards me. "Absolutely perfect," he said, running an extended claw down my cheek and then back upwards to tuck away an errant strand of my hair. I shivered at his deadly touch and felt a flood of heated desire pool deep in my gut.

"Well, before we all burst into flames..." Penina snickered next to me. "Let's play!"

# CHAPTER 65

I COULDN'T TAKE MY eyes off my soulmate. The way she looked at me from across the room moments ago was more than desire. It was an unmasked awe, adoration, gratitude, and so much more that I was scared to even hope.

Currently she was standing twenty paces from Penina with a silver throwing knife in one hand and a blindfold in the other.

"You could at least try to be respectful, boy," Bane grumbled stepping next to me, indicating my stare.

I didn't bother dragging my eyes away from the view. "Fuck off Bane...I don't recall Eve appointing you as her guardian." I smirked and spoke in a low growl only he could hear, "Ah, that's right, she asked *me* to watch over Remnant, not you."

"Eve made a mistake. Dark deserves far better than the likes of you, boy."

I tore my eyes away from Remnant this time and leveled the swordmaster with a lethal look. "I could say the same to you. My mother definitely deserved better than you...and so does Penina. You've never deserved either of them and yet somehow the goddess still honors you with gifts that you continually spit on."

Bane's eyes narrowed.

"That's right, asshole," my voice was low only for him, "I know what Penina is to you. We all do." Growling, I turned my back on him. I despised the bastard to my very core.

*"Careful, fairy boy. Your soulmate was correct when she said Bane will be needed for the Sanguine and if it wasn't for him...you may have never found her,"* Ethereal commented.

I grunted. *"He won't betray us, he just can't admit his unrequited love for my mother wasn't what fate intended. Penina was and that pisses him off."*

*"You cannot help who you love. The swordmaster loved Skylar by choice, he loves Penina by fate. Neither does he feel he can act upon and that makes him dangerous. He may not betray you, but he doesn't have to help you either."*

"Ready Penina?" Remnant cooed and my attention turned back on her beautiful profile. "I'll have ten seconds to throw, you must be ready at any moment." Remnant held out her blade for the shadows to keep before wrapping the blindfold around her eyes. I traced my fang with my tongue, images of what I could do to her blindfolded flooding my depraved mind.

She held out her hand and the shadows gently laid the dagger over her palm.

"I understand the rules," Penina bounced softly on her feet with excitement. She had changed her attire again as she often did. It was a passion of hers and the green jumpsuit she wore now allowed her freedom of movement. If anyone had a chance to dodge a thrown dagger by soulmate it was her.

Remnant inhaled deep. "Riley, countdown please."

"Ten...nine...eight...seven..."

We all held our breath when a flash of silver soared through the air and thunked loudly into the wooden wall.

"Goddess's bitch," Penina snarled, holding her arm where her jumpsuit had torn and blood seeped between her fingers.

Remnant didn't even take off the blindfold. "Just a flesh wound, shifter." She pulled the blindfold off and smirked. "Xi, please heal our friend."

My brow raised. I didn't know the elemental twin had healing abilities.

"Don't get too excited, your majesty," Xi shot over her shoulder at me, "my healing capabilities are basic at best." She waved her hands over Penina's exposed mocha skin, healing it instantly.

"Alright, Nina," Tyr said eagerly and pressed a glass into her bloody hand. "You lost, give us a truth we don't know already, and we'll all drink to it."

Penina's brows furrowed over her deep brown eyes and then smirked. "I don't like pasties."

I choked on my drink and everyone stared. Even my father made a non-committal sound.

Remnant snickered. "What is it with you shifters and your pasties?" She pointed at the elemental twins. "You both as well?"

Riley clutched his arms to his chest wistfully, his hazel eyes narrowed on Remnant. "Freya's pasties are unlike anything you ever had. A golden savory pastry bursting with warm flavors of buttered meat and vegetables, then cooled by the sweet, salty, tartness of ketchup. It is like sex."

Remnant rounded on me and I tore my eyes away from a very stoic Tyr who was staring at Riley with hunger in his eyes.

"You've been holding out on me, shifter?"

I didn't care who was watching, in two blurring steps my hands were in her hair tilting her face upwards. "I would never hold you back from such a delight, little umbra. Watching you eat has become one of my favorite pastimes," I purred and inhaled the flood of desire pouring off her.

With shaking hands she rose her drink between us, her emerald gaze watching me over the rim of her glass she whispered, "Slàinte!"

"Slàinte!" The others said robotically, following her lead.

I watched the pale column of her throat with each long swallow and then slowly pulled the glass away from her wet lips to finish the rest of the contents with a dark grin.

Remnant drew in a ragged breath and spun away. "My turn to dodge. Who's my dagger?"

"I thought you'd never ask, Dark."

Bane sauntered across the room and gave me a smirking glare. I set the glass down slowly before I broke another one today and gave him a warning growl.

*"I hate to say I told you so, fairy boy,"* the panther drawled.

*"Sooner than I expected."* I crossed my arms over my chest and glared at the back of his head.

*"Indeed. In my day, an upstart like this would have been squashed immediately."*

I snorted. *"You were just telling me not to make an enemy of him."*

*"I do believe we are now past any peaceful resolutions."*

*"I cannot kill him. Penina would never forgive me."*

Ethereal sighed. *"Pity."*

I watched the bastard take a silver dagger into his hand.

My father's hand snatched his forearm. "Don't be a fool, Bane. I won't interfere on your behalf this time when my son comes after you."

Bane sniffed and wrenched his hand away. "I don't need protection from your boy, Asher. Besides, Dark wanted to play. This is a perfect way for me to assess where we need to resume her training."

I snarled. "The two hours you trained outside wasn't enough assessment for you, Steelhead?"

His eyes glittered back at me. "There are many ways to assess one's training." He winked at me before pulling the blindfold down and I could still feel his mocking gaze even covered.

Tyr gripped my shoulder and pulled me away. "Fuck him, your majesty. I'm sure his old ass is too slow for Beauty anyway."

I looked at my soulmate who watched me calculatingly.

"Make him lose, Remnant."

Bane snickered.

She raised her brow at me. "Is that an order, your majesty?"

I shook my head. "You don't need an order to beat that bastard. It's merely a request from a fae that cares about you."

A fae that *loves you* I wanted to say.

She tilted her head, staring a long moment into my eyes. Something changed inside of her and she nodded quietly more to herself than at me.

Reaching the wall, she faced Bane. "Count—" Remnant's voice cut off when Bane's arm drew back and the silver knife flew through the air straight at her heart.

Roaring with rage, Tyr could not hold me back when I plowed into the swordmaster. My claws sinking into the back of his shoulders viciously, his face half smashed in from hitting the stone floor from my assault, blood already pooling around it.

A singular steel blue eye glared over his shoulder at me where his blindfold had been knocked off and he attempted to lift his head up.

I snarled and shoved him back down, my claws sinking more into his body. He let out a pained cry and I snapped my fangs just above his exposed artery that pulsed wildly at his neck.

Across the room I heard Penina snarl, "Idiot fossil."

"I could end you!" I raged.

Bane groaned and then spat blood out of his mouth. A look of comprehension suddenly crossing his face. "Impossible!" he wheezed.

My growl abruptly cut short with realization. Bane had...played me.

Shaking with rage at his sick test to satisfy his theory that I was Remnant's soulmate, I roared again, rattling the manor with my fury. Twisting my claws deeper into the swordmaster's shoulders, I reveled in the sadistic pleasure of his tendon's shredding and the painful cries emitting from his smug face.

I leaned lower and dropped my voice so that Remnant could not hear my next words, "You thought yourself an anomaly, that you and Penina were a mistake because you are from two different courts. You rejected your bond and now you attempt to make others suffer but I won't play your fucking games anymore, Bane Steelhead." His eyes narrowed on me and I hissed low. "Out of respect for my family, I will spare your life...again...but know this—I have no reservations about making sure your life is a nightmare full of despair and pain. You think you are familiar with that now but you have no idea how much worse I can make it for you. Consider yourself fucking warned."

Bane gasped, spitting out more blood and with a lethal smile on his lips he whispered back to me, "Must kill you...knowing that I'm the sole reason you even found yours."

Roaring, I dragged his body up on my claws prepared to rip his arms from his body like wings off a cooked chicken.

Then everything went black and shadows swarmed around me.

Breathing heavily, I blinked through the darkness. Bane was gone and now Remnant knelt in front of me. Her hands reached shakily for my face and pulled my eyes down to hers.

"Emon," Remnant cooed at me, like one would to sooth a child.

"Little umbra…" I whispered brokenly. Even in my momentary rage with Bane, I had not scented any blood from her, but I knew my soul would not be calm until I absolutely knew for sure. Retracting my claws, I brought my bloody hands up to her face. "Are you okay, did he harm you?"

Remnant snorted and leaned her face into my hand. "Of course I am okay, Emon. Bane is harmless. I was his novice for many years, nothing he does surprises me anymore. You should have known better."

My puffing sigh of relief blew her hair back into the shadowy darkness.

"I can't—" I swallowed hard, "I can't bear to even think about you being harmed." I trembled. "I need you Remnant, let me show you…let me take you away from here. Just this night, to show you the truth. You said we need to make time."

She frowned in the shadowy darkness. "But the others…tomorrow—"

I kissed her lips softly and groaned when she kissed me back. "We will be back before tomorrow. Let me show you."

Remnant shivered and then leaned in kissing me again. "Okay."

I pulled back and stared hard into her emerald depths. "Be sure, little umbra. Tell me—tell me you choose this."

Her hands reached up and covered my own. "I choose this, Emon. I choose you, shifter."

I released a satisfied groan and pulled her tightly to my chest. "Little fiends," I growled at the shadows around us, "You know what to do."

Snapping, the shadows plunged inward, instantly transporting us to the location I projected in my mind.

# CHAPTER 66

Remnant

T HE SHADOWS DISSOLVED AND I stumbled back from
Emon, staring wide eyed. "Did they just portal us?"

"Yes," he said warily.

I slowly turned and gasped at the large expansive cave we
were in. Crystals of all colors dripped from the ceiling like
icicles. Their glittering points ominously hovered above us. A
gentle waterfall with an aquamarine hot spring glowed in the
center of the cave, its steam curled up from the beckoning
waves making walls glitter like a starry night sky.

Another slow turn and I looked down, to see the smoothly
polished gemstones light up with each step I made. Fascinated,
I tapped my foot and smiled when the floor shimmered with
color from the vibration.

I looked back at Emon who quietly watched me.

"How?" I said with a mixture of wonderment and irritation.

The floor lit up his carefully guarded expression. "I thought you knew. When you never asked how I got back to The West Isles so quickly from The Under. I thought you knew."

I hugged my arms against my body feeling shame from never questioning it before. "I never knew..." I looked up at him frowning, "over two thousand years and I never knew that they had the ability to portal travel," I whispered.

Emon stepped forward and I let him fold me into his body. He kissed the top of my head and I smashed my face into his heated chest. "It seems both our powers have been keeping secrets from us," he mumbled into my hair. "My panther never bothered to tell me he lost his name nor his memories. All those years living with him inside of my head and he never told me either."

I sniffed into his chest, breathing in the security his dominating presence gave me. "Where are we?"

Emon tilted my head up and I was lost in his golden light. He smiled. "It's called the Lover's Cave, a powerful place in the Red Caps. Shifters used to spend their honeymoons here after binding themselves to each other."

A blush spread over his cheeks and over the crooked bridge of his nose.

I giggled the uncommon nervousness pouring off of him, brushing back the hair falling between his eyes. "Not a very creative name, shifter." I watched my hand trail down his face, over the stubble of his beard, and then traced his lips.

Emon chuckled and nipped playfully at my fingertips, his nervousness diminishing as quickly as it came. "And yet very informative. It tells you everything you need to know."

Dropping my hand, I pressed myself closer to his radiating heat. "Is that what we are now, lovers?"

His face turned serious and his demeanor nothing but vulnerable when he whispered. "It is what I wish for and more..." he swallowed, "If you'll have me."

This side of him was one that I wanted to claim myself the keeper of. The one and only keeper of, for this was his heart, a gift that he was freely giving to me.

"It is what I wish for too," I said softly and I felt it then. My carefully cultivated barriers crumbled down, revealing a new me.

I trembled with the infinite possibilities of what this would mean...for us.

Unable to hold back any longer, Emon's lips crashed into my own and he stole my breath much like he had stolen my heart—confidently vicious.

When Emon kissed, he consumed and I wanted to give. Greedily, I pressed my body harder into him, my hands trailing along the hardened muscle I had ached to touch since the day I first found him, and once I did, I could not stop my hands from trailing up his muscular thighs, cupping the arousal grinding into my navel, so deliciously hard and ready.

"Goddess, fuck!" he panted, ripping his mouth away from mine and steadying my hips, creating space between us.

I growled at his resistance, hot desire burning me from the inside out.

His eyes dilated at the sound and he moaned. "Wait, just wait, little umbra. There is something I need to show you...before we—ah fuck—"

I licked a long line up his chest, my mouth moving to swirl my tongue over his beaded nipple. I moaned against his skin, he tasted just like he smelled, like chocolate—hot, spicy, chocolate and I wanted more over it.

"Remnant," he pleaded, his large hands tightening around my hips, still keeping the distance between us.

Slowly I peeked up at him through my dark lashes. "What is it you would like to show me shifter?" My hand teased the low waistline of his leathers, trailing over the ridges of his abs and following that low v right to where I knew I wanted to be.

"Fucking goddess," Emon hissed, scooping me up into his arms and grinning wildly at me when I squealed with delight. He kissed me soundly then, striding confidently across the room. "I want to live forever just to have the chance to hear you laugh everyday."

I grinned up at the awe on his face. "A seemingly easy task, we are immortal."

Emon snorted. "Little umbra, nothing about you is easy but you are worth it no matter how long or how hard I have to work for it. Let us see if I can repeat that lovely sound."

He was successful as his arms released me and I fell into the softest bedding I had ever had the pleasure to lay upon.

My hands stroked the fluffy clouds around me and I tilted my head to see that I was sprawled out on a massive bed made of the same material and it floated in the air around the room. "Where did this come from? It wasn't here before."

Emon watched me with feral hunger. "Like your cabin in the woods, the cave anticipates your needs and provides them."

Wiggling further into the soft white clouds, I hummed.

"Goddess you are so fucking beautiful," he croaked.

I bit at my bottom lip letting his words seep down into my soul. I had heard him utter it before but always rejected it. Tonight, I would allow myself to experience all of what it meant to have Daemon Ash Strider as a lover.

"I think you should get on with what you wanted to show me, shifter," I pouted, "I particularly hope it's of the naked sort and involves much more than kissing. Although I want more of that too."

He barked a laugh and ran his hand through his disheveled hair stalking the edge of the bed back and forth. "It is taking every bit of control I have left, not to tear your clothing off you and rut you like the beast I am—."

Desire clenched low in my belly. "That. Yes. That. I want that."

"But—" He growled, his hands planted on the bed and he stared hard into my eyes, "You wanted my secrets, my truths...this is our time to share them...all of them." His gold eyes beseeched me. "It will require a mind connection between us."

I sat up abruptly, my hair falling around my shoulders as I tilted my head. "A mind connection? You want to show me your memories?"

Emon nodded and licked his lips slowly. "It is the easiest way to give you what you have asked of me and I told you once before, I cannot deny you anything."

I tucked my knees to my chest. "This is important to you?"

Silently he nodded. "You were right. There will be no future for us if we do not confront the darkness of our past. There are things you should know, things from my past that I have not shared with anyone else, things that may change the choice you are making tonight and all the choices you make after."

His eyes watched me with a mixture of fear, longing and resolve and I knew then in his memories were the answers to all my whys.

"Okay," I breathed, lowering my legs and folding my hands in my lap.

Emon exhaled slowly, rustling his hair that had fallen between his brows.

I breathed shallowly when he knelt on the bed, slowly crawling towards me. With one hand he pushed me back and I smiled, the sharp rainbow crystals whirling by me as I fell into the clouds. Blinking, Emon's handsome face hovered over me and he was sweetly kissing my swollen lips.

"Thank you, little umbra."

I snuggled myself closer into him, feeling his bulging erection heavy against my hip, and holding back a moan.

"This is not what I had in mind when you wanted to play show and tell," I teased, protecting the softer side of Emon that gazed down at me with tentative fear on his face.

His eyes shuttered closed and he breathed, "I know." His eyes snapped open with a growl, his hand digging into my hair and shoving me harder into the clouds. "You know how a mind connection works. The sooner you say those words, the sooner I get to worship you in every way you deserve. With my mouth..." He trailed his mouth over my sensitive collar bone, "with my tongue..." He licked lower over the tops of my breast. "And with my cock." He snarled, thrusting his arousal into me, his thigh parting my legs in the process and grinding into my sex.

The words to bind our minds tore from my lips in a worshipful moan. "*Ligare!*"

Emon rose up above me and his hair fell across his molten gold eyes. Pure devotion and love burned brightly in them. "*Te amo mon lidi umbra.* I love you, my little shadow." His forehead dropped to mine. "*Ligare.*"

# CHAPTER 67

## Remnant

### Emon's Memories

*I*MMEDIATELY *I WAS SWIMMING* in darkness. *My consciousness melding with Emon's and separating me from my own body.
He had full control of the memories he would share. I was but a
spectator within them.*

*A stunned speechless spectator left with his words whispering in
my head, a beautiful confession torn from his soul.*

*Te amo mon lidi umbra. I love you, my little shadow.*

*My heart raced and my stomach performed terrible acrobat-
ics—the rush both unpleasant and exciting at the same time...I could
scarcely breathe at the possibilities of it.*

*But looking within his memory, my feelings quickly turned to
one of horror.*

*"No," I whispered, taking in the bright lights and white sterile
walls of a room I had hoped to never see again.*

*Except this time it wasn't me battered and chained with irons,
it was Emon. He lay in a pool of blood on a cold metal table, his*

*chest rapidly rising and falling while roars of agony drowned out any other sound, his gold eyes fixated on the heavy locked iron door.*

*"It can't be," I whispered, hearing the muffled screams resonating beyond that door that drove the chained shifter king to madness.*

*I knew those screams well. They were mine.*

*"Oh Emon." I choked back a sob as recognition hit me like a battering ram. These exact roars, his roars, were the same sound that echoed in my nightmares, telling me something I could not understand, could not remember.*

*It had been him. It had always been him.*

*We both eyed the door when another long scream full of pain and anguish echoed from the hall and then the pleading began. It was my voice, crying out, "Kill me! Just kill me!"*

*Emon's head started to bang against the table roaring his despair, then shifting into a desperate sob. Tears falling from his broken golden eyes and mingling with the blood on the table. "Goddess. No more!" Emon roared out, thrashing again, his skin burning anew in the irons. "Please, no more! I'll give it to you! I'll give it to you. Just stop! Please, please stop—" His chest heaved. "Please make it stop, please, please, please—."*

*Tears filled my eyes. This was his nightmare. The one that left him sweating and vomiting, unable to sleep. The same nightmare I had witnessed in the Balsam Plains when I realized we bore the same painful scar on our souls.*

*But I couldn't help him this time. I couldn't reassure him that I was okay, that in the future he heals me, in the future he loves me, and that we are together.*

*"Tut tut, King Daemon...now was that so hard," a soft musical voice said from the doorway.*

*I glared at the fae standing there. Deirdre. My former lover, former friend, and former queen stood there with a satisfied grin on her face.*

*All I felt for her was utter disgust.*

*Smugly, she strutted into the room, her heels clicking against the tile in a powerful stride that had her hips swaying in a fitted deep blue dress. Her long shimmering legs peeked from two large slits that went all the way up to her hips, and flowing around her were waves of silky silver hair, sparkling in the harsh light.*

*Her eyes, two bright pools of turquoise, hungrily assessed the begging shifter. "You really did make this so much harder on yourself, you know," she hummed, her red lips grinning down at Emon with satisfaction.*

*Everything about her was beautiful and sinful and I hated her for it. Hated that her allure was enough to make any male or female worship her. She reveled in the ability to pull their strings—the ultimate puppet-master.*

*"Stay the fuck away from him," I hissed and stepped in front of her with my spectral form, wanting to cut her from our lives as much as I wanted to cut her from my own heart, but her grinning eyes stared right through me.*

*Emon hissed, and I turned to see his tear stained face full of loathing. "How can you do this...you fucking loved her once!" he snarled, his teeth flashing. "At least honor that memory and cease this cruelty."*

*Turquoise eyes glittered down at him. Her face contorted into a twisted smile. "And if I do, you will give me what I want." She trailed a finger over his rippling stomach. "Everything I want," she cooed.*

*Emon's chains rattled. "Give me your word that no one will touch her, go near her or harm her anymore, including you, and I will give it to you. I will give you the location of the Sanguine."*

*"No Emon...no," I whispered sadly in his memory. "I wasn't worth this. I am not worth this."*

*Desire sparkled in Deirdre's eyes and she trailed her perfectly manicured hand back up his chest, digging into the cuts and burns, marring his body and reopening them until they bled.*

*Bringing her bloody fingertips to her mouth she sucked on them with a deep moan and then licked her lips with satisfaction. "Will you take her place instead?" She circled his body. "Although I have gotten what I need from her I find I have quite enjoyed the process. A fae has her needs after all."*

*Emon's eyes flashed with revulsion and he shook with visible rage. "Your access to the Sanguine gateway is time sensitive. The more time you waste here, means the less time you have to access the gateway."*

*"Of course it is," Deirdre laughed, harnessing her power over wind she floated over Emon to sit astride his powerful hips. Her dress riding up around her waist revealing her naked sex beneath.*

*Emon's chest rose and fell heavily, watching her like a caged predator that was ready to snap.*

"This is a much better position for you to whisper your dirty little secrets to me. Don't you think, your majesty." She ran her hands over her breasts and then down her body.

Emon growled. "I'll have your binding oath before I give you anything."

Deirdre smirked and then dragged a sharp nail over his open wounds watching the blood run down his body and onto the table where her knees were now stained with it. She cocked her head. "You do say the sexiest little things to me King Daemon...and that growl. I love it when you growl. Do it again, growl for me, your majesty. Growl and I will give you the binding oath you so desperately want from my lips."

Bile rose in my stomach when Emon's eyes glanced at the doorway where begging cries continued, hard resolve etched into his handsome features.

"Don't do it Emon." Tears stained my face and I squeezed my eyes shut—unable to witness what I knew he would do...what he was willing to do for me.

When the long low growl vibrated throughout the room and was followed by the delighted heartless laughter of the Queen of Faerie, I shook with fury. Nothing would ever stop me from killing Deirdre ever again. Her life was mine.

# CHAPTER 68

Remnant

Emon's Memories

*R*AGE STILL SHOOK ME *as Emon's mind spun me into the next memory and I narrowed my eyes on the heavy iron door. Stepping back from the tortuous sounds behind it. The sounds of an unwanted rhythmic slapping of flesh. The pleasurable grunting of male satisfaction upon the unwilling.*

*I could taste the bile in my mouth and the beginning of panic clawing at my insides, but a thunderous roar shook me to my core and I spun at the familiar sound.*

*"No," I whispered, staring at Emon running naked with uncontrolled fury raging in his eyes straight for that forsaken door. The iron chains hung around him, his beautiful bronze skin still covered in slashes and burns I had witnessed in the last memory. Deirdre had found a way past her vow.*

*I jumped back out of instinct as he came crashing towards me and then flinched when his large solid body slammed into the door, the iron searing his flesh. I stared when the sizzling sound of his skin didn't even phase him, let alone the pain it must have caused.*

*Snarling and with muscles bulging, he gripped the door, and with a ferocious roar, his hands burning on the cursed metal, he ripped it clear off its hinges, tossing it behind him with such a force that I ducked out of the way quickly. It hit the far wall an thunderous boom that shook the walls.*

*"Impossible," I whispered, following his memory towards the open room, a room I never wanted to return to.*

*I paused at the doorway and closed my eyes.*

*If I passed through this door, then I had to accept two things.*

*One. Emon was much more powerful than anyone could ever imagine. The irons had only stopped him from shifting...but it never weakened his shifter strength, his power had ensured his survival.*

*And Two. I had to accept what had been done to me. I would have to witness it, acknowledge it, and then let it go. There was no room for me to continue to carry this hurt any longer, not with Emon in my life, and I wanted him...in my life. We both needed to move past this moment in time.*

*Trembling, I opened my eyes and stepped through the door with a confident stride despite my shaking.*

*I stared at the drugged version of me in this memory, chained with irons to a sterile cold table—so helpless. Helpless against the human that was forcing himself between my thighs, so caught up in taking his pleasure from my body he hadn't even noticed the roaring shifter until it was too late.*

*Emon ripped the pathetic human off of me with one arm and sent him careening into the opposite wall, his skull exploding on impact. Showering everyone in the room with blood.*

*Growling low, Emon licked at the bright red blood from his lips and stalked towards the dead human. Bending with menacing intent, he ripped the flaccid penis off the body with his bare hands.*

*Then ever so slowly, he turned towards the two other humans in the room frozen in terror with their eyes bulging and their pathetic bodies trembling with fear. Still holding the small bleeding dick in his hand, Emon prowled towards them, his gold eyes swirling with white hot fury.*

*"You," he pointed the severed cock at one of them, "take off your shirt."*

*Shaking violently, the human fumbled clumsily with the buttons of his shirt under the murderous gaze of the king of shifters* towering over their meager height. Emon snatched the shirt from the human the instant it was off, the movement causing his comrade's eyes to roll before he crumbled to the floor, passed out from sheer fear, a wet stain spreading over the front of his khaki pants.

Emon didn't even spare the unconscious human a glance. "Hold this for me, human," he snarled and extended the bloody dick flesh to the still conscious man.

The shocked human paled and promptly bent over, throwing up all over the blood sprayed tile.

Emon hissed and side stepped the projectile vomit, his iron chains dragging across the floor noisily while his flesh sizzled. Yanking on the hand of the still vomiting human, Emon slapped the cock into it.

"If you drop this, I will kill you," he snarled.

The human paused from his retching to look down at the bloody flesh before his entire body heaved to vomit again, intelligently keeping the dick still in his hand.

Disgusted, Emon turned away, walking over to my unconscious body with the blood splattered shirt. The violent rage on his face softened to one of compassion and sadness when he looked down upon me to tenderly drape the shirt over my naked body, pulling it over my shoulders and brushing away the greasy hair that clung to my feverish face.

His hand stilled then, his eyes widening with shock. Time seemed to stop in our awe of each other, the only sound was that our ragged breaths over my unconscious body, and then time started again.

Slowly, Emon turned back to the human, his face shuttered with violent rage and his eyes glowed white with deadly malice—they were going to die.

The conscious human perceived this instantly. "Bbb—but you said you wouldn't kill me if I didn't drop—" He glanced down at his outstretched hand.

Emon cocked his head to the side. His voice was so cold that if I had a body I would have had goosebumps. "I said I'd kill you if you did, I never said I wouldn't kill anyway."

Recognizing that he was about to die, the human attempted to escape, except Emon was already in front of him before he could take another step. The shifter's hand shot out around the human's throat, the iron chains clanking loudly by the abrupt movement.

*Dark satisfaction rose within me when the human released a terrified cry.*

*"Did you rape her?" Emon growled*

*"It was an ooorrd...oorrrder." The human's mouth gaped when Emon's hand slowly squeezed his throat harder.*

*In a blink, the shifter king grabbed the severed dick in the human's hand and shoved it down his gaping throat. He screamed and choked around the bloody appendage, but Emon's hand covering his mouth prevented him from spitting it out as he thrashed to get away.*

*Emon watched the human struggle with a feral grin for a few more seconds before snapping his neck with a sharp twist and dropping him to the floor. The bloody dick tumbled out of the man's dead gaping mouth as Emon stepped over him unaffectedly towards the last living human still unconscious on the floor.*

*With a furious roar, Emon slammed his bare heel down on the man's crotch. The fracturing of his pelvis forced the man to wake up with a blood curdling scream before promptly passing out again.*

*Swiftly, Emon punched downwards, sending the iron chains flying before his fist punched a hole straight into the human's chest—crushing the man's heart with one blow.*

*Brutal. Monstrous. Emon was an avenging animal but this was mercy from a fae. I would have done much worse.*

*Blood dripped from every inch of Emon's exquisitely marred and naked body as he spun and was back at my side with unnatural speed. I stepped closer to watch his memory and the way his trembling hand rose to lovingly cup the side of my face, the blood on them smearing on my pale skin like war paint.*

*"Forgive me." Tears pooled in his eyes and fell, splattering with loud plops on the metal table. "Forgive me, my little umbra. I did not know, I would have come sooner had I known. I would have come sooner."*

*The keening cry that left him sent my heart crashing into my stomach and I watched, unable to soothe him, as his body bowed over my unconscious form, shaking with strangled sobs.*

*"My soulmate, my soulmate," he cried into my unconscious chest, smearing more blood on the white shirt he had covered my body in.*

*"Soulmate," I whispered, my why was before me.*

*Then I felt it, the bond clicking into place between us and I took in a deep clear breath as if I had been holding it my entire life, just waiting for the air that only Emon could give me.*

*Emon rose, wiping the tears from his eyes and stared at the iron cuffs that restrained me on the table. Roaring, he raised his fist and it slammed down hard on the thick iron casing.*

*His knuckles split wide open.*

*Another hit.*

*The iron seared his split flesh clean off, revealing bone.*

*Another.*

*His bones fractured, revealing a mangled fist.*

*Another.*

*The sound of the iron cracking would have been missed by any who were not watching closely.*

*My spectator self rushed over in disbelief, staring down at the iron cuff that had once held me hostage. Emon had done it! Goddess above and below, the shifter had done it...the iron cracked under his broken and bloody fist with nothing more than his sheer will to free me—to free his soulmate.*

*A blaring alarm sounded. Emon turned snarling while chaos broke out within the room. Armed guards attacked him from all angles and he fought like a cornered savage beast but I knew how this ended.*

*Tearing my eyes away, I looked back down at myself in Emon's memory, my gaze fixated on my right wrist and the split iron cuff.*

*A slow smile spread across my face as I stared down at myself.*

*There...wrapping lazily around my twitching fingers was a thin film of smokey shadows.*

# CHAPTER 69

Remnant

Emon's Memories

$D$ARKNESS SWIRLED AROUND ME *again for a new memory and my shoulders slumped with defeated relief when the tortured growls and the sadistic laughter disappeared.*

*I stood in the middle of a massive black marbled throne room, above me a glass dome separated the night sky above from the shadows that swirled below.*

*Instant home sickness gripped my chest.*

*I knew this place well—and thankfully, it wasn't a place of pain. It was one full of love, patience, and understanding. A place that once heard the small pitter patter of my feet, the laughter of my mother while she chased me, and the undying loyalty of a court that I thought I had been lost forever.*

*I was in the Onyx Throne Room of the City of Night, home-land to the shadow fae.*

*And in the middle of the room next to me stood Emon. Proud, despite his deathlike appearance and being covered in iron burns and flaking dried blood, he still commanded a captivating presence.*

*The soft steps of booted feet had me turning to stare at the exact replica of me only in male form. Bright green eyes, dark blue wavy hair, and black swirled ink etched into the pale skin of his muscular athletic frame.*

*"Kade," I gasped.*

*Shadows curled from his lethal hands and weaved around the shifter king. It was a futile attempt to restrain Emon judging by the lack of worry he demonstrated at the shadows binding him.*

*Then the darkness around the room stirred, swirling and materializing into a majestical ancient fae.*

*"Mother," I whispered.*

*The moons highlighted my mother's beauty while the darkness poured off her in gentle waves. Shorter than me but not in presence, her skin was like porcelain, her heart shaped face regal with an air of elegance, her slanted eyes a deep sapphire blue, ringed with green, and outlined by thick dark lashes. Her hair fell in undulating deep ocean blue waves when she moved, mimicking the billowing fabric of her dress that blended into the shadows of the room, whispering across the floor like a dark promise.*

*How could my memory of her ever blurred?*

*Emon's eyes remained trained only on my mother, absent of fear.*

*"Eve," he said, bowing his head subtly.*

*"King Daemon." She bowed her head and then turned to my brother. "Kade, please release the shifter king. He is not a prisoner here...albeit you do look like one." Her eyes narrowed. "Why is that, your majesty?"*

*I opened my eyes and swallowed the building emotion within me.*

*"With all due respect mother. He stormed into our home knocking out a dozen of our guards demanding to see you and only you. I do not feel it would be wise to release him until we know exactly why he is here."*

*My mother snorted, the action comical, with all of her regalness. "He is half dead and still took down our guards." She chuckled and winked at Emon. "You are much like your father, Daemon Ash Strider."*

*Emon smirked at her.*

*Waving a singular hand at Emon she continued, "I thank you for being polite and not killing guards, your majesty. If you would, please demonstrate to my son what a futile attempt it is to restrain you."*

*Emon raised his brows before he broke the shadows binding his hands in front of him with a fierce pull.*

*The cold hiss of Kade's steel blade laid across the shifter king's sword. "How is that possible?"*

*My mother sighed. "I grow weary of this. Kade please lower your sword. The shifter king is not here to harm us. If he was, he already would have."*

*Kade glared at Emon before flicking his blade back into the shadows. "I want to know how you did that."*

*Emon's head slowly turned to my brother and purred. "My secrets are my own, shadow fae."*

*My mother arched a dark brow. "But not all of them." Then she smiled politely at the king, her eyes trailing down to his unbound hands. "Let us cut these pleasantries for now."*

*My mother stepped into Emon's personal space with sudden concern, her pale hand reaching outward to cup his swollen face that was healing very slowly for a fae of his power. Worried blue green eyes looked up into his stormy expression.*

*"Are you in need of medical attention, Emon? Your father's healer was once a great friend of mine. He would be most displeased if I didn't insist on you seeing a healer of our own."*

*Emon shook his head and pulled my mother's hand from his face with care. "I thank you Eve, but I fear there is no time for that. I am well enough for now."*

*I narrowed my eyes on Emon, he was playing with words. He was not well. Not even close.*

*"So be it," she sighed seeing the lie within the truth. She took a step towards my brother who placed his hand on her shoulder in comfort. "Bane sent word that you were searching for my daughter. Tell us. What has happened to my little chickadee, where is my Remnant?"*

*Emon flinched. "She is safe for now, I believe..." His eyes grew distant. "I hope." Then he shook his head. "But you and your people are not. Right now, as we speak, the Faerie Queen has an army marching in this direction to annihilate the shadow fae race."*

*My brother interjected, "Our people can more than handle the queen's meager forces. The City of Night is more powerful than her.*

Answer my mother's question shifter. Where is she, where is my sister?"

Emon growled at him. "Pride will get you nowhere. Your city will fall and everyone in it, if you do not heed my warning. I am here because your sister would want me here to help save you. All of you. You must understand, there will be no mercy from the queen." He stared hard at my mother. "You asked why I look like I was a prisoner? It's because I have been, for three months, along with your daughter."

My mothers voice caught and my brother cursed violently while shadows exploded around him. "That fucking bitch of a queen! I don't know why Remnant ever trusted her!"

"I had to leave her behind to save you." His voice cracked and he bowed his head with shame.

I gasped when Kade's fist connected solidly with the shifter king's face, having not seen him move.

"You left her there!" Kade roared.

My mother's shadows quickly encircled my brother and pulled him forcibly back, away from the furious shifter king. "Settle yourself Kade Stellan Shea Dark!"

Emon snarled through his reopened split lip. "As much as I deserve that...know that I would never leave her defenseless, your sister is strong and I was able to at least break her bindings before almost being overpowered. I barely even made it here." He looked at my mother beseechingly. "She will need you all to recover from what has been done to her. The queen will purge you of Faerie if given the chance, she will wipe your very existence from this world. Her hatred runs that deep. You must leave here before that happens."

Kade turned to my mother with fury. "You cannot believe this shifter scum mother! His own father has been Remnant's enemy for years, slaughtering innocent fae! Allow me to leave here and bring her back to us, unlike this shifter I am not leaving her with that bitch one second longer."

"There are no innocent fae!" Emon snarled. "And if there was, my mother was one of them! My father has paid the price for what he has done."

"Enough!" My mother snapped and suddenly her beautiful face looked very tired. "That is quite enough Kade," she whispered, then straightened. "We must leave. I have seen it, I just didn't know the when."

Kade stared at our mother in horror. "You want to leave her there and leave her behind?" He shook his head. "No. I'm not fucking leaving without my sister."

Emon sighed. "You are not dispensable Kade Dark, none of you are and that is what will happen if you go after her. But if I go, I am. Your sister will still have her family and live a happy life beyond this. Goddess knows she will need it."

Kade's eyes narrowed suspiciously. "You speak as if you care about her...why?"

Emon licked at his bloodied lip watching my brother with indecision.

With a soft sigh, my mother released Kade from her shadows. "Because he loves her."

Emon's gaze turned on my mother. "Yes."

"You're soulmates," my mother continued.

"Yes," Emon said evenly.

My brother cursed again and started to pace uncontrollably.

"I've masked the bond, it is not complete. She does not know." Emon watched my brother pace warily. "No harm will come to her as long as it stays that way. If I fall, then she will still have a chance—"

I knew what he wanted to say. A chance to live, a chance to love, a chance to grow without him.

Tears filled my eyes. Emon had been beaten, experimented on, and raped for three long painful months. He was standing only with sheer will, his body broken beyond the injuries one could see, and even still, he was ready to fight a war alone...for me.

"Then I know what must be done," my mother said softly.

From the shadows, an onyx scroll materialized into her hand and Kade paused with shock when she extended it to the shifter king.

"Daemon Ash Strider, King of The West Isles, Soulmate to the Princess of Shadows, I task you with the guardianship of the shadow scroll, you will deliver this to my daughter so that she may one day join us again."

"And where will you be going?" Emon said, the relief evident in his tone as he took the scroll.

My mother shook her head. "It is best you do not know but the scroll will help my daughter find us when the time comes." She placed a hand on his arm soothingly. "Be careful, my son."

Emon swallowed hard. "I understand," he said gruffly. "I swear to you, that I will deliver this to her with my own hands even through death. Thank you, Eve."

*My brother watched with a stoney expression and his eyes flashed with rebellion. "I will do what my mother asks of me but you will not find me as accepting as her, shifter brother," Kade sneered. "If my sister dies because you fucking left her...I will make it a personal mission of mine to end you. Whatever horrors you have suffered will pale in comparison to what I will do to you should you fail."*

*Emon glared at him but nodded his head with understanding. "I wouldn't expect anything less, shadow brother."*

*I snorted and rolled my eyes.*

*My mothers blue green stare snapped over to me and I froze, my breath held watching her watch me...impossible!*

*She smiled then and I could read the silent words on her lips. "I love you, my chickadee."*

*My tears spilled over. "I love you too, Mama."*

*Then the memory draped in darkness and I was swimming through Emon's consciousness waiting for the next one to come.*

# CHAPTER 70

## Remnant

Emon's Memories

$I$ CRINGED AT THE blaring alarms and the knowledge that we were back in the facility where we had been held hostage.

Except this time, I wasn't greeted with the memory of sterile white walls but of ones painted red. Thick splatters of blood were everywhere, staining the floors, walls, and even dripping from the ceiling. Eviscerated body parts shredded beyond recognition were strewn about along with lump-like forms that resembled very dead humans.

It was a slaughter and my shifter king was in the middle of it.

In a doorway, I spotted him, covered in blood...again.

The room itself was a wreck of overturned tables, strewn instruments, and ripped apart bodies. On the far side of the room, a heavy metal door was ajar, a cool mist pouring out of it, having been carelessly left open in a hurry.

*Dismissing the odd ice box and its empty shelves, I looked back at Emon, who moved to squat low in front of what seemed to be the only human left alive in this goddess forsaken place.*

*I read his blood splattered badge.*

*Dr. Gerald S. Gio.*

*My eyes widened in recognition. I had almost forgotten the only being here that had attempted to bestow upon me some sort of kindness. The only one that had seen past Deirdre's manipulations and tried to help me in any way he could. He never stood a chance against her.*

*"Please," the doctor pleaded to the growling shifter who had his claws placed dangerously close to a main artery of the human's neck.*

*"Worthless human," Emon sneered. "Did the fae you allowed to be abused, assaulted, and raped for your disgusting science ever plead for her own life? Nay! She begged you to end it instead! Yet here you are begging for yours like you deserve a fucking request!"*

*Remorse shone on his wet face. "Please. I tried. God, I did try. Tried to protect her. But I have a family and she...the queen...she used my family against me." The doctor bowed his head, his tears dripping to the floor. "I have a family. Please." His last words were like a whispered prayer from a tortured soul.*

*I recognized it well, having heard that tone escape my own lips.*

*Emon roared with frustration. He gnashed his sharp canines right in front of the doctor's face. "She had a family too! Did you even bother to ask her that? And you treated her like a fucking animal! Worse than that!"*

*More tears streamed from the human's eyes. "I'm so sorr—sorry. I'm so very sorry. God forgive me. I tried...I did try," he sobbed, not even seeing Emon anymore. His eyes glazed over with acceptance of his death.*

*Emon hissed viciously but I could see the change in his blood-thirsty eyes. He did not want to kill this human. Emon was everything light, seeing the best in the fucked up darkness of the world. It was what I loved most about him.*

*I inhaled sharply at my errant thought and my heart pounded loudly.*

*I loved Emon.*

*Warmth flooded into the bond as if Emon had heard my words inside his memories.*

*Growling, he ripped his claws away from the human's throat and watched the doctor slump with relief. Still sobbing into a pool of blood from one of his slain co-workers.*

*"Tell me where she was taken," Emon demanded.*

*The doctor blinked upward against the flashing lights in confusion. "She...she wasss....was able to escape—."*

*A slow predatory smile crept across Emon's blood splattered face and his gold eyes swirled with hope...and pride.*

*If only what had come after had been testament to that hope. Morta was anything but.*

*Dr. Gerald S. Gio stared at Emon fearfully, shuddering when the shifter king spoke.*

*"This will not be the day you die, human. Instead, you will live. Live with the things you have done. It will haunt you day and night, when you kiss your wife, when you hold your children." Emon rose slowly to stand. "Stay away from the games of the fae, human, if you see one of us ever again, run the fucking other way." Turning and walking away, Emon kicked a decapitated head out of his path, straight towards the quietly sobbing doctor.*

*The doctor took one look at the head, its mouth gaping open in a silent scream, before turning away to retch.*

*"Pathetic," growled Emon before prowling from the room.*

*Darkness pulled at me but I resisted it, kneeling before the vomiting doctor with sadness in my eyes.*

*"I forgive you, Gerald." I whispered before I lost sight of him. "I forgive you."*

# CHAPTER 71

Remnant

Emon's Memories

*"**T**HIS BETTER BE THE last one Emon," I said wearily to him through our mind connection when a new memory appeared.*

*I didn't need to see more to know the kind of fae Emon truly was. Strong and gentle, kind and just, vicious and fair, broken but still hopeful, he was the light in the darkness that I was never able to find until now.*

*I recognized the healing quarters with a small smile on my face. It was a place filled with such warmth and acceptance. The essence of the master healer's work.*

*Searching the room, I found Emon sitting on an extended prime root of Riella's bed with a broken expression on his face.*

*Alarm and panic had me rushing over to the faeling, recalling that Emon had placed additional wards on the room. Had he hidden a terrible truth from me, was she not well?*

*Seeing her still sleeping as peacefully as when I last left her, I frowned at the broken expression on Emon's face.*

*It was the most lost and hopeless I had ever seen him. Even through the brutality he had suffered, he always held unwavering strength, but it was absent here. Defeated. My soulmate was defeated.*

*"You are so beautiful...just like your mother," he whispered and reached out to sweep back a strand of raven hair from Riella's face, pausing to study the color of it.*

*I frowned. How could Emon know her mother?*

*Looking down at Riella's hair, I stared at what Emon was seeing. Highlights of blue...I trailed my eyes over the heart shape of her cherub face, her petite nose, the shape of her lips, the soft flutter of her eyelashes.*

*I couldn't move. I could barely breathe. It was as if I was looking down at a reflection of me. How had I not seen it before?*

*Emon smiled reverently at her. "Thank goddess you have her small nose..." he chuckled. "Don't tell her I said this but I think yours might be cuter. Goddess knows your mother already doesn't like me much, but I am trying to change. Don't you worry."*

*Tears filled my eyes.*

*Emon released a sad sigh. "I don't know what I am doing anymore, my cub. I don't believe I have ever felt this lost before."*

*My tear filled eyes could not leave Emon. My cub.*

*Emon sighed and ran a hand through his hair with frustration. "Jar told me that you would hear me if I spoke to you. That it would help you in your healing sleep." He hesitated slightly and then hard resolve crossed his features. "You may not know what it means right now, my sweet little cub, but you have established our bond. It is the bond that all shifter children have with their parents. You are our daughter Riella. Remnant and I are your true parents."*

*I closed my eyes, painful hope blooming inside my chest. We had a child...*

*"Jar also tells me you are equal parts shifter and shadow fae." His voice wavered again. "Although I won't be surprised if you take more after your mother." He smiled softly at that. "They are already regaling the astounding way she ran as fast as a leopard, carrying you with her, through the hills of The West Isles, to save your life. You will find that there are many incredible stories about your mother, and they are all just as fantastically amazing. One day we both will witness this for ourselves together...as a family."*

*My eyes snapped open and I stared hard into Emon's profile.*

*"I don't deserve her, I don't deserve you—" He choked. "But I swear to you, that I love your mother with every piece of my shredded soul...just as much as I love you, my little cub. You both will never know a single day without that love ever again."*

*I collapsed to my knees inside Emon's memory, both agony and joy burning away the remaining vestiges of my old life.*

*I was ready. Ready to feel again.*

*"Ligare." Emon and I both whispered together.*

# CHAPTER 72

Remnant

O PENING MY EYES I fell into Emon's golden depths that were full of worry and hesitation.

"Remnant, I—"

My finger trembled when I pressed it firmly against his lips and my heart raced as I whispered the words we both needed to hear.

"I love you too, Daemon Ash Strider."

Emon inhaled sharply, his eyes searching mine in disbelief. "Say it again."

I grinned and traced his lips. "I love you."

I shivered when he growled low, brushing his nose against mine and then nipping at me. "Again."

Laughing and shaking my head, I nipped him back. "I love you, you dense headed shifter. How many more times do I need to say it?"

"Forever," he breathed and my heart stuttered. "I need you to say it forever."

Crashing his lips into mine he devoured my mouth, groaning deeply when I responded eagerly in kind.

When his large hand trailed reverently down my face, I closed my eyes, feeling the way it shook with the restraint he barely held onto all this time. Not just here in these caves but since that first day in the cabin and even before that.

I gasped when his fingers brushed over the tops of my breasts and dipped into the neckline of my leather vest. "You're wearing too many clothes," he murmured against my lips.

Shivering at the deep growling tone, I reached slowly down his abs feeling them tense underneath the pads of my fingertips, then slid further down into the waistline of his leathers. "I can fix that."

Silently commanding my shadows, they rushed out around us, removing our clothing like thieves in the night.

Looking back at Emon, I bit my lip to keep from laughing at his bulging eyes and mouth hanging open with alarm.

"Fuck," he croaked, closing his mouth and staring at my body with a mixture of horror and awe before swallowing hard. "Future note. Lets keep your carnivorous shadows far, far away from my dick."

I snickered, releasing my lip with a wide smile. "Fair point, shifter. I shall remember that next time."

"Be sure that you do," he growled distractedly, his eyes already trailing hungrily over my breast, down my bare stomach, and then over the source of my throbbing desire, his nostrils flaring, scenting my need for him—goddess help me!

Staring at me with his hair hanging in his eyes, a slow wicked smile spread across his face when he took his cock in hand and slowly pumped it for me to watch.

I was drooling. I had to be. His dick was enormous and thick, his balls complementing every inch of his impressive size back-dropped by the clenching bronze muscle of his abs. Licking my lips, my gaze shot back to him, seeing the challenge alight within.

Raising my brow, I rose up to my knees, pushing him back to the clouds and relishing in his deep chuckle when I slapped his hands away. His laughter changed to a sharp snarl when I wrapped my lips around the object of my desire and plunged his cock deep into my mouth. I moaned around his length, relishing in the taste of him. Emon tasted just like chocolate—hot spicy chocolate and I wanted more.

Sensing my need, his hands wrapped into my hair, guiding himself deeper into my mouth, thrusting shallowly upwards to hit the back of my throat.

"Fuck Remnant," he hissed when I swallowed, gripping my hair tighter to keep me still as he worked himself further into me.

"Goddess, you're beautiful," he moaned beneath me before pulling me off of him to stroke my flushed face, fixated on the rise and fall of my chest while I sucked in ragged breaths. Sweeping my hair aside, he grinned down his body at me, his fangs flashing in the dim light.

I narrowed my eyes up at him.

The shifter wanted to play...and so did I.

Brushing his hand away again, I leaned forward, running my nose along his sex to take a deep inhale, scenting him in the most instinctual way only a shifter would appreciate.

"Fuck!" he barked hoarsely, his cock flexing and slapping softly against my face.

I hummed, turning my head to kiss the tip, my eyes meeting his before I slowly licked his length from his heavy balls, up his shaft, and then the tip again. Giving him a small seductive smile, I bit down on his rock hard member with my blunt teeth.

Emon snarled and removed one of his hands from my hair to wrap around his stiff cock.

"Open," he growled and pushed himself towards my lips without pause. His other hand guided my head again. I obeyed—wanting to taste more of my delicious soulmate, I opened my mouth, watching him. "Suck." he commanded and I closed my mouth around him to suck harder. "So. Fucking. Beautiful." he snarled, punctuating each word with a thrust into my waiting mouth.

I moaned loudly, feeling my arousal building, helplessly wiggling my hips to ease the needy ache created there as Emon used my mouth for his own pleasure.

My soulmate's eyes flashed knowingly when he saw me squirm and ripped me away from him, throwing me backwards onto the conforming bed of clouds. He was between my legs instantly, opening my thighs wide with his large hands and with hungry eyes, stared down at me.

I held my breath, my channel throbbing. Pressing my spread thighs into the bed, he winked at me. "Stay there if you can, little umbra."

"Emon," I moaned his name, biting my lip and wiggling when I felt his hot breath on my core. I stared up at the rainbow colored crystals of the cave trembling in anticipation for what he would do next.

A scream tore from my lips when his mouth finally closed over my clit. Emon growled low into my spasming channel, reaching upwards to grip my breasts, pinching my nipples and sending me into a hard, fast release that left me crying out hoarsely.

My shadow power bursted outwards from the intensity of my pleasure, throwing us into a cascade of infinite darkness.

Not even phased, Emon continued to suck, lick, and drink my release with feral enthusiasm and did not stop until he drew only whimpers from my swollen lips. The darkness rescinded as I collapsed deeper into the puffy clouds, the rainbow hued crystals of the cave glowing over our panting naked bodies once more.

Emon planted one last kiss on my clit, and lifted his head, his golden eyes burning so bright they outshined the caves rainbow light.

He smirked like a man who was pleased with himself and I didn't even have enough strength to roll my eyes as I watched him climb up my body, planting soft kisses along my trembling form as he went. I inhaled when I felt his heavy cock settle between my thighs...my tired body suddenly jolting with renewed arousal.

"You taste so good, little umbra." His muscular arms framed my head, flexing while he kept most of his weight off me. "You've got me so fucking hard. I thought I was going to come all over this bed tasting your sweetness."

He rocked his hard cock against my swollen folds and my lips parted in a soft gasp. As if invited by the sound, Emon's mouth plundered mine, swallowing groans when I tasted myself on the soft caresses of his tongue.

He was mine.

My soulmate.

There would be no other taste on his lips but me. Our bond flared with so much possession that Emon drew back in surprise. I let myself get lost within this fae—lost in his touch and in his love. Tears of awe and wonder filled my eyes and spilled over my heated cheeks.

He consumed me.
He made me burn.
He made me live again.

# CHAPTER 73

**M**Y DESIRE FOR HER raged inside of me. I meant what I said. I nearly came all over these damn clouds instead of inside her where I desperately wanted to be. The way she rode my face as she took her pleasure would have me hard for months, and the taste of her would have me craving her sweet essence forever.

The sexy little noises she made were music to my ears and I reveled in the fact that I was the one that made my soulmate this way, a satiated puddle of lust. She was fucking mine and I was hers.

Except now, shimmering tears filled her beautiful green eyes while our souls melded together in harmony.

Following her tears as they spilled softly over her flushed cheeks I reached out to collect one on my fingertip. "Why do you cry, little umbra? Did I hurt you?"

She smiled softly and shook her head. "No, you feel amazing...you are amazing." She stumbled on her words and a red blush burned across her already flushed face.

I marveled at this vulnerable side of her, slowly wiping more tears from her face. I loved her strong savage side, when she was covered in blood and fierce in her vengeance but this side of her, soft and unsure, full of hope yet trembling with uncertainty...I loved this side even more.

She bit her lip watching me. "I just never...I never thought I could feel this way again."

"And what way is that, my soulmate?"

"Happy, alive, powerful, pure...*loved*," she confessed.

More tears escaped and dripped down to her disheveled hair. This image of her would be engraved into my soul, never fading, permanently there like the soulmate bond we shared.

Leisurely, I licked at one of her tears, releasing a low hum. "You deserve happiness," I whispered heatedly and then licked another. "You deserve to live." Another tear, another taste of salt on my tongue. "You have always been powerful and pure." Her eyes closed and I licked the last of those tears falling down her beautiful face before kissing both her eyelids with loving tenderness. "And you will never, ever, go a single day without knowing just how much I fucking love *you*, Remnant Ezra Soliare Dark."

Her eyes snapped open with so much emotion burning in them that she took my breath away. Goddess. She fucking undid me with those eyes.

"Remnant," I croaked. The emotional moment gave me pause, knowing the past of our abuse. "We can stop this. If it's too much. I am the happiest fae in this universe to just have you in my arms. That is enough."

Her eyebrows rose up in disbelief. "Really shifter?" She teased, pressing her leg up into my throbbing erection. "You think you can stop the beast in you." She nipped playfully at my nose.

A strangled growl escaped from deep in my chest and I narrowed my eyes at her. "Are you challenging me?"

She smiled widely at that and stretched her arms out above her head languidly. The little seductress knew how to play me and it pleased me more than she could ever know.

"Am I?" she purred, her green eyes flashing at me knowingly.

I growled back, looking over her body greedily. Her blue black hair was a halo of darkness against the clouds, a vengeful goddess in my arms. I licked my lips slowly—hungrily.

I looked back up at her amused twinkling eyes. "I think you are, little umbra, tell me you want me."

She bit her lip with desire burning inside her. I hissed and pulled her lip from between her teeth with my own, biting it and keeping it where it belonged—on me.

Her sharp inhale only drove my savage side more.

"I need you to goddess damn say it Remnant," I breathed against her lips when I released them from my bruising bite and pushed myself teasingly against her core.

She gasped and pressed wantonly back, her eyes fluttering closed.

"I know what you need," I whispered in a snarl at the shell of her ear, "your sex aches for me. It begs me to sink deep within its soaking depths." Moaning long and hard, I sucked on her ear. "But you're not getting any of it until I hear those words escaping those sweet lips."

Her eyes flashed open and her head turned, reaching up to cup my face. I leaned into her touch nuzzling against her soft feminine hands and licking at her palm.

Suddenly serious, she exhaled. "I love you Emon. The abuse I suffered in the past will never dictate what is between us. Nor will it ever taint what we have for each other—what we need from each other. I want you and only you, shifter."

Her serious expression shifted, smiling mischievously up at me. Her green eyes twinkling, she slid her hand from my face and tangled it in my hair, her nails scraping against my scalp. I purred, loving the way she dominated me with her touch, yanking me down closer to her, our noses barely touching. Her breath fanned against my face and I inhaled deeply—she was the only air I would ever need to live.

"Now do something with that shifter dick of yours or I will."

I chuckled darkly and gripped her hair hard in return, arching her back against me before using my shifter speed, I rolled to settle her sprawling on top of me. She cried out softly, when I sat her astride my heavy erection, her hands losing their purchase in my hair and slapped down onto my muscular chest.

Sliding my hands over her lean hips, I pushed her wet hot pussy down my throbbing member that desperately needed to be inside her.

"Show me how you're going to use my cock then, little umbra." My voice was thick with lust. She fucking unraveled me, she undid me, she goddess damn exposed me without even trying. I thrusted up against her while I pushed her hips heavily down, and we both gasped with pleasure.

She gushed over my throbbing cock and I moaned as her slick allowed me to easily slide between her folds, resisting every call I had to shove deep inside her, I stretched my arms behind my head—watching intimately for what she would do next.

Despite her words she needed this—the control. To take for once in her life instead of being taken from and for that I was willing to be patient.

My breath hitched when she rose up on her knees, shifting to wrap her soft hands around my dick. Pumping me up and down, I was unable to resist following her motions, thrusting into her hands as she stroked me. She smirked and then moved her hips closer to my pulsing cock, and I couldn't hold back the snarl of pleasure when she rubbed the head of my dick against the hard nub of her clit. Her eyes challenged me this time, seeing my ragged control slip away.

I narrowed my eyes, reaching out to trace the soft curve of her breast with my fingers. "Be careful little umbra, I'm a shifter fae—it's never good to tease the beast."

She snickered again and then dipped me shallowly inside her. Her pussy walls clenched over the tip of my cock, before she raised up, pulling me out of her velvet softness. I twitched painfully in her firm grip as the cool air kissed my cock instead of the welcoming warmth of her cunt.

"I think I'll like the beast no matter what happens, kitten," she said naughtily, her eyes flashing with mischief.

My eyes widened and my hands shot out from under my head to grip her trim waist once more. "What was that you just fucking said?" I growled up at her.

She giggled. "Kitten," she repeated and then raked her nails down my chest. I hissed at the exquisite pain and pleasure that it brought me. "You purr—like a sweet, soft kitten."

I lunged forward bringing my chest up to hers and felt her tits pebble against my heated skin, her sex opened wider to accommodate my girth, and my dick fell perfectly positioned between her greedy thighs. With a growl, I wrapped my arms around her shoulders and plunged her down onto my throbbing dick. Filling her with all of me in one luxurious slide, Remnant cried out, her arms wrapping around my head and holding me there.

I covered her face in soothing kisses while I waited for her to adjust to the size of me. My dick twitched painfully in her channel. When her whimpers changed to soft pants, she opened those fierce eyes and lit mine on fire.

My fucking soulmate was perfect and so was her hot cunt where my cock pulsed with need for her to move. My mouth took hers again and my hands left her shoulders to dig into her ass, lifting her slowly upwards and then plunging her back down again.

My soulmate was a moaning gasping mess as I watched her through my own sexual haze, her tits bouncing every time I lifted and slammed her back down again and again. Latching onto one of them, I sucked her breast hard into my mouth, moaning at the feel of her and the sounds she made with each lavish sweep of my tongue.

I felt the shift within her the moment she took control from me. My hands loosened their grip and allowed her to ride me the way she wanted, fully in control and desperate for more. Using her strong powerful legs to move up and down my cock, I watched her pussy hungrily swallow me up with each downward thrust.

A sheen of sweat coated her pale skin when her pace increased and her breasts were now swollen red from the rough attention of my mouth. When she arched back to grind harder into me, the tips of her black hair brushed over the tops of my trembling thighs, I snarled through clenched teeth to keep myself from cumming too soon.

She looked like a fucking sacrifice impaled on my dick.

"Remnant, look at me," I commanded hoarsely, our bodies trembling in unison.

Her bright green eyes opened and she tilted her head forward, her beautiful gaze crushing me with the need swirling in them.

"I want to see your eyes when I fuck you Remnant."

"Emon," she moaned, lost in her own pleasure.

I flexed my cock inside of her and she gasped. "I want you to see who's fucking you." I reached up and pinched her swollen nipple hard and she let out little mewls of pleasure. "You are mine. This sweet body is mine. I will be the only being to ever own your pleasure," I growled fiercely at her.

Her eyes flashed and I couldn't tell if she was battling my dominance over her or if she was pleased by my words, but either way I didn't give a fuck. No fae, human, or creature would ever have her again. If they so much as even fucking looked at her in a desirous way I would kill them and it would please me to do so.

I leaned forward and kissed her swollen lips. My tongue coaxed her mouth to open and I bit down hard on her lip, breaking the skin, and licking the blood pebbling there before sucking it fully into my mouth. Her blood tasted just as delicious as essence, even better than ambrosia.

Releasing her lip punishingly, I stared into her eyes. "Do you understand?"

She panted against me, her body trembling and her pussy quivering around my dick. "Emon," she said breathlessly, her eyes hooded with lust.

She attempted to move her hips but my fingers dug into her ass stopping her with a warning growl.

"I am yours and no one else's!" she growled back with frustration and her hands gripped into my hair tilting my head back, her teeth bared at me. "And the same goes for you kitten. You are mine, Daemon Ash Strider, your cock that's buried so deeply inside of me? I own it. Now shut the goddess up and fuck me already."

I had her on her back before her words completely finished, pinning her arms above her head. Our eyes stayed locked on each other as I pulled my cock slowly out of her tight pussy and then fed it back into her inch by inch. Shaking, she wrapped her legs around my hips, attempting to increase my pace.

"Shifter..." she warned.

I ignored her and repeated the process again and again. Watching the madness of desire grow as she struggled against my grip to take control.

"Emon, harder, please," she moaned each time I slid slowly inside her.

Reaching down between us, I rolled her clit between the calloused pad of my fingertips, her legs dropping back down to the bed and digging her heels in to press harder against my hand. Pinching her clit firmly she screamed out my name for a second time, her pussy clenching around me and milking my cock.

My restraint broke and I leaned over her to bury my face into her hair before I started to pummel her tight spasming pussy like a rabid animal. Our bodies slapping loudly along with her cries of pleasure echoing inside the cave.

I snarled into the bed—needing to sink so far inside of her that she would feel me for days. I would ruin her for any other and would mark her as my soulmate forever.

Growling I ripped my dick out of her and flipped her on her stomach. Remnant's legs were spread wide and I stared at the mess her release created. Its sweet milkiness smeared over her thighs and coated my engorged dick. The desire to lap it up like the kitten she teasingly called me was so fucking strong I could not resist.

Burying my face into her wet folds I groaned at the wonderful taste of her. If Remnant was my fucking air then her sex was my sustenance, the sweetest most delicious thing I ever tasted.

Satisfied with her hoarse cries and satiated with tasting her, I watched her body tremble and the white knuckled grip of her hands tighten into the clouds. Lifting her head, she peered over her shoulder through messy strands of blue black hair. Her eyes lit with sexual fervor as she watched me slowly crawl over her body to gently brush back her hair from her face, like I always did, since the first moment I laid eyes on her in that terrible place. She closed her eyes at the softness of my touch only for them to fly open with a harsh gasp as I ran her through with my cock. Screaming, she buried her head into the bed to muffle the sound when I took her with savage intensity.

Raising myself up on my arms, I thrusted deeper and harder into her. Grunting into her hair, savoring the feel of her tight sheath around me and my name shouting from her sweet lips.

My pace quickened and I jolted forward, roaring my own release when her pussy clenched around me, drawing another release from her beautiful body. I slammed into her erratically when my seed shot out of my dick with so much force that it leveled me. A second spasm of my cock painted her pussy walls and I cursed in ecstasy before stilling deep within her.

Fuck. She was perfect. Nothing would ever compare to this moment. I finally had everything I ever wanted, our bond, her love, and her panting beneath me, numb from the pleasure only I could give her.

Planting soft kisses on her back, I attempted to control my ragged breathing, groaning when she shivered against me at the soft caress of my lips on her. Rolling us onto our sides, I stayed inside of her. Vowing this was only the first round for the night.

Tucking Remnant's petite body into me—I kissed her sweaty temple and looked down upon her face. Her eyelashes fluttered and then opened, peering over her shoulder back at me.

Kissing her nose gently, I whispered, "I love you, my little umbra."

I blinked at the way her loving smile blinded me. Her hand reached back to cup my face and stroked the scruff of my beard. "I love you too, shifter."

I turned my lips into her palm and kissed it softly. "Rest Remnant, rest my little umbra, my beautiful soulmate."

Her hand dropped from me with a happy sigh. Lowering her head she pulled my arm further into her, using it like a pillow, and instantly fell asleep.

Kissing the top of her head, I closed my eyes. Smiling, when for the first time in a long time, nightmares didn't bid me their welcome.

# Chapter 74

## Remnant

I watched the muscular bronze chest of my sated shifter soulmate rise and fall softly as it pillowed my head. The strong beat of his heart thrumming against my ear and the warmth of our soulmate bond humming happily between us left me in awe.

"You're awake." His husky purr vibrated against my body.

"I am," I murmured, trailing my fingertips languidly across his sculpted chest.

He hummed. "Good. Not that I want you to stop eye fucking me but I was hoping you could maybe tell me what in the Sheol your shadows are doing?"

Lifting my head sleepily off Emon I blinked up at the ceiling where he pointed. "Huh," I said, watching them pulse rhythmically above us.

Emon snorted. "That's not an answer, little umbra."

My black hair fell in a curtain around us when I turned to glare down into his handsome face. Flashbacks of his smug grin between my thighs had me shivering with desire again. I was afraid I would never tire of his carnal hunger for me.

"Listen, shifter. I didn't even know they could portal us until yesterday. So yes. Huh is my answer."

Emon chuckled, reaching up to sweep my hair over my shoulder, then cursed as he rolled me quickly beneath him, shielding me with his naked body when a loud thump hit the fluffy clouds next to us.

"Goddess damn it shifter, I can't see. What was that? Get off me!" I shoved at him but he ignored my demands, snarling up at the shadows.

"It's the scroll. They damn near dropped the fucking shadow scroll on top of us."

"What?" Hooking my leg around him I rolled and slammed him onto his back. Huffing with exasperation, I scrambled off before the gleaming desire sparking in his eyes caught up with his physical actions.

Chuffing he rose into sitting, his carnal gaze raking over me.

Sitting beside the scroll, I stared at it before looking up to see the shadows swirling ominously before popping out of sight.

"Huh."

Shifting closer, Emon tucked my hair back again, letting his hand trail down my arm with a chuckle. "You know I was a little worried that I didn't pleasure you enough last night seeing how you have been awake an hour ogling me, but now I'm starting to think I fucked you well enough that you lost the capability of intelligent speech."

I couldn't stop the crimson blush that crept across my face. "I wasn't ogling."

He snickered and the clouds rose to cradle him. Leaning back he pulled me into his lap. "You are correct. Eye fucking is a better way to describe it."

I squirmed against him to find a more comfortable position between his naked thighs, I clamped my mouth shut. I wasn't about to admit he was right. Emon was gorgeous and he was mine...and the way he fucked me like a depraved beast...

Goddess. My blush deepened.

Emon's chest rumbled, his hand trailing the blush seeping into my pale skin. "You're so fucking beautiful. Especially this way. Unmasked and full of desire. Every piece of you, inside and out, I can see—and it takes my breath away."

I sighed. "You're pretty eloquent for a feral shifter that has been up all night pleasuring his soulmate," I teased and snuggled closer into him, letting my head drop happily against his chest.

Snaking his arm around me, just under my breasts, he growled into my hair. "Here's eloquence. Stop squirming that ass or I'm going to worship it in every fucking way I know how and forget that the shadows just got murdery and dropped a fucking scroll on us."

I eyed the ominous object with pursed lips. "That sounds more preferable."

Emon sighed and kissed the top of my head. "I won't deny you if that is what you really want Remnant Dark but I don't think it is. I'm here with you, what-ever is in that thing, we can face it together. You're not alone anymore and you never will be."

"We don't have time to worry about the scroll." I stared at it mutinously. "The quicker we go through that gateway, the quicker we kill Deirdre, and the quicker we can get back to Riella—to our daughter, to be a family," I choked.

A family. We were a family. I barely had time to digest it. There was so much more we needed to talk about, to figure out.

Emon tilted my head up and kissed my nose tenderly, his eyes a soft glowing gold full of unwavering love. "You know time moves differently here, little umbra. We do not need to leave for a few more hours yet." Kissing my lips he said. "I cannot wait to start our lives together, with Riella, with you and that day will happen. But I also trust your shadows, whatever is in that scroll is something they want us to know now."

Sighing, I turned away from him, pressing my lips into a thin line. "Together then." I blew out a reluctant breath and plucked up the scroll.

He huffed. "Together."

Popping the lid off the black casing, I slid the heavy parchment into my hands. The knobs were made of clear glass, the same glass as the dome of the City of Night and unrolled, the paper was as black as the  throne room itself.

I narrowed my gaze on the silver script and held it up in the crystal light. "Cave, my apologies, I do not know what to call you but I will need more light please." Instantly, the cave's crystals glowed brightly and the silvery script became clearer. "Thank you." I murmured while I read the script with a fast beating heart, my only solace was Emon's steady and strong presence at my back fortifying me to continue.

> *Beware, behave*
> *Darkness takes your life away.*
> *To the city of death*
> *Where love is regret*
> *The end of your soul.*
> *Lives within the Sheol.*
> *Beware, behave*
> *The darkness you will obey.*
> *Beware behave,*
> *Night will lead the way.*
> *An old power rises as the fair one weakens,*
> *Golden becomes the one true beacon,*
> *Blood will run on the darkened moons,*
> *Run child run, I will see you soon.*
> *Beware, Behave*
> *May the shadows keep you safe.*

Emon groaned and his head slammed back into the clouds. "Why is there always a fucking tedious half riddled prophecy attached to shit like this? Why can't it be simple like a human action hero? Bad guy, good guy, fuck up the bad guy, good guy wins...happily ever after. Now that's a better formula."

I laughed dryly, focusing on the words—even the water dragon had told me I should pay attention to them. "Fortunately for you, I grew up with half of this one. I've had many years to try to piece it out."

My fingers traced the chickadee stamped on the scroll.

Emon grunted. "A chickadee..."

I continued to trace the etching of the bird lost in thought. "When I was younger, I would dream of a chickadee singing and playing with me. In my dreams, we would go on adventures to new worlds, worlds I had never been to before but somehow knew they existed despite not ever going through their gateways in real life. I became so infatuated with chickadees afterwards that my family started calling me chickadee. As I aged, the dreams became less and less. Now they have become symbolic for me...a guide in a way."

"For the shifters, a chickadee symbolizes truth and bravery...even foresight. You have chosen quite the powerful guide." Emon nuzzled his nose along my ear then nodded his chin. "Open the rest."

Sighing, I traced the chickadee one last time and then unrolled the scroll further, staring wide eyed at the detailed etching of curved lines, ridges, and ancient text.

"It's a map," I breathed.

Sweeping my hair further back, Emon growled out the one word etched across the illustrated map. "Sheol."

"These markings..." I ran my hand along them at the bottom of the page, "...they look like—"

"Your tattoo brands." Emon reached across to grab my forearm and held it against the onyx paper. "They don't just look alike, they are exactly alike. When did you get them?"

"They appeared when I reached my *centum*. It's very common for the shadow fae to receive brands during their transition into adulthood in their hundredth year."

Emon's hand traced the design on my inner wrist thoughtfully and I shivered at the intimate touch. "Do all the shadow fae have them?"

I pursed my lips. "Not in such detail, not the full arm. My brother and I have the same ones but are the only ones marked this way."

Raising my wrist up, Emon kissed it possessively. "Has anyone ever licked them from here..." He followed one of the swirling brands with his tongue. "...to here before me?" Moving my arm to the side, he kissed the trailing tattoos on the top of my shoulders.

"No," I whispered, remembering the way he had woken me up again for another round of sensual love making hours before and I shifted at the memory of my soulmates talented tongue.

He chuckled. "Still haven't fully gained back your ability to use more than one syllable words I see."

"That's because you completely rob me of words with your sex vibes," I snapped and leaned away from him with an arched brow. "Stop it."

Laughter bursted out of him and echoed off the cave walls. "My soulmate is naked, sitting in my arms and demanding I stop being sexy...I should ask you to do the same," he rasped against my throat and I savored the feel of his beard against my flesh.

I waved my hand up in the air. "I could always have the shadows dress us to help keep you focused."

"Fuck no," Emon growled, "we had an agreement. Keep them far away from my dick!"

"Goddess forbid anything should happen to it!" I teased.

Emon pressed his hard member up into me. "It is in your best interest to protect it at all costs, little umbra."

I grinned up at him before turning my attention back to the map, shaking my head. "We are losing focus." I traced the words with my fingertip. "Sheol. The shadow fae must be in Sheol."

Emon hummed behind me. "When I was younger, my father would always tell me to listen to the words Jarquinn did not say. That day in the study, when Jar spoke of your mother being sent to retrieve the god of death. There were words he didn't say..."

Biting at my lip I nodded. "That, Shea, the God of Death is my long lost father? Yes, I listened to his unsaid words too and it makes more sense now than ever."

# CHAPTER 75

BOTH OUR HEADS SNAPPED up when the shadows returned. Shifting agitatedly in front of us with sudden urgency.

"Remnant?" I growled warily, wrapping my arms around her protectively.

"Emon," she whispered, a tinge of fear in her voice. "I don't have control of them again. They are not listening to me."

Their stormy darkness deepened and swirled faster around us.

Then I heard it.

A soft whisper...then multiple. Each one repeating and interrupting the other. So soft that I strained to hear it appropriately.

"Do you hear that?" I asked her.

"Yes," she breathed, "the shadows are speaking."

Subtly, I moved to place myself in front of her and the whispering shadows. "They fucking speak?"

She rubbed at her temples and shook her head. "They have only done it once before...in Morta."

A chill ran down my spine and my claws unleashed. Cocking my head to the side, I listened. "Mistake. They are saying...*mistake?*"

The darkness swirled faster and their whispers grew louder, then multiple voices all at once, hurried, rushed, urgent.

Recognition and fear bled into my soulmate's emerald green eyes as if she were frozen in time. "Mistake. Take. She will take more," she breathed.

"Deirdre," I snarled harshly.

"Riella," Remnant whispered.

Together we dove off the bed of clouds, landing on the floor that lit up brilliantly in rainbow hues over our naked bodies.

"Dress us!" Remnant commanded and the cave obliged.

Instantly we were both clothed and equipped with weapons. A blade at Remnant's back with knives on her hips, and sheathed at the side of my fitted pants, twin curved blades rested.

I pointed at her. "I am amending our agreement. No more using power of any kind to dress me."

Her smile did not reach her eyes, still watching the swirling agitated shadows with weariness. "Noted."

Tilting her chin to look up at me I stared into her beautiful emerald eyes. So many nights, I had dreamed about the way they would look when I first saw them, but with Remnant every time was a first. Every time I drowned in them.

"This is a trap," I growled low.

A slight nod of agreement. "Yes."

Unable to resist, I swept back the dark strands of her hair to cup her face, running my thumb over her cheek. "Together. We do this together, little umbra."

Her hands shook as they reached up and covered my own. "Together," she said resolutely before looking up at the hovering shadows. "Take us to where we need to go."

The shadows descended, spiraling in a black funnel while their whispers grew to pulsating hisses, repeating one word over and over again.

*Take...take...take...take...take.*

I shivered at the feel of their infinite darkness, there was no end with the shadows, to be taken by them fully was to live a life as an empty shell.

Then it all stopped.

The shadows fell away like a slow falling curtain and I blinked rapidly against the sunlight that highlighted my newest horror.

Jarquinn, the master healer and the fae that was like a second father to me, hung suspended in the middle of the room, his normal ancient blue eyes were saturated red, his mouth gaped open in a silent scream, and his limbs were contorted unnaturally around him.

Possessed. He was being possessed by the Sanguine.

And in front of the healer, barely able to contain my shock, my father stood defensively guarding the other half of my heart—our daughter, our very *awake* daughter.

When her small cherub face looked up at me with gorgeous swirling eyes of gold and emerald, I almost collapsed to my knees.

Nothing prepared me for this. This moment. Time stopped as we stared at one another despite the chaos in the room. Father and daughter...

"Riella," Remnant breathed behind me, stepping cautiously towards her.

"Remnant!" she cried out, her arms reaching out to my soulmate with terror in her eyes, before she collapsed with a sob into Remnant's arms.

Our eyes met over our child's dark hair and Remnant nodded with what she saw in mine.

Stepping cautiously forward, I stood next to my father who had not bothered to turn around, having sensed our bond the moment I stepped through the shadows.

"Father. I didn't expect to see you here."

"Son." My father rumbled without taking his focus off the horrific figure of the master healer in front of us. "I didn't expect to be here. The shadows called to me, the next thing I knew, I was here."

I grunted and palmed my swords, my claws tapping against the metal, watching the healer. My heart was sinking into the pit of my stomach. "What do we know?"

My father snarled, his eyes never leaving the possessed healer. "It's the Sanguine possessing him. There has been no movement, no words but I've seen the likes of it during the blood wars many times. There may not be a way for him to come back from this."

His suspicion was verified when a fierce series of roars and vicious clawing of a leopard slamming at the door broke the morbid silence. Quinn had succumbed to bloodlust, already sensing his father was losing his fight and dying through their bond.

"Fuck," I sighed, swallowing down my own grief and closing my eyes against the keening cries of the shifter on the other side of the door. Yet Jarquinn's wards, the ones I demanded to keep everyone out, still held strong.

Opening my eyes again, I glanced back towards Remnant, staring at the way Riella was wrapped in shadows of black armor. Her swirling gold emerald gaze studied me curiously in her fear and I knew then she had heard every word I spoke to her while she slept.

Dragging my gaze back up to Remnant, I saw her slowly backing both of them up to the open window. Pain constricted in my chest and I gritted my teeth, staring at Remnant's eyes full of tears.

I nodded my understanding.

Remnant would save Riella above all else. Our daughter's safety was what mattered the most right now, but that didn't stop the complete devastation I now felt at being separated from the two things I loved most in this world.

*"I love you. Both of you."* I threaded the words deep into my soulmate bond and the connection I felt to my little cub.

*"If this is your sorry excuse for a goodbye, don't bother shifter, I'll tell you I love you when we walk out of this goddess damn mess together just like you said we would. Together."* Remnant's voice blasted in my head.

I smiled sadly back at her. I wasn't even shocked that our bond had strengthened enough for her to communicate with me. There was no fae more powerful than my soulmate.

*"That makes two of us, fairy boy,"* my panther growled, coming out of his self hibernation.

*"This doesn't fucking look good, cat."*

*"As you always love to say, Daemon Ash Strider...we've been through worse."*

Before I could make a complete fool of myself by saying something truly sentimental to the being that drove me half mad my entire life, a deep ominous cackle came from the suspended twisted form of the master healer, the undertone of the voice I knew well enough.

Deirdre had come and she was playing her sick games again.

"Well, well, well. How very quaint, father and son kings together again, and my former lover—all trembling before me as it should have always been."

I narrowed my eyes on the way Jar's red gaze searched the room, landing on everything and nothing at the same time.

"Where oh where could my golden one be...I've so missed you growling for me, shifter king."

I held my hand up to prevent the others from speaking and shot through the soulmate bond. *Say nothing, little umbra. No matter what. I suspect she can only hear us, not see us.*

I stepped forward loudly and red eyes latched on the sound of my steps, just as I had anticipated. "Alas, there was nothing I missed about you, Deirdre, or shall I call you the Blood Witch now?"

Jarquinn-Deirdre cackled again and I braced against the diseased feel of the Sanguine power pulsing through the room. "I prefer Blood Goddess now." The sickening sound of the healer's body breaking filled the hushed space followed by the anguished roaring of the leopard on the other side of the door. "The power of blood, the Sanguine, allows me to control anything and everything. You were clever to trap me here shifter, but it only allowed me to grow more powerful. Look how I make your powerful ancient dance for me!"

"Your pathetic paltry tricks don't make you a goddess, Deirdre. It just confirms you're still a psychotic bitch."

"Careful, my golden king," the former Queen of Faerie warned from Jarquinn's lips, "I can still make your healer suffer so much more than just this pain...perhaps using him to slice open his own son's throat beyond that door will be needed. His incessant mewling is grating on my nerves."

The roars beyond the doors suddenly changed to squealing shrieks as Deirdre flexed her powers beyond the doorway for demonstration. I had no fucking idea how she was doing it, but it ended now.

"Stop this at once!" I stepped forward again, my entire body shaking with rage. "Why have you come here? What do you want?"

"What I want!" The twisted creature hissed, the Sanguine power pulsed within the room. "What I want is what was stolen from me! What I want is what should have been mine! And I will take it back!"

"Emon!"

I spun with a growl when Remnant cried out, reaching out to her shadows with concentration, attempting to wield them back to her as they were being dragged across the floor, no longer protecting our child. They sputtered and churned at the wooden floor, attempting to crawl back towards us, even gripping onto my booted feet. I reached for them but my hands just fell through their smokey darkness before they snapped up around Jarquinn's body.

*Take...*the shadows whispered one last time.

"I don't have control of them," Remnant cried softly.

"That's because I control them, Remi darling. They are mine now and soon this city will be too! I will use them to destroy it, just like you did to mine," screeched Jarquinn-Deirdre.

"No," Remnant whispered wide eyed as her shadows slowly bled from black to a deep burgundy red.

*"Blood will run on the darkened moons,"* Ethereal hissed and my own blood went cold.

If Deirdre gained the power of the shadows...then there would be nothing left of Finlandia, just like the City of Light.

Nothing could match that kind of power...nothing but mine but it was too violent, too unstable.

*"Release it!"* Roared the panther, but it was already too late.

The shadows had succumbed to the Sanguine.

Before we could react, the burgundy tendrils slammed into both my father and I, sending us across the room like annoying insects instead of the full bodied shifters we were. Grunting, I hit the wall hard, white plaster raining down around me. My father yanked me upright from the wreckage before more of the wall came tumbling down.

I blinked, peering through the dusty sunlight to see my soulmate at the window and I could hear the faint sound of Penina's voice calling to her. Lifting Riella into her arms, Remnant gave our daughter a soft kiss on her forehead, dropping a necklace with an indigo scale over her neck before tossing her into the street below. Slowly, with devastation in her eyes, my soulmate turned back into the room, the ringing sound of her sword being drawn sending a pit of dread deep into my stomach.

"Remnant, no!"

Roaring, I sprung forward out of my dazed stupor to stop her and to send her stubborn ass through that window myself, but again my father and I were slammed back into the wall, this time fully restrained by the red shadows. I roared when my fathers eyes rolled in the back of his head and he slumped in their hold, losing consciousness.

*"Release me! Release me you fool!"* Ethereal clawed outward and I struggled to hold the walls, the power inside of me churning.

*Not enough. Never enough.* This was not happening again. Red shadows sprung forward and a small gasp escaped my soulmate's lips when they penetrated through her body, extending out of her back and lifting her to eye level with the possessed master healer.

"Stop this!" I roared and the walls rattled with my anguish.

"I will take everything from you Daemon Ash Strider—!" Another burgundy shadow sprung forth, this time impaling Remnant through the chest. So fucking close to her heart. I stared, horrified when my soulmate's sword slipped from her fingers and clattered harshly to the floor.

My cries of agony rattled the entire fucking city.

Emerald green eyes met mine.

"No!" I screamed as pure unfiltered power, so gold it was white, released from deep inside me and blinded me from the outside in.

This world was going to fucking burn.

# CHAPTER 76

*Remnant*

I STAYED SLUMPED OVER the stolen corrupted shadows that now impaled me. The pain was almost unbearable but not life threatening...yet. I had no time to tell Emon my plan. The roars coming from him were thunderous but I maintained my focus. Ice cold focus. Despite the terror in Emon's beautiful gold eyes, I had no intention of dying today.

I would see Emon again...and Riella.

I only hoped I had bought Penina enough time to get Riella to safety. Tears filled my eyes at the memory...

*Decision made, I knelt before Riella. "There is no time to explain, little one. I'm sorry it always feels like this." Then I dropped Shen's dragon scale over her head.*

*It's okay, Remnant," her voice trembled, but her chin tilted high. She was goddess damn brave.*

*I kissed her forehead. "Continue to be brave, my sweet little one. There is a shifter below, her name is Penina. Listen to her well. I will find you again when I'm done here," I whispered fiercely.*

*Her tiny hand cupped my face. "You won't have to be alone then either...mother." The gold in her eyes swirled with the emerald green knowingly.*

*Holding back my sob, I leaned into her touch, memorizing every precious feel of her hand on my face, a claiming brand I wish I could have forever. "I'm sorry, my daughter." Then without hesitating, I lifted her and launched her out the alcove.*

*My daughter gave no cry while she flew from the second story alcove into the waiting shifter's arms. Penina caught her with ease and cradled her tightly against her chest, then nodded and turned to run far, far away from here. If Emon was my soul then Riella was my heart. I wouldn't live without either of them.*

*Turning I drew my sword...*

*"Forta."* Called a warm soothing voice.

I blinked back the memory and looked up with tears in my eyes to see bright blue ancient ones staring back at me. Clear of the Sanguine.

"Jarquinn." Sorrow filled me. I could see the pain within him, the fight he was losing, the cost it took for him to speak to me, to hold it off for a moment longer.

I gasped when a fierce golden light blasted around us and the burgundy shadows hissed, releasing us both from their grip as if burned.

Jarquinn and I crumbled to the floor, my hand landing on my dropped sword. Gripping it, I crawled to the healer, dragging it across the floor against the surging power around us.

Jar's pain stricken eyes looked up at me.

"I am at your service, master healer," I whispered.

"It is time to be who you are meant to be, *forta*." His voice was but a mere whisper yet the strength there could raise the sun.

Tears dropped from my eyes and stained the wooden floor next to his mangled body. "A lesson to be had and learned," I whispered back.

"There is nothing more true than accepting who you are but also what you may become." He smiled sadly.

I was neither the hero nor the villain, the monster nor the savior.

Like the darkness, I just *was*. A shadow lost and—a shadow found.

More golden light roared violently around us, Emon had lost control. But it didn't matter, not now. I had a job to do and like the wraiths, there was only one way to banish the Sanguine from its host.

Rising with my sword held high, I looked into those sky blue eyes full of peace one final time before I struck, severing the master healer's head painlessly from his body. With one stroke, I ended his painful torture and banished Deirdre's presence from Finlandia...at least for now.

My corrupted shadows pulsed once before disappearing in a crimson cloud of smoke, summoned by their new mistress.

Slumping over, I gripped my torso both in pain and with a hollowed feeling, like something had just been clawed out of me, leaving nothing but a cavern of emptiness. My shadows were gone.

Lifting my head up with tears in my eyes, I turned to find Emon, but instead was met with the razor teeth of a bloodlusting leopard barreling into my side.

I screamed as Quinn's beserk leopard sent me skidding across the floor, and I rolled with the momentum to find myself in a defensive crouch, holding my side where my open wounds bled.

Keeping my eyes on the avenging leopard, my heart ached to see the replica of Jarquinn's eyes glaring at me full of the need for revenge. Finally set free of the wards from the healer's death, he instinctively scented his fathers blood on my hands.

I palmed the knives at my hip.

"I am sorry Quinn," I choked, spitting out blood that had pooled in my mouth and pressed harder to my wounds to stem the flow. "I don't want to fight you, I don't want to hurt you."

The leopard snarled, so focused on me that he failed to notice Emon had finished his full shift behind us. As he lunged for me I could see behind him where pure white power had gathered in the massive panther's wide open jaw.

"No!" I screamed when it erupted from Ethereal's mouth.

I only had seconds to react. Biting back the pain I knew it would cause me, I crashed into Quinn's leaping form, feeling his snarling teeth snap beside my head, I wrapped my arms around his body and twisted us to the side, away from the instant death that would have taken him and straight out into the streets below.

Losing my grip on Quinn mid air, I could hear the terrified screams of Finlandia's fae as I crashed into a shaded canopy that covered half the street. I lay there for a moment, staring at the uncontrollable streams of white hot power coming from the building above me before the cloth gave way and I hit the ground with a silent cry. Curling in on myself, my consciousness dimmed momentarily from the blinding pain.

Shaking my head, I pushed up, blinking away the rising dust, seeing Quinn's snarling leopard tangled in fabric of his own.

I stumbled to stand, every inch of my body protesting. I could feel my smaller injuries from the fall healing, but my powers were not fast enough to stem the injury I took from the Sanguine.

Uncontrolled, the golden fire exploded into the buildings surrounding us and it heaved before it started to crumble downwards.

"Get to safety!" I roared out to the fae of Finlandia, using shadows to bat down rock and debris assisting them to shelter.

Quinn's leopard snarled, drawing my attention back down to him. "Goddess shit," I spat, the bloodlusting cat was free.

A wave of pain blurred my vision of him and I dropped to one knee gasping, unable to hold myself fully up. Forcing my eyes open, I blinked and then stared at the back of a great blonde wolf, howling defensively into the smokey filled air.

"Asher?" My bloody hand reached outward to stroke the blonde fur while my other hand continued to grip my torso.

Gold eyes of the former king of shifters glanced back at me with a slight nod of his shaggy head.

I sighed with relief. "Thank the goddess."

The wolf chuffed before the city shook with another wave of power and I stared in amazement as Ethereal's giant panther body bursted through the building walls that immediately turned to ash from the sizzling gold fire radiating off him.

*Golden will be your one true beacon.*

The prophetic words echoed in my head as I watched the cobble stone path split when the panther's monstrous paws hit the ground and then it too burned to ash. When he swung his massive head towards me and I inhaled sharply.

Bloodlust stormed in his blinding gaze.

"No," I whispered, before I bowed over my body from another wave of pain.

A low whine from the panther had me looking up to see him staring at the blood that had dripped onto the street. My blood.

"Ethereal. Emon. You can control this," I whispered, reaching out to them pleadingly.

Instead, his raging feline eyes stared hard at my bloody hand.

Snatching it back, I recognized my mistake as a deep guttural roar tore from his chest. More golden power poured from him and up into the sky. I shielded my eyes against the blinding light to watch in awe as his power tore a hole through the lavender sky and out into the universe. Stars collided, planets erupted, galaxies shook under it.

Ethereal was pure, raw, unfiltered life and the power he held was like a supernova star, erupting and destroying everything in its path to make way for something new. A power to destroy worlds.

Slumping forward, I shook my head as spots danced in my vision. A strong hand hauled me upwards and I blinked stupidly at the fae who was shouting at me.

"Go after him!" Asher roared in my face.

I blinked at where the god-like panther had once stood. "He's gone," I slurred.

Dazed, I looked back at Asher who was shaking me violently, behind him Quinn's leopard stumbled to regain himself after Ethereal's light had blinded us all.

The former shifter king shook my body harder, cursing. "Snap out of it Dark! I can handle Quinn. You need to go after Daemon!"

I stared. His eyes were gold like Emon's.

Emon was gone, Riella was gone. The shadows were gone.

My life was crumbling to pieces just like before.

The city was being destroyed...the past repeating itself.

Destruction and death was all my legacy would ever be.

"For fucking goddess sake!" Asher shook me harder. "This cannot be my former enemy I met on the battlefield! If it is, I am ashamed I didn't defeat you!" He shoved me away from him and I stumbled to find my footing. "Save my son or I'll kill you myself, before you even have a chance to bleed out on this damned street, Remnant Ezra Solaire Dark."

His words were like a slap to the face and my soul. I snarled. "Fuck you, Asher Strider!"

Relief lit in his feral wolf eyes. "There she is. There's the daughter in law I'm proud of. Daemon needs you, your soulmate needs you, and he's heading straight for the gateway!"

Realization dawned on me. "He's going after the queen alone?"

Asher growled low. "Not just the queen, she is just the start. He will burn this world from the inside out. Seeing you impaled sent him over the edge, seeing you bleeding out in his city only drove his resolve. With the power controlling him, he will be able to easily enter before the gateway is supposed to open," he snarled, shoving me again. "Now fuck off, Dark. I'm too busy to talk and you're too busy saving my son."

I narrowed my eyes at the former king of shifters. "Bane was right. You *are* a bastard."

Asher barked a laugh. "Then let us hope we live through this day to suffer another moment with that miserable prick. Then you can tell him that in person." He winked and shifted without a moment's pause. His blonde wolf replaced him and he howled one more time before turning back toward a now fully recovered bloodlusting leopard.

Inhaling, I spun, leaving behind the sounds of two ferocious beasts ripping each other apart, and bracing myself against the agonizing pain that set my body on fire. Blood still flowed freely from me, leaving a dripping trail of red while I stumbled along the ash ridden street where the golden panther had blazed through.

I shook my head. Universes...the panther burned universes.

I had nothing that could stop that now. My shadows...the void of all light was the only thing that possibly could and they were gone.

I was more likely to bleed out before I even had a chance to reach Emon to stop him. But giving up was not an option and it never would be when it came to that damn shifter.

He was mine. I was his.

"General Dark!"

Panting, I halted in front of the giant shifter calling to me. "Drey." I clutched my chest and eyed the baker who had been terrified of me just days ago. "Drey, I need you to move please. I must get to the king."

Drey held his hands up with nervous placation. "I know it. I want to help you."

I frowned deliriously. "I don't have time for pastries, Drey, I'm sorry. No matter how fucking amazing that sounds right now."

Drey laughed, a great booming sound. "I can help in a different way, General Dark." Bowing at his giant torso, he shifted, and I stared stupidly at the towering beast in front of me.

"You're a griffin." I gasped and then smiled. "Of course you are."

Almost pure auburn aside from marbled feathers of gray in his wings, Drey's griffin was a masterpiece. His great eagle head cocked to the side and regarded me with striking white eyes. Then he bowed his massive head and sighed his icy breath over my body.

The coldness of his power seeped in and I instantly felt my pain disappear. Finally able to stand fully, I removed my blood stained arm from my wounds, seeing completely healed skin.

A griffin's breath had the ability to heal any creature...but only one time in its lifetime, and Drey—he chose me.

"Thank you Drey. I'm honored," I choked.

His eagle head cocked to the side and he unfurled his marbled gray wings.

My brows rose. "Are you inviting me to fly with you? To reach Emon?"

Drey bowed his griffin head and then flapped his great wings with urgency.

I didn't hesitate, scrambling on his broad lionlike body. Fierce wings pumped with royal elegance against the smoke surrounding us and I gripped his fur harder to stay astride as together we climbed up into Finlandia's lavender blue sky as I searched frantically for my soulmate.

"There!" I cried out against the rushing wind and pointed to the charred trail Ethereal had made. The panther was now out of the city and heading straight for the Red Cap Mountains, straight for wherever the location of the gateway was.

The griffin screeched back his acknowledgement and banked hard, his lion tale snapping to the side, to direct us straight towards the king of shifters. I gritted my teeth and clung low, edging with his turn.

My mind scrambled for something, anything to stop the raging panther. If he succeeded, there would be no Faerie, no us, no Riella.

Closing my eyes, I focused on the shifter I loved, searching for the shared bond between us. *"Emon."* I pulled on our bond. *"You are the light to my darkness. Come back to me, shifter."*

I had no way of knowing if he heard me but I sent my love through the bond anyway; images of him that I saw through my eyes, his snarky smile when I did something amusing, the roguish way he ran his hands through his hair, the way he watched his friends as if everyday was their last together, the soft touches that could soothe and light me on fire at the same time.

Tears streamed down my face while the wind instantly cooled them upon my fevered cheeks. *"Come back to me Emon. You said we would do this together. Never alone."*

Still silence remained.

*"Goddess fucking damn it, shifter. I will kick your dick in again for this."* A sob tore from my throat and the rushing air swallowed up my anguish like a hungry swarm.

Then I felt it. That slightest pull. The smallest whisper.

*"Little umbra. I can't stop. I can't stop him."*

My eyes snapped and then narrowed on the Red Cap Mountains growing larger in the distance. They loomed over these lands, casting shadows over the valleys with its own personalized darkness as the sun set behind its towering peaks.

*"Fight for me Emon. Fight it and hold on."*

I knew what I had to do.

I gave Drey a gentle pat to gain his attention. "I will need to stand. Please keep steady."

Drey's understanding griffin call pierced the dimming skies.

Breathing calmly, I slowly rose up to my feet, standing atop the great auburn griffin. Emon's words from that night in his study echoed inside my mind.

*"Did you really surf the skies upon the wings of the Roc?"*

I hadn't, but today...today I surfed the skies on griffin wings.

Lips thinning, I looked beyond the raging bloodlusting panther to the enormous looming shadows from the mountains. My hands rose and I felt beads of sweat drip down my back. I would need every bit of my concentration for this.

"The sun..." I whispered, seeing the sun sink further still, I beckoned the shadows to me. Eerily they rippled over the lands. "The sun needs darkness." Then with all the power I had inside of me, I lifted them from their rest. Leagues of shadows answered my call and molded forward into a dark tidal wave that I sent careening towards the panther. He roared with light and bursted through it with just the slightest bit of dimming to his blinding power. Gritting my teeth, I tried again. The shadows became thicker, taller, so tall that it rivaled Shen's wall and even the Red Caps themselves. "For it cannot exist without it."

Emon was my sun, but Ethereal...Ethereal was a supernova star ready to burst, and I was both the darkness and the void that could absorb it all.

Baring my teeth, I bent the wall of shadows forcefully into the panther again. The darkness rippled across his body turning him black and for a brief moment, extinguished his light, slowing him to a stop. Heaving more shadows inwards I sent them crashing repeatedly into Ethereal before his light could break through entirely.

It was a terrifying tsunami of shadows versus a breaker of worlds.

More. I needed more.

Vigorously, I pulled the shadows from long outward distances, the smallest blade of grasses, and even from within the mountains, feeding it into the crashing wave that suffocated the panther's light into a huge planetary-like orb within the valley.

Crouching low, with the wind roaring around me, I patted Drey's great eagle head affectionately. "Thank you Drey, but this is where you and I part ways, my friend. Turn back to spare yourself this darkness."

Then I jumped. Straight down into the shadows where I would either burn from Ethereal's light or live under Emon's sun.

The griffin cried out, unable to stop me as I plunged through the orb of darkness, weaving them closed.

I smiled when I heard Emon's voice, now stronger in my mind.

*"And what about the darkness? What does it need?"* Emon's voice whispered back, stronger and clearer in my head.

I spread out my arms to slow my descent, using the shadows to brace my fall. *"The darkness...the darkness does not need the light, it is infinite. But finds it cannot live without the light just the same. To be infinite is to be alone. It does not want to be alone anymore."*

Then I felt him. Strong arms latched onto me, cradling me in his loving embrace. I stifled a cry, burying my head into his chest, inhaling his chocolate spice scent, trembling with relief.

Emon kissed the top of my head and breathed harshly into my hair. "You did it. You stopped him. The moment you weakened his light I was able to take back control."

I hummed, focusing on the steady thrum of his heart and the purring in his chest when he spoke.

"You jumped off a goddess damn griffin and fell through the sky, little umbra," he sounded breathless.

I smiled into him. "Yes."

He chuckled. "So we are back to one word answers again are we?"

I sniffed. "Yes."

"Finally, now I have a story I can write from my own point of view in the *The Unaccounted Life of the Last Shadow Fae.*"

The excited awe in his tone had me drawing back to look at him with raised brows. "Are you serious, shifter? That's what you care about right now?"

He grinned. "I got more than one word this time didn't I?" Then his lips crashed into mine, muffling my snarky response, and kissing me desperately, his hands traveling over every inch of my body as if to check if I was still real.

"I thought, when the Sanguine...then the blood." He choked, inhaling shakily against my lips. "I lost control, I gave into the power, Ethereal's power, he blamed himself for your injuries, and then he couldn't stop...I thought I would never see you again," he whispered fearfully.

I shook my head. "In what universe did you think I would ever let that happen, shifter?"

Emon chuckled softly before taking another deep breath. "I don't know how I will survive you, my little umbra."

I snickered and grinned. "You've been through worse."

He barked out a laugh, brushing my hair back from my face and twirling it around his fingers. "We do this together."

I reached up and drew his hand to my lips, kissing it. "Always."

"Never alone." His steady gaze was so unwavering as he waited for my response.

I peered deep into his adoring golden gaze—eyes of gold that I loathed, then feared, then loved. "Never." I promised.

Never would I be lost in the shadows again—for Emon was my guiding light, bringing me back home.

# EPILOGUE

Remnant

EMON EYED THE COCOON of darkness. "So…" His eyes sparkled, turning to look at the monstrosity I had created. "Is this permanent or will the shadows fall soon."

I frowned at the cascading darkness swirling around us. "I have never powered this much shadow before without my sentient ones. This is all new for me."

Emon watched my face for the pain the separation of my shadows had caused me. "We will get them back, Remnant, we will get the umbras back."

I ran my hands through the wall of shadow, ignoring the deep ache inside. "I know we will, but there is no time to focus on that. Penina has Riella and we need to regroup. Deirdre won't wait long before she strikes again and with the Sanguine using the shadows there's no telling what she can do with them." I swiped at the dormant shadows, baring my teeth at them. "I can't even control these damn things now. Everything is so off balance."

Stepping forward, Emon took my hand and pulled me against him. "Remnant."

Exhaling harshly, I glared at him. "What?"

He smiled sadly down at me. "Thank you for releasing Jar."

I shook my head. "Don't," I choked. The master healer's eyes begging me for death would haunt me for many nights, along with Quinn's.

Reaching under my chin, he tilted my head up to look into his sad eyes. "You freed him. He is with his wife now...his soulmate he has lived without for over two thousand years. He knew his time was near..."

Sighing, I closed my eyes at the memory, his answer to what the knowledge of the God brothers would cost him.

*None that I cannot handle, my clever cub. Do not fret, Sheol will not come for me this day.*

"I know."

Emon's lips brushed against mine. "I'm in awe of you, little umbra."

I kissed him back, feeling his lips move slowly over me.

Groaning, he pressed my body closer into him, extending my head further back to deepen his kiss.

I clutched at his bare chest, needing his comfort, his touch more than ever before. "I need you," I whispered into his mouth and ran my hands down his thighs.

"Fuck." Emon's mouth tore away from mine, tilting his head back in a growling moan. "Take what you need from me then. I'm yours. Yours to use. Forever."

I tore at Emon's clothing, my desire mixing with my sorrow and loss. He soon followed my lead, assisting us both until we stood naked in front of each other, breathing heavily just staring in awe of one another.

Neither one of us moved for what seemed like an eternity, finding peace in baring our bodies and souls with one another.

Reverently I sank to my knees in front of him, tilting my head up to see him watching me like a wary predator before looking back down at his cock, already hard for me.

Emon's hand threaded through my hair and tilted my head back for me to look up at him. "Fuck. You're so goddess damn beautiful."

I smiled and brought my hands up to his trembling muscular thighs, lightly running the pads of my fingertips over the smooth bronze skin teasingly. "So are you, my king." I leaned forward and licked the tip of his weeping cock. A harsh rattling breath escaped him, whether it was from my words or from my actions I was unsure. It didn't matter. I was going to worship my soulmate for the king he was—not of the shifters, but of my soul.

"Perhaps another time. When I am not here." A booming voice echoed around us as if it came from the shadows themselves.

Growling, Emon had me up on my feet, shielding me with his claws flashing. "Who the fuck is there?"

I narrowed my eyes behind Emon's protective stance and watched the darkness stir where a figure began to form—whoever it was, they were weaving shadows.

Stepping out of Emon's protection, I gripped onto the moving shadows and wrenched them back, only to stare dumbstruck at the imposing masculine figure within them.

He was too beautiful to be fae and yet too eerily similar to not be one. His skin shimmered like the stars, short wavy black hair fell across his brilliant green eyes that sparkled like a million faceted emeralds combined into one. He wore black from head to toe, with the sleeves of a silk shirt rolled up, revealing tattoo brands identical to my own.

His otherworldly face wrinkled with disgust. "Fuck really? I have not seen my daughter in over two thousand years and this is the cruel fate I am given? Not only that, but you stole my fucking grand entrance, daughter."

He waved an elegant hand adorned with multiple silver and gold rings. Abruptly, I was covered from head to toe in a tailored black shirt and pants, complete with a thin silver buckle and my favorite laced black leather boots.

Emon growled fiercely with irritation next to me and I snorted with humor—my soulmate was completely covered in *layers*, with an oversized cloak covering his entire person and pooling down onto the shadowed filled ground.

"Much better," the being grinned.

I arched my brow, distracted at how well Emon actually wore clothing. It would be fun to peel those layers off of him...Emon gave me a side glance, telling me he knew exactly where my thoughts had been going.

"You need to learn to school your thoughts, daughter, if you are to survive." The powerful being shook his head and turned towards Emon. "And stop that incessant growling, shifter king.

Despite popular fae belief, not everyone wants to see your shifter dick...especially when it's swinging around my offspring."

*Daughter. Offspring.* I blinked. If Emon and I's assumptions were correct then we were standing in the presence of Shea. The God of Death.

I stepped forward menacingly. I had no shadows, no weapons, but I was not afraid. "You speak as if you know us, but we do not know you. Care to introduce yourself?"

That green gaze, that I realized was so much like my own, perused over my person and smirked. "You know who I am."

"Suppose I entertain the idea you're the God of Death and my father. What do you want? Why are you here?"

My supposed father chuckled and peered at the shadows surrounding us, ignoring my question. "Interesting weave here, daughter. Did you know you made them permanent? You definitely need training but this...this is exquisite work." He ran his hand over the darkness.

My eyes ensnared on his arms again and the identical markings there. "That's not an answer to my question."

Rolling his eyes, he crossed his muscular arms in front of his chest. "You're very much like your mother. So focused on control that you miss out on the beauty."

Emon and I both growled simultaneously.

The God of Death snickered. "Exactly like her. Be at ease, daughter. It is a compliment, beauty is misleading." Smiling, he snapped, "I come bringing you gifts."

Suddenly, our friends materialized with Riella carefully protected in Penina's arms. They acted quickly, like the prepared warriors they were with Bane, Tyr, Xi, and Riley circling around the God of Death while Asher guarded Penina who slowly backed towards us with our daughter.

No one's eyes left the God of Death's who watched them all amusedly.

"Mother. Father." Riella called out when she saw us. Her swirling gold and green eyes alight with happiness as she stretched her hands outward.

There was no stopping us. Emon and I both rushed to our daughter. Taking her quickly from the assassin's arms.

"Penina is nice." She smiled sweetly at us.

Smiling back, Emon and I squeezed her together. "Yes she is." I looked up into Penina's knowing gaze. The shifter smiled and nodded once before turning to guard our little family along with Asher.

Looking back down on my daughter, I smoothed her hair back. "Are you okay?"

Riella straightened and gave me a serious look. "I stayed brave. But he does not scare me." She glanced back to the death god whose eyes twinkled listening to her. "He feels familiar."

"I'm proud of you for being brave, little one."

My father winked at her and then glared at Emon, who had his arms wrapped around both of us. "I give you credit, shifter king. Your people are loyal. Even your swordmaster refused to give up my granddaughter so that I could convince you to trust me. So instead I had to bring them along...unharmed and alive as you see." He pursed his lips in thought.

Emon released us to step forward snarling. "I do not need your praise to have faith in my own people, death god."

"Someone want to explain what the fuck is going on and who the fuck this new asshole is?" Tyr growled, his purple eyes almost bored with a stand off against a god.

My father snorted. "I take it back. I give you credit for all except that one." He waved his ring adorned hand at the grinning Tyr.

Holding Riella to me, my voice was hard. "What is it you want? No one in this world brings gifts without wanting something in return."

His face suddenly turned serious. "We have much to discuss, my little chickadee, and we have very little time to do it." Nodding to the fae that surrounded him he growled. "Step aside."

Seeing the death in his eyes, our group slowly retreated to form a protective circle around my little family.

Muttering with irritation, the death god waved his hand. A portal appeared, bright with a stunning fluorescent night scape of shooting stars, glowing moons, and rainbow hued lights dancing in a darkened sky. Shifting white sands rolled to reveal a silvery pathway that blurred when it shimmered before us. Looking over his shoulder, the death god smiled proudly at me.

"Welcome to Sheol, daughter. Your home and birthright. Come, your mother and brother are waiting."

# Afterword

Dear readers, thank you so much for reading Shadow Lost. Trigger warning: The writing of this book started out as a grief write while I suffered from unbearable, heartbreaking loss. Multiple miscarriages and a diagnosis of unexplained secondary infertility. I bled my heart into words and pages, somehow ending up with a beautiful story that is all about accepting yourself for who you are in the past, now, and what you may become. A healing journey for both myself and the characters. I am excited for you to find out what more is to come! As such please leave a review so that I can share this book with more readers like yourself around the world. Thank you.

# Acknowledgements

None of this would have been possible or even finished if it wasn't for the incredible people that I have surrounding me. A very grateful and special thank you especially goes out to my cousin Sarah—my best friend, my matron of honor on my wedding day, and my batman for life. Her brilliance in editing this piece and taking one of my biggest weaknesses in writing and making it fun will be an experience I'll never forget. The nights we spent discussing this story will always be vivid in my mind. She raced me to this finish line with words like this...
"I love how you were able to take your personal pain
 and funnel it into something creative and beautiful
 while you waited for your own perfect little Ash. You truly amaze me."
And she thinks she's not a writer...please.

Of course I cannot forget my husband who watched me laugh, cry, and throw fits over the final stages of this book. Making me tea and hot chocolates late into the night but also knowing full well what this work meant to me. He held me in the darkness when we could not hold the babies we lost as I wrote my pain into a beautiful story I am so very proud of. I'll never forget that he is the light that always brings me home. Forever and ever.

Special thank you to my boys who have been blessedly amazing as I spent my last months feverishly working on this book in the evening hours instead of playing. They were happy for it...more time to beat up on their Dada!

Big thanks to my sister, a fantasy reader junkie, for also assisting me with revisions and editing, my aunt who graciously listened to all my crazy ideas for cover art and stood by my side with indecisions, and self doubts, believing in me when I didn't. And a very special, heartfelt thank you to my best friend Stephanie. In

2022, we talked about things that we always wanted to do but were too afraid to try. Publishing this book was one of them. We now will forever live by these words.

"So fucking do it then."

And I did. I will. Always.

# About The Author

B.K. Cavaleri is an emerging indie author of dark fantasy romance and a dreamer living in Michigan with her husband and two rainbow baby boys. She works as a doctor of physical therapy by day and a writer by night...that's her moonlit vibe when the babies are sound asleep in their beds and hubby is entranced by The Office reruns. It's during that time she gets to dream amongst the stars and make it come to life on paper. It seemed a shame to keep it all to herself, and her characters are much too loud, so she has decided to step out of the shadows and release her stories to the world. Thank you for joining her on this journey.

For More Books & Updates
www.bkcavaleri.com

instagram.com/cavaleri.archive.author/

amazon.com/stores/B.-K.-Cavaleri/author/B0CVR91XGC?ref=ap_rdr&isDramIntegrated=true&shoppingPortalEnabled=true&ccs_id=4ade8afb-5063-4b4d-97aa-4d8ece56ad6f

goodreads.com/author/dashboard?ref=nav_profile_authordash

# Also By

**_Remnant Archives Series_**
Book 1: Shadows Lost
Book 2: Shadows Ascend
Prequel Origin Novella: Shadows of Air and Earth
Book 3: Shadows Eternal
Book 4: Bloods Fury (TBA)